Bridge to Nowhere is joyously dedicated to my son, Luke Parker, for his unwavering belief in me and support of me through the years, especially when times were tough and it would have been easy for him to criticize or predict disaster. I'm proud of him as a wonderful son, a terrific person, a great husband, a fantastic dad, a United States Marine Corps officer – but most of all – for walking with God.

This book is also gratefully dedicated to my family who continued to believe that I could write in spite of rejection slips, especially sisters Leslie Garcia and Vicky Potter – both talented and gifted writers in their own right.

And the dedication would be incomplete without including my husband, Pastor Alan T. McKean, who brought me to Scotland and gifted me with time to write – and then went on to write and sell his own book!

Go with God and you will find yourself living the dreams you once thought were impossible or only within the reach of other people. God rocks!

May every bridge you
cross in life bring you
joy & strength.

Bridge To Nowhere

A Miz Mike Novel

by

Stephanie Parker McKean

Love & Blessings,
Steph McKean

Aug. 24 / 2012

BRIDGE TO NOWHERE

ISBN 978-1-907984-42-6

First published in Great Britain in 2012 by Rose & Crown Books
www.roseandcrownbooks.com
(Sunpenny Publishing Group)

MORE BOOKS FROM ROSE & CROWN:

Embracing Change, by Debbie Roome
Blue Freedom, by Sandra Peut
A Flight Delayed, by KC Lemmer

COMING SOON:

Redemption on the Red River, by Cheryl R. Cain
Uncharted Waters, by Sara DuBose
30 Days to Take-off, by KC Lemmer
Greater than Gold, by Julianne Alcott
Shadow of a Parasol, by Beth Holland
Changing Landscapes, by Olivia Valentine
Heart of the Hobo, by Shae O'Brien

Chapter 1.

Perhaps I *was* careless, because my mind was chained to my failing Pastor Garth Seymour detective series, but still, it seemed to me the teen driver of the red car was to blame.

I had just left my Three Prongs office when he careened around the corner and barreled down the street towards me, seemingly blind or indifferent to the fact that I was crossing the street in the path of his sports car. I partly leapt, partly tumbled, and totally fell, out of the vehicle's path. As a career, writing is unfortunately a static occupation. One does not get enough exercise – or at least, I don't. At forty-something, I am hearty. Fast movement, like fleeing from a monster car, reduces me to breathlessness. Gracefulness has never been one of my faults at any age or weight, though. I landed in a disheveled heap in front of my long-time heartthrob, Marty Richards.

In my defense, I must add that Marty would be pretty much *any* woman's heartthrob. Even nearing fifty, he was Texas-tall and slim. His wide shoulders and narrow hips shot a breath of life into the Western-cut clothes he wore, from the tooled leather boots and leather belt with his name engraved on the back, and a wide silver buckle bumping up against a flat hard belly, to the pale Stetson that held his cinnamon-brown hair in near-submission. He sometimes complained that his hair was etched with grey, but as he bent down over me to check for injuries all I could see was the red, catching glints of light from the sun and tossing them back playfully; and the fabulous blue eyes, dark as day flowers around the edges and pulsing with yellow around the pupils.

I wasn't sure whether my difficulty in breathing was from Marty's closeness, or my forced rapid movement. My hazel eyes (which I determinedly refer to as *green*) are too big for my face; thus I am sometimes unfairly accused of staring at people. But if someone had accused me of staring at Marty now, it would not have been mendaciously. I drank in the close details of his person like a water-starved plant.

My own light brown-red hair (which I determinedly refer to as *red*) fought its way out of the bun I had stuffed it into earlier with less than expert skill. It fell around my face and blew across my lips as I devoured details of Marty that I was seldom close enough to see. I was thankful that it – my windblown hair – did not block my view of the ex-rodeo-television-movie star. His full lips smiled easily, and the lines around his eyes and mouth hinted at a sense of humor and kindness, but of course I had already memorized those qualities from my dreams.

To his credit, Marty managed not to laugh. Instead he solemnly helped me to my feet, even though his cheeks puffed in and out suspiciously and his full lips quivered under the ends of his cinnamon-sprinkled mustache.

"Good morning, Miz Mike," he boomed in his rich movie star voice that rose and fell with the gusto of a friendly spring breeze. "Are you okay?"

My real name is Michal Rice, but 'Mike' serves to admirably hide my identity as a female writer for the Pastor Garth Seymour series. Critics of the series lament the fact that Seymour lacks the salient grey cells of Agatha Christie's Hercule Poirot. Since I lack the fine brain cells of Christie, I'd have to agree with them. My books win accolade from fans, however, thanks to Seymour's unfailing integrity, unshakable faith in God, and predilection for solving crimes through his *aperçu* in recognizing things nefarious in drag.

Now, with my pantyhose torn, my knee bleeding, and my clothes of dubious labels bundled up around my aching body – there was Marty, asking me if I was okay. I wasn't, of course, but I could hardly admit that to him. His magnetism threatened to pull the truth right out of me: I had been the one who had sent him flowers and candy for Valentine's Day two years prior. At the time, he had jumped to the conclusion that his secret admirer was the girl at the drugstore, and had started dating her.

Remembering that my pedestrian qualities had not improved from a rollicking tumble over the curb and across the sidewalk, I managed to bite my cheeks – hard, on the inside – and stop the ebullient confession from spilling out into the warm Texas air. Instead, I nodded.

That simple gesture sent a blast of pain racing up through my neck to explode inside my head.

My legs tried to shake me loose, although I couldn't tell whether that was a reaction to pain or to the overwhelming effect of Marty Richards himself standing next to me, holding my arm and smiling into my eyes.

Over the years I had linked Marty's name and mine together in my dream life – secretly, of course, as the names could never be connected in *real* life. Since I love chocolate, the voice in my head referred to us affectionately as the 'M&Ms'. Sometimes, while trying to round out a plot or to extricate poor Pastor Garth from some huggermugger of a mess I'd penned him into, I would find myself doodling lines of M&Ms across empty paper.

And then there was my secret M&M game. Even though dark brown might be perceived as a masculine color, my love for chocolate wrote the game rules: brown was for me, and yellow was for Marty. Marty's love, whether real or imagined (and yes, at my age, and with my knocked-about-old-car-looks, it was imagined) spun sunlight into my life. Thus I sorted out the M&Ms, keeping the browns and yellows hidden in a container inside my desk drawer. The other colors were poured out in a dish that sparked my desk with its brightness and invited visitors to my office – and me – to munch and crunch on chocolate rainbows.

Marty insisted on walking me back to my office. By then the utopia of close contact with him had erased from my memory the fact that I had just been *leaving* my office. He need utter no blandishments to win my heart; with his strong arms supporting me, I was in danger of liquefying and falling into a helpless heap on the sidewalk ... again! It took heroic effort to bite back all the extemporaneous conversation that bucked through my mind like a calf at a rodeo: *If I follow you home, can I keep you? ... Marry me, and I'll be a better horse trainer than the Horse Whisperer ...*

The promise of turning myself into a horse trainer would have been particularly spurious, considering that I am rather frightened of the huge, unpredictable animals.

Marty, however, had trained horses for Westerns and television commercials. He owned his own small entertainment business and traveled around to schools, birthday parties, and other large gatherings to give pony rides and display the tricks of his own horse, Cactus, to an appreciative audience.

Marty was a hero of mine for several reasons, not the least of which was his proactive determination to keep our small hometown of Three Prongs Western. Everything he did – including the name he chose for his horse – defined Marty's Western ilk. In a town that boasted of its cowboy heritage, my heart boasted of only one: Marty.

Forgetting the diet soda I had been walking to the corner convenience store to purchase before the rude red car attempted to eat me, I allowed Marty to settle me into my padded desk chair in front of my computer. Ignoring my objections, Marty fetched a wet paper towel from the bathroom and bent down in front of me to mop the blood off my torn knee. I held on to the arms of the chair, lest I be tempted to throw my arms around his broad shoulders.

With his fabulous purple-blue eyes throwing gold sparks at me, Marty pushed his Stetson back from his forehead and chuckled. "You do get yourself into some real pickles, Miz Mike."

I bristled. "I *had* to choose that spirited horse when we went riding! It was what Pastor Garth would have done!"

He laughed. "Yep – some real pickles."

"And you should have told me that horse was afraid of thunder."

Marty shook his head. "Not thunder, Mike – lightning. He's close to being deaf at his age, you know. Thunder doesn't bother him a bit."

I *hadn't* known. Nor had I known that Marty would be the one to rescue me downstream where the horse and I had parted company after a faster, wilder ride than I had intended.

Anger against Marty was impossible to nurse at such close quarters, though, and I found myself smiling mindlessly back at him and forgetting to breathe when he pushed a strand of loose hair gently out of my face. "You take care of yourself now, Mike. I wasn't planning any more rescues today."

Sadly, Marty's coming to my rescue seemed to be part

of a repeating pattern that I was helpless to control – like with my vehicle, Old Blue. Deer are a real threat on late-night drives in Texas Hill Country, but I am usually a careful driver. Thinking that Marty was ahead of me and had already arrived at the children's benefit that he was scheduled to sing for, I had driven perhaps a bit recklessly that night. I hadn't wanted to miss a note of his compelling songs – many of which he had written himself.

I missed the deer. In fact, I missed the entire herd, but poor Old Blue plunged into a series of neck-wrenching spins that would scare the parts out of even a new car. One tire peeled right off the rim.

Marty stopped to pick me up and take me to the benefit with him, since the car was far enough off the road not to be a traffic hazard and there was no time to change the tire.

What a joy it was to spend the evening with Marty and know he would be my escort home! But by the time the concert ended and he took me back, my neck was scream-ing in such pain that I made a less than alluring hostess. Moreover, whereas Blue quickly recovered from the inci-dent after brief treatment consisting of a new tire, I wore a neck brace for several weeks. The brace tilted my chin up into the air, forcing me to strike a constant and unin-tended pose of disdain. At least for the duration no one had noticed my huge greenish eyes and accused me of staring at them!

Now, my insides were quivering like a parcel of startled daddy long-legs spiders as Marty brushed hair out of my face and smiled at me. Fortunately, Marty was not one for light dalliances. If he had kissed me, I would have fainted.

He had to repeat the question twice before I heard it. "Will you be there?" he asked again. "At eleven?"

Because Three Prongs is a small town, I was able to leap to the meaning of the question. Of course, I wished I could believe that I had made the leap because Marty's soul and mine had somehow knit together. Friday was shrimp day at *The Spanish Tile* restaurant, so named both because it had risen up out of immense limestone blocks along the Old Spanish Trail, and because the roof was the only one in Three Prongs that had been constructed with red rounded brick tile.

Filling plates from the seafood buffet on Fridays was a

Three Prongs tradition, due in part to the fact that the town offered limited choices for dining, but also because the food was excellent. It seemed as if the entire town showed up for Friday's seafood buffet. The secret to getting a table was to get to *The Spanish Tile* early. Only on rare occasions had I managed to finagle a place at Marty's table.

So: Marty was inviting me to have lunch with him.

I returned his smile and nodded. "That would be great," I managed in a voice not quite my own. "Marty ..." I wanted to keep him with me as long as possible. "Did you see what happened? Who was driving the car that nearly hit me?"

He stood up, and I immediately missed the close contact we'd shared a moment before. He laughed. "That, Mike, was Three Prongs' newest joke." Then he sobered. "Of course, it's not really funny considering that it's a downright sin."

"Yes," I said, following my own line of reasoning. "If not a sin entirely, at the very least, it is very rude to try to run over innocent people."

He was shaking his head. "No. I mean about the 'long, lean cheating machine'."

"What! Are we talking about the same thing – the car – or did I miss something else?" My face colored at the admission that I had missed his earlier question about lunch.

"I know you're like me, Mike. We stay out of bars and away from the night life and drinking and the like ..."

What a thrill it was to have Marty say we were alike! M&Ms! I knew it! Before long, we would be marching down the church aisle, and then I could finally give up my silly schoolgirl game of holding mock weddings with brightly colored M&Ms lined up as guests, as Brown and Yellow – Mike and Marty – walked the aisle between them.

"But you must know Zolly Gilmore, that feller who owns Borderbound Watering Hole, the bar? You must have heard about some of his antics."

I nodded. "I've heard that he held a bronc-busting contest with live horses in his bar one night and never repeated it because of broken furniture. I think a few people even got hurt."

"Yup. That was just one of many. The taxi is his newest one."

"Taxi? He started a taxi service in Three Prongs?"

"Yep. That was his car, and if you hadn't been so intent

on scrambling to safety –"

"Which was the wise thing to do, surely!"

He nodded in agreement. "If you hadn't, you would have noticed the 'taxi' signs on the sides – magnetic, peels off. He can put them on and remove them at will."

"Why go to all the trouble and expense to start a taxi service and then take the signs off the taxi? Doesn't make any sense, if you ask me."

"You don't understand, Miss Michal Rice, because you have an inner beauty and keep your thoughts on pure things like the Bible tells us to. The taxi isn't a taxi at all, although his wife thinks it is. The whole thing is a ruse. He slaps the taxi signs on that car and runs around with Candy."

"Candy? I thought his wife's name was Carmen."

"Exactly. Candy is that big ... uh, that blonde barmaid of his with the almost-white hair. No one seems to know her last name or anything else about her. She just showed up in town one day and went to work for him, and he keeps her in that trailer behind the bar – the place he lets his band practice in. Well, they don't get to go into the back. That whole half belongs to Candy ... and Zolly, when he spends the night, which he does almost every night."

"No! And his wife?"

"Poor thing hasn't got a clue. She's even taken the taxi around town on a lark, thinking it's legit."

"How awful!"

"Well, I don't believe I've ever heard anyone accuse Zolly of being a nice feller. Anyway, that wasn't Zolly driving just now. It was that kid from the children's home down south of here, Jared Silvers."

"He ought to lose his license," I said darkly.

"Can't lose what he doesn't have. He's too young for a license. Give him a break. He needs one."

"What do you mean? Who is he? Is he in some kind of trouble, or is it just his driving record that's a debacle?"

"Now don't get mixed up in this, Mike. I know how you like to try to find out about everything and help."

How could Marty know that? He must have talked to Ron. My son had the mistaken belief that one of my bad habits was sticking my nose in other people's business.

"Jared's had it about as rough as a kid can, growing up with no parents," Marty continued. "If church folks would have taken him in, I reckon he wouldn't be hanging out with the likes of Zolly now."

Marty had a point. I nodded in agreement, and for a moment, I even felt guilty. My son Ron was an adult, a married man. His wife, Faith, was a nice creature, although plain. She had long, wavy, light brown hair and eyes that were a true clear green; they made mine look hazel by comparison. Her face was oval, and her nose was long and thin, reminding me of a greyhound. Ron thought she was beautiful.

My son was unaware – thankfully – of the secret antagonism I held against Faith. Before Ron married Faith, he had briefly been engaged to my best friend's daughter, Irene. Donna Johnson and I had been inseparable, partly, perhaps, because we had both lost our husbands at nearly the same time … well, we hadn't lost them really, since they were in Heaven and we knew where to find them. Anyway, Three Prongs residents often said of us, "Mike and Don, huh? Hmm. Let's make one of them the chair on this committee. They know how to get things done."

Donna's daughter and I were nearly as close. I liked to think that Irene and I had matching red hair and that after she and Ron married, people would see us together and mistake her for my daughter. Actually, her hair was a rich, dark red, unlike my pretends-to-be-red locks.

Irene had a young, innocent beauty that maintained its breathless quality into womanhood. When Ron met Faith and dropped Irene like a scorpion crawling up into the palm of his hand, I suffered as much heartbreak from their breakup as anyone. I felt I had been robbed of the daughter I'd always wanted and never been able to have.

Donna suffered, too, but she assured me that parents don't make matches for their children in the United States and that Ron was free to choose. She insisted that Ron's marriage to Faith would not ruin our friendship, but she was wrong about that. Shortly after Ron and Faith married, Donna took Irene and moved back to Georgia to be closer to her parents. For a while we stayed connected through phone calls, e-mails, and occasional letters and cards. Then Irene married the high school agricultural teacher in their town and started having children, so Donna became the quintessential grandmother. She and I lost the treasured connection of friendship that we had attempted to maintain.

By this time Ron and Faith had started a family of their own. While I nearly always mind my own business, some grandmothers (like Donna) tend to get carried away and become too involved in the lives of their children and their children's children. Donna put grandmothering Irene's children in front of our long-distance friendship. It was natural, I suppose, since blood is thicker than water and all of that hullabaloo, but I still felt that Donna held a grudge about Ron's cool treatment of Irene. I know *I* held a grudge against my son for a while. Then I discovered that it was easier to forgive Ron and shift that resentment to Faith.

Ron was beautiful for a man. He had blond hair, blue eyes, and chiseled face with a deep cleft in his chin and dimples when he smiled. I would have chosen a matching wife for him – like Irene, with her young, haunting beauty and red hair – but Ron did his own choosing and was stuck with Faith. At least the grandsons – four-year-old Alex and two-year-old Ryan – turned out to be beautiful children who resembled their daddy.

Anyway, as I thought about my grown son and my empty nest I wondered what had kept me from offering a home to a kid like Jared. My husband, Alfred, had died several years earlier, and the big house on the small ranch was ... empty.

"You know," Marty added, rescuing me from the unstable well of memories that my mind had plunged into briefly, "I've been able to get Jared to come to church with me a few times. He likes the kids his age, but he's kind of shy. If you see him around town, you might invite him too."

I bit my lip and nodded. Marty was my hero, and I could never reach the peerless heights he held in my estimation, but I could try to copy his example when possible. "I'll do that," I said resolutely, ignoring the pain zipping through my knee and the slight ache in my neck and back – souvenirs from Jared's driving.

"Great! I'll see you at eleven." Marty doffed his hat, a natural gesture for him, and left.

The room swam large and empty in the wake of his exodus. I sat in the chair, quieting my breathing and urging my mind to people the office again with Marty. My heart skittered around in my chest like a frightened mouse. I felt younger than I had as a schoolgirl, when I'd endured many a hopeless crush.

I looked down at my rumpled clothing that covered the too-much-of-me that existed and decided that I best leave the whole M&M thing to the dream world, where it belonged. In real life, movie heroes like Marty Richards do not fall in love with old frumps like me, and it would be to my advantage to remember that my past had been blessed with a reasonably good marriage, a wonderful son, an okay daughter-in-law (even if she didn't have red hair and wasn't fish-jumping pretty), and two priceless grandsons. That was already more blessing than I deserved in this lifetime. Best leave Marty for someone drop-dead gorgeous who can match his golden qualities. I only hoped it would not be someone like our town's left-over hippie, Hyacinth Walker.

Hyacinth had an aggravating habit of yawning for no reason. She taught yoga and ran an art colony, adopting New Age ideas as her own. She had openly ogled Marty for a long time.

Hopefully it also would not be Three Prongs *Sidelines* newspaper editor Bea Hernandez, whose misanthropic edge tended to shred friendships.

Both women were frankly a bit foolish when it came to Marty. Unlike me, they fawned over him in public. I was one of Bea's rare friends and had, in fact, worked with her for nearly ten years. Hyacinth, on the other hand, I avoided. She attempted to force-feed everyone she met with unpalatable doses of New Age and Eastern religions, fluffed up and scrambled together so their idiosyncrasies were hidden.

No doubt Bea and Hyacinth would both arrive at *The Spanish Tile* at eleven. Bea put the paper to bed on Thursdays and was fairly free on Fridays. Hyacinth, unlike her name, was a virulent burr, trundling her noxious self around town several times a day.

Realizing that my half-date with Marty might fall prey to Bea or Hyacinth made me glance uneasily at the clock. With a sigh of relief, I realized I had time to attempt to make friends with my computer and get some work done. I was writing the seventh in the Garth Seymour series, and even though the number seven is God's number of perfection in the Bible, it wasn't boding well for me. The Pastor Garth series had slowed in sales. As the royalty checks slimmed, my waist continued to expand. I realized that if I intended to continue eating and purchasing necessities like new clothes to house my ever-increasing size, I'd best get the new book finished quickly – and finished well. Searching for new inspiration, I had rented the Three Prongs office and moved into it; therefore it was even more imperative to finish the book and sell it, because rent was coming due.

Of course, if I found myself unable to pay the rent, I could always move my office back to the ranch outside town. However, there were too many distractions for me at home. The dogs enjoyed romping, long walks. Keeping the ranch the unique, picturesque land that God had formed, with live oak trees extending olive green foliage over fields of romping bluebonnets, mandated hard manual labor, sometimes having to spend entire days in temperatures closing in on 100 degrees as I cut down the non-native mountain juniper trees. Cedar was a greedy water-user, not content to go dormant like the native foliage did during droughts. Streams and water levels in wells dropped as cedar marched across the land. The limbs, with their needle-like leaves, shut out sunlight and trapped whatever rain did fall, starving grass and other plants beneath.

An equally noxious non-native resident was the fire ant, so named because its bite stings like fire. The critters are aggressive and will attack savagely if their mounds are disturbed. Besides inflicting pain and discomfort on humans, they prey on native wildlife. Gone were the horned toads that had once called the Texas Hill Country home. Snakes were scarce, and every year kindhearted people rescued fawns that had been partially eaten alive after birth by the venomous ants; fire ants can smell the wetness of baby deer and attack in droves, entering through the baby's nose and killing the fawns unfortunate enough not to find rescue. I waged a harsh war against the marauders, treating fire ant mounds with chemicals that promised to kill them. Unfortunately, those so-called "silver bullets" only caused a mass exodus, and the fiery little beasts simply took up residence in a new area.

I also found myself chasing armadillos in an attempt to get close enough to photograph them, crawling through dry creek beds looking along the banks for animal burrows and taking pictures of wildflowers rioting along the banks.

I was occasionally rewarded for my efforts by getting close enough to take a picture of a shy ringtail or even a grey fox.

At home, it was too easy to forget that I was a writer, not an artist. It was too easy to plant myself on the screened-in porch with an easel and take up paints and one of Ron's borrowed sign-painting brushes and begin painting vividly colored monstrosities that would never sell at any art show. Besides, in Three Prongs, I was close to the post office, convenient for mailing manuscripts back and forth to my agent. It was possible to watch a parade of interesting possible book characters flow past my large plate glass windows, each new and unique person an inspiration for the written canvas expanding under the labor of my fingertips on the computer keyboard.

It was as difficult to close my mind to the memory of Marty moving around the office as it would have been to turn down a chocolate chip cookie with extra chocolate chunks. I placed my fingers on the keyboard and willed myself to remember the book hero I had created instead of the real-life hero who had just left the office.

The door, which already stood open to invite the warm spring day inside, filled with shadow, and I blinked in surprise. My disheveled appearance after the car incident strummed regret through my mind in rude, sour notes as I feasted my eyes on the vision of loveliness before me.

She was a couple of inches shorter than my five-nine, and she was slim where she should have been and full where fullness was no crime. Her gold hair swept over her shoulders like a sunlight-spangled cloud. As she moved closer to me in her tight Western-cut jeans that looked better on her than they would have looked on a sales rack, I could see that her eyes were a light, friendly blue. She brushed her long blonde hair impatiently back over the shoulder of her checkered Western shirt; she was slim enough where she should have been slim that she was able to thrust her hands into the pockets of her jeans as she read the name plate on my desk. "You're Mike?" she asked in disbelief. "You're the Mike Rice who writes about Pastor Garth?"

I managed a nod. I had been mentally comparing the lovely stranger to Faith and thinking that my daughter-in-law would not stack up favorably next to her. If I could have chosen Ron's wife for him after he'd parted with Irene, this young woman was the epitome of who my choice would have been.

"Mike?" she asked again. "A ... a woman writes those books?"

On second thought, perhaps Ron would deserve better. "Gender is not the big kahuna in writing," I said icily. "A woman is –"

She waved my words away impatiently. "I know all that. I'm a woman, after all. I just didn't know that 'Mike' was a woman. Anyway, I need your help, Miss Rice. I'm so ... I'm desperate!"

I gawked at her like a trout-eating bear, then realized that wasn't helping either of us. How could such a lovely girl be desperate about anything? Surely with those looks, the world is hers to command?

"What's wrong, dear?" I asked, hoping I was not about to be asked to stick my nose in someone's business.

I brightened. If she were pregnant and unwed, I could invite her to come live with me until after the baby was born. My overactive imagination instantly conjured up images of helping her raise a beautiful baby who would look like Ron.

"My sister has been murdered, and I ... I need you to find out who did it."

I gasped at first, but then relief drifted over me like pollen from a live oak tree in bloom, smacked by a blast of north wind. This was going to be so easy. I was not dealing with a pregnant, unwed mother, a drug addict, or a person wanting to commit suicide. I had tried to help all those in the past with varying degrees of success, even amidst my son's derisive comments about his mother's inability to mind her own business. But this I could dismiss easily.

I was already shaking my head. "You need to go to the sheriff's department, dear. I don't investigate things. I make up crime stories – make-believe – and let my character solve them in the story. It's fiction, not real. I'm not a detective. I'm only a mystery writer, not a solver."

"I know that," she said patiently, "but I've already been to the sheriff's office, and they don't believe me! They say ... they just dismiss me because they think Julia's death was an accident. I know better."

"Julia, you say?" I mused out loud, trying to remember. "Was that –

"Yes," she said, with tears growing up around the lower rim of her eyes like crystal gardens. "My name is Lynette Clarissa Greene. I'm undercover right now as Clara Greene. I came here from Alabama last week to do my own investigating, since the police are just blowing it off. Julia was planning to divorce Thor. I'm sure you know him – Thornton Dean? He used to be county commissioner, and he sells real estate now."

I nodded. I had known Thor for a long time and had, in fact, a standing invitation to visit his ranch. Even though I always minded my own business, I had just been too busy to make the trek to the southern end of the county where Thor's ranch was located. He had drawn me a map to the ranch a long time ago, but I had lost it. When I had worked for Bea at the paper, I had reported on county commissioner court meetings. Until Thor met Julia, Bea and Thor had dated. That threw the three of us together at community events.

I looked at Lynette and mused, "As I remember, it was a gas leak that caused your sister's death. She walked into her mobile home, switched on a light, and an electrical spark ignited the propane in the house. The whole place exploded. Sheriff Cruz –"

"Doesn't believe she was murdered."

"I've known Brent for years, dear. He's an honest man and seems to be a good sheriff. He's been re-elected three times."

"Her murder was carefully concealed. Money can do that."

In spite of my resolve not to become involved, I was instantly alert. "Whose money? Do you think Thor killed his wife because she was going to divorce him?"

"That was what I thought at first. Julia had written me, you know."

Why do people assume I know things that are none of my business? I rarely mixed myself up in other people's business.

"She told me she was going to leave him, and Thor knew she was planning to. He was the one who helped her rent the mobile home that blew up." Fresh new tears sprouted up in the crystal garden and shed clear liquid petals down her face. "But I got a job with Thor as his secretary. He doesn't know I'm Julia's sister."

I gasped. "Lynette ... or Clara or –"

"You can call me Lynette or Lynn even. Clarissa is my real middle name. Everyone I've met in Three Prongs knows me as Clara, so just don't call me Lynette around anyone else."

"You are playing a very dangerous game!"

She smiled and brushed the garden of tears out of her eyes. "No. Thor's not dangerous. Now that I'm working for him, I know he didn't do it. He's really torn up over her death and feels like it was his fault because it wouldn't have happened if she hadn't been in the process of leaving him."

"Why did she want to leave?" I asked, forgetting to mind my own business.

Lynette apparently did not hear the question. "Anyway, Thor owns this big ranch. His house and office are up near the front gate. He has several houses scattered around the back roads. He lets his help live in them since they're so far out of town. I'm staying in one of those."

Lynnette pulled a list out of the back pocket of her jeans. I was amazed there was room for it there, as nicely as she filled up her denim.

"Thor was my first suspect," she said, flipping open a slim notebook, "but now I've crossed him off the list." She looked up at me quickly. "I only did that because of the facts. Remember when it happened?"

A fresh batch of tears welled up in her eyes. She was waiting for me to reply, and my mind cavorted like a feeding white bass as I tried to remember details. When I was silent, she answered softly, "Two months ago, at the annual Three Prongs Founder's Day Rodeo and Parade. Thor rode in the parade and then participated in the rodeo until ... news came ... about Julia." Fiercely, she rid her eyes of the new tears. "Julia stayed home that day because some people knew about the separation, and she didn't want to be bothered with too many questions from people. But Thor's son from his first marriage, Nat, is still on the list. Nat is a druggie."

I gasped in dismay.

"He lives in San Antonio but comes up to visit. His dad decided to try a tough love approach to get Nat off drugs and threatened to write him out of his will. If that had happened, Julia would have inherited everything, because there are no other children. Thor's first wife remarried and moved to Australia."

I interrupted her. "Lynette, it seems to me that you need to take your list to Sheriff Cruz and explain all this to him."

"He can't do what you can."

"What do you mean, Lynn? As I told you, all I do is write. The sheriff can actually investigate. He has the training and the manpower."

"But you can pray!"

I blinked at her in surprise.

"You can spread this list out and pray over it like Pastor Seymour would. Ask God who killed my sister."

"I need a Diet Coke," I muttered to myself.

"What?"

I shook my head. "Sorry. Bad habit – talking to myself. Also the Diet Cokes. But the caffeine helps me think, and I don't drink coffee."

"Do you want me to run down to the store and get one for you?" she asked. "I'd be glad to."

She was a real find, this young girl whom I would have selected for my son to marry – since he had dropped Irene for Faith. Faith! What kind of a name is that for a person anyway? Faith belongs in the Bible and in a believer's life, but why name a child with an idea-name?

I smiled at Lynette and shook my head. "No, but thanks."

She continued down the list. "My number one suspect is Hollis Newbark."

I thought of Hollis. His white hair was not unlike Candy's – no one knew if hers was natural or contrived – and his crawly caterpillar-like eyebrows tended to rise up over pale eyes in a seemingly constant state of surprise. I couldn't really think of anyone in Three Prongs whom I disliked, but I distrusted Hollis Newbark. I had no objection to his name on Lynn's list of suspects. Besides, he and Thor were former business partners, and now the two seemed to despise each other for, some undisclosed reason.

"Then, of course," she continued, "there's Buddy Turner –"

"Buddy?" I interrupted. "Why would Thor's maintenance man want to kill your sister? What motive would he possibly have? Granted, he is an alcoholic and undependable but –"

"I have to put down every name connected with her," Lynette answered, "just like you do in your books. I have

Neil Peters down, too, because he rented her the house. I even have that barmaid – Candy someone – because Thor said she threatened Julia once."

"Why would she –"

She shook her head, spilling waves of blonde hair around her face. "I don't know! I don't know why anyone would want to hurt Julia. But you can spread this list out and pray over it and let God show you who did it."

"It doesn't work that way, Lynette, honey."

"You mean God doesn't care about my sister or who killed her?"

"Of course He cares! The problem isn't God – it's me! I'm not always good at hearing what He's trying to tell me."

"Can you … just try?" Fresh tears replaced the old pools in her eyes, and she tried unsuccessfully to blink them away. Her courage and quiet dignity moved me. She squared her shoulders and bit her lip.

I took the list and tried to tell myself that I was not really accepting involvement by accepting the paper.

Lynette saw me studying the name on the list that she had crossed out, Thornton Dean. She smiled wanly. "Thor bought my entire family plane tickets for the wedding eight years ago. I didn't get to go because I had chicken pox, so Thor sent me a box of chocolates. Julia sent me a picture of them at the wedding. I thought Thor was the most handsome man I'd ever seen, and I was happy for my sister."

"Doesn't Thor recognise your name?"

"No. Julia and I were actually half-sisters with different last names, and Thor just sent everything to the family and included my first name, 'Lynette,' on the box, which is why he hasn't connected me with Clara."

"I still think you're playing a dangerous game, Lynn. I think you should leave this investigation to someone else."

"Oh good! You will help! I knew you would understand."

I started to protest, but she threw her arms around me in such an ebullient hug that I would have felt guilty to refuse. She would have, after all, been a quintessential daughter-in-law. As a Christian, I knew God hates divorce, which meant I hated it too, but if Ron ever did divorce Faith …

I looked at Lynette Clarissa Greene and was reminded of sunlight beams bouncing over floorboards in the summer, drawing patterns of bright hope on every object they touched. This girl with a halo of bright gold hair and eyes that sprouted tears like crystal flowers was a keeper.

"I will do what I can, with God's help," I agreed. "Nothing is too hard for God, and nothing is impossible for Him, but I am only a clay vessel." I noted her look of confusion and smiled. "The Bible says God took dust and breathed life into it and created the first man. That makes us all … well, never mind. You can read that on your own in the Good Book. I was just trying to explain that sometimes the part of me that is not spirit gets in the way of what God is trying to accomplish through His Spirit."

Lynette was watching me with the kind of nervous trepidation reserved for fireworks when they're about to explode at close range.

I halted my flow of words. "We'll talk more about all this later."

She nodded but still looked uncertain. A quick flash of intuition warned me that perhaps Lynette would not make as good a wife for Ron as Faith did, because Lynn didn't seem to be a Christian; however, that flash was so swift and sudden that I couldn't glom on to it while under the spell of the stranger's sunny smile.

"How does your family feel about your involvement in all this, Lynette?"

"They don't know. They think I just came here for the funeral and stayed because I liked the town and found a job. I had been working with my dad in the family business at home, and they're glad I'm getting a chance to get away from home and get more experience in the job market. They didn't come themselves. They don't care."

"What a thing to say! Why?" I asked, finally getting tangled up in business that was not my own.

"Well, Julia was Miss Alabama, and –"

"Goodness! She must have looked at lot like you. I know her by name, but I don't believe I ever met her. I've known Thor for years, but I haven't seen him much since he married Julia. I don't believe I ever saw her at all, come to think of it. From what I understand, she busied herself taking care of animals and loved ranch life."

"You compliment me falsely by comparing me to Julia," my dream daughter-in-law said humbly. She pulled a picture out of the checkered pocket of her Western shirt, and I suddenly realised that she must not carry a purse.

Crumpled money tumbled out onto my desk as she showed me the picture of her deceased sister. To me, the resemblance was there, even if only a slight one. Julia's hair was the bright red I had always hankered for, and her amber eyes and the slight sprinkling of light freckles across the bridge of her nose gave her face a sparkle of friendliness and good humor.

"They didn't have children," Lynette said softly. "That was one reason for the split. Thor wanted to start another family before he was too old. He's almost fifty, you know."

"Fifty isn't old!" I protested.

She didn't argue but cast a quick glance of surprise in my direction that told me she considered anyone who didn't think fifty was old about as sound as a water bed. "Julia wanted to straighten Nat out before they had their own children. Besides, she wasn't sure if she could get pregnant. That's why my parents didn't go to the funeral."

"Because she couldn't have children!?"

"Because as Miss Alabama, she won all these scholarships and travel opportunities and had the chance to really make something of herself. My dad's business is small and slows down in the summer months."

"What does your father do, dear?"

"Anyway, Julia ran with a wild crowd and had a baby and wasn't even sure who the daddy was. She gave it up for adoption, and our folks had a fit. They only had two daughters and would have given anything for a son to help dad with the business – although he'd be getting pretty old by the time the baby grew up."

"Around fifty?" I suggested derisively.

Ignoring my sarcasm, Lynette nodded. "They did come here for the wedding because they were hoping Julia had changed, but they didn't come for the funeral because someone had written them that Julia was running around on Thor ... drinking and stuff."

I searched my mind. Three Prongs was small, and rumors ran rampant. I had never heard such rumors about Julia. "Do you think it was true?"

She shook her head vehemently. "No! I don't believe that about Julia nor Thor." She blushed. "He's too old for me, of course."

"Yes, I know. Nearing fifty." With a sudden spate of knowledge, I wondered if Lynette's real objective in coming to Three Prongs had been to chase Thor. While it was true that a great number of years separated them in age, Thor was a wealthy man and would be a good catch for the young girl. She would probably outlive him, and Texas community property laws would render Lynn a wealthy widow after Thor's death. Also, she had eliminated his name from her list of suspects rather briskly.

"Thor is all torn up over Julia's death," Lynette repeated, "and he's never said anything bad about Julia, even though she was in the process of leaving him. The sad thing is, Julia let my parents down so often over the years that they believed the lies someone told them about her. Anyway, about Thor ... he got enough from Julia's life insurance to pay for the funeral but very little else. I was able to check that out when I first started working for him. Buddy Turner and Neil Peters insist the mobile home and the gas lines were all in good repair. Surely they wouldn't lie."

And this was where Lynette's deductions were flawed. Neil Peters was a slumlord at best, under investigation by the district attorney's office. An elderly woman in one of his mobile home units had handed her Social Security checks over to him for years with the understanding that he would purchase groceries for her and pay her utility bills. She starved – or froze – to death and wasn't found for several weeks. The electricity had been off for months, the propane tank was empty, and the only groceries consisted of several unopened cans of chili – food she couldn't tolerate because of her aged and frail digestive system. I almost hoped Peters *was* involved with Julia's death because I wanted him put away for life; homicide involvement would seal the district attorney's case against the monster.

Buddy was an alcoholic with an uncertain work record, but violence had never been one of his trademarks.

Lynette was tapping her long, slender fingers against the list. "I don't know Hollis, although I know Thor is upset with him for some reason. I can probably ask some questions and find out more."

"Do be careful, dear."

She nodded absently. "I've seen Nat a couple of times but never got to talk to him. No loss there, I would say."

I summoned up a memory of the unhealthy-looking young man with the long brown ponytail and tattooed body. Anarchy had redrawn the features on his young face

– bar fights and drunken car wrecks were chronicled with scars, a drooping eye, and slashed eyebrow.

"So we agree about leaving all these names on the list?" she asked eagerly. "If Hollis wanted to get back at Thor for something, he picked something devastating that hurt a lot of other people too. And I haven't found any truth about Candy whatever-her-name-is and Thor, but I know it was only a rumor that they were having an affair."

How could Ron possibly say I need to mind my own business? I wondered. Here's yet another rumor I've never even heard.

"I've got to go now," Lynn said, "but I'll leave you with this list. I kept a copy at home." She tore the pages out of the notebook and handed them to me. "I included directions to Thor's house, since Buddy and Neil have places on the ranch. Even though I know Thor's not involved, I figured you would want to talk to him yourself. Besides, you might be able to ferret out information about what happened with Hollis – you know, as a writer. Maybe you can ask questions about their real estate business or their relationship while he was county commissioner."

I nodded.

She hesitated, then gave me a quick hug that warmed my heart before she left.

The room seemed dark and empty without her coruscating presence, and I felt suddenly old and foolish. What could I possibly do to help that beautiful, sweet young girl? I greatly feared that I was destined to disappoint her.

I fell on my knees and poured out my heart to God. Then, forgetting to check the clock and count down the hours until I could meet Marty for lunch, I set out in search of a murderer.

Chapter 2.

It was a raccoon that kept me from making it to *The Spanish Tile* in time to keep my almost-date with Marty. Perhaps Old Blue shared the blame.

Since the big, ancient car did not have air conditioning – or rather, since the air conditioner did not work – I drove with the windows down. Admittedly, this did not improve my already less-than-glamorous appearance. Flyaway, impossible-to-style, nearly-red hair played unruly games of tag around my oval face with the too-big, almost-green eyes that appeared to consume objects passing before their gaze. Still, driving with my hair blowing back and forth across my face put me in a nearly hypnotic state, and I could envision all the thrilling words Marty would never say to me. In my vision, though, he *was* saying them to me, and I was eagerly sharing my own secret with him: the M&M theory.

The directions Lynette had given me suddenly whipped out the window and folded over the top pipe of a chain-link fence that leaned slightly and looked too fragile to hold back the two Rottweilers that were crashing against it and barking savagely. I slowed Old Blue to consider the wisdom of attempting to retrieve the directions. Looking up into my rearview mirror, I realized in horror that a propane truck was barreling towards the back of my car. Earphones hung from the driver's ears, and he bounced around in the seat of the truck with his hands actually leaving the steering wheel as he seat-danced to the beat of his music that no one else could hear. I floored Old Blue and just managed to get out ahead of him before his front bumper connected with Blue's back one.

The close call made me miss the diet soda I had never had time to get earlier in the day even more. The only beverage I had with me in the car was a warm can of Diet Coke that had been rolling around in the front seat of Blue for a few days. Summoning the lost directions to mind, I remembered that a convenience store should be fairly close; that knowledge cheered me.

That hopeful cheer dissipated, however, when I looked down at the gas gauge and realized that Blue needed a drink almost as much as I did. Gas ran through the antique machine seemingly without ever stopping long enough to power it more than a few miles at a time.

I signaled well in advance, but still barely made the left turn into the gas and convenience store without wearing the propane truck on my bumper. Breathing a sigh of relief and whispering a prayer of thankfulness to God, I pulled up to the nearest pump and slipped out of the car. I noted with amusement that I was not alone. A huge raccoon was sprawled on his stomach on the concrete island, soaking up the early spring sun. I laughed at him, and he wrinkled his black nose at me and winked from behind his black-ringed eyes.

"Hi, pal," I addressed him as I attempted to hold Blue's license plate down at the same time I unlocked the gas cap – always a feat for someone as uncoordinated as I am. With the added distraction of the coon, it was even more difficult.

"Hey, lady!" the store manager yelled, approaching cautiously. "You ain't tryin' ta get gas, are you?"

I looked at him in surprise. "Yes. Why? Isn't the pump working?"

"You don't see that coon?"

"Yeah. He's cute. He's not in the way. I'll try not to disturb him."

"Disturb him!? It's you I'm worried about! He might attack you."

I looked at the coon contentedly sunning himself. "I don't think so. He's a beautiful animal, and he looks friendly enough."

"Yeah, well, I've heard that if they look friendly, they have rabies. No telling when he's gonna get up and leap on you. I seen one jump down out of a tree onto a dog once and try to drown it. You'd best get away. I've already called the sheriff's department. They're sending a deputy out to shoot the darn thing."

"Shoot it!? No way!"

"Well, it won't move, and it's scarin' off my customers. People are afraid to come in and get gas with that thing lying there. I've lost a lot of customers already, and look at the line." He gestured to the far side of the pumps.

I grinned as I noted that one of the customers waiting in line was the careless propane truck driver. Untidy blond hair swung around his face as his body jerked in tune to the music that he'd turned up so loud I could hear it pouring out from under the earphones. His fingers beat the side of his truck outside the open driver's side window, and he lifted his wrist and checked his watch nervously between slaps against the metal of the truck.

"Say," the store manager said, looking at me more closely, "since you ain't afraid of it, do you think you can get it to move?" He backed up as he asked the question. It was clear that when it moved, he wanted to be as far away from it as possible.

The coon realized that the solace of its sunny spot had been compromised. It stood up and stretched, then flicked a pink tongue around its muzzle. Several people had left their vehicles and stood with the store manager, watching to see what I planned to do about the raccoon.

"Listen," I told the intelligent-looking animal, "I don't want anything bad to happen to you, so I'm fixing to do something you probably won't like. Don't worry. I would never do anything to hurt you."

I fished around the front seat and nabbed the can of warm diet soda. I shook it vigorously, aimed it at the raccoon, and popped the lid. Hot soda spewed into the animal's face and all over my hands and arms. The coon leapt into the air with a strangled yowl that sounded like a half-growl, half-shriek. It leapt off the concrete and ran for the woods behind the store. I laughed as my audience yelled, screamed, and scrambled in separate directions, opening up a path for the huge, lumbering animal.

"Mad animal!" the propane truck driver shouted above the confusion. "Someone shoot him quick, before he gets away!"

I spun around and ran over to the truck. "*You* should be shot for your driving!" I yelled. "The raccoon is fine.

You're the one who's mad! You almost ran over me twice, and both times I was doing the speed limit and signaling. Are you blind?"

He turned a sunglasses stare on me. "Whoa, baby!" he said. He went back to drumming the side of his truck and jerking spasmodically with his music.

I left him in disgust and returned to the gas pump to treat Blue to a taste of gas. I didn't have enough cash to fill his gullet, but it was something.

Well-wishers lined up between the gas pump and the store to thank me for my quick thinking, and I shamelessly used the unexpected publicity opportunity to remind everyone to purchase my new Garth Seymour book.

When I was nearly up to the store, an elderly lady grabbed my arm and stopped me. She looked somewhat like an upside-down frosted cupcake with silver hair and a winsome smile. "Please, Miss Rice, I know how busy you are with Father Seymour –"

"Pastor Seymour," I corrected automatically. "He's not a priest."

She waved my correction aside with the puffy orange sleeve of her Mexican embroidered dress, reminding me of a butterfly. "Yes, of course, but I need your help. What with you being a detective and everything, I thought –"

"I'm not a detective," I explained, amazed to face two wrong assumptions in one day. "I'm a writer. I only write about a detective. Pastor Seymour is a character I made up for my books. He's imaginary."

"Yes, of course," she agreed cheerfully, still waving fluttering orange cloth in front of my face and rearranging her bowl-shaped haircut with the breeze from her sleeves. "But you see, it's about Romeo. I wouldn't ask you, except that I see you're an animal lover like me since you took care of that poor little raccoon ... well ... I knew you would understand."

So far, I didn't understand a thing.

"My Romeo's a beautiful, fluffy white dog with yellow patches floating on top like butter, and he has the biggest, brownest, kindest eyes you'll ever see. He's my only companion now that I've lost my husband, and ..." She drew a deep breath and dropped her arms in despair. "He's gone. Missing! Right out of the yard. I can't bear to lose him so soon after losing Edgar. You will look for him, won't you, sweetheart? I just know you can find him for me. You're so smart and resourceful, and I just don't know where else to turn for help."

"Where do you live?"

She pointed. "Just over there, across the road and up that hill."

I looked in amazement at the driveway zigzagging up a steep hill. Even at forty-something, I would get worn out walking up and down it. It was so steep I would have hesitated driving up it in Old Blue. Forgetting my resolve not to involve myself in other people's business, I asked, "Have you driven around the neighborhood and looked for him?"

"Oh, I don't drive no more. I'm too old for that. That's why I'm so thankful they built this little store here, so now I can shop. Once in a while, my sister or some friends take me to Three Prongs or somewhere else for things I can't buy here, like wheelbarrows and the like."

Wheelbarrows!? What would this white-haired old woman want with a wheelbarrow? But her blue eyes were twinkling at me merrily, and I could only hope to still be pushing a wheelbarrow at her age. Perhaps this was God's way of getting my attention and telling me I needed to exercise more and take better care of my body? ... but no. Couldn't be. I had heard the voice of God before. If He wanted to talk to me, He could do it quite audibly.

"I would like to help you," I told her sympathetically, "but I'm just not a detective. I only write stories. I invent them." I felt a bit guilty because I knew I was embarking on a secret mission to help my wish-she-had-been daughter-in-law.

Explaining my inability to help the woman reminded me that I still needed the directions to Thornton Dean's house. I would have to ask the manager when I went inside to pay for the gas and get my soda. "I'm so forgetful, I could hide my own Easter eggs," I muttered to myself.

The cupcake lady brightened. "Oh! You'll hide like a dog and try to find him? What a wonderful idea! Thanks ever so much. There will be a reward in it for you, sweetie. I *knew* you were just as nice a person in real life as you are in books! You *are* Susan Seymour in your books, aren't you? I'm delighted to meet you!" Before I could answer, she enfolded me in a blindingly bright hug. "Come on up the hill and visit me anytime. I never go out except to shop and take Romeo on his walks." Tears welled up in her eyes at the mention of her beloved pet.

She wafted across the parking lot and crossed the road. I stood watching her, wondering how I would ever get up that hill, even if I did find Romeo. Then I marveled that she could see me as the beautiful Susan Seymour, Pastor Garth's ingenuous wife and unflappable companion. It couldn't hurt, I decided, to keep my eyes open for a lost white dog with buttery spots.

With a fearful glance at my watch, I hurried into the store to pay for the gas and purchase the much-needed soda. The manager let me pay for the gas, but was so thankful for my role in sending the raccoon back to nature that he gave me the cold drink at no charge. I felt even more blessed when he drew out a crude map of the Dean ranch and pushed it across the counter to me. "It's a shortcut, ma'am," he informed me, and I was thankful for anything that might let me keep my lunch date with Marty.

Surprisingly, the shortcut carried Blue down a hard-packed caliche road. The closest the road had ever come to paving was the traversing of county road trucks with loads of asphalt for patching already paved roads. I steered Old Blue around the worst of the missing chunks of dirt and mused that the shortcut might take longer than keeping to the pavement. Only, since Lynn's directions were gone, I didn't know how to get there on the pavement.

Live oak trees laced fingers of leaf and limb together over the road, draping it in shade. Spring had breathed life into clusters of white and yellow wildflowers and sent them tumbling over the rugged landscape, punctuated by haphazard patterns of boulders and clumps of prickly pear cactus. Yuccas shot wands of white blooms up into patches of sunlight. Old Blue had to halt momentarily to let a herd of deer cross in front of us, leaping effortlessly over brush and fences. The dirt road wound haphazardly down to the river.

Clint Flavors sat on the ledge of the low-water crossing bridge fishing. His long, lanky legs shoved their way out the bottom of soiled coveralls and trailed in the current. He brushed dark brown hair that was drizzled with grey around the edges away from his face and turned a blank brown stare in my direction. Slowly, a light of recognition blinked in his eyes, and his aimless smile spread convincingly. "Morning, Miz Rice. I didn't recognize you in that new car."

I had owned Blue for more years than I could count, but I returned his smile. "Catching any fish, Clint?"

"Naw. They ain't biting today. Dogs up yonder are romping around, playing in the water and scaring away all the fish."

My eyes followed the thick point of his grease-embedded finger. Two dogs frolicked in the water, the male clearly determined to win the favor of the female. Excitedly, I realized the identity of the shaggy white dog with butter patches. "Romeo!" I exclaimed.

Clint hung his dark head. Red patches colored his broad cheeks. "Aw, that's nice of you to say, Miz Rice. I never was much in school for learning from the books and whatnot, but I don't think I'm very much like that Romeo feller, from what I remember about him. Course my girlfriend and me watched the movie once, and I do kinda look like him."

It amazed me to know that Clint Flavors had a girlfriend who watched classical movies. I didn't have the heart to tell him that the white dog's name was Romeo. People in Three Prongs liked to say that Clint wasn't the brightest crayon in the box, but he was a hard worker. With his lack of education and the added burden of an upstairs light that didn't always switch on, Clint could only find labor-intensive jobs: fencing, chopping cedar, clearing rocks out of pastures, and so on. Even as his age increased, Clint never turned down hard manual labor. He pedaled his bicycle into town daily and waited at *The Spanish Tile* for someone to hire him. If no one did, he went fishing.

"Clint," I asked, now completely involved in someone else's business, "how would you like me to get rid of those dogs for you so you can fish in peace?"

"Naw, that's okay, Miz Rice. I don't want no dogs hurt on my account. I can find somewheres else to fish."

I laughed. "I'm not going to hurt them, Clint. I'm just going to take one of them home, and then the other one will leave. I need you to help me catch him."

Clint ran a hand through his closely cropped dark grey hair. "Aw, that's right fine of you, Miz Rice, but there's two of them." He frowned as he considered the situation seriously. "How will you know which one to take home and which one will just leave?"

"Well, I don't know for sure," I told him in a conspiratorial manner, "but we'll get hold of that white one first and try that."

Clint nodded, his dark eyes catching sudden light from somewhere inside as he smiled. He carefully propped his fishing pole on a broken tree limb and took long strides towards the playful dogs.

Catching Romeo proved no easy feat. He led us on a chase that crossed the shallow river several times and took us further and further away from Clint's fishing hole and my car. I looked down at myself in dismay. There I was on the way to an appointment with a well-known community leader who had been county commissioner. My wet skirt hung on me leadenly, my already torn pantyhose sported new runs, and my sandals squished when I walked. Worse yet ... *Marty!* He had already seen me at my worst once that day, and now it looked as if it would be twice. I had no time to drive home and change clothes and still make the seafood buffet on time.

Finally, I managed to ease close enough to Romeo to grab his collar. He whined piteously as his female friend ran off into the woods, out of sight.

"You're a right good dog catcher, Miz Rice," Clint panted; both of us were out of breath. "You sure this is the one you want? I can run after that one yonder."

I gulped air into my lungs and smiled at Clint. "Thanks, but we'll try this one first." I gestured to a huge cement bridge spanning the river in the distance. "What is that? I didn't think this little river had a bridge that big. When was it built?"

Clint squatted down on his heels and laughed. "It's a secret, Miz Rice. That bridge to nowhere is a secret. I know about it because my girlfriend done told me. People in town don't think much of Clinton Flavors, and they sure as heck don't know he knows the secret! They don't even believe Clint can get a purty girl like mine for a girlfriend, but I got her, all right, and I've asked her to marry me five times already." He paused, looking as defiant as it was possible for Clint to look. "She just ain't ready to get married yet. She's younger than me, and her hair is as purty as them yeller spots on that dog."

"I'm sure she's beautiful," I told Clint quickly. When someone hurt Clint's feelings, he could run away inside like wet sand in a river current, and I didn't want to scare him off without getting my answers. "What's the secret about the bridge?" My curiosity overshadowed my promise to Ron to mind my own business. The immense concrete bridge was a mystery, and I – of all people – know that mysteries are for solving.

Clint hadn't disappeared inside, but he was shaking his head gently. "Now, Miz Rice, how could I tell you? It wouldn't be a secret no more, and my girlfriend might get mad. I promised not to tell nobody."

I dragged the unwilling Romeo back to Old Blue, thankful that the dog did not try to bite. Whenever the dog dug his claws into the ground and quit moving, Clint pushed. My legs were weak from exertion by the time I finally hauled the unwilling passenger into the backseat and thanked Clint. I didn't even want to consider how I would get Romeo up to the cupcake lady's house.

Clint was still chuckling to himself over the secret about the bridge to nowhere, and I decided that when I had more time, I would find out about that bridge. It was one of the most deserted areas of the county, and I couldn't imagine why such a huge new-looking bridge would have been built over the meager Three Prongs River.

Once I waved goodbye to Clint, I began whipping my resolution into a strong enough mixture that it would cover me. Since my passenger was still barking and yelping out protests and scratching at the windows seeking escape, I needed to drive Old Blue up that steep hill to the cupcake lady's house. I wasn't sure if I could walk up that hill alone, but I knew I could never drag the unwilling Romeo that far. I was too out of shape.

Breathing a silent prayer, I floored Old Blue and sent the car bucking up the hill, skidding and sliding all the way. I knew that if I stopped Blue before I turned around at the top, I would either be stuck and need a tow truck to rescue me or have to back down the narrow, winding drive to the bottom. My neck wasn't up to looking out the back window and backing up that far, and when the low-slung bumper hit the bottom of the hill, it would dig into the pavement. Blue and I experienced about as much of a nerve-, neck-, and car body part-wrenching as when we'd missed the deer and were rescued by Marty.

I spun the car around on top of the hill, narrowly

missing trees, rosebushes, and a clutter of potting buckets in a wheelbarrow. A cloud of dust billowed up around us, obscuring the little yellow house that was now behind Blue. When the dust settled, I eased out of the car and faced an astonished cupcake lady.

"Oh ..." was all she could say.

My heart was hammering so painfully that I couldn't speak at all.

Then she saw Romeo and threw her arms around me. "Thank you! Thank you, Miss Rice! Oh!" She ran to the car and opened the door.

Romeo looked at me uncertainly before he jumped out to be cuddled by his mistress. He had been as frightened on the bucking rodeo ride up the hill as Blue and I had been.

The cupcake lady introduced herself as Alice Fieldmaster and attempted to reward me for finding Romeo with handfuls of change that I refused.

"No, please," I told her. "It was no trouble at all" – a mendacious statement considering that my wet, uncomfortable clothes hung on me, adding weight for my tired, aching limbs to carry. Romeo's white fur was now enshrined in my wet clothes, and I was aesthetically in no shape to keep my appointment with Thornton Dean or anyone else. Nevertheless, there was no time to change, and if I didn't get to the Dean ranch soon, I would even miss lunch with Marty. "Your dog ran away with a girlfriend, Mrs. Fieldmaster."

"Oh no! Not my Romeo! He wouldn't do that! He's a good doggie."

I wondered why she was surprised that a dog named Romeo would run off with a female. "I'm afraid it's true, ma'am, and unless you take him to the vet and get him neutered, it will happen again. He might get hit by a car or stolen next time and never come home."

"Oh!" Tears washed down her cheeks at the mere thought of losing her pet.

"Plus," I said gently, "we have too many dogs in the county already. Unwanted puppies usually face neglect or worse. If no one claims them, they get euthanized.

"Eutha-what?"

"Put to sleep, ma'am."

"Oh!" She straightened up and wiped wetness from her

cheeks. "Yes, I know you are right, and I am so ashamed of myself. Only ... Edgar only just died, and all the doctor bills are left over. We never could afford life insurance." She shook her head. "I will just have to try to manage it somehow," she said with a note of determination edging into her voice. "Romeo is worth any cost." She thanked me again and then hurried Romeo into the house, still lecturing him in tones of love.

Driving back down the crazy hill, I realized this left me with a dilemma. I knew what I needed to do, but I was totally unwilling to make any of the sacrifices involved, much less all of them. I would be late for my meeting with Thornton Dean, I would miss the seafood buffet, I would miss my sort-of date with Marty, I would be spending money that I could ill afford with the sales slump my books were currently experiencing, and – perhaps worst of all – I would need to walk or crawl back up Mrs. Fieldmaster's impossible hill after I managed to get Old Blue down – an impossible feat for my forty-something and out-of-shape body.

The manager of the convenience store was outside leaning against the building, talking in low tones on a cell phone, and he looked somewhat astonished to see me again. I parked Old Blue out of the way and crossed the road.

I spent the next fifteen minutes scrabbling up the steep hill that the elderly lady had walked straight up in a matter of minutes without even pausing to catch her breath. Fortunately, she was tucked away inside the house with Romeo somewhere, and a scraggly cedar tree met my exigency for rest. When my chest no longer felt crushed from the exertion of climbing the hill, I slipped up to the porch and stuffed the envelope with the money and the note inside into the handle of the storm door. Then I rang the doorbell and slipped around to the side of the building, where I could hear without being seen.

"Why, Romeo!" Alice Fieldmaster exclaimed. "Someone has left you money to get you taken care of so you won't run off again. The note don't have a name on it, but I'm sure it was that nice lady, Susan Seymour in her books. I'll have to see if I can find her phone number and call her to thank her ... or find her address and send a card."

There was the sound of a struggle at the door.

"No, Romeo," Mrs. Fieldmaster said in a determined voice. "I won't let you out to run away again. Come on, boy. Let's go call the vet and get you an appointment. Gladys will give us a ride. It's so good to have her close enough to help."

The storm door slammed, and I heard the decisive click of the inside door as well. I eased out of the shadows at the side of the house and started down the hill. True, I made it down faster than up, but even turning my feet sideways and trying to slow my descent failed at times, and I wound up sitting on my bottom and sliding. My skirt, which was already wet and wrinkled, was now decorated with a mud patch on the back, and my hose were so completely ruined that once I was safely back in Blue, I removed the tattered shards that still clung around my waist and crammed them into the faded "Don't Mess With Texas" trash bag that I kept slung over the radio dial on the dashboard – since, like the air conditioner, the radio was inoperative.

It was insanity to keep an appointment with my clothes and body in such a state of disarray, but I had traveled miles, used gasoline I could ill afford to replace, and spent precious time when I could have been winging my way to *The Spanish Tile* to meet Marty. I was now within a couple of miles of the Dean ranch, and a sudden spate of anger at myself for the dystopia I had created sent me driving between the huge stone gate posts and up the drive to the main house.

The house was prestigious to a fault. It sprawled on a manicured hill, overlooking a private lake complete with a boat ramp. A tennis court dozed in the spring sun on one side of the house, and a swimming pool glittered invitingly on the other side. Expensive lawn furniture was scattered around the pool, and I looked longingly at the tempting water. Bathhouses stood inside the chain-link fence that surrounded the pool. If only I had brought a swimming suit ... but no. I'm here on a mission, not for pleasure. I was on the trail of a murderer in an attempt to bring justice to his victim and closure to a beautiful young xeno who had dropped into my hometown and my heart with all the sudden beauty of the summer sun bouncing out from behind a cloud.

The auspicious surroundings mocked me. I was too pedestrian to find concord in that verdure of riches. I felt like a crudely cut slab of potato that had popped out of grease and landed on a gold serving tray next to caviar. How could someone as totally unsuitable as me possibly find success in this mission that had been thrust upon me? It was about as likely as Clint deciding that he wanted to take night classes and get his GED so he could apply to San Antonio's St. Mary's University and get a law degree.

Chapter 3.

The maid who answered Thornton Dean's door looked at me askance. For a moment, I thought she would close the door on me, as if I were a stray neighborhood cat. Before she could make that move, however, Thornton himself arrived. Thor was nearing fifty, tall and lanky, with swept-back light brown hair that lengthened fashionably behind his ears and darker brown eyes that were intense and brooding. Swimming, jogging, and bicycling kept him in shape, and he was undeniably attractive and virile. Still, my mind was trained on M&Ms and was indifferent to Thor – as a man, at least. To me, Marty was delectable chocolate, a fix I hankered after. Thornton Dean was a vanilla-frosted cinnamon roll, a pastry that I knew would sit too leadenly on my spirit.

Thor's eyes surveyed my soiled, ruined clothing and the added devastation of my body. One eyebrow lifted derisively, and then he held out a hand as thick as a floor plank and invited me inside. "So, you finally made it out to the ranch to visit me, Miss Mike." He chuckled. "I remember that whenever we were in commissioners' court and talk swung around to the critters Julia and I collected, you always said you wanted to come and visit us. It sure has taken you a mighty long time to get here. I wish ... oh, I wish Julia could be here."

Still looking at me with disdain, the maid left with a petulant toss of her head.

I offered no explanation and made no apologies for my appearance as I followed my host into the spacious living room.

After another look at my dirty and disheveled clothes,

Thor directed me to the kitchen instead and parked me on a high-backed wicker barstool, where the mud smeared on the back of my skirt would cause minimal damage.

From my high perch, I could admire the outside view of the twisting lake and wind-tossed live oak trees throwing down patches of shade for longhorn cattle and top-breed quarter horses. A pet llama stood outside the house, looking into the window with its ears perked up curiously. Its playmate, a black and white border collie, circled the llama's feet playfully.

Thor smiled. "Because Julia and I never had children, we adopted a lot of pets, but you already knew that. We've talked about it before."

The inside of the Thornton home was as aesthetically pleasing as the outside. Wide rooms vaulted up into high ceilings, bedecked with crystal chandeliers and quietly whirring ceiling fans with brightly painted blades. Each room was awash with color, from ceiling to walls, and low stonework dividers – not walls – separated the living room, dining room, and kitchen from each other. Live plants beamed at each other with smiling faces along the stone-wall dividers. I looked around at the opulence and sighed.

Thor nodded and said quietly, "Julia did all the designing and decorating. It was her hobby. It meant a lot to her. It made her happy, and that meant a lot to me."

Wordlessly, I nodded, thinking to myself, I could live in a place like this! Then God's voice spoke into my spirit, "Could you really ... and still serve Me?"

I had no answer to the question, but it came so loudly, so audibly that I jumped and looked around to see if Thor had heard it.

Thor was pacing, striking a coiled fist into the flat palm of his hand. "I guess you heard what happened to my wife."

I could see why Lynette had crossed him off her list: He seemed genuinely grief-stricken. "I'm sorry," I said softly, not knowing what else to say.

"Yeah, everyone's sorry – especially me. If only I had known –"

"Mr. Dean, I'm sorry to intrude. I just had a few questions, and –"

"Not if you keep calling me 'mister'," Thor said with a determined smile. "I've known you for longer than I knew Julia. Remember how you and me and Bea used to pal around? Crickets! What a long time ago that was! I hate remembering. It makes me remember my age. Anyway, I know you're a staff writer for Bea at Sidelines." Thankfully, he was unaware of the fact that Bea and I had parted company long ago. "I'd expect you to have a few questions. I'm rather surprised you haven't shown up here before now."

"Uh … yes, well, it's been a busy time and –

He waved my explanation aside. "It's always busy in Three Prongs. When there's nothing going on, creative people invent stuff."

I smiled in agreement. Parades we had – from Founder's Day to pet parades to the annual livestock parade down Main Street before the 4-H livestock show. There was even an annual river parade in the Three Prongs River. In dry years, participants walked on the bottom of the river and bent over to push the entries that were not self-propelled.

Before I could ask a question, Thor asked one of his own. "Are you still writing books?"

"Yes. I'm working on my seventh right now."

"That's great! I'm afraid I can't say I've read any of 'em, as they aren't really my style, but Julia loved them all. Now … what do you need to know?"

I glanced at my watch and breathed a sigh of relief. If I finish with Thor quickly, I'll still be in time to meet Marty. "First, about that bridge to nowhere –

He was instantly startled, and an angry flush colored his broad cheeks. He swore under his breath. "I thought you were here about Julia … to do a story on safety tips for propane heating. What's all this about that bridge?" He seemed to catch his scattered thoughts and marshal them into one unit, like wind filling a sail. "That is not a bridge to nowhere, by the way. It connects a large subdivision to Three Prongs. It's a shortcut."

"Does anyone live there, in the subdivision?" I asked in surprise.

He shifted uncomfortably. "Well, not a lot of people yet, but they will … and then the bridge will pay for itself in the convenience it provides them."

"Who paid for the construction of bridge?"

He quit pacing and flung up his hands. "The Texas Department of Transportation split the cost with the county, but check my record as county commissioner. I didn't vote for it even though Hollis Newbark begged me to."

"How much did it cost?"

Thor's face hardened against me and my questions. "I don't remember. You'll have to look it up. It's all in the records of previous county commissioners' court meetings." My silence prodded him into further speech. "It was supposed to open up a fancy retirement village and shopping mall and bring all kinds of businesses to this end of the county. About all we have is a convenience store, you know. We have to travel miles to shop. The developers – not the county taxpayers – should have paid the entire amount. It put the county budget so far behind in the road and bridge department that some of our roads missed the target date for paving."

I nodded; Blue and I had been on one of those roads that very day. "When is the projected date for the construction of all those dream projects?"

He shook his head and plopped onto a tall wicker stool beside me. "Don't know. It's like you said – a dream project – and the developer must have suddenly woke up and walked out of his dream state into reality. Everyone connected with the XYZ Corporation vanished like letters falling off the end of the alphabet. Unfortunately, old Newbark didn't disappear ..." (Hollis, I knew, was Thor's age and was hardly old.) "... but he never talks about the project. He and I disagreed over project funding, and he's never forgiven me. His part of the project cost him big bucks, and he wanted to pass his investment cost back to the taxpayers. He thought my position on commissioners' court would help him, but I refused to use my elected position to help anyone other than the taxpayers who elected me. Talk to Hollis. He'll be able to answer your questions better than I can, and I'm sure he'll be glad to talk about that bridge." Thor grinned a boyish, engaging grin. "In fact, Hollis loves to talk about that bridge. It gives him more opportunity to bash me!"

"Thanks. I'll do that. Now, about your wife's accident –

"Yes! Please do a story on that. Propane in homes should be outlawed, in my opinion. Propane appliances should sit outside the home."

I tried to image how that would work with a kitchen stove.

Thor's voice broke painfully. "If you had seen what happened ..." Amazingly, tears rushed up into his dark eyes.

My insides quivered in response. I felt almost sick myself as I imagined the grisly scene. "Uh, well, I've heard a rumor –

Thor crashed a fist against the counter with such fury that I jumped in my chair. "So have I! I don't know what to think. Sheriff Cruz thinks it was an accident. If it was deliberate – if my Julia was ... murdered – well, I'm the most likely suspect. I suppose I should be relieved that it's been written off as an accident, but I'm not. If someone did that to Julia, I want them to pay with their life, just as they stole hers. If you had only seen ..." Thornton dropped his head on his muscled arms on the counter, and his shoulders shook.

I was embarrassed to be a witness to this private grief that Thor normally hid from the world. He had forgotten my presence and made no reply when I stood up and quietly announced my departure. I let myself out of the spacious home and headed for Blue, thinking only of getting quickly back to Three Prongs to meet Marty. After my unnerving interview with Thor, I needed the comfort of good, hot food and the even more appetizing companionship of Marty.

I had nearly reached the safety of Blue when a thin hand wound around my arm like tentacles. I bit back a scream and whirled around to find myself nose to nose with the alcohol-ravaged face of Buddy Turner.

"I heard you talking to my boss," he said. "I heard him say you were writing something. I didn't do it." Buddy's light blue eyes swam in yellowed whites with broken red veins. The broken blood vessels at the tip of his bulbous nose and thin cheeks gave his countenance a ruddy complexion. "I ain't drank a drop since it happened," he continued defiantly, although I hadn't recovered enough from the shock of being grabbed to speak. "Tell the sheriff for me. You're a big shot around here and a friend of his too."

I sorted around in my mind for questions to ask him, and he took my silence as an accusation.

"I wasn't drunk!" His fingers dug into my arm painfully, and I reached down and released myself from his grasp. "I loved Julia, Miss Rice. I know that's your name on account of I heard you in there with Mr. Dean. He sent me over there to take care of the house for him since Julia had decided to move out for a spell. I was to see it was safe and comfortable." He grabbed my arm again and peered intently into my face. "It was, Miss Rice. I'll swear before God that it was safe."

Gently, I unwound his fingers again. "I believe you, Buddy. What do you think happened?"

He shook his head wildly. The yellowed-grey ponytail he wore down the back of his neck whipped back and forth over his shoulders. "I don't know. I know what, but I don't know who. I think someone loosened that gas line inside and set it up to blow. Honest, Miss Rice, I don't know who woulda done a thing like that, but it wasn't me. The sheriff's been nosing all over around me like a hound on a coon scent. "

"If you're innocent," I said, "you have nothing to worry about, Buddy."

He shook his head more wildly than before. "That's where you're wrong, Miss Rice. You ain't never been poor."

Considering my present financial state, I found that spurious assumption humorous.

"You don't know how the law bothers folks that ain't got money. It's terrible, Miss Rice. I'm plumb scared." Tears shook loose from his eyes and crawled down the leathery face, wrinkle by wrinkle. "I'm a no-good drunk, sure, but I ain't never been careless in my work. They all think I was careless and got Julia killed. You're a smart lady. You write them books. You can find out what happened. You know who to talk to and what questions to ask. You'll help, won't you?"

"Buddy, this is really none of my business. I mean, I'm a writer, not a detective. I try not to get involved in things that don't concern me. It's for the sheriff's department –

His claw-like hand clutched my arm again, a bit more desperately this time. "Please just try. I'll help any way I can. I can get into Neil Peters' office if you want me to. He's the one who rented Julia that mobile home, you know. I have a key to Peters' office. I work for him when I'm not working for Mr. Dean, and Peters works for Mr. Dean when he's not running his own rentals. Once Peters gets people in his rentals, they usually stay on the account of they can't find no lower prices. That gives Peters time to do Mr.

Dean's bidding."

"You think Neil Peters was behind Julia's death?"

Again, there came the savage shaking of head that bounced the rope-like protrusion on the back of his head. "Like I told you, I don't know what to think, but if he done it ... well, whoever done it, I want them to pay. Miss Julia, she was a nice lady – real pretty and nice and didn't treat nobody like dirt."

"And you think you could find something in Peters' office that would link him to Julia's death?"

"Not if he ain't responsible, Miss Rice. No one could have wanted to hurt Miss Julia, but someone must have, because that mobile home was sound as a dollar," he said sternly, though it was not an intransigent assurance in face of the U.S. economy's record of ups and downs. "I know that trailer was sound," Buddy insisted. "I checked it all myself for Mr. Dean."

"I'll tell you what, Buddy. I've got an appointment now." I glanced at my watch and realized I was already running late, but perhaps I would at least make it before Marty left the restaurant. Perhaps I will at least get to see him again. Twice in one day! What a joyous contemplation! "If you can check out Peters' office without getting caught," I told Buddy, "go ahead. Just don't do anything that will be dangerous for you or cause you to get into trouble. Call me if you find anything. I have an office in Three Prongs now, so you can call there. Meanwhile, I'll see what I can find."

He nodded, and his lips came as close to smiling as was possible with the alcohol-wasted features. "Thanks, Miss Rice. You won't regret this, you know. Buddy won't let you down."

This time he released me, and I fled the rest of the way to Blue and slipped quickly into the seat before Buddy could stop me again. If Old Blue hadn't faltered on a steep hill, I would have kept my lunch date with Marty, but the reason I put "Old" in front of Blue's name was the age, make, and model of the antique machine. Blue sputtered, and I glanced into the rear view mirror. A small red car was behind me, so I eased to the curb to allow the vehicle to pass. Instead, it slowed down and maintained the same distance between – a far enough distance to hide the identity of the driver, but I could tell there was only one person in the car. The more I slowed, the more the other car slowed. When I sped up, it sped up. Regardless of Blue's speed, the red car maintained the same space between us. I was being followed!

The first sliver of fear fled in the wake of excitement! After all, it was broad daylight. What could possibly happen? It was just like something out of one of my books, just like being a real detective! Knowing Old Blue's strengths, I slowed at the dip at the bottom of a hill, then floored the gas pedal of the old car. Blue fairly leapt up the hill, gobbling up yards with greedy tires, a performance the newer, smaller car was unable to match. The red car fell out of sight around the curve at the top of the hill, and I whipped Old Blue off the paved highway and spun around on a dirt road to park neatly behind a billboard announcing Three Prongs' newest subdivision. Sure enough, the red car finally picked up speed; it shot past me and was quickly out of sight.

Laughing, I pulled out from behind the sign and turned down the dirt road where I had found Romeo. If the bridge to nowhere had been open, I had a feeling it would have provided a shortcut into town that would allow me to still be in time to catch Marty for lunch. Clint Flavors was gone, so I thought perhaps someone had come by to hire him for the day – or else the fish had not been tricked into taking Clint's bait even after Romeo and the other dog had ceased frothing up the water.

The bridge looked solid and finished. The barricades stood so far apart that it was easy to pretend the bridge was open. Blue nudged them gently aside. The bridge did indeed lead to nowhere: just a winding, dipping dirt road that separated carpets of wildflowers into small quilts of colors. Smoky blue-black hills folded into each other in the distance, changing colors as clouds crowded in on the sun. Besides chronic drought, Texas Hill Country suffered from two other debacles that I battled diligently at my ranch: the savage wildlife-eating fire ants and pesky, encroaching mountain juniper. I sighed and shook my head as Old Blue nosed past what had once been a picturesque pasture, sporting a bluebonnet carpet in the spring; now it was marred by cedar sprouts and huge fire ant mounds, stripped of vegetation, and swarming with the hostile insects. I was nearly to Three Prongs before I passed the first house, a lovely old L-shaped ranch house with a wide, shady veranda. Two older model pickup trucks were backed up to the porch, and the couple unloading furniture looked vaguely familiar. I was in too much of a rush to pay much attention. Ron always said – albeit unfairly – that I was not observant enough for a writer. He, on the other hand, noticed everything.

I drove into Three Prongs wondering if I had beaten my little red sporty shadow. Wow! Just like a real detective, I had worried someone enough to earn a shadow! I parked Old Blue on Main Street and rushed into *The Spanish Tile.*

I was late. Marty was gone, and so was the seafood buffet. I sank down into a booth muttering "M&Ms" pitifully to myself.

The arch waitress with the flawless figure and dark, full hair framing a pert face attempted to decipher my strange babbling.

Missing my lunch date with Marty was so painful that my hunger was swept aside. Still, for the sake of strength, I knew I should eat something. I ordered a Mexican plate consisting of a taco, two enchiladas, rice, beans, flour tortillas, and chips with salsa. Then, just to round things out, I ordered a plate of guacamole nachos as an appetizer. The day could not possibly get worse, I told myself, but I was wrong about that.

Hyacinth Walker trundled in aimlessly and spotted me sitting by myself in the booth. Pointedly ignoring her was futile. She plopped down in the booth opposite me and yawned. "You should have been here earlier, Mike," she said cheerfully. "Marty was here waiting for you. I think he was disappointed when you didn't show. Not to worry though. I stayed with him so he wouldn't be alone, and then, of course, Bea showed up. That woman has no class. She practically drooled over him in public."

I tried to hide my distaste for Hyacinth as I looked at her. Her blonde hair parted down the middle and hung long and straight on both sides. Today, she had woven bones and feathers into it less than neatly – not even bones, feathers, and artful combing could hide the dark grey roots creeping out to hint at the age Hyacinth took such pains to hide. She was trim, with a knockout figure, but her colorless blue eyes sagged into telling shadows beneath them. I had surprised her secret out into the open some time ago: She smoked. That abuse to her body was beginning to write itself in deep, telling wrinkles and creases that refused to blend into her contrived youthful image.

Without asking, Hyacinth reached over to help herself to some of the hot corn chips and salsa the waitress had brought me to munch on while my meal was being prepared.

I suppressed the urge to smack her slender, grabbing hand.

"So," she said slowly, making no attempt to cover a yawn, "are you and Marty an item now or what? Mr. Nice Guy doesn't involve himself in light affairs. He's looking for a wife. He pictures sitting on the front porch of a cabin with hummingbird feeders overhead and boxes of blooming flowers lined up around the porch rail."

"How do you know that?" I asked indignantly. Marty and I had shared our dreams of living in such a setting once. In fact, that was what had birthed my silent game of referring to the two of us as M&Ms.

Hyacinth smirked. "I told you that Bea and I entertained him when you didn't show up. He's lonely, poor man. I wonder ..." A dreamy, faraway look stole over her face. "I have a cabin at the art colony. It overlooks the river, and I believe it would just about fit into Marty's dream."

I choked on a corn chip in my attempt to act nonchalant.

Hyacinth continued in the same dreamlike state. "There's only one little problem with the cabin, but I think we could work that out." She leaned in close to me. "It's my house."

I could no longer act nonchalant, and my temper flared. "That would never work, Hyacinth! Don't you know the Bible says that believers should not be yoked together in marriage with nonbelievers? You and that wacky religion of yours –

"I didn't say anything about marriage, Mike. I said we could work things out. I think Marty could be ... persuaded."

"Never," I said stoutly, although I was not nearly as sure as I sounded. "You can't persuade Marty into sin, Hyacinth. You don't have that much power."

She clucked her tongue and shook her head at me as if bemused by my mindless innocence. "Mike, Mike, Mike ... by the way, why don't you use your real name? Michal is a beautiful name and much more feminine sounding."

"Yeah, if you spell it for people," I said tersely. "Otherwise it sounds just like 'Michael', Mike for short."

She laughed a light silver laugh like a bell, a laugh that I could easily have coveted if I were given to such sins as covetousness and sticking my nose into other people's business. "You are so sensitive about Marty," she said archly. When the waitress arrived with the food, Hyacinth looked at it with mock horror. "Mike, are you going to eat all that! No wonder you're putting on weight."

I tried to kick her under the table and hit the edge of her bench instead.

"You should join my yoga classes. It's great exercise."

"And you should quit smoking!" I shot back. I drew myself up in the seat. "Marty would never live with someone who smokes." My hero Marty wouldn't, of course, but I had no idea if the real Marty would.

Hyacinth ignored the dig. "I smoke to keep myself thin."

"Why? For a smaller casket? You're signing your death warrant with every cigarette."

She yawned and shook her head. "At least I'll look good in the coffin and at the beginning of my trip to whatever world is next. I eat a lot of salad and fresh vegetables and fruit and exercise a lot. I'm fifty-three, and I've been told I still look like I'm in my thirties."

"I wouldn't say that."

"Marty finds me attractive. At this point, I think that's what matters to me most. Too bad he's so deep into religion, but I believe I could, uh, enlighten him."

"Marty has Jesus, not religion," I told her hotly. "You can't enlighten him when he's the one walking in truth! You could only attempt to peddle your lies to him, and he's too wise to purchase a lame horse."

She laughed. "Dear Mike! Witty even when you're not writing a book. I know you and Marty are against smoking and drinking and hanging out in the dancehalls and having fun like normal people do, but surely even you have no aversion to exercise." She fished around in a denim handbag that was painted in an abstract design and peppered with ill-matched colored beads. I imagined it had been a gift from one of her students at the art colony.

Her twenty-plus acres of land fronted the Three Prongs River. Cement block cabins with cedar-shingled roofs and rustic cedar log porch railings dotted the river frontage and housed some of Three Prongs' most eccentric recluses. I knew one of the families personally since their twenty-two-year-old daughter Samala attended my church. She was often accompanied by Durant Edmonds, a solid young man who worked for the local electric cooperative. I could not envision a happily-ever-after ending for their romance. Samala's artistic parents intended to keep their daughter at home, working for them indefinitely. If she wanted freedom, she would need to demand it.

"Here it is!" Hyacinth exclaimed. She extended a card to me. "You can't refuse this. It's free, a complimentary membership in my yoga classes."

Instead of being my usual wishy-washy self for the sake of politeness, I decided to take a stand. I handed the card back to her. "Thank you, Hyacinth, but no. Yoga is a Westernized form of the Hindu religion. I have my own church and my own beliefs. I don't need yours."

"Don't be absurd, Mike. You've never even been to one of my classes. How can you judge them?"

"I've heard you talking about your yoga classes, about self-realization and reincarnation and becoming a wisdom-seeker. You have a right to believe all that – even to teach it to anyone who will listen to you – but I'm not one of those people."

"Your religion is against wisdom too?"

"False wisdom. True wisdom comes from God. Jesus said He is the way, the truth, and the life."

"Can you prove that this Jesus of yours is right? I think not! Don't judge me until you discover the authority of your divine inner self and tap the universal energy source. Don't you know the peace of letting problems flow away like the surface of a river?"

"God uses problems in my life to strengthen me, like a tree that has withstood many harsh winds. Jesus gives me peace and joy that no troubles or trials can circumvent. I wouldn't want to trade my inner joy and peace for a mindless river."

"Don't attack my religion when you're religious yourself."

"I'm not religious. Jesus hated religion. Religions are manmade. I have Jesus and His Spirit. Being a Christian means being Christ-like.'"

"Mike, you are damaging the flowers of emptiness in your mind by laboring under the false concepts of guilt and sin. The world is dew. Don't worry."

"I'll take that advice, Hyacinth. I won't worry. When I need to make the next payment on my property and the next rent on the office, I'll call you for money."

Hyacinth shook her head and shot me a smile of spurious pity. She pushed the card back across the table to me. "You might change your mind. At least come once before you make a final decision."

I shoved the card back across the table. "That is my final decision. I want no part of anything that's on the beautiful side of evil."

"Evil? Mike, what on earth are you talking about? Are you calling me evil? Are you calling my yoga classes evil? What gives you a right to be so persnickety?"

"Nothing. You're right, Hyacinth, and I apologize. You have every right to do and believe whatever makes you happy. It's just not for me. If I went along with something that I know is wrong for me just to appease you or anyone else, that would be evil."

Hyacinth was good for weight control in a way far removed from her yoga classes; I had lost my appetite. I left a tip on the table and slipped out of the booth, leaving Hyacinth to pick at my tortilla chips. The card with "Retreat Inward to Peace" inked in a bold, flourishing font mocked me as I regarded the food I was leaving behind. Hyacinth believed that Atlantis existed and that people were recycled. If she's been recycled, I thought, it must have been from man-catching flypaper.

With a sigh of relief, I paid for my meal and hurried outside. Work awaited me at the office, and as I left Hyacinth behind, I looked over my shoulder warily. I could almost feel demons snapping around my shoulders and chasing me down the sidewalk. I didn't know out of whose imagination they had been invented: mine or Hyacinth's.

A smile of homecoming played around my lips as I got back to my office and opened the front door. The smile froze when I realized my office had been trashed.

Chapter 4.

News travels fast in small towns. Three cars from the sheriff's department answered the call. Break-ins were rare in Three Prongs. Usually, the once- or twice-a-year occurrence of a break-in happened at night and was connected with a burglary. The sanctity of my office had been compromised in broad daylight, and nothing had been taken. Everything had simply been tossed around, as if the intruder had entered, uncorked a bottle, and let loose a miniature tornado to play skittishly around the office before it was sucked back into the bottle and re-confined.

The wires to my telephone had been cut, and Hyacinth had overheard my end of the conversation from the pay phone at the corner convenience store. She seemed to have a network of contacts, because curious onlookers were arriving at my office even before I rushed back after calling the sheriff's department. Hyacinth flowed around the core of excitement like an exotic flower unleashed in the wind.

Marty shouldered his way through the widening crowd. Being somewhat of a town celebrity, carte blanche was extended to him. He wound up at my side in the office even as others in the crowd were asked by the deputies to stand back. Still wearing my dirty, torn, disheveled clothing, I felt like a bump on a toad's back as I looked into Marty's fabulous blue and gold eyes. He smiled at me, and I felt like an M&M naked of its sugar coating, melting under the kiss of sunlight. "My, my, Miss Mike," he boomed in his famous rich voice. "You do get yourself into some pickles. How did you manage this?"

Chief Deputy John Dion heard Marty's question and stood, pen poised over paper, waiting for me to answer, his pale Stetson pushed up from his light brown hair and blue eyes, which were attempting to tease facts out of me.

Sadly, because of the promise of secrecy I had given Lynette Clarissa Greene, there was little I could say. If the person or persons who had done it were the same ones who had followed me into town, they had to be working for Thornton Dean. That could be proof that Julia had been murdered, and if Julia had been murdered, my wish-she-could-have-been daughter-in-law might be in danger. I had to find a way to warn her.

Meanwhile, I dared not take any action that might alert the murderer before I could alert Lynn. I shook my head helplessly, unable to explain or even invent a likely story. It was humiliating to watch the spectators leave and know that each one was making up his or her own story to explicate the inexplicable.

After deputies had gathered what scant details I could give them, my office cleared of humans, and I was left to contend with the destruction left by the uncorked tornado. Marty stayed to help. We worked together quietly and comfortably as friends, and I fell into a daydream of living and working with him in a cabin with flowers blooming along the porch rail. I pictured the two of us sitting outside together, sipping iced tea as hummingbirds whirred past our heads, fighting over the feeders. It was such a powerful dream that when we finished straightening things up and turned to face each other, the image seemed to be shared for a moment. Something leapt through the space between Marty and me. His eyes darkened, and I quit breathing.

Before anything magical could happen, Bea burst through the door and the rainbow-colored moment evaporated. She looked around the office, hands on hips and a digital camera slung around her neck. "I thought you had a break-in, Mike. I came to get a picture to go with the story."

"There's not much of a story," Marty countered. "Just another of Miz Mike's pickles, I reckon. And the mess is gone because we just got though picking it up."

Bea stomped one foot. "Mike! We used to work together and be such good friends. Didn't you even think of calling me?"

"It wasn't that big a deal, really, Bea. I'm sorry I didn't think of it. It just didn't seem important."

"Everything that happens in Three Prongs during a slow news week is important," Bea said with a toss of her short-cropped dark hair. "You worked with me long enough to know that. What did happen?"

Again, I was unable to answer, so I was thankful for Marty's willingness to run interference for me.

"No one really knows what happened, Bea, but Mike here is about worn out from all the fuss. Let's you and me go get a glass of ice tea and leave her to lock up and get herself on home. As I recall, she's had a bit of a busy day right from the start."

I wanted to go have iced tea with Marty. I didn't want to send my ex-best friend off to drink tea with my hero in my place, but at the same time, I was tired. Marty was too much of a gentleman to mention the tragic state of my clothing, but no one could overlook something so obvious. With a sigh, I watched Marty and Bea leave together. Her dark head bent close to his as she listened to something he said, and I bit back anger and frustration. She was stealing my rainbow, and because of my promise to Lynette, I was helpless to intervene.

Leaving my office – and Marty – behind, I drove home to the ranch. I felt very old and tired for my forty-something years. Even the proudly waving plumes of blooming Spanish dagger and the brightly yellow spring flowers bobbing a greeting to me as I passed them on the road failed to lift the heaviness. The phone was clamoring as I dragged myself out of Old Blue and tripped over my three ecstatic dogs, each more determined to over-greet me than the other. "Abigail, Abner, Prissy," I addressed them breathlessly as I tried to get past them to the phone. They swirled around my legs in collie and mixed-breed colors as I yanked the phone receiver out of the wall holder.

"Mom!" Ron exclaimed. "Where have you been? Faith has been calling you for hours. We were worried about you. You're not getting yourself mixed up in someone else's business again, are you?"

"Ron! What a thing to say to your own mother. As it just so happens, I was … uh, working on my new book."

"But we called the office, and the phone rang and rang, but no one answered."

I remembered both the cut phone line and the fact that I had forgotten to call the phone company to report it.

My son continued to interrogate me, "Where were you really? Whose business are you mixed up in this time?"

"Ronald!"

He jumped to an apology. "I'm sorry, Mother. It's just that you have this predilection for –

"Don't you go using your half-dollar words on me, Ronald James Rice, or I will hang up on you."

"Mother, you're a writer! That's where I got most of my words. Anyway, what I was trying to ask is about Alex and Ryan –

My heart constricted. "Are they okay? What's wrong?"

"They are fine," Ron assured me. "Faith and I are not. We need a break. I wondered if you could watch them for a few hours tomorrow. It won't be long."

I loved my grandsons. They both sported mischievous blue eyes and blond hair like their daddy. They both had boisterous personalities and winning smiles. No one in the world ever had more precious grandchildren. It was a miracle to me that the children could be so beautiful when their mother was so plain – or at least plain in my sight, since I had favored Irene and had now feasted my too-big, greenish eyes on Lynette. It wasn't Faith's fault that Donna Johnson had left Three Prongs to return to her Georgia roots. I knew I shouldn't blame my daughter-in-law for the loss of my best friend, yet the pain was still there. Don and I had made so many plans for the future; plans that had included sharing grandchildren after Irene and Ron married. Faith's most attractive physical quality was her clear, deeply green eyes. Her long, naturally wavy light brown hair was nice enough, I supposed, but her long, greyhound-type nose and thin face just couldn't compare to my new dream daughter-in-law, Lynette Clarissa Green. My meditation made me forget that Ron was on the other end of the line until he repeated his question.

"So, how about it, Mom?"

"Sure," I said unselfishly. "What time?" I secretly dreaded the assignment. My grandsons were about two wood shavings short of hyperactive, and I was feeling old and tired. Unless I rested well overnight, I feared their exuberant romping would be too much for me, and there was no time for rest now. The dogs expected me to take them on a walk.

I managed to mentally lash my body into submission, remembering that moment when Marty's eyes had darkened and I had felt something with an electric quality zip through the space between us. Perhaps it would be a good idea to eat a bit less and exercise a bit more just in case … but that thought reminded me that I was hungry and had eaten very little at lunch, thanks to Hyacinth. I swallowed a huge glass of water to fend off the hunger and chased it down with a Diet Coke. Then I gave into the dogs' demand for a walk and started down the ranch road at a brisk pace, with the canine trio frolicking beside me. "If I ever have more dogs," I told them severely, "I will limit it to two. I only have two hands, you know, and trying to give equal attention to the three of you wears me out."

Abigail, an almost full-blooded collie with one ear that flopped, tilted her head back and forth and waved the plume of her tail in apparent understanding. My words didn't bother her; she intended to be one of the two – and the boss, at that. Abner, a short-bodied black dog of unknown parentage was oblivious to everything except trying unsuccessfully to stay in front of Abby, with little help from his short legs. Priscilla, who was twelve, made no attempt to keep up, and I slowed down the pace to let the black and tan hound catch up. Increasing age had slowed her speed, but not her love of the hunt, and she made the journey down the ranch road with her nose to the ground. Even when she was younger, Prissy could never keep up with the other pups because her hound nature demanded a closer inspection of every new scent.

Even though I was closer to exhaustion following the walk, I decided to do some painting and unwind a bit. My unprofitable fascination with painting had pushed me into renting my Three Prongs office. When I was at home with paintbrushes close at hand, I just couldn't seem to keep my fingers off those long, rounded handles.

Memories of Marty's face kept waving into my consciousness, making me feel slightly lonely and restless. Those were new feelings for me. After the death of my husband, I had buried myself in writing and community events, leaving no time to feel sorry for myself or lonely. I counted my blessings instead: One less person to take care of in the home meant more time to write. I no longer had to tailor my schedule around fixing meals, baking desserts, and offering companionship. I could stay up writing or painting until midnight, listening to musicals and Christian music, with no fear that the lights or sounds were interrupting Alfred's sleep. I could eat chocolate cake for breakfast, drink chocolate milk for dinner, and go a week at a time without using the stove. I could bake a chocolate pecan pie and eat the entire thing by myself in one day. But tonight, with the memory of Marty haunting me, those compensations seemed cursory.

Painting still didn't fill the emptiness, so I tried to expel it with thoughts about spending the next day with Alex and Ryan. Perhaps I would find time to paint some more while they are napping in the afternoon. My son was a sign painter, and even with modern sign technology, he still used sign brushes for some of the work, including a few huge billboards. He had a new brush I was eager to try. When he was in a good mood, he would let me borrow some of his brushes. I tried not to feel smug and superior because he intransigently refused to let Faith use his brushes. Sign-painting brushes are expensive, but Ron's profession as a graphic artist added value to his favorite brushes. The fact that he sometimes shared his expensive equipment with me made up, I thought, for the times when he was rude and insinuated that I had a habit of sticking my nose in other people's business.

E ven after having lost precious time to babysitting, I had made an encouraging start towards solving the mystery of Julia Dean's death. I had called the phone company to restore phone service to my office, and before spending a day with my grandsons, I had interviewed Buddy Turner, Neil Peters, and Thornton Dean.

I had contacted Lynette to warn her again to be careful and to let her know I'd been followed and that my office had been trashed. She was vehement in her belief that such actions were totally separate from Thor, and that made me wonder if, perhaps, Lynn had fallen under his spell. Many years in age separated them, but Thor was an attractive man – and rich. One corner of my mind still harbored a doubt about Lynette's real motives for coming to Three Prongs. Surely an attempt to solve her sister's murder – a murder that had been ruled an accident and might never have occurred – was a weak ploy. Wouldn't it be more likely that Lynette has harbored a secret crush on her sister's husband all these years and decided to take advantage of her sister's misfortune to create her own fortune? Hmm …

The day after I finished my strenuous babysitting sting, Hollis Newbark ambled across my path at the courthouse. I asked him pointblank if he had killed Julia Dean.

His nearly invisible eyebrows rose over his colorless blue eyes, and he replied in a monotone, "What kind of a question is that? Do you go around asking those kind of questions often, and if so, under what authority?"

His question made me realize that I might be getting into what Marty would call a 'pickle', but I didn't allow that possibility to frighten me as I returned Newbark's quiet stare.

He finally denied any involvement in Julia's death, although he admitted, "Not that I wouldn't do anything within my power to ruin Thor's life. However, I am a creative and an imaginative man. I'm sure I could destroy Thor quite neatly without resorting to something as nefarious as murder."

Back at my Three Prongs office, I checked the clock with satisfaction. Monday was not seafood buffet day at *The Spanish Tile*; it was usually Mexican fare. It was, however, as delicious as all other menu choices, and Marty always hit the restaurant at eleven o'clock for lunch. Nothing would keep me from meeting him today.

I scanned Lynette's list of suspects and attempted to ignore my screaming muscles. Every part of my body chronicled the foot chases, games, and stretching-type activities that had been involved in babysitting Alex and Ryan.

One thing that made it difficult to connect a suspect with Julia's death was that it seemed as though out of all the residents in the entire county, only Julia and I had absented ourselves from the Founder's Day parade. The parade gave nearly every local an alibi. Newbark informed me testily that he had driven the Hills of Beauty Real Estate float, and he gave me the names and phone numbers of friends who could corroborate that statement; sadly, they did. In fact, anyone who was anyone had been in the parade or had been connected with it. Lynette had put Zolly Gilmore on her list, but he had been riding in the parade with his barmaid, Candy, in the "lean, mean cheating machine" with "Taxi" signs slapped on the doors and balloons and ribbons trailing from the bumpers and mirrors. Zolly's wife Carmen, unaware of both the joke and her husband's affair with his barmaid, had stood along Three Prongs' crowded Main Street, waving naïvely to her husband. She was proud of her entrepreneur husband who had the foresight to begin a much-needed taxi service in Three Prongs. That poor, blind woman.

I sighed over the impossibility of connecting all the information I had gathered and sculpting it into a recognizable murderer. Since that task seemed hopeless, I tried to make Pastor Garth Seymour come to life on the computer. He was soon there, living and breathing and ready for action, but I couldn't think of a plot to go with my invented character. The impossibility of finding something for Pastor Garth to do released another hopeless sigh into my empty office. The sighs and emptiness sent me out of the office and down to the courthouse to keep a promise to a beautiful young girl who would have done me proud as a daughter-in-law.

The XYZ Corporation was listed as the developer for the undeveloped subdivision at the bridge to nowhere. Idly, I mused over whether the name of the corporation was a play on the infamous incident in American history by that same name. Details in my memory were sketchy. It had, I thought, something to do with a loan to France, in addition to a large bribe for each of the five directors who were then heading up the French government. When the bribe was not paid, an undeclared naval war resulted. I became so active in mental calisthenics that I literally ran into Sheriff Brent Cruz.

"Brent!" I exclaimed in delight.

He was friend as well as sheriff. He backed away from me warily, already shaking his head, his blue-black hair reflecting light from a window and brown eyes darkly imperturbable. "Okay Mike," he said, drumming his fingers on his chin. "What do you need to know now?" He plopped his pale Stetson soundly on his head, preparing to leave the building. It shaded his face, and I was unable to read his expression.

"What can you tell me about Julia Dean's death?"

"Officially or unofficially?" he asked.

I pounced on the words eagerly. "Unofficially, off the record – just for my own knowledge."

Brent threw back his head and blasted the courthouse corridor with laughter. "Officially or unofficially, Ms. Michal Rice, the answer is the same. It was an accident – a gruesome, horrible, tragic, fatal accident, but a closed case. We couldn't even find evidence of negligence on the part of Buddy Turner or Neil Peters. Officially, I don't mind telling you that we were disappointed about not finding a tie to Peters. The district attorney would have been elated if we could root one more human rat out of the low-income housing racket. Course, we're mighty lucky to have so few rats in Three Prongs. Reckon that's why so many new folks are moving in. Growth ... now there's a story for you. In my opinion, that Bea doesn't cover the growth aspect enough in Sidelines. I know you don't work for her anymore, but you might toss that to her as a story idea. She'd take it from you, probably, with the two of you being such good friends."

Guilt scratched me with a sharp metal nail. Bea had been a good friend of mine back when I had time for good friends. But it is not, I told myself firmly, getting involved in other people's business that has taken time away from friendships.

Brent put his hands on his hips and continued somewhat sternly. "Come to think of it, Mike, you and Anna and me have always been good buddies. It's been a right long time since you came out to the house to see us. Anna misses those visits. We were just talking about that the other night. Now that the kids are grown up and in college, we don't get around as much as we used to. How's that boy of yours? Is he still giving you a hard time about snooping around, looking for mysteries like our now-famous lake monster?"

I answered evasively, "His boys keep him busy."

He nodded. "Anna and me are about to get our first grandchild. I don't know which one of us is more excited, but I think the both of us are more excited than the kids. They're a bit worried about finances and the like at the moment. By the way, have you talked to Don lately? Last I heard, that pretty daughter of hers married a local high school teacher, and they're having their first child."

"They have three children now, two boys and a girl. Don

is ecstatic. She's enjoying being a grandma, but it keeps her busy. We don't keep in touch as much as we used to."

Brent nodded. "Yup, life's sad that way. Folks that mean the most to us move off in other directions. Guess we can't lasso up the moments in life that we enjoy the most and pen 'em up. We have to let go and get on. It's hard. I really thought that boy of yours was set to marry her girl. Reckon if them kids had got married, Donna would still be the county's Republican chairman and help run elections. Training new folks is about as easy as parade training a spooky horse to carry a flag." Sheriff Brent Cruz doffed his hat and started to move down the hall. He had no way of knowing that his mention of Donna Johnson and Irene had gorged an old wound and made it bleed again.

"Brent ... wait! What can you tell me about that new bridge on Old Lake Road?"

"Fixing to snoop around and get yourself in trouble again, Mike? Well, I don't mind telling you that a lot of folks are asking the same thing right about now." He drummed strong, thick fingers on his chin. "Like I tell folks, growth is coming on us all over the county. That bridge will save a lot of travel time for folks in the south end someday when there are folks in the south end, but at the moment – thanks to that monster bridge – the county's out of money for paving projects, and no one has moved in on the old Griffith place, even though some big corporation out of Dallas bought and subdivided it. Might run that by Bea, too, if you really want to know. I believe she was doing some investigating on her own when we all got sidetracked by that monster hoax."

I thanked him and left the courthouse deep in thought. The monster hoax! I had forgotten about that. It had turned out to be a clever tourism scheme by some city folks who had bought a restaurant and boat marina on Old Lake. No clear-written county history existed to explain how Old Lake acquired its name. The best guess was that the name referred to the ancient cypress trees along the river and shores of the lake. The lake was not a fixed-level lake. Thus, in times of drought, the water level dropped, and water sports enthusiasts fled to Canyon Lake and other more dependable lakes. When the city folks saw their business falling off with the water level, they invented a monster and engineered a string of sightings that kept their business swimming. Unfortunately, I had accidentally solved that mystery, and while it did gain Marty's notice of me briefly, it had also given Ron the idea that I had a tendency to nose around where I shouldn't.

I sighed and checked my watch. There was time enough for Bea before attempting to run into Marty by happenstance at *The Spanish Tile.*

Bea greeted me like the long-lost friend that I was, which sent a new thrust of guilt twisting up into my chest cavity. "Give, Mike," she said after a few moments. "What are you mixed up in now? You ignore me unless you want information." She knew me too well, this former co-worker who had given me enough belief in my writing ability to launch the Garth Seymour series.

"I want to know about that bridge to nowhere."

A shutter clicked over her dark features. "Michal," she said, which let me know I had offended her, "what does that bridge have to do with you? Now that you've sold so many books, are you plotting a new career in politics?"

"Heavens, no!" I exclaimed with too much feeling, considering the fact that Bea Hernandez and Thornton Dean had been engaged before he met Julia. I could understand how Bea might still be wounded by the past. Ron and Faith's marriage had rocked my world as surely as Thor and Julia's had rocked Bea's, but like Sheriff Brent Cruz had so wisely said, it was impossible to lasso time and life and send them tracking along one's preconceived trail drive. God had engineered the route.

Bea's broad, intelligent face was unlined for her age. Her dark eyes brooded behind heavy, mauve-framed glasses. Her dark hair, cobwebbed with grey, fell around her head and face in a pleasing, thick curtain that came to life and bounced with her every movement. Briefly, I wondered if she planned on re-staking a claim on Thor. She watched me guardedly, waiting for an explanation.

"Just curiosity," I assured her. "I saved close to nine miles coming over the bridge, and –

"Over the bridge? I didn't know it was open."

Deftly, I changed the subject. "All the wildflowers blooming reminded me, Bea. I really enjoyed the spring travel guide you published this year. And it was a nice touch, adding that bit for folks who live here on how to conserve water by replacing formal gardens with xeriscaping. Century plants, red yuccas, lantana, silvia species – why, they are all interesting and unique as well as having beautiful blooms. Mountain laurel doesn't bloom for long in the spring, but I love that sweet grape smell ... and of course agarita is everywhere, with its lovely yellow blooms and intoxicating, sweet fragrance. The leaves are scratchy, and they remind me of holly. But anyway, I'm glad you included it as a plant to keep in your publication."

A smile chased away the closed look on her face. "Thanks, but it was more fun when we worked on special editions together." She and I smiled at each other, remembering shared deadlines, successful stories, and the times we sailed too close to a scalding sea of controversy.

"That new writer you have is good," I added.

She nodded. "Yes. He's not really new. He's been with me for two years. Still, it's not the same as when you were here. Besides, he wants to leave here and go work for a bigger newspaper now that he has some experience. Truthfully, I expect him to quit any day now, so if you know of a good writer who is looking for a job, send them along. No sense in asking you to come back. I know you'd refuse because you're so busy with your books now."

We visited for a few more minutes before I headed to the door.

Bea's voice stopped me. "Mike ... I'd advise you not to advertise your mileage savings on that new bridge. The sheriff's office is investigating a case of vandalism. Some vehicle crashed through the barriers, and –

"I didn't crash." I paused in embarrassment, and Bea's laughter propelled me out the door. I left in such a hurry that I ran – quite literally – into Hyacinth. She waved my apology aside and clutched my arm. I was amazed to see her usually unreadable face traced with lines of worry.

"Mike! You must help! Samala is missing! That Edmonds boy has been smuggling her to your church, and –

"Smuggling? He brings her openly."

"Well, now she's missing. Her parents are alarmed about all this religion and –

"We don't have religion at our church, just Jesus."

"Listen to me, Mike! She's missing!"

"She's also twenty-two, if I remember correctly. She has a right to be missing."

"We're worried. She might be with that Edmonds boy."

"If so, I'm sure she's fine. Durant would never harm her. He loves her wildly. But if I see her, I'll let her know y'all are worried about her."

"Please do. She's been gone two days, and Sheriff Cruz won't investigate because she's –

"An adult?" I suggested. "If she's with Durant, I'm sure it's all legal. This 'religion' you deplore so much teaches a strong set of moral values."

"You mean," Hyacinth whispered, "they might be married or something? But she's just a baby! So impressionable ... and all this religious nonsense –

"Might teach her to question her parents' lifestyles ... and yours?"

"Oh, Mike! How wicked you can be!" Hyacinth fled down the street away from me.

I had to laugh, sad as it was. Samala's parents, along with others at the retreat, swapped partners and sometimes even families. Raids by the sheriff's department over the years had uncovered an epidemic of drug use and underage drinking. Hyacinth had been arrested several times herself. I knew Samala was embarrassed by her home life. She had tried to be an obedient daughter and witness Jesus to her parents through her example. I knew that if she had left home, it would only have been because they had tried to force Durant out of her life. Durant had even offered the old-fashioned courtesy of asking the man now living with Samala's mother for "his" daughter's hand in marriage. No one knew for sure if he was her dad – not even Samala.

As I stood on the sidewalk laughing after Hyacinth's retreating figure, an image rose up in my mind. I suddenly saw an L-shaped farmhouse. I rechecked my watch. It was not that I wanted to get mixed up in anything that didn't concern me, but I thought I had just enough time – that is, if I risked another venture across the unopened bridge. No one had stopped me last time, after all.

Samala herself answered the door, astonished to see me. "Ms. Rice? Wh-what are you doing here? I mean, hi. It's ... it's okay. We're married. We had to because they wouldn't let us see each other anymore."

Durant joined her at the door, and his lack of welcome was complete. "Did they send you after us? It's too late. We're legally married, and we're buying this house. I've been saving for it secretly for over a year, and we put the down payment on it yesterday."

"Congratulations!" I said warmly. "On your marriage and the house. I just wondered, Samala, if you might let your parents know you're okay. They're worried about you."

"For now," Durant said darkly, "while they're sober. They'll forget all about us in a little while, when they start drinking again."

He was probably right, but I tried again. "I remembered seeing furniture being moved into this house when I was by here earlier, and I thought –

"Earlier? What were you doing on this road?" Durant asked. "The bridge isn't even open yet. How did you find us?"

"Well, I'm glad you're both fine. Let me know if you need anything. I'll see y'all at church Sunday."

"Ms. Rice," Samala said, "would you take a note to Valerie if I wrote it … to let her know?"

"Certainly." I waited while Samala wrote a note to her mother and slipped it in an envelope.

Durant looked disgruntled but voiced no objection.

Samala's bright smile of thanks made me feel good all the way back into town. I was so eager to give the note to Valerie that I pushed Old Blue past *The Spanish Tile*, forgetting about Marty.

Valerie was already engaged in what sounded like a drunken brawl with the man who had won the title of "husband for the day," so I left the note with Hyacinth instead. Her concern for Samala had apparently been genuine. She was so thankful to receive news about the girl that I had to convince her all over again that I had no interest in joining her yoga classes.

Breathlessly, I rushed into *The Spanish Tile* just in time to see Marty paying his bill and preparing to leave. I felt as deflated as a bicycle tire with a thorn in it. I slipped past Marty before he saw me and settled despondently into a booth by myself, determined to enjoy the always-excellent food. After I paid for my meal, I realized again how important it was becoming to be mindful of expenses.

Locking doors when one was only going to be gone for a short time was unheard of in Three Prongs, Even the previous day's break-in had not broken my careless habit of leaving the door to my office unlocked when I ran errands, so Lynette was waiting for me at my office when I got there. I related my investigation to date, including the happy chapter of solving Samala's disappearance.

Lynette listened with rapt attention, and then her lovely features sagged. "But my sister's murder," she asked quietly. "How are you getting along on that? Who killed my sister?"

"I haven't a clue, dear," I replied truthfully.

The lovely, dreamlike vision of the girl I would have welcomed as a daughter-in-law dissolved into tears.

I felt old, tired, and defeated.

Chapter 5.

After Lynette dried her tears and left, I spent a few minutes berating myself for my lack of xenia. Lynn was, after all, still a xeno in Three Prongs, and I had found myself unable to console the stranger, for all of seeing her as the quintessential daughter-in-law that had been denied to me when Ron had tossed Irene aside for Faith. I yearned for an outing with my best friend Donna. Entirely free of judgment, Donna would have listened to me and encouraged me. In fact, Don would likely have joined me in the search for a murderer. Some claim there is safety in numbers, and Donna would have doubled my effort. The two of us would have been traveling together on that dangerous quest if Ron had never met Faith. The officious tone of the phone interrupted my pity party. With a histrionic sigh to let God know that life was mistreating me (in case He had an unexpected surplus of time), I grabbed the offending instrument and barked into it.

"Mom," Faith's voice quavered, "you don't have to yell at me. I haven't even asked you yet."

I apologized quickly.

"I need your help," Faith continued. "You have to help me!"

"Faith," I said patiently, "if you and Ron are having a disagreement, just talk to him. You know I don't get involved in other people's business."

"But we haven't," she wailed, "not yet anyway. I mean ... he doesn't know yet."

"Know what?" I asked, experiencing a sudden vision of Faith confessing to an affair with another man. If she divorced Ron, then maybe ...

"It's the brush, Mom. You have to help me find it."

"What brush, Faith? Let's get on the same page ... oh no! You don't mean you've used one of Ron's brushes and lost it. Not that! No one can help if that's what you're talking about! Sometimes I think Ron is genetically linked to his brushes."

"That is what I mean, Mom, and you can help. You can come help me find it before Ron gets home. Besides, you know how much Alex and Ryan would enjoy seeing you."

My grandchildren needed a rest from me, and I started to tell Faith that when I remembered that Nat Dean was one of the suspects on my list whom I hadn't talked to yet. He lived in San Antonio, so perhaps I could combine the dubious pleasure of romping with Alex and Ryan again with a business trip. "I'm on my way," I told Faith cheerfully. I grabbed my notes, thankful that I had already taken time to look up Nat's address.

Old Blue's gas gauge robbed me of my initial cheerfulness. I had enough gas to get to San Antonio, though, so I would worry about how to fill the tank on my way home.

Faith met me at the door. Red blotches on her long, narrow face testified to recent tears. With tragic green eyes weighed down by a load of unshed tears, Faith looked more greyhound than human. I tried to thrust aside the comparison with Lynette that rose to the surface of my mind like natant floral life on a pond. I tried to forget that before Faith had called me, I had been regretting Ron's decision to marry her instead of Irene, reliving those sad days in my life again. I tried to forget that except for this teary-eyed, greyhound-faced, child-woman, Donna would be with me right now. The two of us would have tackled Nat Dean together. When I had looked his address up in the phone book and compared it to a San Antonio map, I had discovered that Nat lived in an unsafe, unsavory neighborhood.

"Thanks, Mom." Faith's smile was sweet and sincere, as was her engulfing hug. "I was antiquing that furniture Ron and I bought at the open air flea market last time you watched the boys for us, but I've learned my lesson. I'll never borrow another one of Ron's brushes! I've been sick with worry. If you can keep an eye on the boys, that'll give me a chance to search every inch of the house."

Bravely, I agreed to the arrangement. It was a long time until naps were due, and the boys tumbled over each other like heedless collie pups. I tried to collect them for a story. Alex was intent on leaning forward in my lap until he tumbled off, then blasting the living room with laughter. Ryan was soon following his example, giggling rather than shouting when his head hit the floor. Afraid that one of the boys would break his neck, I put the book aside and tried to interest them in blocks. Ryan was interested, as he liked throwing blocks at his brother. We switched to molding with clay at the kitchen table. Except for the mess, the project showed real promise – unlike Faith's quest.

Faith failed in holding back the tears as she explained that the brush was seemingly nonexistent. "How much will a new one cost, Mom? If you watch the boys, I'll go get one."

"You watch the boys," I directed. "I'll get the brush. You can't find sign brushes anywhere, you know. It has to be at an art supply store. So few sign-painters use them now. They've switched to vinyl lettering."

With deft intervention, Faith prevented Ryan from smashing his clay invention over his brother's head even as she smiled and nodded her thanks to me.

She was a good mother, my daughter-in-law. I made myself meditate on that fact as I drove through heavy traffic on unpredictable streets to the art supply store. Since I was stuck with Faith, I was fairly sure that God expected me to start appreciating her more. Finding the right brush was easy; paying for it, however, made me bite my lip. I certainly hoped there would be a check in the mailbox when I got back home, and it would need to be a sizable one to cover the purchase I had just made. The sales clerk had looked exasperated when I had asked for the third time, "Are you sure this is the right price?"

It was necessary to wind deeper into the city on unfamiliar roads to find Nat's street. I crossed several railroad tracks on the way. Broken-down chain-link fences, graffiti on every sizeable object, and debris rained down on street and shoulder made me wonder briefly if I might be entering a gang war zone.

Suddenly, a large group of bare-chested, leather vest-wearing, tattooed youth formed a human fence across the road and stopped Old Blue. The profanity spilling out of their mouths matched the obscene emblems and signs on their vests, and my chest felt like the elephant sitting on it was wiggling around to get comfortable. Gang members – a few of them female, wearing skimpy halter tops under leather vests – pounded out clashing music on Old Blue's hood

I knew I had to hide my fear, but even being slightly overweight, I wasn't big enough to hide that much. I forced my trembling lips into a smile and leaned out the open driver's side window. "Hi. Jesus loves you!"

"What!?" The group fell away from the car, jostling each other and attempting to fathom the craziness of the old lady in the big car.

I floored Blue and thudded down three streets with the thump of my heart matching the bump of the pavement. The matchbox-style houses along the weed-infested street sported peeling paint, broken window frames, and porch rails and yards with patches of bare dirt. Few of the house numbers were intact, so I had to guess which house was the one Nat Dean called home. I knocked boldly on his door and called his name.

With the speed of a striking rattlesnake, a thin, wiry arm reached out from the opening door and snatched me. I was hauled into a dark, foul-smelling room, and the door slammed behind me. "What do you want?" Nat hissed with alcohol-flavored puffs of breath. "Who are you trying to get killed, me or you?"

Nat Dean failed in every aspect to mirror the rugged good looks of his father, Thor. He was painfully thin and wormy looking, with anemic brown eyes whose dilated pupils shouted drug abuse. His sharp, slight nose was red and wet from snorting cocaine. His reddish-brown hair hung limply around thin, undeveloped shoulders. His movements were jerky and uncoordinated. My heart cried out in despair for this weed-like young man who slept in the enemy's camp, ate the enemy's delusions, and breathed out death. He didn't know he had been deceived. He didn't know about Jesus and that Jesus had the power to set him free. He didn't know, and that lack of knowledge had sealed and stamped his death certificate.

Nat eyed me narrowly. "What do you want anyway?" he asked suspiciously. "A nice old lady – a xeno. Didn't you see that gang down the street?"

"I'm not old," I told him testily, "nor am I blind. I outran that gang in Old Blue."

"In what?"

"Never mind."

"Listen, stranger, whoever you are ... don't you know them gang members eat old ladies like you for breakfast and pick out the bones before lunch? If you're looking for Xanadu, you're lost."

"I'm not old!" I yelled, inwardly marveling at his usage of correct verb tenses and the literary term "Xanadu." He was using some of my favorite words. I had memorized the "X" section of the dictionary because it was the shortest. I planned to use some of those words someday to introduce a new character in the Pastor Garth series. I said in a more reasonable tone of voice, "I'm here to talk to you about Julia Dean."

"She's dead. Why would you want to talk to me about her? I hardly knew her."

"I have some questions about her accident."

"Then you should talk to my dad. He was married to the woman. I told you already, I hardly knew her." His eyes narrowed more, squinting at me from dark slits. "You mean questions the old man wouldn't answer ... like did he do her in?"

"Did he?" I asked eagerly.

"I hardly think so," Nat considered. "He ain't got the guts to go against the law. He's too highfalutin to risk slammin' his butt down in metal furniture for the rest of his life. He was kind of fond of Julia, you know. He got into some knockdowns with me because she disapproved of my, uh ... lifestyle." He gestured around the room, where empty beer cans swarmed over the ashtrays that had long ago given up any attempt to hold the squashed stubs – not all of them legal tobacco.

I could understand the objection to his lifestyle. I summoned up my courage. "Actually ... I came to ask you if you killed Julia."

"Me?" His reddish eyebrows rose into question marks. "You are a very crazy xeno to risk your life coming over here to ask me a question that I might never answer. I didn't, but why should you believe me? No one has ever believed anything good about me." Truth echoed in the directness of his words.

"I believe you, but have you any idea who would have wanted Julia dead?"

"I wanted her dead," he said without hesitation. "Dad was transferring all my inheritance to her – tough love and all that, trying to get me to straighten up." He shrugged thin shoulders. "But I didn't kill her. I'm about to get kicked out of this pad, and I lost my car a long time ago. I'm not exactly set up to finance a long-distance killing." He had a point.

"You lost your car before Julia's death?"

"Yup, just before. So maybe that's one good thing about it. Can't hardly convict me of a crime I ain't got no way to get to commit, can they now? Look, crazy lady, you'd best go. Them dudes out there play rough, and I wouldn't stop them if they broke down the door and dragged you out for fun and games."

"Why don't you move to a better neighborhood?"

He laughed bitterly. "Yeah, right. I'll just run down to the bank and get a loan on a little place of my own. Until my dad dies and frees up a bit of the cash flow, I'm stuck here. It's all I can afford."

I motioned to the full ashtrays and empty cans. "Because of that?"

"That and a lot of other things that a nice old lady like you don't know nothin' about." His speech transformation from educated to uneducated struck a discordant note.

"Can't you get a job that pays well? You sound well educated when you want to. You use words that most people don't even know."

"Yeah, well, that's one more failed dream of mine – to be a writer. I put out the college newspaper before things in my life went bad. I started out memorizing the dictionary. I started with the 'X' section because it was so short."

"Me too!" I exclaimed. "See, we have more in common than you –

"We have nothing in common. You better get out of this neighborhood before you wake up feeling as if someone worked you over with a xyster, if you wake up at all."

I cringed, thinking of how painful it would be to have a surgical instrument scrape my bones. "Look, even if your Earthly father won't help you move out of this neighborhood, you have a Heavenly Father Who will."

"Don't come breaking into my pad spouting off religion to me. Lies!"

"I'm not talking about religion. I'm talking about Jesus.

Religion can't help anyone, but accepting Jesus as Lord and Savior can change a life. Jesus walked on this Earth like we do, Nat. He faced the same trials and temptations and never sinned. Then Jesus took our sins to the cross so we could begin life again without them and go to Heaven when we die. Don't you want that? I want to help you."

"What I want is for you to leave before your friends ..." His voice broke off as blows fell on the front door. "Look, crazy lady," he hissed, "when I open this back door, you run like a squirrel. I can't be responsible for what happens to you if they catch you, and I won't try to stop them, or they'll kill me too."

"But what about you?" I asked. "I don't want to leave you here. They might –

Dean's fingers dug into my arm. He shoved me roughly through the house to the back door. "Leave me alone, lady! I don't need your help. You just run. I'll be right behind you. If they catch you, don't expect me to stop." And with that, he propelled me out the back door.

I tripped over bags, boxes, and the collection of loose debris on the back porch and nearly fell.

Nat grabbed my arm again, arresting my fall, then shoved me in the center of the back. "Run like demons is on you, because they is," he hissed. "Don't look back!"

I didn't. I managed to draw the gang members around several houses much like Dean's and double back to Old Blue without getting lost. My breath was still exploding in ragged puffs, and my heart was still knocking on my ribs, crying out for attention when I pulled up into the driveway at the neat little house with a well-kept yard many miles away from Nat's neighborhood. I breathed a sigh of relief as Faith and the boys poured out the front door and ran to meet me. Faith had never looked more beautiful, I thought. Her green eyes were happy orbs, and her long, light brown hair floated around her shoulders in a shiny cloud. After hugging the boys, I reached into Old Blue to retrieve the brush.

Before I could hand the brush to Faith, Ron's truck pulled up into the driveway. He bailed out of the truck and engulfed me in a hug. My son, who had outgrown me by several inches, swung me around in apparent delight. "Mom! What a wonderful surprise! Why didn't you tell us you were coming?"

Faith made an attempt to divert Ron's attention by issuing an invitation to me. "Won't you stay for dinner? I have a taco salad all fixed."

For some reason, salad made me think of Hyacinth, and I lost my appetite. I shook my head. "Thanks, Faith, but I need to get home and walk the dogs and –

The diversion failed. Ron noticed the bristle end of the brush sticking out of the small brown bag and slipped it out of my hand. "For me? Thanks, Mom." He engulfed me in another hug. "You shouldn't have, you know. These brushes are expensive." How well I knew that! "How did you know I needed this brush?" he asked, puzzled. "I lost mine on the job and haven't been able to find it anywhere."

Relief wrote itself in capital letters in Faith's bright eyes, and I smiled at her. She was okay, my daughter-in-law.

Our silent communication was lost in Ron's cheerful banter as he took turns swinging the boys around while he talked to us. "I'm glad you're here, Mom, and not sticking your nose into other people's business. You're getting too old to get mixed up in mysteries, you know. It's dangerous. Speaking of danger, I saw the strangest thing on the way here. This gang was chasing this scarecrow of a kid down the street."

"Did he get away?" I interrupted breathlessly.

Ron fastened a penetrating stare on me. "He was still out in front when I lost sight of him, but why do you ask? You couldn't possibly have a personal interest in a gang fight ... could you?"

"Ron! What a thing to say to me, your own mother! How could I have a personal interest in anything – besides you and your family – in San Antonio? I don't even live here!"

Faith threw a quick look of interest in my direction. She was intelligent, this daughter-in-law of mine. She was loyal and liked me well enough to harbor the secret she had guessed. She, Ron, and the boys all seemed genuinely sorry that I was unable to stay longer.

Now that I had interviewed Nat, I was convinced that he was innocent of his stepmother's murder. He might have been guilty of many things, including faulty judgment, but I couldn't picture him as a murderer. Nat had risked his life and safety to save mine, and I was a total stranger. He had acted with no expectation of reward. Thinking of that made me wonder if there was some way I could reward him.

Engulfing me in one last hug, Ron admonished me, "Now, Mother, I'm going to watch which way you turn when you back out of the driveway. I don't trust you not to get mixed up in someone else's business. Let someone else rescue that young man."

Rescue? I thought about that word as I drove dutifully towards home. Nat does need rescuing. Perhaps I can find him a job. I knew Bea would give him a trial at the paper if I asked her – or at least she might. I would have to latch on to him like chocolate day and night to keep him away from drugs. I had room at the house now that Alfred had changed his residence to Heaven, and I thought perhaps Nat could stay with me for a short time. Old Blue read my thoughts, and suddenly, I found myself back in Nat's neighborhood, scanning the derelict houses for some sign of the anemic youth. I found him sprawled across the broken concrete paving of a driveway. The lurch of my heart matched Old Blue's as I stomped on the brake pedal and skid to a stop. He's dead! They caught up with him! Still ... he looked intact, and I saw no blood.

Nat's labored breathing spewed out beer fumes. His eyes rolled around, seeming to find it difficult to focus on me. Hearing loud ranting in the distance, I demanded physical action from my body that my body was ill equipped to provide. I lifted Nat up and half-carried, half-dragged him to Old Blue. I propped him against the rear door on the passenger's side and tried to open the front door. It might as well have been welded shut for its lack of cooperation, and now I spotted black-clad gang members rounding the street corner in our direction. I grabbed the back of Nat's grease- and dirt-painted jeans and hoisted him through the open window. He tumbled off the seat and landed headfirst on the floor. There was no time to help him into the seat: Gang members swarmed across debris-littered ground towards us. Thankful I had left the car running, I bailed into the driver's seat and floored Old Blue.

Nat remained semiconscious during the drive back into the hill country. I wondered if he needed medical attention. He finally made a worm-like crawl into the seat when Old Blue bucked down the ranch road, met with welcoming barks from the dogs. "Where are we, crazy lady? Why did you pick me up? Why do you care? Who are you anyway?"

"I'll answer all those questions while we take the dogs

on a walk," I said firmly, "and after I've fixed you something to eat. You look about as starved as a stray pup. And while I fix dinner, you can take a shower. You're filthy, and frankly, you stink. I think Alfred left behind some clothes that will fit you."

"Who's Alfred? Your husband? Did he run away because he realized you're crazy?"

"He died of cancer. He lost a lot of weight in the end, so I'm sure some of his things will fit you."

"Great. Wearing a dead guy's clothes. But, hey, I'm sorry for … well, I mean, sorry he died."

"Yeah, me too. He was pretty wonderful."

Grumbling about not liking dogs, Nat accompanied me and the dogs on our walk. The people-loving pooches were ecstatic. When we returned to the house, Nat dutifully showered while I cooked. Even after the meal was on the table, my circular-chasing mind found no rest. Now that I have Nat, whatever should I do with him?

After dinner, Nat and I spent hours talking. I listened to his wavering excuses for the wrong choices he had made and tried to explain to him that I had a friend Who could help him. "Jesus loves you and is waiting to forgive you and direct your life, but you have to make the choice to let Him. You've made a lot of other choices that have left Him out. Why don't you make a choice now that includes Him? I want you to stay here, Nat, until you get on your feet and until you want to leave. I want to help you, but I can't do it alone. You will have to help me help you. If you stay, there will be rules."

"Yeah, like, is that supposed to be a newsflash or something? First you dress me in a dead guy's clothes. Now, I'm supposed to shape myself after him, Mr. Nice Guy, right?"

"Keep your own shape, by all means," I said a bit tartly, biting back the addition of, "no one else would want it." Instead I finished, "I'm going to get you a job at a newspaper with a friend of mine. I used to work there."

Nat couldn't hide the quick spark of interest that brightened his eyes. "I don't like work," he said flatly, hunkering down into his dead guy clothes.

"And while you are here, no drugs, no smoking, no alcoholic beverages, no profanity –

"Sheesh. I'd be better off dead. Why didn't you let them finish me off?"

"Nat, how can you say that? With all your potential –

"Yeah, I'm a winner – dressed in a dead man's clothes and talking to a crazy lady with a bunch of stinking dogs messing around me."

Before I could fashion a stinging reply, Nat's head lowered on the thin string of neck, and he fell asleep on the couch with his body twisted uncomfortably like an ocean-dipped pretzel. I straightened him out, pushed a pillow under his head, and covered what little there was of his body with a brightly colored quilt that Faith had made for me. She was talented, my daughter-in-law, even if her looks could never match the sparkling, fresh beauty of my dream daughter-in-law, Lynette Clarissa Greene, and even if she wasn't my best friend's daughter.

I called Abigail, Abner, and Priscilla away from Nat and turned out the lights.

Russian thistle and Norwegian sage," I muttered to myself the next morning, looking with disbelief at the brush Ron was missing – the one I'd replaced at great expense. The brush was sitting where I had left it after borrowing it without asking. "I don't know if tumbleweed is really from Russia or if sage grows in Norway," I told the curious dogs, "but I do know I could hide my own Easter eggs and then forget where to look for them! Now what? Do I tell Ron the truth or let him keep on thinking he lost it?"

"Stall for time," the dogs replied, winding around my legs. "Take us for a walk first!"

It seemed like a good idea. I checked on Nat, and he was still asleep. I put the breakfast tacos I had made for him where he would see them if he woke up before I returned with the dogs. He, however, was still asleep when I got back to the house. Taking a deep breath, I called Ron.

Ron said a bit more than "Russian thistle and Norwegian sage," although to his credit, he never used profanity, that son of mine. He just made me feel like a snake's belly. "Mom! I don't mind you borrowing things if you ask, but I started out blaming Faith for this! Then I decided it was my fault, and I went back to the job site twice to look for it. At your age, you should be more responsible. You're a great mother, and I don't mean to make you feel bad, but you need to quit borrowing things without asking ...

and you need to quit getting yourself mixed up in other people's business."

I decided not to mention Nat, who suddenly made an appearance and crammed a taco in his mouth as he shoved his way through the dogs and disappeared into the bathroom.

Ignoring Nat, I settled myself at the kitchen table for my morning Bible reading. Before long Nat reappeared, his thin body swallowed up in a new set of dead guy clothes. He ambled over and began reading over my shoulder. Acknowledging his presence or his interest in the Bible would, I knew, turn Nat away in embarrassment, so I read more slowly and pretended I had no idea that a shoulder-reader was sharing the words with me. After I read one chapter each out of the ten places that I kept marked in my Bible, I started to pray. Nat refused to join me in prayer, but I prayed aloud for him anyway. "Let's go," I said after I finished praying.

"Where?"

"To the paper, of course … to get your job nailed down."

"What makes you think anyone would hire me? Do you own the paper?"

"You have talent," I said. "Bea recognizes and appreciates talented writers, and she's about to lose the one she's had for the past two years. I used to work for her, and we've remained friends." Thinking about how crazy both of us were about Marty made me wonder if I had just uttered a somewhat mendacious statement. Hiding my doubt from Nat, I patted the dogs goodbye and bundled Nat into Old Blue; this time, he sat properly on the seat.

Marty himself met us in Bea's office. I liked to imagine that his eyes lit up with gladness when he saw me, but I couldn't tell because I couldn't breathe. Marty seemed to expect to stay and become a part of the conversation, so I plunged into an enthusiastic account of Nat's talents.

Nat openly smirked at me.

Marty threw back his head and laughed. "Right smart of you, Miz Mike, being so quick to help other folks. If you come up with any ideas about how to help Jared Silvers, let me know. That young'n sure needs a hand up."

"I don't know who this dude is y'all are talking about," Nat enjoined unexpectedly, "but I do know one thing. I ain't babysitting, if that's why this crazy lady brought me here." Nat spat the words out defiantly as Marty's eyes left my face reluctantly and focused on the pale, anemic youth.

"If you plan to work for me, Nat," Bea said briskly, "you'll need to use correct grammar, even in speech. Come on and let me show you around. Marty and Mike would probably like a chance to visit. They both seem to be too busy these days to keep up with old friends."

Those last words were, I knew, a dig directed at me for neglecting our friendship, but she had said "Marty and Mike," and our names sounded so delicious together that my mind was awash in rainbow streams of M&Ms. It just has to be! Marty and I are meant for each other. Other women were arguably younger, more attractive, and in better shape than I was, but I didn't believe any of them could love Marty as fiercely as I was prepared to love him or be as faithful to that dream as I had been to that dream for the past several years.

Marty slipped an arm through mine and drew me outside. "Let's leave Bea and that kid to get acquainted. He's Thor's son, isn't he? Where did you unearth him from? I thought he left town a couple of years ago."

"Well ..."

"Mike, you and your pickles! I know you're just trying to help, and I admire that." His warm tone of voice melted the cartilage in my knees, and it was hard to stand beside him with sunlight pouring over his head, throwing red sparks around him like a halo. Each spark found its mark in my heart. Then, without warning, the tone of his voice chilled. "But, Mike, I trust he's not staying with you in your house. You are wise enough, I'm sure, not to let that happen, no matter how much you want to help that misfit druggie."

I looked at Marty in confusion.

"With your husband being gone and you being a Christian, I know you've thought of how it would look to have a strange man living at your place. Even with the difference in your ages, some people will be bound to think the worst ... and people talk."

No, I hadn't thought of that. One of my worst – or best, depending on individual point of view – personality traits was total indifference to the opinions others held about me. I always tried to be kind, fair, and nonjudgmental. I was too busy to worry about what other people thought.

"I'm headed into San Antonio," Marty added, "so I'll miss you at lunch today, but surely I'll see you at church tonight." He doffed his hat and strolled away, his long legs swinging with a strong, free stride that constricted every muscle within my chest.

Church! I brightened. I had forgotten about the midweek service, and I had forgotten to acquaint Nat with one more important rule of the house: church attendance. Nat would rebel, I was sure, but I was afraid to leave him in my house alone. I almost forgot Old Blue and left the car outside the newspaper office in my rush to get back to my office and launch Pastor Garth Seymour on a new mystery before church started. That was one thing about Three Prongs: It was such a small town that a person could literally walk from one end to the other and find every place they needed to go. Parking was scare. When one found a good parking place, it made sense to leave the vehicle parked and walk. However, in my case, it was easy to forget where I had parked. I turned back and retried Old Blue and parked him outside my office until it was time to pick up Nat for church.

Rebel proved a mild word for Nat's reaction to my announcement about church. However, after a Mexican plate special at *The Spanish Tile*, he was more amenable. He even admitted – with embarrassment – that he had enjoyed his first day at work. "It's hard," he said with relish, "and I've got a lot to learn. Bea can come down pretty hard on mistakes, but she's fair. So few people I've known in my life have been fair."

I was suddenly glad that Nat was with me, in spite of what Marty – or anyone else – would think if he knew I would be taking the young man home with me after church. My job was to live for God as fully as I could at my age and state of health and let Marty and other people who might disapprove be responsible for their own thoughts. I could take responsibility for my actions, but I could not accept responsibility for their thoughts. Keeping track of myself was a big enough chore. If God wanted Marty and I to be together, nothing strong enough to separate us existed on planet Earth. If God did not intend for us to share a future, none of the weapons I possessed were strong enough to ring victorious. But M&M? It must be. So I showed up at church with Nat in tow, feeling totally confident and prepared to face Marty.

Joy found me first. I entered the sanctuary and found Lynette there. Her bright beauty robbed Nat of speech, and forgetting to train myself to appreciate Faith, I thought again with a pang of how good she would look at Ron's side. I was glad to see her in God's house, since I had been concerned about her spiritual bent.

How short the lifespan of joy. Marty strolled into church shaking hands and greeting friends, making his way steadily to my side. Just when I tried to suck in enough air to revive myself, his eyes hit Lynette and stopped. By the time the first hymn began, Lynette and Marty were sitting together, sharing a hymnal, and Nat and I sat together, with me holding a book that he pointedly ignored. After church, Marty and Lynette disappeared together so quickly that I was unable to say goodbye to either of them. I drove home with Nat, carefully guarding my hurt.

"I'm sorry," he said quietly as a chorus of doggie welcomes met our ears.

"Sorry?"

"I can tell how much you like him. He's seems nice enough, except for being so old – much too old for her. But she's ... well, she is really pretty."

"Yes, she is," I admitted, keeping bitterness out of my voice. "Marty's a good friend. I want what's best for him, and I want him to have what God has planned for his life."

"Even if it's not you?" Nat asked in disbelief. "I've never had the chance to be in love. From what I've seen, it makes people act kind of foolish. Still, I think if I did fall in love, I would fight for it like a pit bull defending a bone."

I couldn't let Nat know that at the moment, I felt like physically attacking Lynette Clarissa Greene and pulling the lovely golden hair out of her head. She was young and beautiful and could have any number of men in her life. For me, though, there was no one except Marty. He wasn't just my dream lover; he was the total of all my dreams.

As Old Blue drew up to the house, I realized that the dogs' barking sounded enclosed. "You didn't shut the dogs up in the garage when we left, did you?" I asked.

"Hey, crazy lady, I told you I don't like dogs. I probably never will. But you've been nice to me. Why would I do something like that unless you told me to?"

But Abigail, with her long, loose, floppy ears, and Abner,

with his short black legs pumping as if riding a bike, were in the garage. They rushed out to meet us, clearly relieved to have been restored to freedom. Poor old Priscilla, the senior member of the group, was missing.

Leaving Nat to rest after his first day of work and church attendance, I went looking for her. The black and tan hound was nowhere in sight, and she failed to respond to my calls. When I found her, it was with a cruel, shocking twist of disbelief. She had been shot in the head and pushed over an embankment halfway down the drive. Her teeth, even in death, were closed around a strip of material. With tears running down my face, I realized that faithful Prissy must have been protecting her home from an intruder and had paid the ultimate price for that loyalty.

Surely it had to be an independent act of violence and had nothing to do with my investigation of Julia's death. I didn't even know anything yet!

Sobs tore out of my chest as I looked down at the hound I had never wanted, but the one who had proven herself in a long, rich friendship. Alfred had made fun of my "soft heart" when I'd brought the gangly-legged pup home. She had been shivering in pounding rain at the side of the highway, looking hopefully at each passing vehicle to see if it held a familiar face. Alfred said we would keep the hound pup until we found a home for it, but she found a home in our hearts first.

As I stooped down to gather Prissy to me, wiry arms wrapped around my shoulders. "Don't," Nat said softly. "Let me take care of her. I'll dig her a real nice grave. I won't let you down, crazy lady."

Feeling every bit as crazy as Nat's accusations, I fled to the house in tears.

Chapter 6.

E
ven after having supervised the nighttime burial, Nat was ready for his second day on the job with time to spare. Both of us were silent on the drive into town. I was thinking about the strip of pastel-plaid material that I had eased out of Prissy's teeth before Nat had buried her, and I was still touched by the kindness he'd demonstrated towards me, but I knew he would be embarrassed if I mentioned it again.

"I don't get paid until tomorrow," he said shyly as I dropped him off at the Sidelines office, "but I'd like to take you out to lunch and pay you back then."

I smiled and thanked him for the offer. "It's a date. Make it eleven o'clock so we can get a table. I'll meet you at *The Spanish Tile*. We can both walk there from our offices."

He looked so happy at my acceptance that I was thankful I had hidden my first tendency to refuse. Marty was the one I really wanted to see at lunch – not the skinny youth with untidy hair and unhealthy skin.

Hyacinth breezed into the office, interrupting my flow of thought and the stream of typing taking place beneath the tips of my stiff fingers. "Do you think Jared really tried to save her?" she demanded. "Or do you think he held her under?"

Clueless, I stared at her.

"No one's told you? Even with that kid you dragged out of some storm drain working for your old pal Bea? A woman drowned at the children's home early this morning. Jared Silvers said he saw her swimming across the lake and that she called out for help and went under. He said he doesn't swim well, but he jumped in to try to save her because he knew there wasn't enough time to go get help. So what do you think? Hero or villain? You're tight with Brent and Anna, so I bet you could find out. I don't have the sheriff in my pocket. He seems to disapprove of me."

Hyacinth had no further details about the incident, just aimless questions. As soon as she took her white-blonde hair and cigarette-thinned body elsewhere, I jumped into Old Blue and headed out to the children's home. Thankfully, I found there was no need to fear letting Nat down at lunch. He was on the scene with Bea already, taking pictures and interviewing witnesses. Elusive joy returned to me as I saw real interest written into that apathetic young face for the first time. He was so intent on his job that he failed to notice me at first.

Brent nodded a welcome to me, not surprised that I was there, even though it was clear that I was not covering the story for Sidelines. He tossed out brief details about the incident to me before returning to his investigation.

I angled over closer to Nat, impressed both by the quality of the questions he was asking and the thought that had engineered them.

Opinion on whether the drowning had been accidental or deliberate seemed equally divided; Jared's reputation as a troublemaker was well established. Witnesses agreed that he had hated the victim, house parent Renee Davis. Davis had, in fact, ordered the teen to quit working for Zolly Gilmore. The children's home rightfully took a strong stand against alcohol and encouraged its students to make wise choices in life, including abstaining from damaging – and damning – lifestyles.

When I watched Nat tactfully question the young boy, I was even more undecided. Jared was badly frightened, and I wondered if his fright was a portent of his guilt.

Nat caught me by the arm as I was leaving. He used my name for the first time, albeit shyly. "Mike ... uh, I'm sorry, but I won't be able to meet you for lunch. Bea wants me to interview a few more people, especially the other house parents."

I nodded and smiled at him. "Thanks. I understand. I'm proud of you. You've thought of solid questions, and you're doing a professional job of interviewing."

His face flushed with pleasure. "That's what Bea said. Maybe this job will work out." He released my arm. "But,

Mike, I can see it on your face. He didn't do it. That kid –
he didn't do it. He's afraid because he knows he will get
blamed. He's like me. He gets blamed for everything …
well, I guess we both deserve a lot of blame at times, but I
swear to you, Mike, he didn't do it. I can just … I can tell."

I wasn't convinced, but I nodded. "I'm glad to hear what
you think about all this, Nat. Good luck with the rest of
your interviews."

With careful maneuvering, I managed *The Spanish Tile*
within a few steps of Marty and made it seem fortuitous
rather than deliberate. Gentleman that he was, Marty
invited me to join him, although I had the uncomfortable
feeling that he was less than ebullient about the invitation.

Just as I slipped a sugar substitute into my ice tea and
prepared my large, greenish eyes for feasting on Marty's
face, Lynette bounced into the restaurant and up to our
booth.

Marty slipped over on the hard, polished wooden bench
to give Lynette a place to sit.

"I'm sorry," I said breathlessly (wasn't I always breathless around Marty), "but I didn't know you were expecting
someone."

"Stay," Marty ordered as I started to slide out of the
bench on my side of the booth. "I think you met Clara at
church Wednesday. She's new in town and could use a
couple of friends."

Lynette smiled at me. "Yes, please stay, Miss Rice. I love
your books, by the way. Are you working on a new one?"

"Mike has an office here in town," Marty answered for
me. "I don't know how much writing she gets done, but she
sure lands herself in some real pickles. And that reminds
me, Miz Mike … I dropped off some papers from Hyacinth
at your office. The door was unlocked."

It sounded almost like an accusation. I knew Marty
probably thought that after my office had been trashed, I
would keep it locked. He didn't understand that I was on
the track of a killer and that if I were coming close to the
truth, having my office trashed again was the least of my
worries. "I ran out to the children's home today when I
heard about Jared," I replied evasively. "Nat and Bea were
there, and –

How could that soft, heart-rending cowboy drawl turn
so cruelly cold? I thought when he interrupted, "Jared!

Are you still on his case just because of that near-accident in front of your office? I'm disappointed in you, Mike. I've always appreciated your kindness to others, above all things. Like Clara here, that boy needs a good friend – not more maledictions from yet another person."

Miserably, I buried my too-big eyes behind the menu that I was unable to read through the blurry window of unshed tears. Clara and Marty were too interested in their semiprivate conversation to notice my despair. Despair seemed more effective for my secret program of body trimming than working out in a gym or dieting. Simply put, the delicious smorgasbord offered at *The Spanish Tile* suddenly resembled natant floral life on a green-scummed pond to my lovesick eyes. To their credit, Clara and Marty tendered spurious regret when I excused myself from their table. Before I made it up to the cash register to pay, they had already forgotten the empty place and untouched food across from them.

Pastor Seymour had never seemed as flat and uninteresting to me, his creator, as he did that afternoon when I attempted to recapture the pace of the story. The debacle of lunch with Marty had made me forget how I planned to solve the mystery that my character had obediently discovered. I was ready to go home long before Nat phoned to announce that he had to work late.

"Bea wants this story finished. I'm new at this, so it's going a bit slow. I'm sorry, Miss Rice."

"Mike, please. That's fine, Nat. Don't give it a thought. I have more work to do here, and the extra time will give me a chance to run to the store for groceries." I kept to myself the secret fear that the check might bounce.

"I'll pitch in some grocery money tomorrow, when I get paid," Nat offered. "Only, if you could ... could you get a bit extra tonight? I mean ... well, I didn't really have time for lunch, and now that I'm not ..." His voice dropped. "Well, you know what all I was doing before. You were there in my pad. Now that I'm clean, I'm getting kind of hungry again."

After hearing his confession, I would gladly have bounced ten checks to feed the anemic youth!

On the way to the store, I spotted Marty. Actually, my heart was capable of finding him anywhere in town, at any time of day or night even at times when I wouldn't have expected to see him. His truck – the same color, make, and model as perhaps fifty others in town – leapt to sight from blocks away down Main Street. It was one of those inexplicable facts of life.

Marty turned in the direction of our church, and I noticed with surprise that Lynette/Clara was not with him. From their involvement with each other at lunch, I had expected to see the two of them glued together as romance bloomed around them like early spring bluebonnet swells. I felt ashamed of the little lift of hope in my heart – hope that Lynette had already proven disingenuous to Marty. I tried to remind myself that love, as written in the Bible, demands that even people in love should put the other person's welfare above their own, a demand that some-times means letting go and letting someone else grasp the blessing. But how can I let go, when Marty and I belong together? M&Ms!

Even after groceries were stowed in Old Blue, Nat had not turned up at my office yet ready to go home. Since my new book had stalled after lunch, I had spent hours in the courthouse, shuffling through minutes and records from past county commissioners' meetings. True to his denial, Thornton Dean had not voted for the bridge to nowhere, but I did manage to uncover a fact he'd neglected to mention: He had been a partner in the XYZ Corporation at the time. The bridge, although it now benefited no one – least of all the taxpayers who had funded the multi-million dollar project – would add value to real estate near the bridge, land still owned by XYZ. The bridge cut miles of travel from our strangely shaped county and made the county seat of Three Prongs more accessible. This newly accumulated knowledge made me ponder Thor's possible involvement in his wife's murder. If Julia had found out about the project, she might have attempted to use it as leverage against Thor, especially if he contested the divorce she had appar-ently been all too eager to file.

Still waiting for Nat, I paced aimlessly around the night-time streets of Three Prongs, reminding myself somewhat of Hyacinth. At least I was getting exercise. Combined with the lunch I had not eaten at noon, I was at least making an effort to trim and shape up my forty-something body.

Even though I was on the other side of the street, my ramblings took me past Zolly Gilmore's Borderbound

Watering Hole. To my amazement, I saw Lynette Clarissa Greene approach the door to the bar, with one arm wrapped possessively around Thornton Dean. Just before reaching the door, the couple paused on the sidewalk and swallowed each other in a slow, intimate kiss that made my insides hurt a bit. Lynette and ... Thor!? I was right! Lynette Clarissa Greene had not come to Three Prongs for the noble purpose of solving her sister's murder. Rather, she'd come to steal her deceased sister's husband! She didn't want justice for Julia; she wanted wealth for herself! My mind leapt to the pastel-plaid material I had pried out of Prissy's mouth. It looked like it might have been from the kind of clothes, in style and color and fabric, that Lynn would have worn. Is it possible that Lynette and Thor were both responsible for Julia's death? I wondered. I had known Thor a long time and didn't want to believe it, but if it were true, I didn't even know how to prove it. Would it be possible to find out more about Lynn, or had she cleverly covered her tracks to Three Prongs? I rued the fact that it was too late at night to launch an immediate investigation.

Fortunately, by the time I had retraced my steps to my office again, Nat had materialized. Feet planted apart, he faced me with such a look of steeled determination that I was amazed. "I know I only just met you," he said. "I know I was rude to you at the start, and you don't owe me a thing. You can tell me 'no' and send me away, and I won't even be surprised or hate you for it."

"Whatever are you talking about, Nat?"

He looked quickly around outside the office, then took a few steps back inside towards me. "It's Jared. They kicked him out of the children's home until the investigation is completed."

"Oh! How terrible. I'm sorry, Nat. You seemed to hit it off with him. Does he have family somewhere? Where is he going to go?"

"That's just it. He doesn't have a family – leastways not a family who claims him. His mother is dead, and he doesn't know who his father is. He doesn't have anywhere to go, and they are talking about sending him to the juvenile detention center for a while until they sort everything out. That's a bad idea, Miss Rice ... Mike, I mean. Dad sent me there. It was where I learned to hotwire cars and strip them down and disarm a security system. Jared tried to save that Davis woman. I know he did. Now he's being punished for trying to do something good. It's not fair!"

"I agree, Nat, but what can we do?"

"We can take him home with us."

I gasped.

"He's out there waiting right now. I couldn't leave him alone. I couldn't let him down like everyone else has. Sheriff Cruz says he knows you and that if you will take responsibility for Jared, he can stay with you for a little while." He paused and directed a malevolent gaze at me. "Jared's expecting you to say 'no,' and so am I."

Hadn't Marty wanted me to help Jared Silvers? I dismissed the nagging thought that now I would have two strange young men at the ranch, living in my house and – as Marty had pointed out – no husband to contradict rumors or false impressions. My lips twisted into a smile as I thought about possible gossip. Would those other people who Marty worried about decide we're holding orgies at the ranch? With spurious confidence, I asked Nat, "Why would I say 'no'? Get Jared and put him in the car. We need to get the groceries home. I bought them quite some time ago, and I don't want anything to thaw or melt."

Nat closed the space between us and threw his arms around me in a wormy hug. "Thanks! You won't regret this. Jared's good at fixing things. With your husband gone, maybe he could work for you on the ranch. You wouldn't need to pay him much, you know – not as much as a regular person. Maybe just a bit of cash and some grub." Understandably, Nat did not know how practically impossible it would be for me to pay anyone for anything.

Jared slid into the open doorway, looking at everything except me. He was almost as thin as Nat, but he lacked a few inches of Nat's height. His eyes, I supposed, were blue, although the color was impossible to surmise with the downcast head. His blond hair, long in the back, looked dirty.

"She said 'yes'," Nat told the frightened boy. "Now let's go before the sheriff changes his mind and takes you with him."

On the ride out to the ranch, Nat and Jared talked about rock and rap groups whose names I was totally unfamiliar with. I smiled to myself remembering Nat's request for extra groceries. In spite of what he had said about figuring I would refuse, he must have expected Jared to come with us – or perhaps he would have smuggled Jared along anyway.

Both Nat and Jared helped carry the groceries into the house, a new luxury for me. Even when Alfred was alive, he rarely helped with that chore. He was usually off on a tractor somewhere or out working in the shop when I came home from the store.

Unlike Nat, Jared liked dogs. He sat down on the floor in the kitchen and petted both dogs while they covered him with kisses. Nat looked shocked that someone would allow dogs that luxury, but Jared's raucous laughter testified to his merriment. Nat switched on the television in the next room and plopped down on the couch with his long legs resting on the table of magazines in front of him.

Jared, however, jumped up from the floor, washed his hands, and began helping me with the tacos I had planned for dinner.

I hid my amazement.

Praying before meals was apparently standard for Jared. He bowed his head readily as I prayed. Eyes open, Nat slouched uncomfortably at the table, ready to grab food as soon as it was passed his way.

After we were through eating, Jared instructed Nat to help clear the table, and he did. I left the two young men to wash dishes and clean up the kitchen while I carted forgotten – and unpublished – manuscripts out of both spare bedrooms and prepared the rooms for their new inhabitants.

Neither Nat nor Jared wanted to come with me to take the dogs on a walk. Remembering Prissy's fate, I wasn't sure I wanted to go either; however, I wasn't going to let fear steal my life.

It was hard to drive away from the ranch the next morning and leave Jared there alone. He was a total stranger to me. What kind of trouble might the teen find with no supervision? Still, Nat was depending on me for transportation to work, and I needed to get back to work too.

"I'll make a list of repairs you need," Jared informed me as Nat and I prepared to leave. "Then I'll make a list of supplies. You can decide what needs to be done most and get some of the stuff you need. I won't let you down, honest. I did a lot of work for Zolly." The boy's voice broke a bit when he mentioned the older man's name, and my heart lurched.

Poor kid. The only one who had taken time to befriend him was apparently one of the least desirable residents of Three Prongs, and there I was adding to that insult by worrying about leaving him alone at my house. Momentarily, I was ashamed of myself.

"Jared," I asked gently. "What about school? You should be in school."

"I quit," he replied shortly. "I'm old enough to quit."

"No one is ever old enough to quit learning," Nat and I found ourselves objecting in unison. Still, there was no time to argue with the young man at the moment and get Nat to work on time. "We'll talk about school later," I promised, "after you've had a chance to settle in and make some decisions."

This time as I delved into the mystery I was attempting to finish for my publisher, the dark patch in the doorway transformed itself into Clint Flavors. White tufts of hair stuck out of his overall dark hair, and his dark eyes roamed around my office without an accompanying hint of recognition.

"Clint? Hello."

The big, sturdy man shuffled into the office, still looking around him as if he were lost.

"Clint?"

His eyes finally found me, and he nodded quickly. "That you, Miz Rice? Is this here your office?"

"Hi, Clint. Yes, this is my office. Are you working today or fishing?"

"I come here looking for you."

"Well, you've found me. Come on in and sit down."

Clint shuffled further into the room, twisting his grease-stained cap between long fingers. His body was apparently not well suited for sitting in chairs. "Miz Rice," he said, still standing, "I come to see you because my girlfriend left me. I thought you might could help."

Not knowing what to say, I said nothing.

"Folks here in town are laughing at me. They don't believe I had me a purty girlfriend. They think I made it all up, but she stayed with me in my cabin for quite a spell. She used to laugh and joke about hiding out with me. I kept asking her to marry me 'cause I knew nothin' else would make it right. She kept laughing at me in that pretty way of hers, sayin' she would, but it wasn't the right time ... and now she's gone. How can I get her back, Miz Rice? I don't read good, but I hear tell that in your stories, you always got someone falling in love and getting married, so I figured you would know. I gave her money, I bought her stuff, and I wanted to marry her. I even bought her season tickets to the rodeos what's starting up. Now I've got two seats at the rodeos and not even one of her. What did I do wrong, Miz Rice?" The man's lugubrious countenance dissolved suddenly. Still standing, he held his scraggly head in his hands and began sobbing.

Shock traced cold fingers across my shoulder blades. What should I do? What *could* I do? I hadn't felt so helpless since Lynette Clarissa Greene had walked into my office and asked me to help her find her sister's killer. Not knowing what else to do, I tried to put my arms around Clint to comfort him.

He shrugged off that gesture like a big dog shaking off bath water. "Don't, Miz Mike. She might see us and think the worst. She might be around here. She ain't at the cabin no more, but I think she's still around town. She liked it here, and she said she planned to stay. That's one reason I asked her to marry me so many times. What can I do? I can't even sit out around *The Spanish Tile* and wait for someone to pick me up for a job. I can't sit still long enough to wait for someone to hire me. I keep walking around looking for her. I can't keep my mind on nothing."

`"Clint, I really don't know what to tell you. I never even met this girl, and –

"But you're smart, Miz Mike. You must know. 'Sides, ain't no one done met her. That was how she wanted it. She was hiding – something 'bout some checks she wrote, she said. I don't have no bank account, so I don't know what she done wrong."

"Clint, perhaps you can help me and I can help you. Do you know Jared Silvers?"

"Yup, and I know a secret about him. I learned it from her – my girlfriend what I had, only I ain't telling. I promised not to tell."

I shook my head. "I'm not asking you about a secret. I have Jared out at the ranch. He's going to do some work for me, but he's pretty young. I think he needs someone like you to supervise him. If I take you out there, will you help me while I look for your girlfriend?"

"Supervise? That means like telling him what to do? Aw, shucks. I ain't never been nobody's boss before. They always tell me what to do, not the nother way around."

"But you're a good worker, and you know what to do. Could you try helping him?"

"Sure. I'll try anything to get my girlfriend back."

"Good. I'll run you out there right now. You can tell me more about this girlfriend of yours on the way. For instance, what's her name? Is she from around here? What does she look like? Do you have a picture of her?"

Clearly, I had asked too many questions at one time, and Clint had slipped away from me into some pathless dimension where I could not follow. "Supervise," he said doubtfully. "Can't Alfred supervise both of us? Oh, I'm sorry, Miz Mike. I forgot. He's up there in Heaven with my mama and daddy, ain't he? I wonder if they've seen each other yet. Can't you stay and tell us what to do? I listen real good. I'm a good worker, I am. Clint Flavor's not all stupid like some folks think ... and I had me a real purty girlfriend once, and they can't nobody say nothin' different about that!" His voice ended in a belligerent tone.

By the time we reached the ranch, I still knew very little about Clint's girlfriend.

I had a picture of her," he said. "I took lots of pictures of her 'cause she was so purty, but they's gone. I reckon she took 'em when she runned away."

"Why would she take pictures of herself?"

"Her name was Veronica. Ain't that a pretty name? It's a hard one to spell. I called her Vinny mostly, and she used to laugh at me – but it was a nice laugh, like she liked me, and not a mean laugh like they laugh at me in town when they're making fun of me. Vinny. Ain't that a pretty name?"

"What was her last name?"

"She never told me. Said it didn't matter 'cause after we got married, her name would be the same as mine ... and our kids if we had any."

I tried not to cringe as I thought about a family of Clint Flavors hiding out from the law because of hot checks, unable to cope in the modern world because they were a few fries short of a kid's meal. "What did she look like?" I needed to at least know that if I were going to search for an unknown "Vinny" with no last name.

"She was right purty," Clint said. He brightened as we drew up to the house. "Them yonder your dogs, Miz Mike? They look purty friendly. I get along good with dogs."

"Clint, I need to know what Vinny looks like if I'm going to find her. What did she look like?"

"What's them dogs' names? They won't bite me, I'm sure. I get along good with dogs, 'ceptin fer when they's scarin' away my fish." He climbed out of the car and got down on one knee to pet Abigail and Abner.

The commotion brought Jared around the house at a run. He looked so amazed to see us that I felt guilty. I didn't want him to know I didn't fully trust him, but he knew. As I explained about Clint, Jared's face darkened. "You can trust me, Miss Rice. I've already made the lists, just like I promised."

"I do trust you, Jared," I lied. "I just thought that with Clint's help, the work will go even faster."

"Why would I care about that?" he asked. "I've got nowhere else to go and nothing else to do. I'm in no hurry, unless you are." He had a point.

"I'll tell you what, Jared. Take Clint and me around to see what you've planned, then give me your list of supplies. I'll try to get some of the things on your list before I get home tonight." Old Blue would also need gas, but I tried not to think about the math equation that matched a dwindling bank account against increased expenses. "Besides, like Nat said, you need to consider getting back to school." Nat hadn't said that exactly, but I knew Nat's words would carry more weight than mine.

I had momentarily gained approval from both Clint and Jared. Clint clearly had no desire to be in charge of anyone except himself. Jared straightened himself importantly as he showed me needed maintenance on the ranch buildings, things that needed repair that I hadn't even noticed. I left Jared and Clint to discuss the best way to paint the eaves of the barn. The dogs were delighted that even though I was leaving them, human companionship remained.

I never saw the small red car until it shot out from behind the sign where Old Blue had previously hunkered down when we had outwitted the driver before. It came straight at me, and I swung the big old car onto the shoulder in an attempt to avoid a collision. It wasn't until glass exploded around me that I realized the driver – who wore a Halloween mask under a red cap – had tried to shoot me. Instinctively, I ducked when I saw the gun barrel leveled at me again. When Blue stopped, it was with a horrendous grinding and tearing of metal.

Like a somnambulist, I unfastened my seatbelt, then fell out of the mangled metal and stood swaying in shock as I looked at my good and trusty friend of so many years. I seemed to be alive, but Blue didn't come out unscathed.

Already, other drivers had stopped to help, but the red car was gone. The world of modern technology had left me behind; while I owned a cell phone, I never seemed to have it with me when I needed it. It was too easy to forget something so small that I used so rarely. I had no fondness for talking on phones anyway; I preferred to speak to people in person, which had benefited me when I was working with Bea on the newspaper.

Other drivers, however, had already called.

Sheriff Brent Cruz answered the call himself, arriving just ahead of an ambulance and two deputies. Brent discounted my story. "Mike! Really? Halloween masks and drivers shooting at someone here in our quiet county? You write too many mysteries or read too many or watch too many violent TV shows. Tell the truth … it was a deer, right? You swerved to miss a deer and parked your car up against this cliff."

One of the deputies, however, found three ragged bullet-shaped holes in the driver's side door. "It's a good thing you drive such a heavy old monster, ma'am," he said. "The bullets didn't go through. We're going to have to impound this car for evidence."

"But it's my only transportation, and I take someone else to work, meaning it's his only transportation too."

Brent clasped my shoulder gently with his wide hand. "Steady, Mike. Anna has a car we've been trying to sell because I bought her a new one. Her old car still has insurance on it, and I'm sure we could let you borrow it for as long as you need to. It's about time you bought yourself a new vehicle anyway. Why, I bet you can't even find parts for this one."

"I don't want a new car. I want Blue … and why would I need parts? He works fine, mostly."

Brent's dark eyebrows climbed up towards his Stetson.

"Mike," he said gently, "your car is totaled. I don't think you could even buy new parts for it if it was worth fixing. Do you realize how old that car is? I haven't even seen one like it in a junkyard for probably ten years. Now come on over to the EMS unit and get checked out. In fact, I'd feel a lot better if you'd take a trip to the hospital and –

"I'm fine," I said, a mendacious statement. My knees were wobbly, my neck hurt, and fear was beginning to turn my entire body cold and shaky.

"Look, Mike, I know about Nat and Jared and how you've made them your responsibility, but –

"You gave Jared permission to stay with me, but how in the world did you find out about Nat?"

Brent laughed. "Mike, have you forgotten just how small Three Prongs is and how quickly news travels? Thank you for having the guts to help those two. They desperately need a hand up, and you were the only one with spunk enough and faith enough in God to do the Christian thing and try to help them."

I could only hope Marty would feel the same when he found out they were staying at the ranch with me. I wasn't sure how he'd really feel about me living alone with two young men and no chaperone. Acting in all those Hollywood Westerns had engineered an old-fashioned attitude in my cowboy hero.

"But, Mike," Brent continued sternly, "you have friends – including Anna and myself – who would be glad to help out while you get checked out at the hospital. Don't think you have to go through this alone."

I checked out the parts of my body that I could see or feel and decided that, unlike Blue, I was fine. Brent gave me a ride back to his house to collect Anna's old car. I tried to be brave and not cry when I watched the indifferent tow truck drag Blue off down the road in the opposite direction. It was just a car, but it was such a faithful friend.

At least Brent and Anna lived far enough from Three Prongs that if news of my crash had circulated around town, Hyacinth didn't know where to find me. Anna rushed out of the house and listened in disbelief to her husband's tale. Imperiously, she dragged me into the house to the bathroom and closed the door behind us. Then, disrobing me, she checked me for injuries herself before allowing me to rejoin Brent outside.

"Now, this car is newer than yours, so you'll have to get used to it," Brent told me. "Anna has always loved it." The car was already running, and Brent motioned to me to get inside.

I opened the door to get in, and a deep male voice announced, "A door is ajar."

With a scream of terror, I bailed out of the car, landing on my rear end beside the driveway.

Brent and Anna clutched each other, laughing hysterically. Brent was still wiping tears from his eyes when he reached down with a strong arm and lifted me to my feet. "It's just the car, Mike. Relax."

"The car talks? I don't want a talking car. I want my car! I want Blue."

This time, Anna took over. She held me until my trembling quieted. "Give the car a chance, Mike. It will get better gas mileage than your monster did."

I brightened in spite of my adamant decision to keep Blue and get him fixed. Good gas mileage was a plus, especially given my current lack of finances and the three hungry men – and two hungry dogs – back at the ranch.

"At least drive it until you find out how much it will cost to fix yours," Brent added. "Anna and I will be insulted if you don't let us help."

So, within a couple of hours of my accident – really an attempted murder – I was trying to cope with a car that unexpectedly shouted at me, "Your gas is low ... Check your engine ... Fasten your seatbelt ... A door is ajar."

When I finally reached my office again, I dropped my head down on the computer keyboard and slept soundly until Nat shook me awake.

"Mike, your car's been stolen!"

I jumped up and rushed outside with Nat. Then, spotting Anna's beige car, memory swept back and I sat down on the sidewalk outside my office and sobbed. Poor Nat.

He finally prised the story from me, bundled me into the passenger's side of the car, and drove me home. "Hope we don't get stopped," he bantered cheerfully. "I let my driver's license expire since I lost my wheels."

Both Clint and Jared met us when Nat eased the car up close to the house. Words seem to have failed me, of all people, a writer who made somewhat of a living with words. Nat answered questions as he ushered me into the house and eased me into a puffy living room recliner.

"We'll get dinner," Jared said, propping a pillow behind my head.

I smiled at them, still unable to speak.

"And," Jared said, shuffling his feet, "I hope it's okay with you that I made a decision today when you were gone. I tried to call you at the office, but no one answered the phone."

"Yeah," Nat said, "because she wasn't there. She was out trying to get herself bumped off so she wouldn't be stuck with us anymore."

Clint hovered by the chair, his big body swaying awkwardly as he tried to fathom the conversation. "I found it!" he said to no one in particular.

I scanned the room around me, searching for clues. What decision? What's going on with Jared now?

"What I decided," he said, as if reading my mind, "is to let Clint stay here."

"What?"

"Yep, in the barn. He asked. He rode his bicycle out to his cabin and brought back some clothes and stuff. He said that with his girlfriend gone, he's too sad and lonely to be alone. Says he's been wanting to kill himself so his girlfriend will be sorry she left him!"

I gasped and looked at Clint.

"I found it," Clint said, looking off into a corner of the room and nodding in a satisfied manner.

"I know I'm young," Jared continued, "but when I was fourteen, I fell in love with this girl. She was really nice to me when I first got to the home. We talked a lot. In fact, we could talk about anything and everything. Just being with her made the flowers burn with color. Being with her made it summer, even when it was cold outside." He looked at all of us looking at him, and his face flushed. "Forget the drivel and all this mush. All I mean is, she ... uh –"

Nat clasped his shoulder. "Hey, man. I know what you mean. I've dreamt of feeling that way. Don't apologize and don't try to pretend it didn't happen."

Thinking of Marty, I laughed. "Yes, Nat's right. We do understand. Even old folks understand about love, Jared. Don't be embarrassed."

"I knew it was somewhere," Clint said, rocking up and down on his heels and addressing a picture of Alfred. "I found it."

We looked at Clint, looked at each other, then shrugged in unison. "What happened?" I asked, turning back to Jared.

"They found a relative of hers – an aunt up north some-where – and she had to leave the children's home and go live with the aunt. We wrote for a while, then she moved again. We lost touch with each other. Anyway, I remember how cold and empty and devastated I was when she left. I thought I would die. I wanted to die. Actually, I thought about swimming out into the pond until I got tired and couldn't get back across. I'm not a very strong swimmer."

"Jared!" I exclaimed.

"Anyway, I know how Clint feels, and since you helped me, I wanted to help him."

"He can stay, but not in the barn! Alfred and I built this house together when we were young. We had one child, a son, but we always hoped for more children. We built extra rooms both for the children we hoped we would have and for family when they came to visit. I use the screened-in porch as a sort of art studio, but if you and Nat will help me move my paint and easel out, Clint can stay there. It's comfortable. I like sleeping there in the summer myself."

My words had barely dropped into the room before Nat and Jared flew into action, followed by a still-muttering Clint.

Weakly, I leaned back in the chair to rest my eyes. It was a brief rest. In fact, I thought I was dreaming when I heard the rich badinage, "Well, Miz Mike, quite a pickle this time! The whole town's talking about it."

Convinced I was dreaming, I sat bolt upright in the chair and blinked.

Marty dropped down in front of me on one knee and peered into my face. "Are you really okay? Anna said she checked you out."

Wordlessly, I nodded.

"Why would someone shoot at you, for heaven's sake? Was it one of those drive-by shootings we hear so much about on the San Antonio news stations?"

Before I could answer, Clint, Nat, and Jared trooped back into the room, and Marty just stared at them.

"I found it," Clint told his new audience member. He pointed to me. "She's looking for my purty girlfriend, so I found it."

"Well," Marty said, easing his tall frame back up from the floor, "I must say, Mike, you are scarcely alone. Are these your new bodyguards?"

"I'm staying on the porch," Clint Flavors announced proudly. "She moved me out of the barn into the house."

"Jared got kicked out of the children's home," Nat added. "Miss Rice is letting him stay here until the investigation is completed."

"And you?"

"Oh," Nat said cheerfully. "I live here. I was already living here before they came."

I groaned and sank down into the chair as Marty doffed his hat sarcastically and left without speaking to me again.

"Hey, did I say something wrong?" Nat asked. "Or was he leaving anyway?"

Before I could answer or even think of the correct answer, Clint dropped a picture into my lap. "I found it … under my pillow – a picture of my girlfriend Vinny. She didn't know. My girlfriend. I loved her. I wanted to marry her. That's why I hid Vinny's picture under my pillow – to keep her with me always. But now she's gone. Why did she leave me? Have you found her?"

The photo rendered me more speechless than I had ever been in my life. I looked down at the picture in my lap, and the flirting smile of Lynette Clarissa Greene looked up at me with bright mockery.

Chapter 7.

Perhaps my nascent speechlessness was fated to become permanent, for it hit me again the next morning as Nat and I prepared to leave for work in the talking car – with me driving this time.

Clint shuffled out to the car with us. "Ma'am," he said, looking up into the grey-green tops of the live oak trees.

"Yes, Clint?"

"Ma'am," he repeated, shifting his gaze to a blooming yucca plant near the car.

"Yes, Clint," I said again, striving for patience.

"I gotta tell you on account of you trying to help me find Vinny."

I gritted my teeth and said nothing.

"Jared thinks you kidnapped him."

I blinked.

"On account of keeping him away from Zolly. But it won't work, Miz Rice, on account of Jared is Zolly's kid. My girlfriend told me not to tell anyone, and I ain't except now on account of you're smarter than me." He waited expectantly for me to solve his dilemma.

"Does Jared know that Zolly's his dad?" Nat asked.

"Don't rightly know. Vinny never said nothin' about that, but Jared likes Zolly 'cause Zolly's nice to him. He's sad he can't see Zolly no more."

I hadn't known that Jared was particularly sad; despair had most definitely not nipped his appetite. "Why doesn't he live with his dad?"

"Don't know. Vinny didn't say nothin' about that – just that she knew the secret and not to tell anyone, or Zolly would be mad at her on account of money or something."

"Child support," Nat said bitterly.

I looked at him sharply, wondering what hurts he carried from his childhood. I left Clint Flavors to study the sky and ran inside to talk to Jared. "Listen," I told Jared, "you're not a prisoner here. I want you to stay for as long as you need to or want to, but you can come to town with us anytime you want. Do you want to come with us today?"

"Naw. Thanks, but someone should stay here with Clint to keep him from doing himself in. He's real low about his girlfriend. Besides, I found a couple of good cans of paint in the barn. We can get that old shed painted today. But, Miss Mike, could you do me a favor? If you see Zolly, let him know where I am and that I'm okay. I usually work for him several days a week, and if he's heard what happened ... well, just let him know I tried to save her. I did. I really did."

I nodded, hoping my face didn't betray my own doubt. I hurried back out to the car and found Clint scuffing his toes through the leaves next to the car. Nat had already started the engine, so I opened the door on the driver's side and the deep male voice shouted, "A door is ajar."

Nat and I both laughed as Clint jumped. We couldn't help it, for poor, confused Clint was still looking around for the source of the voice as we drove away from him.

"Wonder how long it'll take him to figure it out?" Nat chuckled.

"He still hasn't understood that his Vinny is Lynette Clarissa Greene and not a very nice person."

"You're sore about her and that movie star guy, aren't you?" Nat surmised.

That wasn't true – exactly – but I let him think that.

Amazingly, Marty was waiting for me outside my office, which I had thankfully locked for once. He followed me inside, then took my elbow and spun me around to face him. Rapid knocks from my heart bruised the inside of my chest wall as I imagined his lips claiming mine. Instead, a teasing smile lifted the corners of his cinnamon mustache. "Mike, I owe you an apology."

"Kiss me instead," my hormones suggested, but I was unable to speak.

"It's real good of you to take in that trio of misfits and try to help them. It woulda been better if a man in our church had stepped in and acted, but none of them did –

not even me. So I'm as guilty as they are."

"I forgive you," my hormones screamed.

"Anyway," Marty said, twirling a strand of my hair. "You're the greatest! I had no right to act like I did. I don't even know why I did – jealousy, perhaps."

I nearly fell down.

"So please accept my apology."

Wordlessly, I nodded.

"Seafood buffet today, my treat. We'll talk then." For the briefest moment, he looked into my eyes as if he were tempted to follow the invitation with a kiss. Then, like sugar melting in the rain, the breathless moment slipped away. Marty smiled at me again, then left.

I deflated. I sank down behind my computer, but it was a long time before I could breathe well enough to pull out the keyboard and start typing. I managed by mustering anger against Marty, forcing myself to remember how quickly he'd turned away from our chocolate-flavored friendship to court Lynette. Still, my fingers slowed as I remembered my promise to Jared. Being a Christian, I had never ventured into any of the Three Prongs bars. However, the only place to find Zolly would be at his bar.

Three Prongs was small enough that the entire town was accessible by foot. With my renewed zeal for exercise and reducing my bulk, I headed for Zolly's place on foot. Casting a glance around to make sure no one saw me, I darted through the front door of the Borderbound Watering Hole. The dim interior painted over the panes of my eyes, and I paused until I could see well enough to navigate through a sea of polished wooden tables, sticky with stale beer. Sawdust cushioned my steps. I made it to the long barnwood bar, with silver coins embedded in knotholes, before Zolly noticed me. By this time, my curious eyes had swilled details: the rough cedar bark wall panels, topped with reflective wall paper; neon beer signs swinging over the two pool tables; head mounts of wildlife from whitetail deer to a moose; and one stuffed black bear standing in the corner, holding a beer bottle up to its snarling lips. On the bar, a dead armadillo reclined upside down on his armored back, holding a beer bottle in his paws, forever guzzling the dry contents.

"Cute, huh?" Zolly commented, gesturing to the dead armadillo, though that would not have been my choice of adjectives. "So who are you, darling, and what are you doing here? We're not even officially open now, though this place will always be open to you, doll. But you don't look like the usual early morning barstool decorations." He laughed at his wit.

I countered with a direct attack. "Are you Jared Silver's father?"

He blinked. "What brings you in here asking a question like that? My last name's Gilmore, as I recall."

"Perhaps that's so," I lied evenly, "but I also have proof that you are Jared Silvers' dad. So why has he been staying at the children's home? Why haven't you taken responsibility for your own son?"

His ruddy color deepened on the slack features of his face. His eyes were amber in color, reminding me of Jared's, now that I had seen Jared's eyes and had discovered that they were not blue as I had expected with his fair mop of hair. Zolly's hair showed traces of the amber color it had been before grey had cobbled a web over it. Had it not been almost snarling at me, his face would have been attractive. "You think you know all the answers, don't you, fine lady? What are you doing in here hassling me then? I ought to call the law and have you arrested for criminal trespass. I'm not even open yet."

"I dare you."

"To what?"

"To call the law. I wonder if they know that Jared's your son and that you choose to let someone else support him."

He sputtered, "What do you want from me? I spend time with the boy. I even pay him for working for me."

"Perhaps, but he's in a spot of trouble right now and could use a real parent."

"What makes that your business, lady?"

"Unlike you, I've given him a home – even though he's not my son and not even related to me."

The bar owner's face relaxed. "So that's it," he exclaimed. "Wait here."

Wondering what I was supposed to wait for, I watched Zolly bail out the back door and lumber across the weed-infested space between the bar and the trailer where he reportedly hid Candy from his wife. I wondered if I should run in the opposite direction while I had the chance, for he had seemed rather angry. This was, however, a once-in-a-lifetime chance for me to acquaint myself with a beer joint, and I realized that information might someday filter into a story. The smell of smoke and stale beer combined nause-atingly. I decided I hadn't missed anything important in life by shunning such establishments. Lifeless stares of what had once been proud wild animals fell on me from the trophy mounts on the wall. I shivered. "Listen," I said, hearing Zolly's sound tread approaching, "I only wanted to give you a message from your son. He wants you to know that he tried to save that woman at the children's home."

"Of course he did," Zolly said confidently. "Was there ever any question of that?" He fixed me with a belligerent stare. "Has somebody been saying something bad about my kid?"

"I certainly believe him," I answered quickly, hiding the fact that I was far less than certain. "Apparently, Jared doesn't know you're his dad, but he's very fond of you. He wanted you to know that he's fine and that he'll be back to work for you when everything settles down. Why doesn't Jared know you're his dad?"

"This is no kind of a place to raise a kid, so why should he know? They tried to turn him against me at that fancy home he was in just because I run a bar. If he's in some kind of trouble – which your visit here portends – then I should think the last thing he needs is a father like me dumped on him."

Actually, I agreed with Zolly, yet I said, "Mr. Gilmore, he was at the children's home only because he had – or every-one thought he had – no family. He misses having a father figure in his life. I think he would be glad to know you are his dad, regardless of your occupation. What a lonely feeling to have not even one family member in your life!"

Zolly leaned forward into my face.

Instinctively, I backed away from him.

"But now he has you, fine lady, so he'll be okay, won't he? My parents split when I was a kid, and I grew up without a dad. I made it okay. Jared doesn't need an old man with a reputation like mine. I even have a rap sheet. I had to get my liquor license through my wife. That's why I can't divorce her and marry Candy. And Jared? Well, me and his mother were never even married. She didn't want him to have anything to do with me. She was worried I'd be a bad influence on him. But after she got killed in that car wreck ... well, I felt I needed to make an effort to at least see the kid once in a while and spend some time with him. I figured it wouldn't be going against her wishes as long as he didn't know the truth, right? And be very careful, nosy lady, because Carmen don't know about Jared being my kid neither."

"Or a lot of other things," I almost said. For a moment, I warmed to Zolly and his reasoning, which seemed to be respectful both of his son and of his son's deceased mother. Then common sense stepped back into the chamber of my mind. "It was a convenience in terms of not paying child support, too, I imagine."

Zolly shook his head like a black bear that had been stung on the nose by a bee. "Oh, no, nosy lady! You ain't gonna go around town starting those kind of rumors about me, ruining my business. Here's his support for now! Come back when you or the kid needs something else." He grabbed my hands in his and pushed a roll of money between my clenched fingers. "Now, get outta here! I have work to do around here before I open."

"No! I'm not here for money!" I tried to return the wad of cash.

He grabbed it from me and thrust it rudely into the pocket of my denim skirt.

I gasped in dismay and tried to fish it back out.

Zolly grabbed me by the shoulders somewhat roughly and marched me to the front door.

I tried to plant my feet, but they slipped in the sawdust, unable to find purchase.

"You and me never had this conversation," he said. "Get out before I get tired of you. When I get tired of people, I get cross. If you doubt that, ask my wife." And then, before I could reply or react, Zolly shoved me out into the daylight of Main Street.

I heard the lock on the door click behind me.

When my eyes adjusted to the return of natural light, I spotted Marty across the street. He looked at me, shook his head, and followed a group of coffee drinkers into *The Spanish Tile*. Had I blown our seafood date by getting into ... another pickle? Straightening my shoulders, I found a hole in Main Street traffic and sprinted across the street. It was beyond my ability to control Marty's thinking process or to take responsibility for it. I would be at *The Spanish*

Tile at eleven. What did or did not happen after that would be up to him. With courage and determination wrapped around me like a mantel, I forgot my too-big eyes that had a tendency to assume the appearance of staring until one of the coffee drinkers shouldering his way out of *The Spanish Tile* almost ran into me.

"Sorry, Mike. Hey, you mad about something? What are you looking at? Are they putting up the rodeo banner yet?"

I left the coffee drinker scanning the space above Main Street for the nonexistent banner he expected to see and hurried down to the Sidelines office. Bea and Nat were surprised to see me. I explained my mission to Bea, and she waved a generous hand towards the back of the building, where the archives rested in mostly uninterrupted peace. It took just over an hour to find the information I sought. I was so elated by the success of my research that I sprinted the four blocks back to my office, forgetting that I was forty-something and out of shape. In a few moments, my phone connected with the right party at the other end. By the time I hung up and headed to the courthouse, I knew the truth. But wait ... if I had solved the mystery of Julia's murder, why did I feel dead inside? Why did my mouth feel as if it was lined with dry cardboard?

Sheriff Brent Cruz met me at the door to his office. "You must be psychic, Mike, he said. "I was going to call you at your office. I've sent a deputy out to the Dean ranch to arrest Thor. I thought you would want to know."

I stared at Brent Cruz. "Arrest Thor? Whatever for?"

"Your attempted murder, for one. The red car that sent you into that cliff belongs to him. We got a partial plate number and traced it to the ranch. The Halloween mask and gun were still inside. Pretty careless of him. The gun had been fired several times."

"It wasn't Thor! You've got this all wrong, Brent. I –

"You'll be glad to know we've reopened our investigation into Julia's death. I figure you were getting too close to the truth, and Thor tried to stop you."

"Not Thor. You've got it all wrong!"

"We have a solid case against him, Mike. We have a witness who can place him at the scene of your accident and who saw him holding the gun out the window aimed at your car. That same person witnessed the threats he made against Julia when she told him she was going to divorce him. Thor was having an affair with Candy what's-her-name – the broad who shacks up with Zolly now – and Julia found out. If Julia had gone through with the divorce, Thornton Dean stood to lose half of everything, including his holdings in XYZ Corporation."

"But it wasn't Thor!" I shouted again.

"Mike, I'm sorry you're taking it this way. You and Thor aren't … uh, romantically attached, are you?"

"Certainly not, but I know who killed Julia and why, and I'm telling you you've got it all wrong. See –

"What I see is that you need to stick to writing your books and let my department handle crimes," he said severely. "Now, Mike, you'll have to excuse me. The problem with living in Three Prongs is that it's so small that everyone gets to be friends. I don't understand why Thor has done what he has, and I don't condone it, but he and I have been friends for years. Right now I have to put aside my role as sheriff and be there as a friend when they bring him in for booking." He doffed his hat and brushed past me.

I breathed for one last time, "But it wasn't Thor!" Glancing at my watch, I realized it was time to meet Marty at *The Spanish Tile*, if I hadn't ruined my invitation with my exodus from Zolly's bar. Besides having been a good friend of mine for years, Marty was intelligent and resourceful. I decided I would tell him what I had discovered and ask him for advice. Marty and Brent were close. Marty had helped run his campaign during his first term in office, so I thought perhaps Marty could talk to Brent and convince him of the truth.

"Here she comes," Marty announced to the early lunch crowd, "Miz Mike, the woman of a thousand pickles." With that crooked smile that rocked my heart, Marty seated me in the booth opposite him with a flourish. He plopped his elbows on the table and leaned across the table to look into my face.

I held tightly to the bench to keep from melting and slipping under the table.

"Now, Mike, what jar of pickles were you opening up at Zolly's place?"

Without asking, the waitress arrived with our iced tea and silverware, then expertly dropped a bill for two seafood buffets in the small space of table between Marty and me – again without asking if we were having the buffet.

In a voice that shook slightly, I told Marty, "It's a long story. Why don't we fill our plates first?"

"Excellent thinking, Mike." Marty grasped my hands in his, and we both bowed our heads as he prayed aloud.

Silently, I reminded the Lord about Marty and me being M&Ms and belonging together, just as surely as dark chocolate over milk chocolate.

Then Marty and I joined the line already forming at the buffet table, which was actually a real antique chuckwagon. One side of the wagon housed electrical heating elements to keep the food hot, and the other half was refrigerated for salads and desserts. Three Prongs prided itself on its Western heritage, and much of the credit for keeping the town Western belonged to Marty.

With our plates full of fried shrimp and stuffed crab, Marty and I reclaimed our table.

"Now, Mike," he said after both of us had eaten a few bites, "the story."

Obediently, I started. "Did you know Jared is Zolly's son?"

"Don't tell me you're messing around with that!" Marty's quick anger rendered me speechless. "I knew his mother. She was just getting her life together and trying to make something out of it when she had that accident. She protected Jared from knowing who his dad was because ... well, actually, Zolly was in prison when Jared was born. First Kathy was killed in that car wreck, and now you plan to kill her dream of protecting her son."

"No, Marty. I haven't told Jared. I haven't told anyone except you. I found out by accident. Well, Clint told me because his girlfriend told him, and, Marty ... well, this part is hard to tell you –

"Just so long as you don't betray Kathy, I can take about anything else you have to say. As long as you're willing to think about what's best for Jared, I reckon we're on the same team."

The same team? M&Ms! I knew it all along! The day grew so bright that I would have been walking in a yellow glow in the middle of a thunderstorm. I savored a few more bites of lunch and took a deep breath before telling Marty, "The girlfriend Clint had is Lynette Clarissa Greene. You know her as Clara, and –

"What? What are you talking about, Mike? Are you

plumb crazy?"

"It's true! Clint kept talking about his girlfriend and how she left him. Then he showed me her picture, and it's Lynette … Clara."

Marty reached across the table and placed a wide hand on my forehead. "No fever," he muttered. "Mike, what's gotten into you? I mean, we all like Clint, even though he isn't the brightest bulb in the string, but Clara? A beauty like her – a young girl with talent and intelligence – with Clint?"

"It gave her a place to hide out here where no one knew her."

"Hold it, Mike. A girl like that doesn't need to hide! She could pose for billboards. She could be a pinup girl on a calendar. She could make it on a movie screen. I used to be in Hollywood, remember. I know what it takes, and Clara has it!"

I sighed and shook my head. "She was hiding out while she planned her sister's murder. Marty, she's here under-cover! Julia Dean was her half-sister. She wanted to get in good with Thornton and –

Marty pushed away from the table in anger and slapped his pale Stetson over his thick, wavy hair. "Mike, I don't know what in heaven's name has gotten into you, but when it finds its way out, let me know. Meanwhile, this lunch date is over."

Just like that, he was gone. Just like that, the seafood buffet in front of me turned to brown rocks. Gentleman though he was, Marty's anger had made him forget the bill. I would be paying for two meals that sat uneaten on the table. I decided that perhaps I could use one of the bills in my pocket to pay for lunch, since I had been buying groceries for Jared with no help from Zolly. I pulled the roll of bills out of my pocket and gasped. All of them were hundreds! I had been walking around town with more than a $1,000 nestled in the pocket of my skirt.

Chapter 8.

After I had opened a savings account in Jared's name with most of the money, I stopped at the lumberyard and bought some of the items on Jared's list. Since my borrowed car was smaller than Old Blue, I couldn't get everything on his list. I had to save room for Nat!

Working in my office had never proven more difficult. Clint Flavors was installed at my house for treatment of a broken heart, but with Marty so furious with me, I wondered who could possibly help me mend mine.

Shuffling papers mindlessly around my desk, I uncovered the papers Hyacinth had sent me. She was hosting a meeting for the local Democratic club. Hyacinth actually embraced no political views of her own. She wrapped the confluence of nature so tightly around her thoughts that it shunted the mundane away from her trackless mind. She had adopted the Democratic platform recently because she resented everything the local Republican Party endorsed. Republicans stood against abortion, and Hyacinth was all for it. The libertine cast of her life, including her philosophy of "free love" in spite of all the publicity about sexually transmitted diseases, sent her looking for a platform that condoned her own liberal views. Abortion wasn't the only sticking point: She hated talk about religion and family values and claimed traditional family values limited her self-growth. She thought of babies as tiresome and time-consuming, and she believed it was pedantic to stick with one man for life and not sample the wide selection of men looking for change and adventure. As for religion, Hyacinth hated anything Christian most of all: She didn't want God to exist because she wanted to be Him. She wanted to make her own laws – laws that would benefit her generously and limit everyone else. I thought if nothing else, it might be entertaining to attend the meeting. It would at least take my mind off Marty. Drowned M&Ms ... washing down the sink drain with the dishwater. Shaking my head, I grabbed my purse and a note tablet and headed out to the tirelessly talking car. It was always a bit of a shock to see it sitting outside where Old Blue used to wait so patiently.

The meeting was outside on the banks of the Three Prongs River in the pavilion Hyacinth used for teaching yoga. Neil Peters was there, and the sight of the slumlord who had managed to keep himself just out of reach of prosecution sparked my anger. I thought about slipping away before too many people noticed me, but Hollis Newbark joined Peters. Sunlight glinted distractingly off Newbark's white, caterpillar eyebrows. I edged closer to the men, attempting to hear their lowered voices.

"Thor's in jail," Newbark said in a tone of protest.

"Too bad for him."

"Look, Holl, we need ..."

I never got to hear the rest of the whispered conversation. An arm wrapped around mine imperiously, drawing me aside, and I found myself looking into the laughing face of my one-time dream daughter-in-law, Lynette Clarissa Greene. Knowing as I finally did that she was a cold-blooded murderer who'd helped organize the explosion that killed her own sister, my first impulse was to jerk my arm away and run, but that would only tip her off to the secret knowledge I possessed. I had already lost Prissy and Old Blue, and I decided that perhaps I'd better play along. I attempted a smile.

"You don't look your sunny self today," she said brightly. "I hope it's not over Marty. Everyone in town says you two are stuck on each other. I didn't know that. Marty is attractive and amusing, but actually, Thor and I have become close. Thor has a lot more money and a wonderful ranch."

I had seen evidence of Lynn and Thor's closeness in the lingering kiss they had shared outside Zolly's bar, so I really didn't need her confession.

"So I'm returning Marty." Lynette laughed at her joke.

My face flashed with color at hearing Marty described with the same carelessness as a defective product that could be taken back to a department store for a refund.

Not my Marty! He's worth more and was more desirable than all the chocolate in the world!

"Hmm. You still don't look happy, Miss Rice," Lynette said brightly. "I thought you'd be glad. Anyway, I'm glad you're here today. I'm going to be the speaker. Hyacinth invited Bea and Nat to cover it for the paper, but I guess they both had better things to do."

"The speaker?"

She laughed and leaned in closer to me, her grip tightening on my arm. "Like you, Miss Rice, I have many talents." Then she released my arm and headed up to the makeshift podium at the front.

Amazement left me too weak to leave. I practically fell into one of the folding chairs and grasped the cold metal of the chair in front to reacquaint myself with the space and time around me.

Other people, small group though it was, also settled into the uncomfortable chairs to listen.

Lynette coruscated with beauty. Her graceful movements enchanted the listeners, even if her words were somewhat redundant. She knew how to survey her audience and draw each of them into her theme with intimate glances and smiles. She was good, that cold-blooded murderer, and I didn't notice Hyacinth yawning even once. "We've got to get rid of the sheriff in the next election," she told listeners. "We must select a candidate from our ranks and get an early start pushing for victory. If Brent Cruz isn't removed, tourism will be as dead in this town as The Rafter."

Heads nodded sagely. Those who remembered the burned-out drive-in movie theatre, The Rafter, at the edge of town smiled.

"Deputies stake out the bars," Lynette continued, "waiting for patrons to leave and then arresting them for driving under the influence. You know how tourism has already dropped. The merchants are screaming in pain. They can't even pay their bills."

I tried to remember if I had heard any complaints. Business at *The Spanish Tile* certainly had not suffered; it was nearly impossible to find a table unless one arrived early.

Hollis Newbark surprised me. "You mean you want law enforcement to leave the drunks on the road?" he asked Lynette. "You have no problem sharing the road with someone like Buddy Turner coming at you in another car?"

The image drew a hearty round of laughter from the assembly.

Lynette made a swift recovery. "What I'm endorsing is fairness, Mr. Newbark, not lawlessness. Some patrons are never stopped because deputies recognize their vehicles and let them go, so tourists and minorities and ..."

Lynette's speech droned on for several minutes, but I was impervious to the words. Not only was Brent a friend, but he was a fair and honest man and a fair, honest, professional law enforcement officer. I didn't think the group's mendacious accusations would affect the next election. In fact, looking at the Byzantine members, I doubted they could field a candidate of their own.

It was then, seeking a discrete escape, that I accidentally solved a longstanding mystery. With Lynette's speech at an end, cans of beer were fished out of iced tubs as the club planned strategy for the upcoming election and canvassed their group for a candidate. Slinking away, I managed to reach the borrowed car, then groaned in dismay. Some inconsiderate driver had pulled another vehicle up nearly against the bumper of mine. I could ease forward and back and cut the wheel enough to get out, I thought, but another car – double-parked – blocked me from the side. Well, surely the gathering won't last much longer. Work that my mind was too tormented to complete waited for me back at the office. Hasn't Hyacinth issued me many invitations – all of which I've refused – to tour her art colony? And haven't I been earnestly engaged in my own personally engineered weight loss program? Already my skirt hit my legs further below my knees and fit my waist more loosely, and more walking would equal more weight loss. Cheered by this thought and by the progress I had made, I set off at a brisk pace to explore.

My progress, however, came to a sudden halt in front of a twelve-foot high fence made out of corrugated roofing metal. Why would anyone with Hyacinth's artist bent create such an unsightly fence along the beautiful river bottom? Hearing movement and whines behind the fence, I deduced that it had to be an animal pen. Curiosity and a love for animals drove me into rare action, since I was a person who usually minded her own business. I traversed the metal pen and discovered that if I waded out into the river, I could reach a chain-link fence that would afford a view. Pulling up my skirt, I stepped into the water, shoes and all, and edged around slippery rocks to the fence. What I saw made me gasp in horror. Pit bull dogs lay staked on short chains outside shoddily constructed shelters, circling a dog-fighting arena. Blood-darkened, clawed-up dirt was in the ring and smeared on the metal rails around it. Following the evidence of my nose and a swarm of flies, I scaled the fence – at the cost of torn hose and scratched legs – and found a heap of dead, bloated dog corpses that no one had bothered to bury. A small tractor with a wide blade was parked close to the dead dogs, so surely it would not have taken long to bury the animals decently.

I knew Brent had heard rumors about a dog-fighting arena but had been unable to substantiate it; now I could lead him to the truth. First, however, I had to get out of the fence and back to my car without being seen.

If the dogs had ignored me, if they had kept sleeping, I would have made it, but I was a stranger, and those short-tempered canines had been taught to hate from their puppyhood. A white male with a brown patch over one eye and a torn, bloody face rushed at me. I eased back towards the fence along the river, but the dog continued his powerful lunges. I was almost to the fence when the stake he was chained to jerked out of the rocky ground, releasing the furious animal to make his pursuit. With a savage growl, his paws churning up ground and tossing clods into the air as he ran, the pit bull shredded the distance between us. I threw myself over the fence, but my skirt caught on the twisted wire at the top of the chain links and stopped my descent.

Savage teeth tore into the metal fence. I yelped in fear and jerked my skirt off the fence, tearing it in several places. When the fence released the fabric, it released me. I tumbled backwards into the river. Swift water rushed over my face, holding me down. My back slid on smooth, rounded rocks, and I couldn't regain my footing, even though the water was shallow. Coughing up water and sputtering like a boiling teapot, I finally turned myself over and crawled out of the river. Frenzied barking met my ears, and I hoped the loose dog would not attack the others. My job was to regain my car without being seen and then get to the sheriff's office.

As I had surmised and hoped they would be, most of the crowd was gone. The aggravating yapping car stood alone, unhindered in its ability to travel, but Hyacinth was sharp, and I was sure her ears had probably picked up the racket down by the river. My torn skirt and wet clothes did not escape notice. "Why, Mike! If you wanted to go swimming, you should have asked. I keep extra swimsuits on hand. I think I have some large enough to fit you. Besides, we never swim in the river. I have a heated pool. There're fish and snakes in the river ... and frogs. Ick!"

"I thought you loved nature, Hyacinth."

"I do, but not slimy critters like snakes and frogs." She peered at me suspiciously. "Where were you, Mike?"

"Thanks for the invite to the meeting. It was, uh ... informative. I was really surprised at Lynn ... er, I mean Clara's speech. She's been here such a short time, and –

"Yes! Isn't it serendipity, her showing up in Three Prongs like this just when we needed her to energize us? Where are you going now, Mike? Home to change?"

Grasping that idea with alacrity, I nodded. "Exactly. I think I have enough time to get back and pick up Nat. Bea's been giving him some long hours."

"I must say, Mike, I'm surprised at you. I thought you were too staid and self-righteous to let someone like that druggie into your house. You can't trust him, you know. The moment you do, he'll let you down. It's an old pattern, and it always happens. Not even you can break it."

"You know very little about me, Hyacinth, and you know even less about the Christian way of life. Jesus told His followers to walk in love and to judge the heart, not the exterior. Besides, I'm not in charge of changing Nat's life. No person can do that. I've put Nat into the hands of Jesus in prayer." I pushed past her and eased myself into the car, realizing for the first time that my body was sore and hurting and that my wet body and clothes were not, perhaps, good for the leather seats and carpeted floorboard.

It wasn't that I didn't trust Brent's deputies; it was just that I had been less than fair to Brent and Anna as of late. I hadn't spent enough time with any of my friends. Brent and I had talked about the mystery of the dog-fighting ring that seemed to move about the county. The sheriff's department had obtained search warrants and visited several locations, but they'd never found evidence that indicated that a dogfight might have been held. The land-owners had offered other explanations for anything that seemed suspicious, and no fighting dogs had ever been found. I wanted to tell Brent about my discovery before disclosing it to anyone else, so I settled myself into a chair in his office across from his desk, waiting for him. Then I fell asleep.

When Brent shook me awake, it took me a few moments to recover from my dream of chasing flying M&Ms. I sat bolt upright and spilled out the solution to the mystery so haphazardly that Brent stopped me and made me repeat the story twice.

"Let's get Bea in on this," he suggested, calling one of his deputies. "She can bring a camera and record this for the Sidelines and for us. And since you finally solved this case, I suppose you want to come along."

"Yes. I usually try to mind my own business, but –

Brent roared in laughter. "When have you ever minded your own business, Mike? Life around here would be plumb dull if you did. Never mind ... let's go! I've waited a long time to make this arrest."

Within an hour, our entourage arrived at the art colony: two patrol cars from the sheriff's office, my borrowed car, and Bea's vehicle. Nat rode with Bea.

Surprisingly, Hyacinth greeted us like a gracious hostess, covering up the inevitable yawn with a slender hand dripping with assorted mismatched rings. When Brent informed her of our mission, her pale blue eyes opened in wide, innocent surprise. "Are you sure you found a dog-fighting ring on my property, Mike? You know what a runaway imagination you have, with all those stories you write. Like Marty says, you get yourself into some real pickles. By all means, Sheriff Cruz, have a look around. If someone is using poor, helpless animals to fight, I want them caught. I have nothing to hide." Smiling, she trundled her noxious self back into her art studio, giving all of us the freedom to roam around the grounds.

I led the party down to the river to the dog-fighting compound, but when we got there – where I knew it was – it was gone! Sheet metal was stacked up against a shed I had not noticed earlier, and rolls of chain-link fence were inside. The ground was scraped and disturbed, but the dogs were gone, the chains were gone, and even the shelters were gone.

"Mike …?"

"It was here!" I told Brent desperately. "You have to believe me!"

"That's a little hard without proof," he said dryly. "You even told me I should have arrested that pretty new blonde in town for Julia's murder and not Thornton."

Nat looked disgusted. "I knew you had it in for her, Mike, but really! Once you slay a person's reputation, it can be permanent. That's a lesson I learned years ago. I don't think that used-up cowboy is worth that cost – ruining a person's reputation."

"Who?" Bea interjected. "Marty? How did he get into this conversation?" She laughed. "Actually, Mike and I think alike where Marty is concerned. He's worth just about any price."

"What about the dog ring?" Brent asked in exasperation. "I thought we were here about fighting dogs, not romance gone sour."

Stubbornly, I led the way around the area, pointing out patches of what looked like blood-darkened soil.

"We have to have proof, Mike," Brent said each time I pointed out more possible evidence. "We don't even have so much as a broken dog's tooth!"

Remembering the corpses, I rushed over to the spot and pointed. "Look! They must be buried here. The tractor was sitting here, and so were four dead dogs." I shuddered, remembering the mangled, blood-frothed bodies. "The dogs had been killed in a fight, torn to pieces. It was horrendous!"

Brent shook his head. "It doesn't look like the ground has been disturbed enough to have buried four big dogs, but we'll give it a look, just in case." He motioned to the deputy. "John, I saw a shovel over by that shed. Bring it here."

It took very few moments of digging to prove the validity of Brent's surmise. The dogs – even the dead ones – were gone.

I knew that in a minute, everyone would likely be distrusting my sanity. They might conclude that I had imagined the whole incident.

"Maybe they pushed the dead dogs into the river," John

suggested. "The water's running pretty swift right now."

"Yes!" I responded eagerly, remembering how the water had held me down in an attempt to drown me.

Our party scanned the shallow river along the property edges but found nothing.

By the time we all left in our respective vehicles, I was feeling about as welcome as a cold grilled cheese sandwich on a picnic.

Bea, having been a friend and former employee, seemed to understand my desolation. "I'll bring Nat home tonight if you need to leave now."

Wordlessly, I nodded to her, but once we were in our vehicles heading back to town, I let the others get in front of me. Then I turned down the road leading to the bridge to nowhere. Even though I usually minded my own business, it was a time for action. There was a mystery to solve, and I wasn't sure of my future status in Three Prongs if I didn't attempt to solve it. Neither Samala nor Durant was at home since they both worked. Hoping their hospitality could be trusted, I parked in the shady yard and walked down to the river. Then I began a painstaking search of the riverbanks on both sides, working my way back towards Three Prongs.

It took two hours, but I found what I was looking for. Now the problem was to mark the spot so I could find it again. Being made a fool of twice in one day was too much even for me. Someday, I told myself, I will remember to carry a cell phone with me everywhere like other people do. I always forgot mine, leaving it safely resting in strange places that mandated a search anytime I needed to use it. Erecting a rock pillar presented itself as the best idea. I hauled smooth river rocks out of the rushing water, placing the biggest ones on the bottom and making it too tall and broad to be easily missed when I brought the sheriff. Long before achieving that goal, I was seeped in sweat and puffing like a woman in the throes of natural childbirth.

"Mike!" Brent exclaimed when I drew up in front of his house. "You're in a worse mess than you were last time I saw you. Whose trouble have you been mixing yourself up in this time? Anna and I are about to eat. Won't you join us?"

"You've got to come! I can prove it!"

"Prove what? Now what mystery are you poking your

nose into?"

"Brent, please. I found those dead dogs I was telling you about – all four of them. They were dumped in the river, just like your deputy said."

Brent groaned.

Anna joined him at the door, and I quickly explained the situation to her. "If what Mike says is right, you should go, honey. We should both go. The food will keep. I'll grab our digital camera to take pictures. I hate animal abuse! Any abuse! If you get proof ... well, we've heard these rumors for a long time. This might be the chance you've been waiting for!"

Sadly, Brent shook his head. "We'll go, but Anna, darling – and Mike – don't get your hopes up. Dead dogs in the river miles from where the incident reportedly happened won't be enough proof to make a court case. We won't be able to prove where or how the dogs were killed ... or who was responsible."

Deflated, I realized he was right. Still, he and Anna came with me. Both Durant and Samala Edmonds were at home. They not only agreed to let us park in their yard, but they also accompanied us on the long trek down the river to the rock column I had erected. The sad sight brought tears to Samala and Anna.

Brent kicked loose dirt along the bank angrily. "Some people aren't fit to live," he muttered darkly. "Using poor, dumb animals like this ... for entertainment? Put the cowards in the ring and turn the dogs loose on them! Now that'd be worth watching." He looked at us, his rapt, appreciative audience. "Sorry. I didn't mean to spill out like that. Durant, do you have some rope and a shovel? We should pull these animals out of here and bury them, both for decency's sake and to protect the water quality."

We all helped with the project. Digging in the rocky Texas Hill Country with a shovel is never easy, but digging a large enough grave far enough from the river to bury the bloated corpses was especially difficult.

It was after dark when I got back home to the ranch, and I knew intuitively that something was wrong. So much for attempting to save others from their self-destructive lifestyles. So much for starting to trust Nat and letting down my guard. So much for proving the noxious Hyacinth Walker wrong. She was right all along. Nat had apparently used his paycheck to purchase marijuana and booze. My nose tingled from the thick, noxious smoke even before I opened the front door. Loud music poured out around me, shoving me back.

Nat, laughingly, was urging Jared and Clint to join him. He banged energetically on the bottom of one of my large pans, using it as a drum.

Jared, much to my surprise, strummed soundly on an electric guitar hooked up to an amplifier. I didn't even realize he had such musical equipment or that he had brought it with him.

Clint Flavors had earned a reputation as a sober, dependable man who never drank alcohol. This time, however, he must have joined in sampling the spirits offered at the impromptu party, because he was reeling around the living room in a crazy, loose-limbed dance, rocking his head and shoulders as the music rocked the airspace.

Wordlessly, I walked into the room. I unplugged Jared's guitar and the DVD player that only a moment before had been ranting and spewing filthy rap lyrics out into the air. Sudden silence assaulted my eardrums. I grabbed the pan from Nat and threw it across the room. It hit the wall and bounced back into the middle of the room, hitting Clint. Clint, shoulders slumped and arms askew, gaped at me as if I were an alien life form; to the drunken trio, I probably was. I stomped viciously on empty beer cans and kicked them around the room. They pinged off the legs of furniture, and occasionally a sailing beer can hit a human. Then I swept up the remaining full cans of beer and the joints of marijuana and carried them out to the car. Leaving the suddenly sobered trio staring after me, I drove off into the night, more hurt and angry than I had ever been in my life.

Chapter 9.

I spent the night in my office after I disposed of the grass and beer. I left the joints with a mystified dispatcher at the sheriff's department, explaining that I had found them; after all, it was true. I gave him my name, address, and phone number. "Ask Brent about me in the morning or call him at home," I said. No one stopped me, so I left the sheriff's department and entombed myself in my office.

Once settled in my Main Street digs, I opened the cold beer and poured the contents down the bathroom sink, flushing the sink with water. Then I bundled up the empty cans and carried them outside to the rollaway trash container. It took a long time to clear the office of the stench. The office was equipped for work, not sleep. I wrapped one of Faith's bright quilts around me, more thankful for my talented daughter-in-law than I had ever been before, and bedded down on the hard wooden floor planks. My resulting lack of sleep met my expectations. By the time the office lit up with natural light, I was still undecided about how to handle the situation at what had once been my home. My disheveled state negated going anywhere in town where I would be seen.

I was still pondering the situation when the pounding began on the office door, which I had actually remembered to lock. When I opened the door, three abashed men practically fell inside. Once facing me, none of them seemed up to the task of speaking. "How did you get here?" I asked in surprise, countering their silence.

"We used Clint's bicycle," Jared said. "We took turns riding and walking and running and pushing."

"It's nearly twenty miles from the ranch!"

"Yeah, we traveled all night. We finally got a lift after daybreak."

"We know we blew it," Nat added, "but we had to come and find you and tell you we're sorry, even though it won't do any good."

"Bad," Clint Flavors said, nodding at the computer. "It tasted bad, and I feel bad, and it was bad what we done." He looked at the other two men suddenly. "How come we done it?" They had no answer for Clint, so he repeated the question to the computer and waited for illumination.

I looked at the humbled trio. "I don't even know what to do or say," I told them severely.

"Neither do we," Jared said with asperity.

"It was my fault," Nat admitted. "I bought the stuff and made them try it with me. You shouldn't be surprised, nice crazy lady. You know I'm a miscreant."

Someone had been teaching Jared at the children's home before he had been ousted. "What you did was your fault," he told Nat, "but you didn't make us try anything. That was our decision, our fault. We're guilty too. You're not big enough to carry your guilt and ours. Only Jesus can carry someone else's guilt, and then it has a purpose – so that person can be forgiven and go to Heaven … like my mom."

Tears condensed in Nat's eyes at the conclusion of Jared's speech.

"We gotta leave Miz Rice's house," Clint announced, nodding at the desk lamp. "I'll go back home and do myself in."

"I'll ask Zolly if I can stay in that trailer in back of the bar – the one musicians use for practice. That way I can work when he needs me."

"I've already lost my pad in San Antonio," Nat said. "I was overdue on the rent anyway. I want to keep my job here, but I haven't seen any street people around to hang with. I know! Bea said that ditzy yoga woman has some kind of place where she lets people hang – artists mostly."

"Yep. I'll do myself in," Clint repeated with satisfaction, looking at the computer again.

"What we are going to do," I said severely, "is attempt to put Clint's bike into the trunk of the car. Then we're all going home. As I recall, I've been feeding you boys for quite a few days. You promised to do some work around the place, and I'm going to hold you to that promise."

"You want us back?" Jared asked in amazement.

"Either that, or I'm stuck with you for now," I said coldly. "I don't want you hanging out behind a bar. You should be back at school."

"School? I quit. I'm old enough to quit."

"No one is old enough to quit learning unless they're dead. You can at least take GED classes at the library and get your diploma. I've got a savings account set up in your name at the bank. There's not enough in it yet for college, but it's a start." I turned to Nat. "As for you, I will not have you mixed up with Hyacinth Walker. There's reason to believe she's connected to illegal dog-fighting, something you know, Nat. I should think you've had enough brushes with the law already."

"I wouldn't have anything to do with making dogs fight," Nat said hotly. "I don't like dogs, but I don't want to see them hurt. Hurting is not fun." His words silenced the group as each was reminded of private hurts.

Clint recovered first. "Yup. It hurts. It all hurts. I'm gonna go home and do myself in. Her picture! I forgot her picture."

"Fine, Clint. You come home with me. You can't go back to your cabin and do yourself in without her picture to remind you of why you are doing such a foolish thing, so you might as well come back to the ranch with the rest of us."

Before we could leave, the patch of morning sunlight bouncing across the floorboards darkened as Sheriff Brent Cruz, in uniform, crowded the doorway. He doffed his hat to us collectively.

Three guilty men instinctively drew closer together, offering each other the buffer of their presence.

Brent addressed Jared. "I've been looking for you, young man."

"It wasn't his fault, Sheriff, sir," Nat said quickly, stepping forward.

"I know. That's what I've come to tell him."

Nat, looking confused, stepped back.

"Jared, the entire community – save Miz Mike here – owes you an apology, young man. We just got the autopsy back on Renee Davis." He looked around at all of us. "That's the name of the house parent who drowned. Seems she had a heart attack. Jared couldn't have saved her even if he'd been an Olympic swimmer, and he certainly didn't cause her death."

"But she was too young to have a heart attack," Jared protested.

"She had a heart attack because she'd taken drugs the night before at a party - Cocaine. Quite a bit of it apparently."

We all gasped in unison.

"Needless to say, she would have been fired if they had known about it at the children's home, but each house parent gets one weekend a month off from duties. She left saying she was going to visit her parents and went to a weekend party in San Antonio instead. There was a lot of drinking and drugs involved –

"Bad," Clint interjected. "Bad stuff. I feel bad."

The two young men threw a glance of fear at the older man, who was rocking aimlessly back and forth on the heels of his shoes.

"Yes," Brent said, "very bad and very illegal, and it killed a young woman named Renee Davis. She had her whole life ahead of her. She had won a music scholarship and was planning on attending college in the fall. One of the songs she wrote had been released on a CD, and she had just received her first royalty check. She and her boyfriend were planning to announce their engagement. They were going to get married the day after he graduated next year, but instead, he had to help carry her coffin to the gravesite. It's all because of drugs and alcohol. Although most people don't realize it, alcohol's also a drug."

Casting surreptitious glances at each other, three men found sudden fascination in the planked floor.

Brent cleared his throat. "Now, I'm gonna mosey on out of here and let you folks do whatever you planned with the weekend. I've got a new case to look into. Someone walked into the sheriff's department last night and left off a bag of marijuana joints and then claimed to be Miz Mike here to get her into a major pickle. Can you imagine? That person isn't in trouble for finding the drugs and turning them in – although she might be in trouble for falsely identifying herself to a law enforcement officer – but my job is to find out where they came from. The user – or users – they are the ones in trouble." He doffed his hat again and left.

I hid my smile. The three men were huddled together in abject misery and fear. I let the suffering continue for a moment, then picked up my purse and headed to the door. "Let's go. We have a lot of work and a short weekend."

They followed me out.

Clint put the bike in the car trunk, and Jared scouted around a few Main Street buildings until he found a piece of wire that had probably bounced out of a pickup truck. He ran back with the wire and fastened the trunk lid down across the bike since it wouldn't close with the bike sticking up.

"Mike," Nat said shyly, scuffing the toe of his shoe across pavement, "I never got to take you out to lunch and ... well, like you said, we've got a lot of work to do when we get back. I didn't blow my whole check. What I mean is ... well, I want to take everyone out to breakfast."

"Breakfast? Look at me! I'm a mess. I didn't get to take a shower or change clothes. I'm still wearing the torn skirt that got caught on the dog-fighting fence, and you want us to go out in public?"

"Bad," Clint added. "All of us look bad and feel bad. We were bad."

With Clint's words, we all looked at each other. No one had showered or changed clothes, and the men had run and ridden Clint's bicycle for most of the night. Clint's red striped shirt was pulled out of his belt on one side, hanging loose. It was buttoned wrong, and two of the top buttons were missing, exposing a torn undershirt. Clint's dark hair, with its grey weaving, sat as haphazardly on his head as his shirt sat on his chest.

Jared had spilled something on his blue shirt, and it clung stiffly to him in places, relaxing into crooked folds in other places. His wind-rumpled white-blond hair spiked up from waves around his head, and his face was dirty.

Neatness had never been compliant for Nat. His thin body, still swallowed up in Alfred's clothes, wore anemic brown eyes beneath an untidy mop of reddish-brown hair. Nat was a walking synonym for dystopia.

Suddenly, after studying each other, we collapsed into helpless laughter. Jared and Nat fell to the pavement, and I reeled backwards into the driver's seat of the car.

"The trunk is open," the vehicle announced.

Clint jumped and looked around for the source of the

voice, and that made everyone laugh even more. Clint rocked unstably on his heels, his laughter bringing a rare hint of clarity to his face as if he might have suddenly solved the mystery of the speaking voice shouting from the car.

"You win," I told Nat. "We'll go to breakfast and let people stare at us and wonder what sort of huggermugger they've missed. What's important in this life isn't what other people think of us. It's what God thinks, and He looks beneath the surface, down into the heart."

"Bad," Clint said, making a wrong word association from the word 'heart' that I had so carelessly tossed into the room. "I miss her bad."

With more compassion than I would have expected, Nat took Clint's arm and handed him into the backseat of the car.

Before Nat and Jared could get in, Brent reappeared, causing Nat and Jared to visibly stiffen. "Glad I caught you, Mike," Brent said. "Forgot to tell you, but since you were right about that dog-fighting ring – oh, I know, we didn't get enough proof to make an arrest, but it seems pretty clear to me – I decided to do some more checking into that Thornton Dean incident in case you were right about that too."

"Dad would never have killed Julia," Nat said, fishing up enough courage to face the sheriff, in spite of his long distrust for law enforcement officers. "She meant too much to him – way more than I ever did." The bitterness in Nat's voice tumbled out into the still morning air.

Brent clasped a hand on Nat's shoulder, and the young man drew back slightly in fear. Brent let his hand rest lightly on the narrow shoulder blade. "If you and your dad had a good talk, son, I'm sure you would find out how wrong you are about that. Your dad talks about you to the jailer, the other inmates, and anyone who will listen. His biggest regret seems to be not having spent more time with you while he could."

"Yeah, whatever. He planned to change his will and leave everything to Julia, to cut me out completely. He said it was tough love."

"And you don't see the love in that?" Brent asked gently.

Nat could not look into the sheriff's face.

Brent removed his hand from Nat's shoulder and, hands

on hips, looked at me. "I found out that the key witness against Thor is now out at the ranch, acting as manager in his absence and going through a lot of money. Seems she and Thor were secretly engaged before this happened, and he gave her legal status to sign checks and make decisions. After I found out about that, we rechecked the Halloween mask and gun. See, it bothered me all along that neither of them had any fingerprints on them. They had both been wiped clean. Now, why would someone take the trouble to wipe fingerprints off but leave the mask and gun in the car to be found? It didn't make sense. When we rechecked the mask with that in mind, we found blonde hair –

"Lynette Clarissa Greene," I breathed.

"Clara? Are you talking about Clara Greene? You're down on her because of that Marty guy," Nat objected. "I know Dad didn't kill Julia, but I can't believe that pretty blonde girl did it. Why would she? She even came to church that time."

"So did you," I countered sternly.

Nat fell silent.

"She did it because she wanted Thor's money and the ranch – maybe even Thor himself."

"That old guy?" Nat questioned in disbelief.

I bristled. "He's not old, not even fifty yet. He's only a little older than I am."

"Let's get this straight," Brent said to me, drumming his fingers on his chin. "You know this Clara person, and you believe she's guilty?"

"I tried to tell you when you said you were going to arrest Thor, but you wouldn't listen."

"I'm listening now."

"She's been here for months longer than anyone knew. She was hiding out with Clint in his cabin."

"Clint!" Brent's dark eyebrows threatened to fly off his forehead. "This Clint? Clint Flavors?"

"Vinny?" Clint's voice questioned from the car. "My girl-friend Vinny was. She left me. I guess I'll go do myself in," he muttered, but no one was paying much attention to Clint.

"I called back to Alabama and talked to her parents," I told Brent. "Julia had a different last name before she married Thor because she was the child of a previous marriage. Lynette was always jealous of her sister, even though she belonged to both parents and they say they gave her plenty of attention and love and just about anything she wanted. She was a tomboy growing up –

"That girl was a tomboy?" Nat asked in disbelief.

"She helped her dad in his business and even drove the trucks. Brent, it was a propane business! She used to fix heaters and gas stoves and even fill propane tanks."

Brent whistled. "That's a pretty good case. If only we had evidence."

"Her parents are sending me a picture of her in her business uniform with the propane company logo."

"That won't wash, Mike. We have to place her at the scene of the crime, or Julia's death will remain just what it was ruled – an accident. And perhaps it was just an accident. Sibling rivalry is rarely, I think, a motive for murder."

"But how about Thor's money? And the ranch? From what you've told me, Thor's come to trust Lynette completely. With Julia gone, they can marry ... and even if they don't, she has pretty much what she wants right now."

"That's true, but I just don't see how we can prove any of this. All we have is a long blonde hair caught in the mask, and even if we were to match it with hers, it wouldn't prove she drove the car and shot at you – much less that she blew up her own sister."

"We have to prove it, Brent! We can't let her get away with murder ... and attempted murder." My voice dropped. "And Prissy's murder."

"Prissy? Who's Prissy, and why don't I know anything about another murder?"

"She couldn't have shot your dog," Nat broke in. "I couldn't shoot a dog, and I don't even like them."

"Mike, explain." After I told him about Prissy's death, Brent groaned. "So now the evidence is buried. We might still be able to find the bullet. If we could match it –

"Wait ... you wanna dig up a dead dog?" Nat was horrified. "She's at peace. She shouldn't be disturbed."

"Well, son, I suppose it's true that she's not going anyplace. We'll leave her for now and concentrate on getting your dad out of jail. Meanwhile, I would recommend that all of you stay clear of this Lynette/Clara person. If Mike is right, she's dangerous. If any of you come up with an idea of how to prove this, uh ... improbable story, please come see me."

Nat, Jared, and I talked quietly among ourselves at breakfast, attempting to formulate a plan. Clint, his flat brown eyes focused on an invisible distance, stuffed food in his mouth at an amazing pace and seemed barely cognizant of his surroundings.

We were nearly through eating when Marty entered *The Spanish Tile* and sauntered over to our table. He surveyed us in frank amazement. "I see Miz Mike's been involving everyone in some new pickle," he said. He eschewed our table, possibly because we looked so disreputable.

Fortunately, Alfred had built our home with two bathrooms, complete with showers. The men showered in one bathroom, I showered in the other, and we met again outside to begin working in less than an hour. None of us noticed that Clint had disappeared on his bike. We were all stationed at our work duties. I was even more distracted when a truck drove up in the drive and Ron and Faith spilled out with the children.

"I see you have company for lunch," Ron said, engulfing me in a hug. "That's fine, because Faith and I planned to barbecue for you today. She even made that potato salad with mustard and brown sugar dressing that you love, Mom."

When I hugged Faith, I wanted only her for a daughter-in-law. All thoughts of Lynette Clarissa Greene's outward beauty had been banished, swept away by the realization that under her good looks, Lynette was heartless and unbelievably evil. Amazingly, even my grudge against Faith for having replaced Irene Johnson in my son's life seemed to be gone. I was thrilled to claim Faith as a family member. Why, what if Ron and Irene had married and then Donna had taken them to Georgia with her? Distance would have swallowed up all my family members and separated me from my grandsons. Perhaps God knew what He was doing after all, working away with that master plan of His. Perhaps when God sets the lasso and pens up moments of time, our job is to trust whatever winds up in the corral with us.

To their credit, Nat and Jared continued working until the barbecued brisket and chicken were ready and the outside picnic table was decked with gold-colored potato salad, sliced onions and pickles, and Ron's secret recipe beans. We clasped hands as Ron's deep voice led us in prayer.

As we began filling our plates, I realized that Clint was missing.

Jared ran to look for him. With worried face, he returned and explained, "He's gone, and so is his bike. Do you think he went off to kill himself, Miss Rice?"

"What!?" Ron and Faith exclaimed.

"He's morose about losing his girlfriend, but I imagine he's just gone after some more of his things."

"Wait ... he's staying here?" Ron asked.

"We all are," Jared replied cheerfully. "Nat lost his pad in San Antonio, and I got kicked out of the children's home for killing someone I didn't kill, and Clint was going to do himself in over his girlfriend, who Mike thinks is a murderer."

Faith gasped, and I noticed for the first time that she lacked her usual hearty appetite. Uneaten food lined her plate, and she had pushed the plate away after feeding some of her leftovers to Alex and Ryan.

"Mom, explain," Ron ordered. "Now whose business are you mixed up in?" He looked at Nat suspiciously, and revelation washed across his face. "Hey! I saw you, running down the street with a bunch of thugs chasing you. Someone better explain."

"Your mother saved my life, and then she got me a job at the newspaper in town. I – we – all of us let her down last night. We had a party while she was gone, but it was my fault. And today we've been working around here like we promised at the start."

"Party? What kind of party? What's been going on around here?"

"Ron, don't worry. Everything is fine here."

"Fine? You, a widow, living alone out here in the middle of nowhere with three men and having some kind of party that no one wants to explain? You call that fine?"

"She wasn't at the party," Jared interjected helpfully.

"You sound like Marty!" I told my son.

"Who is Marty? You have someone else here?"

"Marty is the guy Mike's stuck on," Nat explained. "That's why she was so angry about Clara taking him away. Only now it seems Clara has dropped Marty for my dad, and my dad's getting out of jail because it might have been her – not him – who killed his wife Julia. Meanwhile, poor Clint doesn't even know who Vinny is and what terrible things she's done. Anyway, her real name isn't Vinny or Clara. It's Lynette."

"Say what?"

"Yeah," Jared assured Ron. "Nat's telling the truth, and she might have even killed Prissy."

"Prissy!" Faith exclaimed. "Oh, Mom, I'm so sorry you lost Prissy. I know she was old, but she was special. Even at her age, she was so gentle with the boys. I wondered why she wasn't out here visiting with us like Abigail and Abner."

"Forget the dogs!" Ron thundered. "I want to know what's going on around here!"

"He told you, sir," Jared said, "and even though his dad is getting out of jail, we can't get her arrested without proof."

"Mom?" Ron asked in a shocked voice.

"No, Clara, but Mike says her real name is Lynette Clarissa Greene. She knows because she solved the whole mystery herself, even better than the sheriff. She just kept on prying into things until she found the box that contained the truth, and then she dumped it out."

Ron groaned and plopped his head down on the table.

While Jared and Nat refilled their plates, I tried to explain everything to Ron and Faith while still swinging Alex and Ryan between my legs, a game they loved.

Amazingly, Faith wiped tears from her eyes when I finished the story.

I turned a puzzled look in her direction.

"Sorry, Mom. It's just that Ron and I had this idea, and now I see it won't work. What I mean is … well, you've done a wonderful thing opening up your home like this, and –"

"Mom," Ron said, "we're going to have another baby."

"Oh!" Overjoyed, I swept Ryan and Alex aside and hugged Ron and Faith. "That's wonderful! Praise the Lord!"

"Well, we agree that it's wonderful, but Faith has really bad morning sickness this time, and –"

"Faith, honey, I'm so sorry. Is there something I can do? Do you need me to keep the boys?"

Ron laughed. "Mom, I should say you've outdone yourself in the keeping department already. Actually, what we needed was for you to keep us here ... all of us."

I gasped. "You would stay here with me? Our whole family would be together?"

"You know how I've been thinking of starting my own sign business and getting the boys out into the country, where they have room to run and play without being in danger or aggravating the neighbors. We thought that if we could stay here, you could help Faith with the boys, and I would have extra cash – from not paying that high rent – to start my business."

"Of course! That's a marvelous idea!"

"Mom, where would we stay? I should say you've about filled the house up by now with your collection of, uh ... challenged individuals."

"Oh! Well, Ron, God always supplies when there's a need. Give me a chance to pray about this. Meantime, how soon can you get here? We have plenty of storage space in the shed and the barn for items that won't fit in the house. That's what Jared and Clint and Nat have been doing today, making repairs and painting." I suddenly remembered that Clint was missing.

"Maybe we could bring in a mobile home," Faith suggested.

"That would cost more money than paying next month's rent," Ron pointed out.

Before we could discuss the situation further, we were interrupted. The tall, solid figure of Thornton Dean joined us.

"Dad!" Nat exclaimed. "What are you doing here? I mean, hello. I'm glad you got out of jail. I tried to tell them you didn't do it. Honest, I did."

Without replying, Thor swept Nat into his arms and hugged him so tightly that Nat winced. "Son, can you ever forgive me?"

"It would help if you'd quit choking me."

We all laughed.

Thor released Nat and looked at me. "I've heard Mike preach that the Bible says to give thanks in everything and that everything works out for good to those who love the Lord. Well, I believe it now. They carted me off to jail, shouting and protesting that I was innocent, but when I got there and had time to think, I realized I've been guilty of many things – most damning of all, not being a good father to Nat here. Now, I'm hoping to change." He turned his attention back to Nat. "Son, if you will let me, I want to practice being a father. It's not too late, you know. I expect I have a few years left. And, I'm sure proud of how well you're doing at your job. Bea's been bragging about you all over town. Anyway, I want you to come home to the ranch with me. I have a spare car you can drive, and –

"Dad, I don't even have a driver's license."

"We can fix that, and I can drive you back and forth until we do. You didn't lose it through drunk driving or anything, did you?"

Nat shook his head. "I just didn't bother renewing it on my last birthday. The car had been repossessed, and I didn't have a job, so I figured, what the hey?"

Jared addressed Nat. "I'll miss you, man, but if you move out, Mike will have room for her real family ... and she's done a lot for all of us."

I knew one reclaimed room would not be enough for Ron, Faith, and two active boys, but Jared was right. It was at least a start.

Thor looked at Ron and Faith in horror. "You mean my son has pushed you out of your own home by staying here?"

"No, sir," Ron said quickly. "We have an apartment in San Antonio. We were just thinking of moving in here to keep track of Mom. She has a tendency to, uh ... well, to get mixed up in other people's business."

"Ron! What a thing to say about your own mother," I protested hotly. "I never do that! Writing and running this ranch keeps me too busy to get involved in other people's problems."

Everyone looked at me, but no one said a word.

"Anyway," Thor finally added, looking at his son, "you have to come with me now to protect me. I left that ... " He noticed Ryan's and Alex's rapt attention focused on him and reconsidered his words. "I left that golden-tongued serpent, Lynette – I thought her name was Clara – in charge of the ranch. If I'm left alone with her, I will be guilty of murder, and I'll wind back up in jail. I need you there to run interference for me, Nat, and to help me get rid of her ... legally."

"And I can keep my job at the paper?"

"Wouldn't have it any other way, son. If I remember

correctly, you've always wanted to write. You've always demonstrated a flair for it, ever since you were just a little older than that one." He pointed to Alex.

Nat smiled at his father. "Well, can you come back for me, Dad? I was helping Jared."

"You go now," Ron said decisively. "I'll help this young man and the other if he ever shows back up here. I don't know you at all, and I've only seen your dad a few times, but from watching you and your dad together, I'd say you two have some big-time fence-mending to do. And, like your dad says, he needs you to help him get rid of that girl – although I admit I still don't quite grasp the whole story. It sounds like it should be a plot in one of Mom's books, not something all of you are actually involved in somehow."

Since he was dressed in Alfred's clothes, Nat had very little in the way of possessions to collect. He and Jared embraced as they parted.

"We'll get you some clothes that fit you better, son," Thor said, seeming to notice his son's attire for the first time.

"Yeah. And not more dead guy's clothes," Nat said without explaining further. "And, you know, Dad, Bea's gonna let me cover county and city stories now that I've kind of proven myself. I'm thinking I should get a haircut so I look good for the paper. Of course, I've learned a lot from Mike. One thing is not to trust the way people look on the outside – like that girl with the pretty face being so evil. Mike says God looks at people's hearts, not their outside appearances. I'm glad, 'cause I don't think I'll ever look real good on the outside, even with new clothes and a haircut. Also, Clint's a pretty good guy, but folks make fun of him and say he's not the brightest crayon in the box. He sure works hard ... and he knows when something's bad." Nat turned his attention to me. "Thanks, Miss Rice. You've saved me in more ways than you'll ever know."

"Jesus has saved you, Nat. I was just the human instrument."

"Whatever. Thanks ... and I'm really sorry." Without explaining that comment further, he engulfed me in a wiry hug, then followed his dad around the house to Thor's truck.

"We better pray," Ron announced. "I don't pretend to

begin to understand everything that's happened here, but I gather Thor could explode and get himself in trouble." Ron had always displayed natural leadership abilities.

We all gathered around him, holding hands. Even Ryan and Alex joined the circle, although I knew they didn't understand what we were doing. Ron prayed with quiet assurance and conviction. Faith prayed after Ron, and my heart embraced her more than ever because she included dimensions in her prayer that Ron had overlooked in his. They were a good team, my son and his wife. I was blessed.

After the prayer break, we started back to work.

Clint's bicycle creaked to a stop outside the shed as we were working on condensing the contents to make room for Ron and Faith's furniture.

"Clint!" Jared and I exclaimed in relief.

"You didn't do yourself in," Jared added. "We're so glad. Nat left with his dad, so we can really use some more help … and you're strong."

Clint nodded in satisfaction.

Ron looked at the empty face with an expression of mild exasperation.

Faith drew Clint into her words with a friendly smile. "Mom and I were just clearing off the table from lunch. We left plenty of food for you. Come grab a plate."

"That's food?" Clint swept a glance over the table.

Alex and Ryan were considering him with bright blue stares.

"Them's your kids?"

"Yes," Faith answered simply. She took his arm and smiled at him. "You can help after you eat. There's a lot to do, and it's still early in the day." She was a treasure, the daughter-in-law God had blessed me with.

Clint propped his bicycle up on its bent kickstand and followed Faith to the table. He had been to his cabin: A bungee cord strapped a broken plastic milk crate crookedly to the handlebars. Well-worn clothes spilled out from under a box of papers. The weight overbalanced the bike, and it clattered to the ground. Papers flew up into the air.

Ryan and Alex danced in excitement at the unexpected circus. I gathered the papers up without looking at them and pressed them back into the box. Then I collected Clint's clothes and let Ryan and Alex help me carry them into the house.

Clint was still sitting at the table eating with relish. He nodded and smiled. "It's good," he said. "This is good, not bad. We were bad, but this is good."

I smiled at him, knowing we shared a secret.

For a moment, his eyes focused on me, and when he smiled, he was really smiling at me as a friend. Then his eyes wandered to the treetops, and he rocked back and forth on the bench. "I got it!" he told the trees. "I got it. I ain't got her. I ain't done myself in, but I got it now for the sheriff."

I should have questioned Clint then, but Ron was calling me, so I darted to the shed, leaving Clint to rock back and forth on the bench and talk to the trees between bites of food. How could my son possibly think I stuck my nose in other people's business? If I had been nosy then, I could have solved a mystery and prevented another crime – a horrendous and terrifying crime.

Chapter 10.

The ranch house took a crowd well, I decided. Having Ron and Faith and the boys stay for the weekend had been exhilarating – if not a bit tiring – for me. Forgotten was the new Garth Seymour mystery that my agent had been clamoring for me to finish. With two young boys rollicking about, the house took on its own clamor and wore it well. Jared was young enough to frolic with Ryan and Alex. Having spent years in the children's home, he'd been introduced to children of all ages. Clint was more reserved, but if the children became too rambunctious for him, he possessed the gift of removing himself to some distant place where none of us could follow.

Before Ron and Faith left on Sunday, we had agreed on a plan. They would move to the ranch within two weeks. First, they would bring everything they didn't need to unpack immediately and store it so that the final moving day would be easier and not put too much stress on mother-to-be-again Faith. Meanwhile, I felt Jared and I could both keep Clint busy and begin urging him to return to his cabin. Clint had lived in his own cabin peacefully and happily for many years before Lynette had arrived to claim, torment, and discard him. If we could find the key to making Clint understand the truth about his Vinny, perhaps he would be ready to move out and live on his own again. I had seen no evidence that he was prone to suicide, in spite of his childish insistence that he planned to "do himself in".

It seemed like a good plan, but it turned out that it had been very fortunate that Clint had slipped away from us to bike back with his meager possessions. I had just arrived home a bit early on Monday when Jared pointed out a thick cloud of smoke to me. Thinking about how pleased Bea would be if I got a picture for the paper, I scoped up the digital camera that had enhanced my abilities as a photographer and headed in the direction of the smoke, with Jared and Clint accompanying me. The closer we got to our goal, the more I regretted having brought Clint along as a passenger. If it were not his cabin that was on fire, it was a fire very close to his cabin.

"That's my fire!" Clint said in wonderment as we swept around the last curve. "That's my cabin what's on fire." He staggered out of the car, and Jared and I held him back out of the way as fire-fighting equipment rolled into the neatly kept yard.

The little three-room house bloomed brightly in its secluded cedar tree location. Before water pumped out of trucks, the roof collapsed, and standing walls toppled. The excitement of the fire swept all memory of possession from Clint's mind. He clapped and cheered as water knocked down flames and smoke billowed in front of us in a blinding screen. Even when the cabin was reduced to wet charcoal briskets, Clint's enjoyment remained intact. Volunteer firefighters took time out to come and personally extend sympathy. Clint had possibly never had so much attention in his life.

The fire marshal, looking grim, found us. "Son," he said to Clint, who was probably about the same age he was, "I have some bad news for you. This fire was deliberately set. I understand you were gone when it started?"

Clint pointed to me. "I live with her on account of so I won't do myself in."

The fire marshal covered his surprise smoothly, but his eyebrows still asked the question held back by his lips.

"Clint's girlfriend left him," Jared offered, "so we're keeping him for now. He took it kind of ... hard."

"Vinny," Clint said nodding. "My purty girlfriend, Vinny."

"Where is this girlfriend now, Clint?"

"My girlfriend left me. My Vinny's gone." Tears eased out of the corners of his flat brown eyes, and I wondered if they were for the lost Vinny or the lost home or both.

How much does Clint really understand?

"Clint," the fire marshal said gently, "do you know who could have set this fire or why?"

But Clint had traveled far away; words could not reach him, and questions could not disturb his inner peace. Jared drew Clint back to the car.

I promised the volunteer fire chief that I would keep in touch and call with any information I could ferret out of the stunned Clint.

The fire presented a major hurdle for me in my private life. Plus, I couldn't help feeling that there was something I would know about the fire if I could just concentrate better. My concentration during the week following the fire was a debacle. I never heard how Thor had dealt with Lynette, but she was alive for sure and had reclaimed Marty as her hero of the moment. They paraded before my eyes everywhere I went in Three Prongs. In self-defense, I began to take my lunch to work and hide myself away in my office, where I couldn't possibly see them unless – as sometimes happened – I looked out the large plate glass windows at the precise moment they either drove or walked past.

Obviously, Marty had not heard about Lynette and Thor – or if he had, he had chosen not to believe it. Brent, I knew, was circumvented from talking about the case. Not only was it still under investigation, but there was absolutely no proof connecting Lynn to anything illegal.

So, with one week to prepare for my son's move to the ranch, I was less prepared than when the possibility had first been discussed, and I had no more room to offer at the ranch house. Pastor Garth was plodding along through his story so slowly that the action bored even me, its very creator.

Nat and Jared remained in touch. Jared had signed up for GED classes at the library. With a little time, I thought he would return to school and attend regular classes. He was a bright boy, not a bad student, and I coached him in whatever areas I could; math was not one of them. When I took Jared into town, I dropped him off at the Sidelines office to visit Nat before classes began. It seemed as if everyone's life – except mine – was the star on top of a Christmas tree. I didn't even rate as the rusted stand hidden under a worn white towel.

Marty and our link as M&Ms were outside the reach of my thoughts ... mostly. I attacked the computer keyboard with a vengeance, proving my ability to dissemble and earn my keep through writing lousy stories. Thus engaged, I let out a yelp when a thin hand stroked my arm.

He claimed to have quit drinking and perhaps he had, but Buddy Turner's wasted face had yet to recover. The whites around his light blue eyes were still yellowed, and his thin cheeks cast a ruddy glow in the darkened office. "I keep my promises," Buddy informed me. "I told you I would poke around Neil Peters' office and find stuff."

"You found proof of who killed Julia?"

"Naw, sorry." He shook his head. "I couldn't find out nothin' about that, but look here, Miss Rice. I heard you were looking for that dog-fighting ring ... how you found it and then it was gone."

"Yes," I said eagerly.

"It's Peters' money that makes it move."

"Explain, Buddy."

"Well, he charges admission. He moves the ring around his circle of friends. It was at the art colony until you discovered it. I know where it is now, and I can take you to it. I even have some papers here that I think are important. I ain't good at reading, but it seems to be about the dog fights."

Quickly, I took the papers from Buddy and examined them. He was right: Peters had kept detailed accounts of expenses and profits. He had listed the dogs by numbers, not names, and written down details about their strength and viciousness. Being somewhat of an egotist and cocky as well, Peters had foolishly signed his name to the papers. In fact, he seemed to enjoy writing his name in bold, sweeping letters.

I smiled at Buddy. "Thanks! You're right about this, Buddy. It's a gold mine! Now let's go get Brent and –

"Oh no!" He backed quickly away from me. "I don't have no truck with the sheriff. He thinks I done something to that trailer and caused it to blow up on Miss Julia."

"He doesn't think that anymore. Buddy, we think we know who did it, but we don't have any proof. We think it was a girl who moved in with Thor –

"Clara? I knowed she was no good! I knowed she tricked the boss! I tried to tell Thor, and he almost fired me, but she's gone now. The kid's back. He's doing good, that kid. I always liked Nat. He's kind of like me. No one else likes him."

"You knew Clara when she was at the ranch. Did you

find out anything about her that might tie her to Julia's murder?"

Slowly, he shook his head. "Nope. Wish I had, but there might be something in that book. She wrote everything down in that book."

"What book?"

He sighed and shook his head. "Don't rightly know where it is now, but she never let it get away from her. She was always writing stuff down in there, but I don't know what.""

"What did the book look like? Was it a diary? A book like a photo album?"

"Coulda been. It did look something like that, but she never lets go of it or leaves it anywheres. She took it with her when Thor kicked her off the ranch. Boy, was he mad! If he ever got that mad at me, I reckon my heart would attack and die."

"Buddy, I have to go to Brent, or we can't get Peters, and he will keep on fighting those poor dogs."

"I know. I hate that. I love dogs. I saw it once 'cause he made me watch. Then he made fun of me for getting sick to my stomach. He told me he'd get me fired from Thor's and that he'd never come up with no more jobs for me. Then he did, only he said if I ever told anyone he wouldn't. But I had to tell you, Miss Rice. I can't stand knowing about it and not doing nothing. He was laughing about the last fight. Four dogs died, he said. I didn't see that one, and I'm glad 'bout that."

"Buddy, I don't know how to thank you enough. I wish I did."

"It's okay, Miss Rice. My gut will thank me. It won't hurt no more."

"Buddy, the Bible says a wise man regards the life of his beast. That means God expects us to be kind to animals. I don't know how to thank you, but I really believe God will reward you."

"Thanks. You just pray for me. If God has enough time, ask Him to mix up Neil so he won't know how them papers got away."

I nodded as Buddy slid out of the office. Then I called Brent. My fingers shook as I dialed his office. After what seemed like an eternity, his voice answered. I explained quickly.

"Be right there, Mike," he promised, and it was a promise he kept.

God kept His promise to Buddy too. Armed with a search warrant, Sheriff Brent Cruz stormed Neil Peters' office and seized files and computers. With all that evidence hoisted out the door to waiting patrol cars, Peters could never have imagined that Buddy had been there first and had confiscated some of the material to present to me.

Peters tried intimidation, thrusting his stocky rancher's figure between deputies and his desk and threatening the county with a lawsuit for harassment. His blue eyes snapped as the truculent man spewed profanity out of his mouth as freely as brown water aerating at the sewer plant. He blasted everyone – me included – for the invasion of his privacy. He flatly denied any knowledge of a floating dog-fighting ring, even when Brent waved the proof in front of him. When he became abusive, Brent called for backup. "I wasn't in this alone!" he shouted. "Why don't you go after the big fish instead of the small fry?"

"I'll go after every fish I can catch," Brent answered evenly. "Reckon you're providing the bait on your computers and in your files. Meanwhile, Mr. Peters, let me assure you that my office and the district attorney will prosecute you to the fullest extent of the law. Animal cruelty is a felony in this state … and if I find proof of elderly abuse, neglect, or fraud, you'll stay in prison until the palms of your hands dry up and fall off the bones."

Peters lost some of his bluster under the sheriff's imperturbable stare. "You cops are always picking on me! It's not fair!"

"A jury will decide about the fairness, Mr. Peters. John, read him his rights and cuff him."

Brent's chief deputy, John Dion, complied with relish, removing his Stetson and running fingers through his mop of brown hair. His blue eyes failed at their determination to maintain what he considered a lawman's equipoise. He loved dogs. He was smiling as he read the Mirandas, and his eyes smiled right along with him.

Even the room seemed to sigh in satisfaction that slumlord Neil Peters had been caught in his nefarious dealings. Once he was escorted outside, Peters got into a shoving match with John and tried to break away and run. Brent shook his head in exasperation as he listed more charges in his notebook.

My own ebullient state at having finally solved a real-life mystery lasted until I sank down in the desk chair in front of my computer at the office. Garth Seymour's pragmatic character questioned, "Okay, Mike. What now? I can't move the story on my own, you know. You are the writer-creator-inventor. Don't expect me to do your thinking – or punch the keys for you."

I couldn't think for my fictitious book character Garth or for anyone else at the moment – not after having seen Lynette and Marty strolling down Main Street arm in arm. Her upturned face had laughed into his as they'd shared a private moment in a very public place. Surely there's a limit to the amount of pain a heart can suffer before it simply quits beating and, thus, hurting. Surely a logical mind like mine can only spend a certain amount of time planning a losing romantic campaign strategy. Surely a person like me – who eschews getting mixed up in other people's business – can find a way to think past this latest and greatest hurt.

The sudden intake of air in the office as Bea and Nat jerked open the door and entered was a welcomed distraction. Nat draped himself over a chair casually. With clothes that fit him and a haircut, his looks had improved enough that he didn't hurt the eyeballs.

Bea, her short, dark hair bouncing with vitality and her dark eyes sparkling, pushed me playfully out of my chair. "Get up and walk around and exercise," she directed, plopping her full figure down into the chair. She propped her tightly jeaned legs up on my desk. "This is payback time. Don't look surprised! You finally remembered your old friend. You sent Nat to me, and he's a real prize."

Nat looked away, his face flushed with pleased embarrassment.

"Then you brought me pictures of Clint Flavors' fire. Poor Clint! Is he still staying with you?" Without waiting for my reply, she continued, "And now you've helped break the story of the year!"

"How do you know about that?"

She laughed. "The police scanner we keep in the office in case there's an accident or fire we need to shoot, remember, Mike? You should! I used to send you out for photos often enough. Anyway, when the sheriff called for backup,

Neil Peters' name went out after they called in the license plate on his truck. Then that code, '10-95 one time with a white male,' was a dead giveaway. There were people celebrating in the streets when they heard about his arrest. He's hurt a lot of people and has been getting away with it for a long time."

"Did you get a picture of his arrest?" Nat asked eagerly.

"No. Sorry. I didn't have my camera with me."

"No matter. You still came up with the story of the year!" Bea interjected. "I'll get a mug shot from Brent, or we may have some old file pictures. I know we have the crime scene where that poor elderly woman he was supposed to be taking care of died. Brent hasn't released the details about the dog-fighting yet, but he's already working on the press release. He gave me permission to question Peters, but I doubt he'll talk to anyone except his attorney. Anyway, Mike, he gave you credit for breaking the case. He said you are a real fine rat trap." She and Nat laughed. "Or perhaps that's what Nat and I said! So, Mike, it's payback time – a fun event for you."

I groaned.

"It will be fun," Nat urged. "My first one when I was sober enough to know what's going on anyway."

"What in the world are the two of you talking about?"

"The Annual Chili Cook-Off to raise money for the senior center," Bea explained. "The Meals on Wheels Program. Something like that might have saved that poor woman Peters starved. And you know, Mike, it won't be long until me, you, Brent, Anna, and even Marty will be senior citizens. We might all be hanging out at the center together."

I groaned again.

"Sidelines is sponsoring a booth," Nat explained excitedly. "It will be the greatest fun! Dad's cooking the chili. He's so glad to be out of jail and cleared from suspicion that's he's volunteering for every community event someone dreams up!"

"And we're going to win the showmanship trophy thanks to Nat's idea. See, Mike, the booth will look like the front page of Sidelines with a picture cut out. The picture will be the counter, of course, where we serve chili to customers. We'll all be dressed up in newspaper-related costumes."

I groaned again.

"Nat is so thin that he's going to be a paper. I'm going to

be a computer, to represent the modern world of newspapers. You can work out a costume from the past. And quit groaning, Mike! Use your imagination. Don't waste it. You can come up with something."

I was already shaking my head. "No, I can't. I don't sew. It's a self-imposed law I follow. I sit too much already writing books. If I'm going to sit, I'm going to write. That at least makes me some money. I'm terrible at sewing. It doesn't earn me anything but frustration because it's boring and I do it so poorly."

"You can invent something to wear that doesn't have to be sewn," Bea pointed out patiently.

"Sorry, but I can't, Bea. See, Ron and Faith and the kids are moving in with me in a little over a week. I have to get the place ready. The biggest challenge will be to figure out what to do with Clint now that he's lost his cabin. I don't have time for any more projects right now."

"Let's make a deal," Bea offered. "If we can solve your problem about Clint, will you help us?"

It seemed like a fair offer, albeit a most improbable one. "Sure."

"Good. It's settled. So get your costume made. Nat's going to take Clint out to the Dean ranch. Clint can live in one of the ranch hand houses. Now that Nat and his dad are getting along so well, Thor has decided to build a house for his son and his son's future family."

Nat squirmed uncomfortably and turned red again.

"So Thor's hired a crew, but even with Buddy helping out, they're one man short. Clint will love it! He loves hard work and fishing and animals. He'll find everything he loves there."

"Bea, that's cheating! You cheated! You already had this figured out before you made me promise –

"Oh, get over it, Mike. You need a social life, and we need your help. It's a perfect match. Now get your costume together, but remember that I have dibs on the computer screen. See you Saturday. You won't have to do anything but come up with a costume and help us dish out chili and rake in dough for the senior center. We'll have a blast!"

I groaned and shook my head.

Before I could formulate another protest, Bea jumped up and grabbed Nat's arm. "Come on, buffalo hunter. Let's hit the trail. We've rounded up all the strays at this campsite."

Laughing, she and Nat left.

Buffalo hunter? Has Bea been hanging around with Marty too? My scandalized heart, hardened by too much hurt, throbbed with renewed vigor. The pain was so intense that after my friends left – imagine me thinking of Nat as a friend – pain drove me out of the office and down the street to Zolly's bar. This time, I didn't care who saw me enter, nor did I care that the bar was filled with boisterous afternoon patrons. I marched through the bar and up to the counter. Slapping both my hands palm down on the counter in front of the startled bar owner, I announced, "Zolly, you must do the right thing. It's not fair to keep that secret from Jared."

He blinked and licked his lips, unable to engineer an answer.

"He can stay with me for as long as he needs a home," I added. "Actually, I wouldn't want him hanging around here."

The buxom barmaid, Candy, drew herself up behind Zolly, her obvious female attractions pointing at me in anger. "What do you mean by that?" she asked tartly. "Is there something wrong with this place? And if there is, what are you doing here?"

Ignoring Candy's pale blonde hair that was being tossed in my direction indignantly, I finished my speech to Zolly. "No one deserves to suffer from heartbreak when there's a cure. Jared needs a father. He needs family. He's had more fathering from a rescued drug addict and a day laborer with darkened upstairs windows than he has from you. Are you proud of that? A successful businessman like you? You should be ashamed!"

"I thought you didn't like me or my business."

"You thought right. I'm not fond of you, and I hate your business. If I could, I'd close down every bar in the country. I'd bring back prohibition."

Candy stomped angrily behind the counter. Zolly ignored her, although his face mirrored the imprecation of a spurious fortuneteller.

"If I had my way," I continued, "I'd plaster scenes from drunken car crashes on every billboard in the nation. I'd cancel every media ad created to push alcohol at those who haven't any better sense than to drink poison. But how I feel about your business has nothing to do with the fact that Jared needs and deserves a father. You are his father, and it's time you accept that responsibility and started acting like it. You have one week. If you haven't told Jared the truth by then, I will." I spun around and trounced out of the bar, ignoring the whistles and drink invitations that followed me.

Marty and Lynette were outside on the sidewalk engaged in a heated argument. I walked briskly past them, not sparing them a look, even though my heart felt as slashed and smashed as grated cheese. From the words I over-heard, Lynette was urging Marty to accompany her into the Borderbound Watering Hole. Marty was telling Lynette that he "held no truck" with alcohol or places that served it.

Good! It's about time Marty realized what Miss Perfectly Drop-Dead Gorgeous is really like on the inside. He belongs with someone more like me. After all, we would be M&Ms! We would be as compatible as chocolate icing on a choco-late cake. Marty and I belonged together, and yet, because Lynette Clarissa Greene had come to town and shined a false brightness on the horizon of Marty's dreams, that could not happen.

Once I was hunkered down back in my office, I resisted the imperious temptation to leave early. The dogs, ever loyal, would appreciate me if I did. They loved me unques-tioningly. Clint and Jared would probably appreciate me because they were probably both hungry. It would be fine to get home and see the ranch under strong daylight. Nevertheless, I was immobilized. My life had been robbed. Something valuable and irreplaceable had been stolen now that I had released the dream of Marty and me sharing a future. Brightness had bled out of colors. Songbirds raved about strange joy. A cloudless sky looked mundane. A cloudy sky roiled dark and heavy.

Dutifully, I sat at my desk staring at the clock on the wall until it hit exactly five o'clock. Then I rounded up everything, including enough enthusiasm to get me out the door. Thankful again for the loan of Anna's car – even though the talking irritated me as Old Blue never had – I drove towards the ranch more slowly than usual. I barely noticed other drivers shoving their vehicles past me on the highway.

A strange vehicle sat in the driveway. Fear tightened the walls of my chest, preventing breathing. Are Clint and

Jared okay? Will I be shot when I exit the car? Are my dogs ... oh, thank you, Jesus! The dogs at least were okay. They rushed at me with such joy that I felt guilty in having prolonged my trip home.

I ran haphazardly through the yard, searching for the driver of the strange car. As I rounded the corner of the house, my feet slid to an abrupt stop, and I eased back.

Zolly and Jared faced each other across the picnic table. I couldn't hear the words, but Zolly was addressing the teen in a low, earnest voice. Overjoyed, I knew that Zolly had finally accepted his son!

When joy swooped back into my heart, it refilled nature's colors with bright hues. Joy harmonized the songbirds and piled the clouds into fascinating, fluffy white shapes. I had finally done something right! I might have lost Marty, but I had gained a father for a lonely son. Usually I minded my own business, but this time I had stuck my nose into someone else's business and embraced someone else's problem and had been able to help. Whatever happened now – even if I were to die a natural or deliberately caused death that very night – my life would have been spent accomplishing at least something worthwhile. Zolly was giving Jared what he needed most – a father – and all because I had grabbed courage by the horns and wrestled it to the ground.

Whistling to the dogs, I set out down the walking trail at a run, leaping over tufts of grass and tripping through clusters of rock. The dogs must have been amazed, but they were game for a sprint. What finally slowed my joyous pace was remembering that father and son might need more private time.

Zolly had left by the time my carefully slowed footsteps made it back. Jared saw me, flew down the driveway, and threw himself at me. He whirled me around dizzily.

"Whoa!" I gasped. "I'm about to fall down! What is this all about?"

"Oh! Miss Rice! Mike! Oh!" He grabbed me and spun around with me again. "I have a father! I have a ... dad." He breathed reverence into the word "dad." He quit dancing and released me, stepping back with a sober look sliding down over his face. "You won't like it much when I tell you who he is, but I finally belong to someone, someone who is real family. I don't have to go back to the children's home and wonder what I did so wrong and terrible that I would be left alone, with not even one person in the world to claim me as their own. I finally get to use that word I've always hated because other kids could say it and I couldn't. I can finally call someone ... Dad."

"That's wonderful, Jared!" I hugged him joyfully. "Awesome! I'm so happy for you!" Tears crawled out of my eyes faster than I could blink them back.

"My dad is Zolly Gilmore, Mike. We have different last names because my mom used her last name for me. Dad told me more about my mom than I had ever heard before – good things. Her name was Kathy. Dad never told me before because he didn't want me to feel bad about him and my mom not being married, and he didn't want me to feel bad because he owns a bar. I don't much like the bar, Mike, but I'm so glad to have a dad! He said we can start doing a lot of things together – even take a vacation, just the two of us. He is married, you know, to someone named Carmen. I've seen her a couple of times, but I've never met her. Anyway, she doesn't like camping, but Dad does, so he said he will take me camping next time he gets to go. I can still work for him and get paid, but I can see him now even when I'm not working, and the money he gives me will go into that college fund you started for me, Mike. Dad's real proud that I'm taking the GED classes and thinking about going back to school and that I'm wanting to go to college. He says he wishes he had gone to college. I've got to go tell Clint!"

Clint was inside watching television, a novel experience for him since he had never owned a TV set. Jared told Clint about Zolly. Neither Jared nor I could tell if Clint understood, even though he smiled happily and nodded.

Jared followed me into the kitchen and began setting the table. "Mike," he said shyly, "Zolly ... er, I mean Dad, said I could stay with you for a while if you don't mind."

I hugged him, amazed at how my initial distrust of him had transformed into something approaching love. "I want you to stay, Jared. You've been a great help to me, and I love having you here just as yourself."

He looked surprised and gratified.

"You also get along great with Alex and Ryan. I'm sure Faith will be delighted that you will be around to play with them sometimes while they get used to their new home."

Jared drew his shoulders up straighter and looked important. "Yeah. It's tough to get used to moving into a new place. I learned that a long time ago. I'll be glad to help, Mike."

"That's fine. I think we can be a real family. You'll have two! You and your dad when you are with him, and all of us when you are here."

Fresh tears swam out of the corners of my eyes like released tadpoles when Jared threw his arms around me in a fierce hug. "I'm so glad God sent someone like you into my life," he said simply.

It was all I could do to keep from blubbering like a mindless idiot.

While we were eating, Jared asked me if I thought he should change his last name now that he knew Zolly was his father.

"You and your dad should talk about that, Jared. I'm sure it can be done fairly easily, although to be legal, I think it would need to go through the court system. I can check into it for you if you'd like."

Jared smiled at me and nodded.

Then I broached the subject of the job at the Dean ranch with Clint.

Clint nodded. "Thor's good. I'm a good worker ... strong."

I agreed. "You've been very good and strong for me, Clint, and I thank you, but I haven't been able to pay you much money. Thor is a rich man. He can pay you more money for working than I can."

"If I go work for him," Clint announced, "I will need to go stay with him. He lives too far for me to ride my bike. He lives too far for you to take me, Miz Mike. You would be late for work."

And that simply, my problem of needing more space in my home was solved by Clint Flavors, the person some suspected of missing at least one flight of stairs.

Chapter 11.

To my credit, I did get my chili-cooking costume together, complete with visored cap and vegetable ink smeared on the tips of my fingers and on the white printer's apron. For some inexplicable reason, the closer it drew to Saturday, the more reticent I became about joining the festivities.

Clint and Jared both planned to accompany me. Clint was so excited about the proposed outing that he opted to wait until after the weekend to move to the Dean ranch. Meanwhile, he had been around to help Ron unload, arrange, and store the household belongings he'd brought in preparation for moving day.

Clint, constantly forgetting that Thornton Dean had volunteered as chili cook, spewed out suggestions for our booth like wind-blown popcorn. Most were ingredients he wanted added to the chili pot. "Mama used to do that, I think," he said, nodding sagely.

Jared and I gave up telling Clint that our collective responsibilities would be to look "newsy" and help Sidelines take home a showmanship trophy.

By Saturday, I was so uneasy about leaving the ranch that I was jittery. Ron and Faith would probably be bringing a few more loads of their belongings. I would have preferred to stay home and visit with them, but neither Jared or Clint could drive (I had been the hapless near-accident victim involved in Jared's illegal attempt at driving, as you may recall), and both were so excited about the Chili Cook-Off that I couldn't let them down. Partly, I dreaded the crowd that I knew would attend the event. Crowds and I have always been inimical towards each other.

I knew that part of the apprehension sprang from the visit Lynette had made to my office. She had charged inside, her coruscating beauty infused with such anger that it had transformed her perfect features into an ugly mask. She had stomped across the floorboards, dislodging dust and rattling the plastic keyboard of my computer. When she ground to a stop at my desk, I looked up in astonishment. "I hate you!" she spat.

My philosophy is that when a person doesn't know what to say, the best thing to say is nothing. I followed that advice, which angered her all the more.

"I hate you!" she screamed. "I hate you! I hate you! I hate you! Do you hear me? I hate you!" She waited for me to respond.

"I imagine even the rocks in this building heard you. I'm sorry you hate me ... but why do you hate me?"

"You know! You know you turned Marty against me! I hate you!"

I blinked. Watching she and Marty stroll around Three Prongs arm in arm, one could hardly conclude that anything had power to turn Marty against Lynette. My role was that of the injured party. The hurting below my ribcage had lessened to resemble open, lacerated skin and hammer-bruised organs. Thinking about how desperately I loved Marty and how quickly Lynette had whisked that relationship out of my sphere, I said nothing. My silence again infuriated Lynn further.

"I hate you!" she screamed again. "I want Marty, and I aim to have him. I usually get what I want, and I want him. You can't stop me!"

That's true enough.

"And I'll tell you something else, Miss Fancy Pants Storybook Writer,, you'll be sorry! You're gonna pay for this! If I can't have him, no one can!"

"Do you plan to kill him like you killed your sister?"

She gawked at me.

"I know the truth, Lynette Clarissa Greene. I know you killed Julia, and I know how you killed her and why you killed her, and I plan to prove it. Don't look so surprised, Lynette/Clara. You asked me to find out who killed your sister, didn't you? Well, I have."

"You lie!"

"Sometimes, but not about this. I know about your dad

and the propane business and your work repairing gas furnaces and hot water heaters. I have a picture of you in uniform with a tool belt around your waist, looking very proud about the unit you were servicing. I called your parents in Alabama and had them send me the photo."

"That doesn't prove anything! Don't try to scare me with your lies. It won't work!"

"You should be scared, Lynette. Texas imposes the death penalty for capital murder. I plan to have you found guilty and sentenced to lethal injection. You left behind more evidence than you realize."

"I left nothing behind because I didn't do it! You can't prove something that didn't happen! Why don't you spend your time getting the real criminals arrested instead of messing with me – like that retard drug addict you're so chummy with or Buddy Turner or Thornton Dean? Why don't you get one of them arrested and quit trying to scare me?"

"You would be wise to be scared, Lynette. You're going to Hell. You probably don't know much about the place, so let me fill you in. You will never die, and neither will the worms eating your flesh and torturing you. You will be separated from everything you loved on Earth, and you will beg to die, but you won't be able to. Frightful, isn't it?"

"I don't believe in Hell, and I don't believe in you! You lie. You even admitted that you do sometimes."

"God doesn't lie. You told me to pray and ask God who killed your sister. I did, and I know it was you, Lynette."

"I don't believe in God!"

"Whether or not you believe in God doesn't make Him any less real. He's not depending on your belief or asking your permission to exist. He just does. He just is."

"I don't believe in God or Hell or Heaven ... or you!" she shouted again. Then she jerked around, knocking pages of my manuscript to the floor as she tore out of the office.

Remembering that incident as the weekend approached nurtured my unease. I had called Brent. Legally, there was nothing he could do. Lynette had not injured me, and she had not destroyed property. I had no witnesses to her threats.

After a few moments of thought, Brent suggested a plan. "We could set a trap for her, Mike, with you as the bait. She's pretty angry with you. Agree to meet her somewhere, and when she does, tell her you will tell Marty the truth about her. I'll be stationed close by to witness the whole thing – and to keep you safe if something happens. If she becomes violent, we've got her. We can arrest her on a misdemeanor charge and hold her while we finish the new investigation into Julia's death. It's the only plan I can think of right now that might get you out of danger. She can't do much damage in jail."

So, I had asked Lynette to meet me at the art colony. Brent had arrived first and slipped into the men's dressing room by the pool. Lynnette had stormed towards me so aggressively that I had been tempted to flee, even though I knew Brent was installed nearby for my safety.

She stopped just short of where I stood, hands on hips. Anger flushed the beauty from her face. Even her body looked less than quintessential, with her form-fitting Western wear shaking in rage. "Well?" she demanded. "I already said everything to you that I had to say, so why are we here?"

"Lynette, we started out as friends –

"We were never friends. You were just … convenient."

"For what? For bringing you information about how close officials were to solving Julia's murder and arresting you?"

She was too wily for such an obvious trap. "Get real, Mike. Why are we here? Talk quick."

"But I thought we were friends."

"Then you're a fool!"

"I'm giving you a chance to confess and turn yourself in. It will go better for you in court. You know you are guilty, I know you are guilty, and Thornton Dean probably knows you are guilty. Most of all, I have proof."

"You have no proof. You couldn't possibly. What you do have is an overactive imagination. You live in a backwater town where nothing ever happens, so you've got no outlet for your imagination. So when I came along – a pretty stranger who stole away your boyfriend – oh, yes, Miss Michal Rice … I know you want Marty for yourself. When he fell for me and you realized you didn't stand a chance against someone young and beautiful like me, you targeted me for your lies and harassment, because you're a mean, jealous woman. Isn't that how it really is, Miss Rice? It sounds like a solid case to me, and this conversation is finished!"

Lynette had turned and walked briskly away, her heels clicking angrily on the concrete pool surround.

I was left standing, rooted to the hard surface, feeling very much the fool even before Brent joined me.

"So much for that plan," he said wryly. "Still, it was worth a try. Mike, I hate to even ask, but are you sure about Lynette? I mean, she did make some valid points. You do have a wild imagination. It's what makes you a great writer. And everyone in town knows you've been stuck on Marty for years."

"Yeah – everyone except Marty."

"The point is, Mike, do you think you might have imagined some of this? Any of it?"

Remembering how I had once coveted Lynette as a daughter-in-law, I almost wondered myself. Slowly I shook my head. "I wish that were the answer, Brent. Honestly I do."

"Yeah, me too, but if she is our cold-blooded killer, she'll slip up – or at least I hope so. Don't you have any evidence, Mike? Can you think of anything other than that picture you showed me from her folks?"

I frowned. "I keep thinking I've heard or seen something important, Brent, but the harder I try to remember, the faster the memory gallops away from me."

He sighed. "Yeah. I've heard memories do that. Mike, quit trying to remember. If you are right about this girl, other people – including you and possibly Marty – could be in danger."

The thought of Marty in danger made me gulp in big mouthfuls of air. Not Marty! Lynette couldn't hurt him! I won't allow it! But ... how could I stop her? Marty doesn't even believe she's was dangerous. "Oh, Brent, I hadn't thought of that ... about Marty, I mean. I'll quit trying to remember and go by my gut."

"Mike," Brent said, dropping an arm around my shoulders, "I'm concerned about you as well as Marty. Please be careful and take care of yourself. Look over your shoulder when you're alone." He ripped a piece of paper out of his notebook and scratched a number on it. "Here, my cell phone. I'm never without it. Call if anything seems wrong. I don't care if it seems as ridiculous as a wrong-colored cat crossing the street, you just holler." He paused. "And, Mike, start keeping your cell phone with you. Please.

No one has an excuse to be out of reach nowadays when we have cell phones – not that we get service in all areas around here, what with all these hills."

Touched by his concern, I had nodded. Then I had tried to remember where I had left my cell phone and whether or not the battery needed to be charged. Now, as Clint and Jared loaded up the car for the Chili Cook-Off, I remembered what Brent had said about off-colored cats. I looked around my peaceful ranch home, trying to use X-ray vision to see behind cedar brush and through clumps of live oak foliage tossing shadows to the ground. As a precaution, I locked the dogs in the garage. Prissy's cruel and senseless death still rankled.

The Sidelines booth was already set up on the festival grounds near the Three Prongs River. Making a quick survey of other booths, I felt confident that Nat and Bea had hatched a winning idea for our booth. We were certainly in the competition. One booth was set up as an outhouse, with unused and unplugged modern appliances strewn around it as half of the outhouse door swung open at the top to let the pajama-clad cook dish up samples. "Everything was better in the olden days?" I asked with sudden illumination.

He looked startled. "No. I just like outhouses, that's all. I think they're funny."

Mama's Flowerful Chili operated out of a booth smothered in potted blooming plants and hanging baskets. Mama wore a flowered dress and bonnet and served the chili with a garden spade.

A Native American-owned business from nearby Thunder Falls brought a real teepee and hung racks of drying herbs that released spicy fragrances into the summer air. It reminded me of Marty all over again. He had not neglected the role of Native American culture in his zeal for keeping Three Prongs Western. Indians had helped write our history, too, and Marty had embraced that. Thanks to his efforts, Three Prongs hosted annual Pow Wows that showcased different tribes and their unique craftsmanship, customs, and beliefs.

The White Water Rafting Company cooked their chili inside a kayak, stirring it with a paddle.

All the ideas were clever, but I still felt that Bea and Nat had wrangled the winner. Nat made an outstanding walking newspaper, and Bea's computer screen was awesome. The rest of us could not compete with them, but altogether, we were indeed showy.

After inspecting the other booths, however, I couldn't settle down at ours. I felt like an allergic reaction had set in to fire ant bites, and my skin was inching up into hives.

Even Clint noticed my agitation. "You look bad, Miz Mike – like someone stole eggs out of your Easter basket and hid them again, and you don't know where to look for them."

Suddenly, I knew everything. Ron was right! He'd often said that anyone who earned a living through writing – as I did, or at least tried to do – should learn to be more observant. How did I miss comprehending that past salient remark of Clint's? Now I smiled at him. "Thanks, Clint," I said and ran for the talking car, leaving him staring after me as if I were a fish he had just spotted climbing out of a tree. Perhaps I was a fish out of water, but I knew what to look for and where to find it. Bea and Nat shouted at me to come back, but I knew I didn't even have enough time to explain my haste to them.

I kept carefully to the speed limit, but no cars passed me. Instead of pulling up in front of the house, I pulled the car around back to see if Ron and Faith were unloading things into the barn. Silence fell around me as I heaved myself out of the car. Without Jared and Clint, the house was bathed in emptiness. For a moment, I dreaded going inside alone. Then I shook off that silly feeling of impending doom and hurried through the back door to the screened porch I had given Clint as a room. His few clothes hung in a huge cedar wardrobe in a corner. The box of papers he had brought back from his cabin just before it burned sat untouched at the end of his bed. It took only a few moments for me to find what I was looking for. I hugged it to me in excitement and almost whooped for joy. Fortunately, I suppressed the urge at the last moment, because before I could even open the book I held clutched to my chest, I heard the front door opening surreptitiously. A brief pause and careful steps eased around living room furniture. Quickly, I jerked open the wardrobe and stepped quickly inside. The door closed on me just before I heard the intruder enter the room. That was when I berated myself for stupidity. In my haste, I had closed the door completely. Now I couldn't see the intruder and if I tried to open it, I would disclose both my presence in the room and my location For all I knew, the intruder might be armed and unequivocally dangerous.

I heard Clint's belongings rudely tumbling to the concrete floor of the porch. I had just decided to surprise the intruder and rush out of the wardrobe when I heard the careless click of the back door. Ron! I'm safe! Now I can see who was in the room with me. But even as I pushed on the heavy door, footsteps clattered across the floor into the other room. I fell out of the wardrobe and landed in front of two well-laced track shoes. Looking up fearfully, my eyes met the incredulous stare of my son. "Ron, there's no time to explain," I cried as he hauled me to my feet. "Someone was in the house! Quick! We have to see who it was. I have to have proof!"

The two of us sprinted through the house to the front. We were in time to hear, but not see, a vehicle leaving.

Ron crashed back through the house and jumped into his loaded-down truck. Faith and the boys watched in amazement as he sent the truck careening around the house and hurtling down the driveway while I explained his mission to Faith. Unfortunately, when Ron returned, he reported that he had lost the vehicle.

"Didn't you even catch a glimpse of it? Didn't you even see what color it was?"

"Mom, I know how you feel, and I'm sorry. We have a long driveway, but it empties out on a major farm-to-market road, with a lot of traffic. How would I have even known which way to turn?"

With a sigh, I apologized. Then I explained to Ron and Faith about Lynette. I left out the part about having coveted her for a daughter-in-law. I opened up the book, and the three of us read the chilling narrative together.

Today, I finally did it! I finally got rid of Julia! I killed her. I blew her up in that new mobile home she was moving into. Serves her right for leaving Thor. No one will ever know because it was such a clever idea. I fixed it so that if anyone is suspected, it will be Buddy. He deserves it. He drinks too much. Sometimes he skips out on work.

I might even fix it so Thor looks like a suspect if he disappoints me. I can't wait to try him out. Oh, he thinks he's heartbroken right now over Julia. He'll get over her quickly enough. She was stupid. After he meets me, he will know how stupid she was.

I've hated Julia for a long time. She won all those beauty contests. She married the man I wanted for myself ... rich! Rich! Rich, foolish Julia. She didn't even know what to do with all that money. She could have bought furs and diamonds and taken vacations to other countries, but she stayed on that stupid ranch with a bunch of stinking animals and never had any fun. I hate animals. I hate everything – especially Julia for being so stupid. I'm the smartest one in the family. Now everyone will know that. Hey! Now I'm the smartest AND the prettiest, because I'm the only one left! That's funny!

The whole thing was so easy except for using that dimwit Clint as a cover. He really thought I was going to marry him. Imagine that! He has this idea that marriage is the only decent thing to do since I moved into his cabin with him. I've had a time keeping him quiet. He talked about his girlfriend around town. It gave me a bit of a fright until I realized that no one believes him. Besides, I stayed low, and no one even saw me until after Julia was gone. I'll be okay now if Clint doesn't start talking again. He knows a lot of people, but who would listen to him anyway? A dumb retard! A nitwit! Surely no one will believe Clint Flavors.

See, what I did was ..."

"I think she's the one who shot Prissy too," I told Ron and Faith grimly.

Faith gasped.

"I found a piece of pastel-plaid material in Prissy's mouth. I showed it to Sheriff Cruz, but he said it wasn't worth anything as evidence unless we could match it to the rest of an outfit and prove who was wearing it. Brent didn't believe it was Lynette at first either. He was convinced it was Thornton Dean because Lynnette came forward as a witness. She called herself Clara, and Brent had no idea that the Clara who said she was an eyewitness to Thor threatening Julia and shooting at me –

"Mom! What in the world?"

"Another time, Ron. That's what happened to Old Blue. So I guess you could say that Lynette is a murderer several times over – Julia, my Prissy, and even Old Blue. Anyway, I still have the material scrap. Maybe it will come in handy as evidence yet. I never could get anyone ..." My voice dropped. "Not even Marty would consider it as evidence or consider Lynette/Clara as a suspect in anything."

Ron snapped Lynn's diary shut and fixed me with a penetrating stare. "Mom! I just can't believe you're mixed up in all this! Do you realize you could be in danger? Do you think that was her in the house, looking for this book? It must have been, but how does she know it's here? It's a good thing Faith and I are moving in to take care of you. I don't like this at all. I'm scared to death for you!"

"It's okay now, Ron. We'll call Brent and turn this book over to him, and the whole nightmare will be over. Once they have this evidence, they should be able to arrest Lynette ... as soon as they can find her. It's a confession written by her own hand, and she hasn't exactly been hiding," I added, thinking of her peremptory claim to Marty. "As long as she doesn't know for sure this book is here and she doesn't know we're on to her, she probably won't run. See, she burned Clint's cabin down to the ground, and –

Faith gasped and stared at me as if I were an exhibit in a freak show.

"Well, she can't possibly know for sure that the book is here," I explained to Faith and Ron. "She knows there's a chance it burned in the fire. I think Lynn only wanted to check to make sure, probably because I told her I've got proof."

"Mom! Have you lost your senses! Talk about dangerous games! You mean you bragged to that deranged girl that you have evidence against her? No wonder she broke in here looking!"

"I was trying to trick her into coming into the open."

"Well, it seems it worked," he said dryly.

"So that's what happened to Prissy," Faith said softly and sadly, shaking her head and sighing. "How can a person be so utterly evil? How sad. How terribly, terribly sad." She pulled her cell phone out of her purse and handed it to me.

I called the personal phone number Brent had given me. Time was crucial. Something inside Lynette's mind was as twisted as a live rattlesnake on a skewer ... and more dangerous.

Apparently, the sheriff agreed with my deduction. Even though it was Saturday and he was one of the Chili

Cook-Off judges, he said he would pick up Deputy John Dion and come out to the ranch immediately. "Don't do anything, Mike, until I get there. Just sit still. You say Ron and Faith are there with you? Good. They can keep an eye on you until I get there."

What none of us knew, though, was that it was already too late to stop the advancement of evil that had found a creeping, slithering vehicle in the outwardly beautiful shell of a young woman named Lynette Clarissa Greene.

Alex climbed up on the bench of the picnic table next to us, and Ron planted a kiss on his head. "What's that in your hand, son?" he asked.

"Candy."

"Candy!" Faith exclaimed. "Where did you get candy? Did you have that hidden, young man? You know Dad doesn't want you eating candy in the truck."

"I got it from the nice lady," Alex said, taking another bite. "She gave it to me and Ryan, but I was a good boy. I didn't get into the car with her like Ryan. I told Ryan not to, but he did anyway. He wanted the candy."

For a stunned moment, we sat in paralyzed fear. Then the cell phone in Ron's truck jingled. He used the phone for work, and the number for his sign-painting business was painted on the door of the truck. Ron jumped up and ran to the truck, swinging the door open and yanking the phone from its holder.

Faith and I were right behind him and crashed into him when he stopped.

A clear female voice laughed chillingly. "Mike, I know you can hear this. You thought you were hidden from me in that closet, didn't you? But you started to open the door before I left. Not very smart, Mike. It tells me something. It tells me you found that book I left with Clint, that it didn't burn in the fire. Well, Mike, if you want this kid back, you'll get the book back to me without showing it to anyone else – especially Brent. Oh, and, Mike, I will know if you cheat. If you do, the kid will get this." The phone crackled, and her voice, fainter now, said, "Cry, kid."

Ryan let out a yowl of pain, and his pregnant mother fainted right on the spot.

Chapter 12.

Faith had crumpled to the ground in a twisted heap among leaves and dirt when she fainted. Ron and I dropped down on the ground beside her, inspecting her for injuries. Dirt and leaves clung to her long, wavy, light brown hair. Her long face, with its greyhound nose, was alarmingly pale. Other than that, she seemed sound. She groaned, and her green eyes flew open. "No!" she whispered.

Ron brushed his fingers lightly across his wife's face. "Yes," he said, almost as softly, "but don't forget our secret weapon. Ryan is protected."

"Jesus," Faith breathed. A slight smile lifted the corners of her lips. "Oh, Ron!" Tears slid down the sides of her face, mingling with the dirt and leaves in her hair.

I helped her sit up, then threw my arms around her. "You are beautiful," I told my daughter-in-law ... and I meant it.

"Mom," she said with a shaky laugh, "imagine you saying a thing like that at a time like this! And me with my skirt hiked up in the air and leaves and dirt all over me!"

"I should have told you a long time ago," I replied, hugging her fiercely after Ron and I had helped her to her feet. "You are a quintessential person, a marvelous wife to Ron –

"Amen to that!" my son interjected, kissing the top of his wife's dusty head and brushing leaves gently off her shoulders.

"And a terrific mom to those boys."

Tears glazed a shine on Faith's pale cheeks. "Yeah," she said bitterly. "Such a terrific mom that I wasn't paying any attention to the boys while one of them was kidnapped. It's all my fault!" Her voice rose in desperation.

Ron took her roughly into his arms. "None of us were watching the boys," he said. "This is the country – Three Prongs, for heaven's sake! It's supposed to be a safe place to live and raise our family. That's why we're moving here, remember? You're not supposed to have to keep your eyes glued to the children every moment. What happened is as out of character for this place as Mom would be if she minded her own business. Now, listen ... no one could watch those boys closely enough to keep them out of danger with this twisted, evil Lynette/Clara person involved. Rational people like us are at a cruel disadvantage because our minds can't follow the serpentine path her mind takes. So quit blaming yourself. All of us, I know, are blaming ourselves right now, but that's wasting energy that we need to use to find Ryan. Right now, let's all agree to quit blaming ourselves – or, heaven forbid, each other. Let's get into the house and start planning our strategy while we wait for the sheriff."

Alex had started to cry softly, not realizing the virulent turn of events but intuitively sensing danger. Ron swung the boy up to his shoulder and led us, a somber, tearful troop, into the house. Once inside, he paced through all the rooms, holding Alex snuggled to his chest. Faith stared out the front window with sightless, tear-washed eyes. I let the dogs out of the garage and sat mindlessly petting them as we waited for Sheriff Cruz to arrive. When he did, it was me who fell to pieces.

Ron handed Lynette's diary to Brent. Suddenly remembering her threats, I jumped up from the couch, pushing the dogs away, and snatched the book from Brent's hands. "You can't have this!" I yelled into the startled room. "She'll know! She'll hurt Ryan! She won't give him back!"

The fear packed into those words alarmed Alex. Even Ron's arms could not comfort him. "I want Ryan," he sobbed. "I want Bubba back, my Bubba. Don't let that mean lady keep Bubba. Don't let her hurt him! He's sorry he didn't listen. He's sorry he took her candy. He didn't mean to go with her. I tried to stop him, but I couldn't hold on to him any tighter. She was too strong. I'm sorry I didn't hold on to him good enough."

All of the adults in the room, including Brent and John,

looked at each other in horror. If Alex had continued clinging to his little brother, Lynette would have kidnapped both boys.

"I should have hit that mean woman!" Alex said, suddenly fierce. "I knowed she was bad. Ryan didn't know 'cause he's just a baby. He didn't mean to do something bad. He didn't mean to."

Faith took Alex from Ron. "We know Ryan didn't mean to do anything wrong, Alex, and we know you tried to help." She kissed him. "Remember your favorite Bible stories? They remind us that God wants people to want to be good like Him, but He won't make people be good. God could have made people like puppets. Remember how you like to put your hands inside your puppets and make them talk and play together?"

Alex nodded. "I make my puppets do stuff to make Bubba laugh."

"Well," Faith explained, "God could have made all of us like puppets so we would have to be good and do whatever God tells us to, but God gave us a gift, Alex – the gift of getting to make choices. We get to decide if we will obey God and be good like God wants us to be or disobey Him and be bad."

Ron reached over and ruffled Alex's blond hair. "Your mom is right, son. God loves us, and He wants us to love Him, but God knows that if we were just puppets, we might only pretend to love Him. So God gave us the gift of making choices. That mean woman who took Ryan made a choice to be bad like Satan, who is God's enemy and our enemy too. Never forget that, Alex. The devil hates us and wants to hurt us. God loves us and wants to help us."

Alex rubbed his eyes and butted his head against Faith's shoulder. "She was mean to take our Bubba! She was bad! Why was she so mean and bad?"

That was a question all of us in the room wanted answered.

Faith kissed Alex again and held him tightly against her. "Alex, it's like your dad said. Satan is God's enemy, and that makes him our enemy. That woman – her name is Lynette – decided to be friends with the enemy instead of friends with God. That's why she's so mean. That's why she's done this bad thing, stealing your brother. But Ryan is God's friend. All of us in this room, including you, Alex, are God's friends. We're going to pray for your brother. That will make God's heart glad. Jesus will protect your brother and bring him back."

I loved my daughter-in-law fiercely at that moment. Having lost my best friend ceased to matter. Donna Johnson would likely have moved back to Georgia to take care of her elderly parents, even if Ron had married Irene. I dredged up a memory of Irene and decided that her face had worn the mask of a simpering young woman, not the inside-out loveliness that Faith's mature trust in God painted on hers. True, Faith's hair was not red, but of what importance was hair color? God judges the heart, not the outward appearance of His creations. God expects us to follow His example. I loved Faith's imperturbable faith. I loved the quiet assurance of spirit that settled an ambiance of peace over the room, touching all of us. Alex quit sobbing, and all of us, including Brent and John, clasped hands and prayed.

The others seemed calmer after the prayer, and I realized I was the miscreant of the family. I couldn't force myself to believe. For all my bright words of faith on paper, words that had spilled out of Pastor Garth Seymour's mouth over the years and had turned his series into a successful one, I discovered that I was really a hypocrite. My fear for my grandson rose up into my throat in swells of foul-tasting bile, and my insides quivered like startled daddy long leg spiders. My insides hurt from clenching and unclenching, and I tried to stop Brent from calling the San Antonio branch of the Federal Bureau of Investigation. "She'll kill Ryan," I whispered to him desperately. "You've seen the book and her confession about killing Julia. Just hide somewhere and let me give the book back to her and get Ryan back. Lynn won't know that anyone knows her terrible secret. After I get Ryan back, you can arrest her. You'll have the book and Lynette, and we'll have Ryan back. Doesn't that make sense, Brent?"

Gone was my kind friend of many years. The efficient lawman in Sheriff Brent Cruz brooked no opposition. He told Ron curtly to get me out of the room. He issued an Amber Alert on Lynette and Ryan, even though we didn't know whose car she was driving or what it looked like. Less than two hours later, everything – from having the phone lines tapped to having Ryan and Lynn's description floating out over the airwaves – had been completed, and a team of FBI agents were installed in the living room with us.

For the first time in my life, I discovered that prayer had frozen somewhere inside my body, chilled to an inert mass by fear. I felt like an empty caricature of myself. "We can't let her know," I kept insisting. "Lynette's no fool, and she's dangerous! We can't let her know she's walking into a trap!" But everyone was too busy to listen to me, and all my protests were swept aside like broken egg shells.

One of the FBI agents was examining the cover of the book. "Unusual," he said, noting the bright bird and flower pattern. "Too bad we couldn't pick one like this up in San Antonio and switch them, but it even has 'Alabama' written on it." He turned to Ron. "Son, do you have something like a carpet knife?" Armed with the sharp tool, the agent cut the pages out of the book and handed them to another agent to bag for evidence. He handed me the cover of the diary. "Go check around the house and see if you can find some pages to put in here so she won't notice that it's empty."

"She's not stupid!" I protested. "When she opens it –

He ignored my outburst. "We won't give her time to open it. As for you, just hurry. Don't get too far from the phone. When it rings, you have to be the one to answer it. Keep her on the line as long as you can so we can trace the call."

Fortunately, as a writer – who was now feeling like a debacle-creator and not a paper crime solver – finding pages the right size to fill the empty cover was not challenging. What was challenging was to pretend the same imperturbable qualities that the others seemed to be exercising. When the phone rang, I discovered that I was too paralyzed to answer it for so long that I was afraid Lynette would hang up. Then I pounced on the phone receiver so quickly that it clattered to the floor. I dove for it, aware of Brent's and Ron's frowns of disapproval. "Lynette!" I screeched, without waiting to make sure the caller was really her. "Lynette, don't go away! Don't take Ryan! Don't hurt him! I'll do anything you say! Just don't hurt my grandbaby!"

If the caller had not been Lynette, my frantic words would have left him or her confused, but Lynn's silvery laugh – so deceitful in its sweetness – lacerated my eardrum. "Dear

Mike, the friend I never really had. I thought you would make the right choice."

"Keep her talking," Brent mouthed to me.

I tried to slow my erratic breathing and think of something useful to say. "Lynette, is Ryan okay? Is he with you?"

She laughed again, that sharp-toothed serpent in the curvaceous form of a lovely woman. "Mike, I'm disappointed in you. As clever as I am, do you think I would be irresponsible enough to leave a young child unattended? Of course I have the brat. He's my insurance policy." She must have turned towards Ryan, because her voice grew more distant. "Speak to your grandma, kid." For a moment, there was silence, and Lynette repeated the command.

Suddenly, Ryan screamed.

I nearly dropped the phone.

Ron grabbed me and steadied me as tears blazed trails down my face.

"Lynn!" I whispered horrified. "Don't hurt him!"

Lynette laughed. "Stopping me is a bit difficult at your distance, isn't it, Mike? Don't forget that. I've made up my mind to ask for a ransom for this kid to go along with the return of my diary. Thanks to you meddling in other people's business, Mike, I've lost all the riches I expected to get from Thor. He's turned against me and is trusting that wormy-looking kid of his. You got me kicked off his ranch, Mike. You, with your infernal meddling! It's a shame you didn't just mind your own business. Thor was a lot older than me, but he was a good catch – an attractive man and oh so rich! The house was so beautiful. I felt so elated to walk about in that place that my sister had decorated so lovingly, never expecting that I was smart enough to come along and take it away from her.

"But I did! I almost had it all. I would have had it all if you hadn't interfered and messed things up. I planned this for years – probably since I was a kid, when they got married and I saw his picture and pictures of the ranch. I wanted him even then – even when I was too young to know what to do with a man or what a man could do for me. Then you came along and screwed it up, Mike. So don't expect me to be kind to this kid on your account. I owe you big time. Hurting the kid, knowing it hurts you, will give me great pleasure, Mike. And since you've robbed all the other pleasures from me, this one is about the only one I have left. So you better listen to me about my diary, because I might find that I really enjoy making the brat scream. Since I have the kid and you don't know where I am, I don't think you or anyone else can stop me!"

"God can ... and will." My frozen faith thawed suddenly, coursing warmly through my chilled body like electric heat. I believed. I could trust again! God was still in control, even though I was not. God had never moved even a breath away from me. I had just forgotten to reach out and touch Him. But now I remembered! Anger against Lynette fired frozen faith, and it flowed freely, pulling my shoulders erect and flashing fire in my eyes.

Even Ron noticed the change in me. He came softly across the room and clasped a hand on my shoulder, smiling down into my face from his trim height.

One of the FBI agents nodded, and everyone smiled. They had a fix on Lynette's location.

With quiet movements, police units were dispatched.

"Lynette," I said in a voice suddenly more like mine, "just tell me where to meet you. I have your diary here, and I can use my credit card to get cash for you up to my limit. I'll bring it to you immediately. Just don't hurt Ryan again. Please."

"I don't mind hurting kids," the nefarious creature whom I had once been blinded enough to covet for a daughter-in-law said, "especially your grandkid, but I do want that diary back, Mike. It has some embarrassing confessions in it – especially if I decide to hang on to Marty. Marty's a bit old fashioned, Mike. He has strange ideas about wrong and right and silly trammels like not boozing and getting married. So here's the deal. Meet me at that deserted house outside Three Prongs – you know the one I mean. It's the only empty house in Three Prongs, a house that will stay empty because it's been gutted by fire and attracts snakes and rats – even big rats like you, Ms. Michal Rice. Oh, and bring cash. I want $10,000 in cash so I can make my escape after you get the kid back. How you get the money is your problem. Don't show up without it, or you will really hear the brat scream."

The phone clicked.

I gasped and grabbed my purse, prepared to run out to the borrowed talking car.

Brent held me back. "She called from a pay phone booth at the far edge of town. Wait a minute and see if we got someone there in time to pick her up. If we didn't, you go. We won't let her see us, and we won't let you go into danger."

"She wants $10,000 in cash," I lamented. "I haven't got ten dollars to take with me, and I don't really have a credit card. I cut them all up a long time ago so I wouldn't be tempted to overspend. I just told her that so she wouldn't hurt Ryan again. It's Saturday! How am I going to get the money? And if I don't –

"We're going to get Lynette Greene before you turn over the diary or any money," one of the FBI agents assured me, "if we miss her in town at the phone booth. We should know that within a few minutes. Just hang in there, Miss Rice. Everything's under control."

But it wasn't. Lynette had somehow slipped away from the phone booth and disappeared. Faith bravely fought back new tears when she heard that the insane woman was still on the run with her little boy.

I sprinted to the car, my shadows close behind. For the safety of the child, they had promised to remain invisible while I kept the meeting with the bat-fowled human pretending to be a lovely young woman.

My insides spun like a washing machine wringing water out of clothes as the fire-darkened building rose up through its screen of wildly overgrown vegetation. Snakes! Spiders! Rats! Creepy, crawling things jumping out of a nightmare and walking through the empty building during daylight hours. I shuddered. I didn't want to get anywhere near the house, yet, strangely, I was more frightened of Lynette Clarissa Greene and what she might do to Ryan than I was of possible wildlife intruders.

Forgetting to watch out for snakes or spiders, forgetting even to look and make sure I had been discretely followed by law enforcement, I parked the car in the patch of weedy driveway in front of the house. I threw the door of the car open and almost fell out of the driver's seat in my haste. I regained my balance and battled through overgrown weeds with a vengeance calculated to scare both rats and snakes lurking in their possible habitation.

Yelling for Ryan, I frantically searched outside the fire-chewed house, then ran inside. Not even the skittering

noises of scattering critters as my feet hit rotten floorboards stopped me from zipping through broken rooms
of the house shouting. The house was empty. Blinded by
tears, I nearly missed the scrap of white paper fluttering on the end of a rusty nail near what had once been a
kitchen door.

Mike, the neatly rounded writing warned, *you blew it.
You told someone. I almost got caught making that phone
call to you.*

I gasped in horror: Ryan had been so close to safety, yet
so far away!

Now, Lynette had written, *you may never see the brat
again. It all depends on if you pass this test. You know by
now that neither the kid nor I are here in the house. We never
were. Since you blew it when I called you, I had to give you
a test. For the sake of the brat, I hope you've passed. I hope
no one has followed you. I'm watching to see.*

With renewed cries for Ryan, I crashed outside the
ruins, almost running over one of the officers following me
in my haste. "Get away!" I shouted at him rudely, waving
the paper. "She's watching us! She's a murderer! She'll kill
our baby!"

Brent materialized from overgrown vegetation and took
me by the shoulders. "Hush," the big man ordered. "Mike,
we need your help since she seems determined to get back
at you. You are apparently the only one she's willing to talk
to at the moment, but if you can't keep it together, we can't
use you. Get a grip. If she's in the area, we'll get her. We
have officers crawling through this overgrown mess right
now. I don't believe she's here. I think she just wants to
scare you, and she's succeeded. Now, Mike, can we count
on you to calm down and help?

"You need to get back to your house and wait for her
to call again. She's bound to. She's not the type of woman
to enjoy babysitting, and she needs money to make her
escape since Thor kicked her out. Also, of course, she
wants her diary back. It contains a confession of murder,
and considering the fact that she wanted to steal Thor's
ranch and wealth, that could even be legally construed
as 'murder while in the commission of a felony' – a capital
murder offense. It would slap her on death row, in line for a
lethal injection. We can get her without your help. We're all
trained and efficient, but it would be easier with you. Now,

do you think you can pull yourself together and help us? I've seen you come through some pretty sour pickles over the years, Mike. I think you can take this one in stride."

I nodded and dug tears out of my eyes with the corner of my t-shirt so I could see.

"Are you calm enough now to drive?" Brent asked gently, releasing my shoulders and drumming his fingers against his chin. "If not, you can leave the car here and –

"I'm fine!" I assured him hastily. "She might come back here to check. She said it was a test. If the car is here, she'll know I wasn't alone. Besides, she knows where I live. She could even check up on me there." I grabbed Brent's arm. "She's dangerous," I breathed. "She's a cruel, heartless, dangerous woman. I'm frightened of her. I'm frightened by what she's capable of doing."

"You won't get an argument from any of us about that," Brent assured me, "but you're a pretty special person to a lot of people, Miz Michal Rice. My priority right now is making sure that it's safe to let you get in your car."

"We have to have the car back to the ranch, where Lynette expects to see it."

"I can't picture her getting that close with all of us on guard, but perhaps you're right. Are you sure you're okay, Mike? As a lawman and as a friend, I can't let you get into a vehicle if you're not fit to drive it."

It was beyond my power at the moment to summon a brave smile, but I nodded again. Brent opened the door for me, and I slipped into the beige vehicle. "Thanks again for letting me borrow this car," I remembered to say.

Brent nodded. "As soon as we get all this behind us, Mike, Anna, and I will go car-shopping with you. That way you can get a good deal without getting ripped off. I'm no expert, but I know what to look for and what amounts to fair pricing and finance options. And, while we're in no hurry to get the car back, Anna thinks she may have a buyer for it."

"Brent, if you have the car sold –

"Don't give it a thought, Mike. We've got more important things to think about right now. When we know the car's sold for sure, we'll let you know. Meanwhile, treat it like it's yours. Considering how long you drove that old blue car of yours before you got mixed up in a murder mystery, I should say you know how to take care of a car."

I realized that Brent was keeping me there, holding a mundane conversation, while he judged my fitness to drive. He was a good lawman – and a good friend.

Thankful for many things, including good friends who could be counted on when they were needed most, I nodded at Brent, then backed the car carefully down the driveway that displayed its rutted trace briefly in random gravel patches between tall weeds and blooming wildflowers. I had always considered myself a careful driver, and I usually did my best not to crowd the speed limit to the point of reinventing it. However, knowing that several law enforcement vehicles were following me at a discrete distance made me nervous. My hands were wet on the steering wheel and my body felt clammy from a combination of fear and exertion-induced perspiration – more accurately, sweat.

Somehow, I made it home.

Ron and Faith took the news of Lynette's escape with Ryan more calmly than I had. "I don't believe she will hurt him," Ron assured me. "She's in so much trouble already. What she really wants is money. It's what she's wanted all along – what she came here to Three Prongs to get. I know she didn't ask for much ransom in exchange for Ryan, but she's probably counting on her good looks to get her in with some new guy somewhere else. She just wants enough to do some fast, trackless traveling."

"Besides," Faith added, "Jesus is protecting our baby. That's the most important fact. We can't forget that. If we do ..." Her lips trembled and tears glinted in sea-green eyes. "If we forget that, we'll all fall apart. We can't let that evil person win. If we lose hope and become helpless, she's won already." Faith stomped her foot. "I won't allow her to win!"

Waiting for the phone to ring again, I paced aimlessly through the house. Ron couldn't fault my lack of observance this time. I saw every nail print in the wooden trim, every scratch on the painted walls, every particle of dust on furniture. I knew I should find something constructive to do with my time, but my body refused obedience to my mind and continued its nonproductive strolling.

When the phone call finally came, I pounced on it with only a little more grace than before. "Lynette, where's Ryan? Why didn't you meet me at that creepy house?"

She laughed. "It's rather fun toying with you, Mike. You deserve to suffer like you've made me suffer. I could have had everything I ever wanted from Thornton Dean if you hadn't messed it up, sticking your nose where it didn't belong. But I'm getting tired of this kid. Here ... listen." She held the phone up to Ryan, and he screamed.

I gasped. My knees failed me, and I plopped down on the floor, managing to keep my grip on the phone. "Lynette, don't!"

"You passed the test at the house, Lynette."

Now I realized that the law enforcement officers had been correct: Lynette had been nowhere near the house.

"I'll give you another chance. Have you got my money?"

"Yes!"

"Good, Mike. You're smarter than you look. Now, you know that big bridge that doesn't go anywhere? The one where that nitwit Clint Flavors likes to go fishing?"

My heart thundered within my chest, almost deafening me. The bridge! The bridge to nowhere! It was only a few miles away if one approached it from the backside and crashed through the barricades. Ryan is so close! "I'll be right there."

"No, Mike, let me finish. Meet me there in ..." She considered. "Make it an hour ... and, Mike ..." Her voice was so cold and hard that chills shook my body again. "You'd better be alone, or you'll never see this kid again – not alive anyway."

Silence cut the connection, and all my yelling into the receiver resulted in dead quiet.

Ron grabbed me and shook me. "Mom! It's okay. They've got a trace on her again. Surely they can get someone to her before she slips away again."

"Slips is the operative word," Brent muttered darkly. "She's at another phone booth – in the next town! We weren't counting on that. There are so few pay booths anywhere anymore with cell phones. How on earth did she manage to find two of them in one day? We still don't know what Lynette Greene is driving, but we'll set up a roadblock and stop everyone. Hopefully, she doesn't know about the ranch roads that cut off from the main road. She shouldn't unless she and Thor did a lot of traveling together. She's not from here."

"But she was with Clint Flavors first. He knows every

back road in the county!" I exclaimed.

"Maybe, but he doesn't have a car," Brent reminded me. "She doesn't strike me as one to go for riding on the back of a bicycle. Besides, she was hiding out when she was with him. In any event, we'll get her."

But for all of Brent's assurance, they didn't. Word bounced back to us within thirty minutes that no one had spotted Lynette or anyone who looked like her. Cars had been stopped, children had been eyed, but none of the stops had yielded either Lynn or Ryan. They seemed to have evaporated just as surely as water from Old Lake.

"Listen carefully, Miss Rice," one of the agents said, "we'll hit that road from the opposite direction you'll be taking. If she gets on that road, we've got her. We'll have her tailed to your location." He looked at Brent. "You'll have to give my men directions."

"I'll take you there," Brent said with steely determination.

The agent nodded. "We're going now. We'll stash the vehicles and get out of sight. Now, Miss Rice, you just meet her there at the agreed time and don't do anything foolish. We're dealing with a dangerous person – perhaps a mentally unstable one. You could get seriously injured."

"Just so she doesn't hurt Ryan."

"Can't I go?" Faith whispered. "Ryan's bound to be frightened and upset. He needs his mother. I'm not afraid of that monster!"

Ron grinned and hugged his wife. "I can keep Alex here with me," he told Brent. "Since y'all have this figured right down to stashing your vehicles out of sight, what would it hurt if the boy's mother went with you to calm him? She would be out of sight too." He laughed. "And, if you find you need reinforcements, just turn this angry mother loose on Miss Lynette Greene. I think my wife would tear her from horn to hoof, like a jungle cat."

The officers consulted briefly, then bundled Faith out to one of their vehicles.

I sighed in relief. After Lynette's cruel, heartless treatment, Ryan would need all the comfort he could get. I was thankful that Faith would be there for him – and for me.

Time, which usually shot past me like a horse race, turning me around in a melange of confusion, plodded on turtle legs. Ron pulled me back every time I attempted to shoot out the door after the officers had left. One agent stayed behind to protect Alex and Ron in case Lynette suddenly changed her plans and returned to the ranch. Lynette had called Clint Flavors a "nitwit" and had made fun of him after having used him for her deadly game. She was a frightening creature because something inside her mind was as ruined and twisted as old barbed wire. She was also as unpredictable as the twist and turns in a broken barbed-wire fence. The only name I could think of to call her was "evil," and even that could not encompass the bat-fowling scorpion strumpet who called herself Lynette Clarissa Greene.

Even with Ron's intervention, I arrived at the bridge ten minutes early. Every buzzing insect rang painfully in my ears, like music from a hard rock band. Even the sun sliding through the sky over the empty expanse of bridge seemed to radiate with noise. My body ached from tension, and my throat was so constricted that I could barely swallow my own spit.

I looked around a bit uneasily. No vehicles were in sight, and I felt alone and unprotected. Is anyone else really at the bridge with me? I thought about searching, but was afraid I might accidentally give away their location to Lynette if I knew where they were hidden.

Finally, I spotted Lynn approaching – at least, I figured it must be her since the bridge had yet to open to traffic and the approaching trail of dust came from the direction of Three Prongs. Somehow, she had stolen Thor's little red car again. Idly, as I waited for her to reach me, I wondered if Thor knew the car was missing. As the car drew closer, I ran for it and was nearly hit by Lynn as she braked to a stop. She did not have Ryan with her; Lynette was alone in the car.

Chapter 13.

Tears broke out all over my face. I pounded on the hot metal roof with my fists. "Where's Ryan? What have you done with him?"

Lynette laughed up at me through the open window of the car. "Now, Mike, your grandson – brat that he is – is okay. I haven't hurt him, except just a little when I needed him to scream for me to make you listen good. I told you that brat's my insurance policy."

"Ryan is not a brat. If you want me to listen to you, you better quit calling my grandson a brat. He's a blessing from God, a gift to his parents and to me – not that a twisted, evil person like you would know anything about God's gifts, Lynette Clarissa Greene. I'm almost sorry for you."

She blinked at me as if I were a fragment of sleep that could be whisked out of her corroded imagination. "Whatever. Don't feel sorry for me, big-shot writer Michal Rice. I'm the one with the kid. I can get him back to you within an hour, but I don't intend to hand him over until I have my diary, the money, and know that I haven't been followed. I see you have everything I asked for. Give it to me."

And then I did something totally out of character for me – or perhaps I was acting like any child-bereaved human. I jerked the door of the car open, grabbed the startled girl by her striped Western shirt and hauled her out of the car. When she scratched and tore at me, trying to release herself, I gave her a mighty shove that tumbled her painfully across the concrete floor of the bridge. Blouse material covering her elbows tore, and she yelped in pain as the hard surface of the bridge abraded her skin. Before she could recover her footing, and before I could leap on her and scratch her face and pound her head against the concrete – which I fully intended to do – Brent and one of the agents tore out of the cedar brake beside the bridge and clapped handcuffs on her. When she spat at them, I tried to get in at her and slap her face for that rudeness, but I found myself restrained by Brent.

"Easy, Mike," he said in a grim voice. I knew the grimness was directed at the nefarious, bat-fowled human-pretender Lynn and not at me. "Don't forget, you're a lady. She's not. She doesn't know any better. Don't sink to her level."

"Too bad you betrayed me, Mike," Lynette said acidly. "Now you'll never get the brat back. I won't tell anyone where he is. You can lock me up, but you can't force me to talk."

"You won't have to," Brent informed her. "Now that we have you, we'll test your clothes to find out where you've been. That will give us a pretty good idea of where you've been hiding Ryan. We can study the plant fibers and seeds we find on your clothes under a microscope and match them to the area in the county where they grow. We don't need your help. We can recover Ryan using scientific techniques. You might think of Three Prongs as a backwater town, Miss Greene, but we are privy to big-city law enforcement techniques. The game's over for you. You've lost. You might as well save yourself a lot of trouble and save us a lot of time by telling us where we can find the boy."

Lynette laughed scornfully. "The game's not over for me, and I intend to cause you all the trouble I can, not save you time. I can get a good attorney, and he'll prove that diary Mike has wasn't real – just me letting off steam, an exercise of my imagination … to keep me sane." It was chilling to hear Lynette Clarissa Greene call herself sane. "But if my attorney doesn't win my case, I might wind up on death row. So what do I have to lose? You can only kill me once. I have no incentive to cooperate." She batted her eyelashes at Brent. "Unless you big guys want to give me an incentive. Then I'll think about telling you where the kid is. Oh, I'm sure you can find him with all your scientific techniques, but that will take time, won't it? And where I left the little brat, he doesn't have that much time." She tossed her head defiantly as she was lowered into the caged back seat of the patrol car.

My knees fell out from under me, and I was the second human casualty on the bridge to nowhere. I had forgotten that Faith had come in Brent's car. She was apparently being held out of sight until Lynette had been captured. Faith suddenly tore out of the bushes beside the bridge and flew across the concrete to me. She dropped down on her knees beside me on the heated cement and cradled me like a child. I clung to her. The two of us shared tears and comfort, then helped each other to our feet. "Come on, Mom," my brave daughter-in-law said stoutly. "We have work to do."

"Work?" I questioned weakly. My head wobbled around on my shoulders like a melting patch of ice cream on a Popsicle.

"We have to work on being strong in the Lord. This is war. I know we have troops fighting wars on foreign soils, and we pray for them daily, but this war is on our turf, and you and I have been enlisted to fight in it."

"I don't want to fight. I just want Ryan back. I just want to go back to where I've always been, minding my own business, and ..." I brightened suddenly. "Wait! You're right. This is war, and it's one war I can enlist in and no one can tell me to go back home because I'm too old. Being forty-something isn't old, but that's what they would tell me if I tried to enlist in the military."

Faith laughed. "Undoubtedly, but only because they don't know Michal Allison Rice like God does ... and like her family does."

Brent had overheard Faith, and he chuckled. "I don't know, Faith. I believe I would hire your mother in my department. Sticking her nose in other people's business has sure led to some interesting developments around these parts. Life without her here in the country would sure be dull."

"I never stick my nose in other people's business," I protested. "I wish Ron would quit spreading those rumors about me, his own mother! That wicked Lynn creature came right to the house and stole Ryan. I wasn't –

Brent held up his hands. "Okay, Mike, chill." He turned to one of the FBI agents and explained, "That's what our kids are always telling us." Then he turned back to include Faith and me in the conversation. "Now let's figure out where everyone needs to go from here and what the next action needs to be. There's no point in any of us lawmen returning to your house, Mike, with Lynette in custody. She won't be calling you again. I guess we need to map out a radius within an hour of here and start the search there, since she said she could have Ryan to you within an hour."

"An hour?" Faith said in horror. "That could be anywhere in this county and several more besides – even San Antonio is less than an hour from where we are standing right now. How will you find him?" Faith's lips trembled, and tears seeped out of the corners of her eyes.

It was my turn to comfort her, and I was thankful the two of us had each other at that devastatingly painful moment in time.

The FBI agent who had been the first to arrive at the ranch surveyed the wide concrete expanse spanning the Three Prongs River. "Where does this bridge go?" he asked in amazement. "I don't even see any houses out there."

Brent chuckled. "Even a small town like ours is prone to political embarrassments at times. Miss Mike here calls this the bridge to nowhere, and that's a pretty apt name for it. Voters were so outraged by the money spent to construct it that they elected a new county judge and commissioners' court all in one election. Reckon if I'd been in on it, I'd have been impeached. Anyway, it's a shortcut to town." Brent smiled at me and winked. "Some unknown person we've yet to catch has already discovered that by trespassing."

The agent looked mystified.

Brent pointed to the barricades. "Someone in a big car sort of nosed everything out of the way and took the bridge. The Texas Department of Transportation put up money for the bridge, and our county matched the grant. The grand opening is scheduled two weeks from now – a big shindig." He fixed a stern look on me. "The concrete is still curing at the moment."

I felt redness creeping over my face, even though I was unable to see the betraying color myself. Faith treated me to that quiet, measured look of hers that let me know she had guessed my involvement but wasn't going to tell anyone. God had blessed me with this daughter-in-law that He had chosen for me, because I would not have been wise enough to choose her for myself.

The agent chuckled. "Well, I should think that barri-cade-busting is a bit out of our jurisdiction. Let's go find the boy." He doffed his hat in my direction. "For now, we'll let these young ladies go home. Then we'll sit down with you in your office and map out that search. What about volunteers? Does your county have any who'd be willing to help?"

"I imagine people with scanners have already ener-gized our volunteer emergency medical service and fire departments and they are waiting for a word from us to get started. This county's backbone was hammered in by volunteers. Thankfully, that seems to be an inheritance that gets passed down to each new generation."

The FBI agent nodded. "That's great. We depend on that in our line of work. Honest, helpful volunteers in Small Town USA."

"God-fearing," Faith said decisively.

All of us nodded.

Brent came over to us and put one sturdy hand on each of our shoulders. "Mike, are you settled down enough to drive?"

I nodded, hoping that was true. Each time I had a flash-back of Lynette sprawled on the pavement of the bridge, I felt a renewed desire to leap on top of her and pummel her head against the concrete. I had never known before that I possessed such a vicious streak in my character or could be moved to such acts of violence.

"You take Faith back to her husband and son. I'll be in touch with y'all at the ranch and let you know our plans. Even though she sounded defiant, we may be able to convince Ms. Greene that it's in her best interests to just tell us where Ryan is."

I shook my head but didn't voice my doubt: Lynette Clarissa Greene would tell them nothing. Behind bars, revenge was the only action she would have the freedom to exercise. She planned to punish me for ruining her future with Thornton Dean and Marty Richards. I suspected that her warped mind had written herself into a drama in which I was the villain and nothing she had done had been her fault.

Faith drew me towards the waiting vehicle. "Sheriff Cruz is right, Mom. Let's get home to Ron and Alex. We can't do anything here, and Ron will want to know what's happened." Tears squeezed out of her eyes. "I wish I didn't have to tell him. I mean, I wish what I had to tell him was completely different." Her voice broke. "I wish I was taking our baby home to him!"

"We both wish that," I breathed, slipping an arm around her. "In fact, Brent was right. I'm sure there's a whole community wishing that right now. They'll help, Faith. You'll see. I imagine people will be out searching for Ryan within an hour. We'll find him. You and Ron can stay with me until –

"No. If I know Ron, he'll go back to work Monday so he won't let his crew down. He loves Ryan as much as any of us, but we can't all sit around waiting for the phone to ring. That would be ridiculous."

Sudden decision stiffened within me, drawing my body up into a rigid line. I knew what I intended to do. My abrupt intent didn't even swing close enough to sitting around waiting for the phone to ring to swish a draft across such idleness. I remembered that I had left Clint and Jared at the Chili Cook-Off. Needing to pick them up and bring them back to the ranch would work right into my planned action.

Faith and I faced Ron together. I knew my son loved his family, but until I saw his over-six-foot frame collapse in grief, I had never realized how deeply. It was the first time I had seen Ron awash in tears since he was a five-year-old and had put his pet grasshopper in with a pet preying mantis, not understanding that the smaller insect "preyed," not "prayed."

Realizing that it was Faith's job to comfort Ron as a wife, not my job to comfort him as a mother, I left the two of them alone and took Alex up into my lap. I rocked with him held tightly against my chest while I read his favorite story to him. When the phone rang, I almost dropped him in my haste to answer it. My heart hammered under my ribs so violently that I was as breathless as if Marty had just walked onto the stage of my life and kissed me. "Hello?"

"Mike, this is Don."

"Don who?"

There was a moment of silence on the other end of the line.

"Don, Donna Johnson – your best friend Don. Or have I been replaced already?" she asked playfully.

"Don? Oh, Don … I'm glad you called." I told her about Ryan's kidnapping.

"Mike! No wonder you were so out of it. I can't even imagine what you're going through – no, I can. That's what makes it so scary. Look, Mike. I want to be there for you. That's what best friends are for. I can help. You said volunteers are going to search, right? I'll get a flight out tonight or in the morning. Don't worry about picking me up at the airport. You've got too much on your plate as it is. I'll rent a car at the airport. If you're still driving that old blue hunk of metal, I'd feel more comfortable in a rental car anyway."

"Old Blue got shot at – killed by the same lunatic who swiped Ryan."

"Say what?"

"Never mind. It's a long story. I'll tell you some other time. But everyone's safe now. They caught the sheep-biting, toad-spotted strumpet. Oh, Don, it's great that you want to come. I'd love to see you again. I've missed you, girlfriend. But don't come for this. I mean, I hope we will have already found Ryan by the time you get here, then you'll be making the trip for nothing."

"You call visiting together and renewing our friendship nothing? I'll be there, Mike. Expect me when you see me. Bye, darling."

I hung up the phone, more alarmed than relieved. The ranch house was bursting at the seams already with extra people. Where will I stash one more? But, oh, to see Donna again!

"Is it …?" Faith whispered, afraid to finish the question.

Ron stood behind his wife, his broad hands resting gently on her shoulders.

"I'm sorry," I told the anxious parents. "It wasn't about Ryan. It was an old friend. She's coming for a visit and to help look for Ryan if he hasn't already been found before she gets here."

"Donna Johnson?" Ron hazarded. When I nodded, he explained glibly to Faith, totally unaware of the antagonism that had sprung up between best friends because of his actions. "She's Mom's best friend. She had a pretty redheaded daughter whom Mom wanted me to marry. If you hadn't come along in time to rescue me, I guess I would have married Irene Johnson. Something tells me that would have been a disaster, though, so thanks for coming along when you did, Faith. I think Donna was a bit put out about it at the time, but I'm sure she will have forgiven me by now."

Donna wasn't the only one put out about it, but Ron could not be expected to know that since, minding my own business as was characteristic of me, I had never told him.

Ron wound a thick strand of Faith's hair around his finger playfully. "I'm sure Irene recovered quickly and completely and is happily married to the man God intended her to find in the first place. I know God has given me the most amazing wife in the world in you, honey."

Even with my best friend's voice echoing through my memory, I could almost agree with Ron. "Look," I told my fully grownup kids, "I have to go to Three Prongs to pick up Clint and Jared. I almost forgot them. I left them at the Chili Cook-Off with Bea."

"Couldn't Bea bring them home?" Ron asked. "So you can stay here with us? You've had a horrendous enough day already. I don't think you need more stress."

"Bea could bring them, and if she calls, please have her do that."

"I thought you said you were going –

"I am, but I want to look for Ryan along the way."

"Mom," Ron said, his eyebrows lifting questioningly, "where in heaven's name are you going to look for him? If you know anything about where he might be, you better call Sheriff Cruz. It's his job right now, not yours."

"Finding Ryan is everyone's job right now … and as quickly as possible. I don't know where he is, but I know of a place where I want to search."

"Mom, where? You must tell us! What if you get hurt? What if you get lost? Faith and I can't handle any more lost family members right now. We're fighting to keep from falling apart now, even with you in plain sight."

"That deserted house just out of Three Prongs. Don't worry."

"I'm worried already, and you haven't even left. Mom, I wish you wouldn't. I don't think it's a good idea."

"Lynette can't hurt me. She's locked up. I'll be fine."

"Mom, I can't let you go running off into danger like this –

But Faith put a hand gently on Ron's cheek. "Darling, let her go. You know Mike. She can't just sit here doing nothing. It would drive her crazy. A lot of people are going to be looking for Ryan. I'm sure Mom will be fine. She'll probably run into other searchers."

I smiled at Faith, finding myself more thankful for her by the moment. I fled to the aggravating talking car before Ron could voice any further objections. I was still a bit sore from my impact with the bridge, and I noted a few scratches on my legs, but I was ready for action. In fact, I realized with amazement that I not eaten all day, and I hadn't even thought of food! If I keep this up, I might be able to beat my forty-something body into a reasonable shape and condition that would be more appealing to Marty. Visions of M&Ms in bright, glorious colors kept my mind occupied up until the ugly torn hulk of building rose up out of its hiding place amongst the trees. I parked the car and approached the building carefully. Clumps of prickly pear cactus had miraculously attached themselves to what was left of the abandoned house's roof. I paused briefly, wondering how the cacti had achieved such height. Then I ventured into the unstable hulk.

The late afternoon sun slanted across the fire-bitten ruins, throwing bars of light and dark across the rotting floor. I stepped carefully, calling Ryan softly and listening intently for any answer. Room by room, I searched for any clue that my earlier haste might have hidden from my eyes. With the scrap of paper removed from the nail, the ruins had nothing to tell me.

Outside the building, I fought my way through choking vegetation, still calling Ryan. Several deer crashed away through the brush in front of me, but no small boy answered my call.

I pushed deeper into the woods. Like so many places in the Texas Hill Country, juniper had staged a campaign for the land and won. The cedar trees branched out broadly, clear down to the ground and laced brittle, scratching branches to the sky, shutting out sunlight. Feeling every bit of forty-something, I dropped to my knees and crawled through the unfriendly maze of juniper. I called Ryan but quickly decided that I was wasting precious time. Lynette would never have plunged through that saucy, warped forest to hide Ryan. She was too careful of her beauty to expose herself to the slapping limbs and thrusting branches. I felt like throwing myself under the low limbs, where I would be safely hidden from human eyes, and venting the storm of tears and despair collecting in my emotions like dark clouds.

Remembering that fire ants searched for motionless targets, I crawled instead back towards the car. At least I hoped that was the direction my low crawl was taking me. With the sun flirting with the blue-rimmed hills and the juniper warding off any subdued light left in the sky, I couldn't be sure. I knew I had to make it back to the car: Ron would never forgive me for getting lost and adding to everyone's worries. Come to think of it, I wouldn't forgive myself. What if my selfish decision to search for Ryan on my own costs the searchers – mostly volunteers – to be pulled off a search for Ryan to look for me? To make matters worse, as was typical, I had forgotten the cell phone, a useful communication tool that Ron had purchased for my safety in his flawed deductions that his mom stuck her nose in other people's business and could easily get into trouble as a result.

Frantically, I beat the brush above my head and around my abundant body and fought my way into a clearing. Dust and cedar pollen rained around me, hazing my face and making me sneeze.

A lanky, emerald-green snake slipped through the grass in front of me, stopping briefly and raising round pupils in an effort to identify the human intruder in its path. I had heard that except for coral snakes in the U.S., snakes with round pupils were always harmless. Certainly the snake seemed to have no desire to get close enough to me to bite, but I had even less of a desire to tread the same ground with the green serpent. I crashed back through the weeds, hammering heart and heaving chest, and practically fell over the hood of the parked car. Cedar limbs had reached out to slap me in the face and yank my hair. I could feel welts inching up along the sides of my face. I put my hand up and felt my hair; it stood out all over my head, held stiffly captive on broken juniper limbs.

I had spent longer in my fruitless search than I had intended. I was sure Jared and Clint would probably wonder why I had deserted them, unless Bea had thought to call the house. I tried to brush dirt and debris off my person and my clothes. Then, pulling a few of the cedar pin-like sticks out of my hair, I slid into the car and headed to the Chili Cook-Off.

Most of the booths had already been dismantled, and Bea and her crew where taking apart the newspaper stand.

Clint saw me first and danced in excitement, holding up a first place showmanship trophy. "We won, Miz Rice!" he exclaimed. "And we done wonned a second place for the chili." He threw a sideways look at Thornton Dean. "Even if him didn't use my mama's recipe, he makes good chili. He says I work good, and I'm gonna work for him from now on."

I managed a smile for Clint's benefit and nodded.

Bea turned around and glared at me. "It's about time, Mike. Thanks for nothing! That was very rude of you to run out on us without even an explanation, but we managed quite well without you. And where on earth have you been? You look like something the cat dragged in and the dog was afraid to touch." She motioned me away from the booth. "Don't get near the chili until we get it stored in a container with a lid on it. What a mess you are! Stay back so you don't drop trash into our award-winning chili that you were supposed to help us with and didn't."

Somehow, Nat recognized what my disheveled appearance portended. "Hush," he said, grabbing Bea's arm briefly. "Something's wrong – bad wrong. Mike, what is it? What happened?"

Jared and Thor stopped taking apart the booth and crowded around me.

I sank into a lawn chair and burst foolishly into tears. When I tried to wipe the tears away so I could answer, salty wetness that stung the scratches on my cheeks mingled with dust and painted muddy streaks across my face. "It's Ryan," I finally managed to explain. "She kidnapped him, and now we can't find him."

"Lynette/Clara ... whatever her name is?" Thor questioned through gritted teeth. "I'll kill her! I should have killed her when I found out what she did to Julia." He was shaking with rage.

Nat grabbed one of his arms in an attempt to calm him. "Please, Dad. Chill. Get a grip. Mike needs our help, not one more worry. Act like what you are, a good man who can be trusted in a crisis."

"Vinny?" Clint questioned piteously. The wiring in his brain was beginning to connect.

Work on the chili booth stopped while my friends gathered around to hear the entire story. The dusky hues of evening were dropping shadows over the hills by the time I finished.

"We'll all help in the search," Thor promised, speaking for everyone. "We'll get all this stuff put away and call the sheriff's department to see where we're needed most." He turned to Bea. "Why are we just now hearing about this?"

Bea bristled. "I'm just one person. I've been here all day, for heaven's sake. How am I supposed to know everything that happens? We don't have the scanner out here with us. I may run a newspaper, but even I take days off."

"Sorry, Bea. I didn't mean it that way. I'm not blaming you. I'm just trying to find out why no one's been around with the news already. I would think it'd be all over town."

"I don't think Brent wanted the news out until after they arrested Lynn," I told Thor. "People with scanners knew something was going on, but not the details. I think volunteers from the fire department and EMS know now and are busy organizing. Brent was going to call them and get search parties lined up."

Thor clapped his hands. "Okay, everyone. Let's go! We've got to get this mess picked up and stowed away so we can help. Bea, I imagine you're going to keep the trophy at the office so everyone can see it. How about this leftover chili? Besides having proven itself to be award winning, it's just doggone good. It should be refrigerated."

"Send it with Mike," Bea said readily. "I doubt she and her family have had the time or inclination to think about food and cooking."

"Clint," Thor said, "I know you were planning on staying with Miz Mike until Monday, but I need you out at the ranch now. You can come with Nat and me wherever we search. I'll get hold of Buddy Turner. Since he's quit drinking, he's become more reliable. He knows the county like the back of his hand. He might have some good ideas where to look. Besides, Clint, Ron and Faith will probably be spending the rest of the weekend with Mike. They probably need more room."

Clint nodded importantly. "I can help twice. I can help look, and I can give them family of Miss Mike's my bed."

Thor smiled at Clint. "Good. That will be a double help, just like you said." He turned to me. "I don't mean to be highhanded, Mike. Is that okay with you?"

I nodded and smiled at Clint. "Thanks for wanting to help me, Clint. I will miss you, but Thor is right. I do need the extra bed. Also," I paused, remembering, "Thor, you remember Don Johnson, don't you?"

"Your other best friend besides me?" Bea asked. "Your son was going to marry her daughter, wasn't he?"

"Yes. I thought I was the only one who'd remember that. Anyway, Don called today. I told her about Ryan, and she's flying in to help search. She should be here tonight or in the morning. So, Clint, thank you for being so thoughtful. I do need extra space with her coming and Ron and Faith and Alex already there."

"I can stay with Zolly," Jared offered.

I managed to drag up a shaky laugh and shook my head. I hugged Jared. "Thanks, but I think we can find room for you. Besides, if everyone leaves at one time, I think I'll be too lonely. It's been kind of nice having someone around to go home to."

Thor swept a glance up to Nat and smiled. "Isn't that the truth?" Nat smiled back at his father.

For a moment, deep peace tried to settle down into my spirit as I noted the quick play of affection between father and son. Ron might have accused me of meddling, but some good had sprung from that very fault – if it was, in fact, true. Then I remembered that Ryan was still missing and that daylight was folding into the nighttime canvas of Texas Hill Country. I panicked all over again. I leapt out of the lawn chair and paced frantically, twining my arms together and wrapping them across my chest. "I'll take you home," I told Jared. "Then I'll join one of the search parties."

"No. I'm going to stay in town and search now," Jared said, taking a defiant legs-parted stance. "I've been eating chili all day, and I'm stuffed. I don't need to go home with you to eat or anything. You need to do what Miss Hernandez says. You need to take that chili she's going to give you home with you and feed everyone and get some rest. I don't mean to be disrespectful, Miss Mike, but you look like a mess."

"Tuckered out for sure," Thor agreed. He picked up a heavy container of chili, opened up my folded arms, and plopped the container down into my hands. "Now you take this to the car, Mike. Nat, bring those left over tortillas. Good, son. Just put them in her car for her. Clint, what about those corn chips? Alex will probably like chili over corn chips. Okay, Mike, you're all set. Off you go." Thor directed me towards the car, as if I was a feckless child.

Still, I resisted his trundling and stood as if rooted to the spot, foolishly clinging to the still-warm container of chili. Mud and tears streaked my face. Limbs stuck out of my hair at improbable angles. My too-big, greenish eyes stared at nothing. I heard the horse and recognized it before I noticed the rider; it was the same horse that had thrown me during that electrical storm years ago. I reached up absently with one to pat its nose as it stopped in front of me. The container tilted against me in the other hand, dribbling wet, brown chili slime across my already mangled t-shirt. "You still around?" I asked the horse like an idiot. "I didn't know horses lived so long. Do you remember what you did to me? No, I suppose not. Well, if you're in on a search for Ryan, I forgive you."

"He's in the search, Mike. We both are. Someone has to be around to rescue you and look out for you with all those pickles you get yourself into."

With my ruined face flashing red embarrassment, I tilted my head and looked up into the grinning face of my neatly pristine idol, Marty Richards.

Chapter 14.

After we put Alex to bed on time, all of us – Ron, Faith, and I – swore to each other that we were too bruised by the maelstrom of emotions unleashed by Ryan's abduction to sleep. As predicted by Thor, Alex had enjoyed his dinner of chili over corn chips. The rest of us ate mechanically, mostly to fill in some of the long, bleak night hours that had suddenly stolen into our halcyon existences.

Little Alex broke into tears when Faith tried to put him to bed. "I want Bubba," he sobbed so pathetically that emphatic tears sprouted in the eyes of us adults. "Where's my Bubba? Why didn't that mean lady give Bubba back?"

That was a question that not even Faith, practiced in her quotidian walk with Jesus, could answer. Faith sat with Alex until he fell asleep, then joined Ron and me in the front room. None of us wanted outside distractions to intrude into our family tragedy. The television remained a blank, reflective eye on the room, catching our images and tossing them back to us as we paced aimlessly.

At some point in time, the human body acknowledges its water-filled, clay frame and collapses. When Donna Johnson swept into the room with her luggage shortly after six in the morning, Ron was draped uncomfortably over both arms of the recliner, snoring lightly. Faith was crumpled up on one end of the sofa. I woke up when the front door opened. I discovered that I had been sleeping on the other end of the sofa with my legs pushing Faith into a more tightly wound ball.

I leapt up and hugged Donna like the long-lost friend she was. I helped her carry her bags into the screened-in porch that Clint Flavors had so recently vacated. I refused to look at the wardrobe and recall the role it had played in our crisis. If I had stayed quietly hidden in the wardrobe and not tried to flounce out and catch the intruder, perhaps Ryan would not have been missing. If I had just minded my own business ...

I spoke to Donna to break off that fruitless regret. "I'll get the bedding washed later today, Don. I haven't had time yet. We had someone camped out here until last night."

"Hush, girlfriend," Don ordered. "Not another word about bedding when you have bigger worries. Has your grandson been found yet?"

Unbidden, tears climbed back into my eye sockets, and I rubbed them away determinedly. I had falsely thought I'd already cried out every ounce of moisture my body had retained in its lifetime.

Donna herded me into the kitchen and shoved me into a chair. "Sit. I'll fix breakfast for everyone. I'm afraid I've lost my touch with breakfast tacos since I left Texas, but I can whip up a mean Georgia omelet."

"What's in a Georgia omelet?" I asked curiously. "I've never heard of that before."

"Anything you want, girlfriend ... and since I'm still a Texan by birth and at heart, I imagine it will be plenty spicy. I'll make a smaller one for your other grandson. Alex, isn't it? The one who tried to stop that insane kidnapper? Good for him! He must be a gutsy little guy. Knowing you, I imagine they both are."

I laughed. "Gutsy is right, but not any credit to me. God has blessed me greatly. Ron and Faith are both quintessential parents."

Donna grinned at me. "Same old Mike, huh? Still using your writer's words that make me feel dumb and uneducated."

"Sorry. I forget."

"It's good to be home," Donna said with a sigh of satisfaction. "At times, I wish I had never left Three Prongs. I especially miss it on Fridays. I remember the seafood buffet. We don't have a restaurant like *The Spanish Tile* where I live. Even if Irene hadn't married Ron, maybe things would be better now if I'd have stayed here. If nothing else, I could always look forward to seafood buffets on Fridays!"

"Don, what do you mean? Is something wrong?"

"Just about everything at the moment. What's most wrong," she said with a metallic bite to her voice, "is my daughter. I don't know what happened. I raised her right. I haven't had any problem with the boys. I set a good example for her – right up until the day her father died. You know that. You know what a faithful, supportive wife I was. I never ran around or –

"She's running around on her husband?" I asked in shock. That fact was incompatible with the visual image of young, innocent beauty I recalled from my memory whenever I thought about the redheaded Irene, who had almost been my daughter-in-law.

"Was ... Eddie caught them together and divorced Irene."

I gasped. "Oh, Don, I'm so sorry! I didn't know. That must have been terrible for you."

"It still is. I think Eddie's recovered better than I have. I have to deal with disappointment over my daughter and the guilt of wondering what I did wrong to cause her to act that way. It's been rough. The worst part is that she didn't learn anything from it. She and Eddie have three children. She ruined his career at school when she left him. Understandably, he sort of fell apart for a while. He got transferred to a lower-paying job in another school district. She married the guy she was running around with. Oh, Mike! It was awful! Her new husband hated the children because they weren't his. He was so mean to them, and they were so young to have to go through all that trauma." Donna turned to me, spatula in hand.

I ran across the kitchen, threw the spatula into the sink, and hugged my friend. For a long time, we stood there holding each other. Then I released her and stepped back. "Child abuse, or is he just mean? Can you get him arrested?" I wasn't sure that arresting a child abuser would help, but I was quite sure that anyone who hurt a child should be held accountable for the destruction of that child's innocence and trust.

"I never could get enough proof together at the right time." She shook her head. "It doesn't matter now. That marriage broke up after only four months. Now – thankfully – Eddie has custody of the kids. I moved again. I wanted to be closer to them so I can babysit while Eddie's at work. I quit my regular job and just keep the kids. Eddie really appreciates it, and I really appreciate spending time with my grandchildren. Of course, I don't make as much money as I used to when I worked a real job, so I've had to cut down on expenses. Bruce's life insurance paid for a nice funeral and gave me enough money to get myself and Irene to Georgia so I could look after my folks, but there wasn't much left over after that."

Looking at the trim figure of my best friend, I realized that expenses must not be the only thing she had cut back on – or perhaps she had cut back on expenses by cutting back on food and meals. After having seen how slim she was now, I was thankful I had shed a few pounds of my own over the past couple of weeks.

Donna pushed her short-cropped brown curls away from the frame of her glasses and sighed. "Remember when we were in high school and we thought that as soon as we graduated and gained the freedom to begin our own lives, the world would be ours and all our problems would be solved? We actually wanted to leave home and leave our parents. I went back to care for Mom and Dad, though, and I'm thankful I did. I really miss them – both of them. Especially now, when I feel like I need to talk to someone about Irene. Mom was what people without careers call 'just a housewife,' as if staying at home and raising a family is something to be ashamed of. Mom was one of the wisest women I've ever known – even smarter than you, Mike, no offense."

"Not offended in the least. You'll get no argument about that from me. I only met your parents once, but they both seemed pretty wise and special. But back to Irene. Why doesn't she help keep the kids?"

"Irene," Donna said with bitterness, "is too busy with her own life. She's pregnant now with the man she's living with. They're not married and probably never will be. He's an ex-con with a background of spousal abuse. He's not divorced yet from his second wife. I don't know what happened to wife number one."

"Oh, Donna!" Not knowing what to say, I embraced her again. My secret thoughts were filled with thanksgiving to God that Irene and Ron had not married. I felt that my life had been spared a dystopia that I would have been too injured and weary to endure. Ron, I felt, had been rescued from a hell on Earth that would have lasted until death parted Irene and him. I shuddered, thinking about what insults and hurts my son might have been subjected to in a marriage with the capricious Irene. The most devastating thought of all was that if Ron had married Irene and not Faith, Alex and Ryan would not have been born. Spending time with my grandsons always illuminated the qualities that each of them had inherited from each of their parents. They were a unique creation of God's and of Ron and Faith. At one time, I would have willed my friendship with Donna to rob me of my grandsons! I was so thankful that God was wise enough and kind enough to sometimes answer prayers with an emphatic, "No."

Finding less personal and more cheerful topics of conversation, I set the table and watched Don whip up a batch of her famous Georgia omelets. They looked Texas ranch style to me and smelt so appetizing that we were quickly joined by Alex, Ron, and Faith. Ron hugged Donna jovially and introduced her to Alex and Faith. When I looked at Faith in the bright kitchen light and saw a beautiful young woman without even a hint of a greyhound's face, I knew I had been healed from my resentment against the unexpected turn of fate that had thrown her into Ron's arms, displacing Irene.

Over breakfast, we discussed plans. Someone needed to stay close to the phone in case Ryan was found. The morning sky crept over the ranch in a thick grey sky cover that I tried to ignore. I tried to pretend that the distant rumbling causing the oak tree leaves to tremble on delicate new spring growth was from highway noise, not thunder. It would be unbearable if inclement weather caused a halt in Ryan's search. Finally, however, the storm approached with such aggression that not even I could ignore it. Grey turned black, and white, zipping electric bolts shot holes through the curtained sky.

Sheriff Brent Cruz, who proved to be a mind reader as well as a friend, called to reassure me. It was too dangerous to send volunteers out until the electrical storm passed, but the search had merely been halted, not called off. Weather forecasters promised the storm band was small and moving rapidly.

I told Brent that Donna was with me. "Where do you want us? Which search party?"

"Well, someone has to stay by the phone."

"Faith is staying here with Alex. She also has her cell phone. We gave you the number yesterday. Ron wants to search, too, if you just tell us where you need us."

"All of you ride horses, don't you?" Brent asked. "I know Donna does. She was a rodeo champ in high school barrel-racing."

It was amazing what different facts people remembered; I had forgotten about Don's horseback skills.

"Marty's leading the horseback search," Brent continued. "I think they're out at the park waiting for the storm to pass. He's loaned out all his horses, but he said to tell you not to worry if you want to join them because he's the one riding the old spirited horse to protect you from any more pickles. He said you would understand what he meant by that."

I grimaced. Yes, it was one horse, one ride, and one rescue I would never forget. I gasped. That horse was frightened by thunderstorms – or at least by lightning, according to Marty – so I hoped Marty would be okay. My stomach, which was already clenching around Donna's Georgia omelet when I thought about my missing grandson, roiled even more when I imagined Marty in danger. My heart seemed to have forgiven him already for his momentary infatuation with the evil Lynette Clarissa Greene.

Brent added, "I know you and Don want to hang out together, but since there are so few extra horses in Marty's group, Ron might want to check out the Old Lake area with fire department volunteers or help out at the Dean ranch. Thor's organized a search there, in case Lynette sneaked back and left Ryan. She did sneak back and steal Thor's car – that we know for sure. Anyway, that gives all of you some choices. I gotta run. We'll call immediately if we get any news – even just a smidgen of news. Oh, and Mike – for heaven's sake – remember your cell phone for a change."

Don and I were ready to fly out the door together like birds out of their parents' nest and were frantic to find safety elsewhere, but Ron's pragmatism held us back. "It's pouring down rain," he pointed out. "Just wait a few minutes and see what happens. You couldn't see well enough to do any searching in this downpour. Look at Don. She wears glasses. She'd have her hands full just keeping the lenses clean enough to see anything."

"Thanks for noticing," Don said sourly. "It happens after age forty, so I've been told." She looked suspiciously at me. "Why aren't you wearing glasses, Mike? Have you gone and gotten contact lenses?"

Ron answered for me. "Mom won't admit that she needs glasses. She says people already accuse her of staring at them because her eyes are too big and that it would be worse if she wore glasses. She squints at the computer screen and does okay with her writing, but you should see her try to look up a number in the phone book or read the lettering on a medicine bottle or business card."

"Ron! How did I raise such a rude son?"

He grinned at me impishly, reminding me of Ryan. "You taught me to be truthful, Mom, and I quote from you – something you claimed to be quoting from the Bible – 'A lie lasts only a moment, but truth is forever.'"

"That sounds about right," Donna agreed. "That's another thing about Irene. She's quit going to church, Mike. She seems to have turned her back on God."

"Irene?" Ron said with shock. "I'm so sorry for you, Donna, but if you'll forgive me for saying so, I'm thankful I didn't marry the girl."

"We all are," Donna said grimly, and I realized she was speaking truthfully for me too.

When the rain held back the grey sheets of water and unleashed lightly chained drops instead and the thunder pushed off in the distance to frighten other people's animals, Ron decided he would join Thor's search party. He knew without asking that Don and I were heading to Three Prongs to find Marty, and we did. We arrived just in time to see him being loaded into an ambulance.

I ran, slipping and sliding over the wet ground. "What happened?" I demanded, skidding to a stop in back of the ambulance and falling seat-first into mud.

One of the volunteer emergency medical technicians reached down and pulled me up, then answered, "Thunder spooked his horse, and he got thrown, but he'll be fine."

From the back of the ambulance, I heard Marty's querulous voice. "Lightning, not thunder. That old horse is about deaf."

I laughed in relief. "Yes, he sounds like himself. Sounds like he's going to be fine."

"Mike, is that you?" Marty called. The EMT moved aside

and let me peer into the back of the ambulance at my fallen hero, who was strapped securely to a backboard.

"Yes, Marty, I'm here. Do you need something?"

"If you promise not to laugh at me for getting into one of your pickles, I'd like you to come to the hospital with me. Can you?"

I looked questioningly at the EMT.

She shook her head. "I have to ride back here with him, county EMS rules, but you can take your own transportation to the hospital."

Donna, who had wisely made her way more slowly to the ambulance and had not fallen into mud, squeezed my arm. "Go ahead, Mike. I've already run into a lot of old friends here. Someone will give me a lift back to your place. We can visit more later. We wouldn't get much visiting done right now anyway, riding around in this mud and slime looking for your grandson."

So as the orotund tones of the ambulance warbled down the winding highway to San Antonio, I followed more slowly in the borrowed car, trying to ignore its aggravating, always unexpected bursts of conversation: "Please fasten your seatbelt … Your fuel is low." Brent had been right, I realized, when he'd told me that after we found Ryan, I needed to find a new vehicle. He and Anna were too close to me to ever pressure me for the prompt return of their car. In return, I owed them enough consideration to return the borrowed car quickly and get my own vehicle to drive. The economy was less than booming, and most people I knew were strapped for cash. I was sure that while he and Anna were not in a crisis situation, they would welcome extra cash from the sale of the car. Besides, I was worried that my carelessness – like the fall into the mud that had slime-painted the seat of my pants – might ruin the car's upholstery or cause some other damage.

Because I usually avoided driving in San Antonio, except for Ron's neighborhood, I soon lost sight of the ambulance. I knew approximately where the hospital was, so the loss was not unnerving. My meandering choice of roads took me past a huge car dealership, and a bright yellow pickup truck whistled at me as I drove past. Momentarily forgetting about Marty, M&Ms, chocolate and Diet Cokes, I turned into the paved driveway and parked. I left my purse and keys in the vehicle – forgetting that I was now in a big city and not Three Prongs – and answered the truck's whistle just as surely as if I'd been a border collie herding cattle.

I knew it was foolish to select a vehicle on the basis of color, and Alfred would have been scandalized, yet as I walked solemnly around the truck, I found that it pleased me from every angle. Alex and Ryan – for we would find Ryan and there would always be a Ryan – could ride in the back seat. I could let the dogs jump in the bed and take them down to the river for a swim. I could fill the back of the pickup with the lumber and building materials needed to finish the maintenance work at the ranch. I could give up my Three Prongs office and move my writing back to the ranch to save money for truck payments. At the ranch, I could find all sorts of things to move around in the back of the truck. Of course, I admitted to myself with an unusual spate of honesty, moving things around the ranch in back of the truck would probably provide one more distraction to keep me from writing – and already existing distractions at the ranch had sent me into Three Prongs to rent an office in the first place.

Before I got concise directions to the hospital and put the borrowed yapper back out on the road, I held a sales estimate in my hand for the bright yellow pickup truck. Ron, I knew, would never understand. His approach to life was slow and cautious – not given to impulse buying – and he liked sober, somber colors older than his years. He had thought Old Blue was a fitting car for his mother. My paintings and the brightly colored clothes I sometimes wore caused him to physically shudder.

"Mom," he would scold, "who do you think you are? A teenager? A rock musician? Some kind of circus performer? Why can't you learn to mind your own business and to dress and act your age? I never know what to expect from you. Someday I'll find you in Indian headdress, living in a teepee." Then he'd pause and frown at me. "I won't really, will I?" a question for which I had no answer at that particular time in my life. Life is an adventure, and my motto is: Never let an adventure pass by unmolested.

It would be smashing to drive up to the ranch in the bright yellow pickup and watch Ron's dawning look of horror when he realized I had purchased a vehicle that was not beige or white! Of course, financing would be a problem, but my next royalty check was due any day now, and I had a draft of the next book almost completed and ready to send. Alfred had left some money in a savings account. Just before he died he had instructed me to forget about the account so I wouldn't be tempted to spend it foolishly. (I suspected that like Ron, he would have thought purchasing a bright yellow pickup truck was at the pinnacle of foolishness!) Alfred had been almost as bad as his son when it came to doubting my wisdom. I had proven Alfred wrong by having almost forgotten about the savings account. It took the clear whistle of a bright yellow pickup truck to remind me.

Even after I reached the hospital, I had to wait to see Marty. He had been sent for X-rays, scans, and lab work. When he was finally installed in a bed, I was directed up to his room.

Marty Richards smiled at me wanly, looking less cowboy hero and more like an oversized, frightened young boy. "Thanks for coming, Mike. This hospital thing is new to me. I've always gone to visit friends at the hospital, but I've never been the patient. So far, it's been less than amusing." His voice was low and shaky, unlike the fabulously rich voice that could still be heard in old Westerns.

I suddenly realized that Marty Richards, ex-actor and still famous in his small hometown, was indeed as frightened as I had surmised. That knowledge made me realize that for all the years I had jealously guarded my passion for Marty, I had learned very little about him as a man or as a person. I knew him only as the romantic impetus behind my dreams, the nonfattening M&Ms that flavored my life.

"My leg's broken," Marty told me glumly. "Fortunately nothing else, but I'm bruised and shaken up a bit. They are keeping me overnight for observation," Marty added in his newly uncertain voice. "I'm so sorry, Mike, about not believing you – about that that … that horrible … that …" His voice trailed off. He twisted angrily on the bed. "You have every right to be angry at me. I'm plenty angry with myself. You should hate me." He raised up on his elbows from the pillows behind his head and searched my face with those fabulous pulsing blue eyes. "Perhaps you do hate me," he suggested in a small voice, totally unlike his usual rich, assured tone. "You just came along to be nice because that's the way you are."

He sounded so tragic that I did something totally uncharacteristic for me: I bent down and kissed his forehead gently. "No, Marty. I could never hate you."

"But I was so stupid, Mike! How could I have been so blinded by that ..." Again his word basket came up empty. "And you, Mike – truly beautiful inside and out, the truest friend any man could have, a treasure, a woman any man would be proud to have as his wife. Mike –

Whatever Marty planned to say was interrupted by the floor nurse who came rushing in with brisk efficiency to check machinery and tubes.

I felt like kicking her, for by the time she left, Marty's thoughts had returned to the search.

"The worst of it is not getting to look for Ryan, Mike. You were counting on me to help find him, and now I've messed up and have to miss out on the rest of the search. But with so many searching in so many different areas, perhaps they've already found Ryan by now. If you want to use my phone card to check, you can call home from my room. They've already told me Three Prongs is long distance, and my calls won't go through without a card." He grimaced. "I would let you use my cell phone if you don't have yours with you as usual, but the blasted horse threw me down pretty hard, and I landed on it and smashed the thing to smithereens."

Marty motioned to the phone resting on the bedside table. "Go ahead and call from that thing. Get my wallet out of my jeans – if you can find them. I've asked the nurse for my clothes twice already, and she hasn't given them to me. I guess she's afraid I'll get up and run off." He sounded as if he had actually contemplated that action.

"Marty," I said, putting a hand on his arm.

He quickly clasped my hand with his other hand.

"Please don't give missing the search a thought. Like you said, they may have already found Ryan. I do have my cell phone for a change, and I will call in a few minutes. Even if they haven't found him yet, with so many people looking, I'm sure they will soon. I appreciate what you've already done. I mean, you organized the whole horseback search and even let riders borrow your horses. If you hadn't been trying to help, you wouldn't be here in this bed with a broken leg. So thanks. Although those words can't begin to express how much I appreciate your efforts, I just haven't found any better words yet. It's frustrating."

"I wouldn't be here if I hadn't forgotten about that horse and lightning," Marty said glumly. "I should have remembered. I trained that critter – 'cept I didn't train him to be afraid of storms. Mike, I had a book with me when I got thrown – under my shirt so it wouldn't get all wet. Do you think you could find out what they did with my clothes and that book and read some to me? I think it would calm me down some – not that I'm nervous or anything. It's just a broken leg."

"I'll be glad to," I said quickly, feeling closer to Marty than I ever had in all my improbable dreams. Seeing him as a man with real strengths and weaknesses instead of a peerless superhero who was untouchable for someone as mundane as me built a foundation of real love under what had been my shaky attraction. I realized that now.

Even though I was an avid reader, I had never heard of the slightly damp book I found with Marty's clothes. I pulled a chair up close to his bed, eager to begin reading and learn more about Marty's literary tastes.

Marty smiled at me fondly. "Thanks, Mike. I'm being a selfish beast to take up your time like this. I know you're worried sick about your grandson, so just read a few pages to me and go. Otherwise, I'll feel guilty about keeping you away from your family for too long. It's mighty nice of you to even come visit me at a time like this, especially after the way I was so rude to you about … her … and other things. I mean, I acted kind of down on you before I found out you were helping Three Prongs misfits when no one else could be bothered. And then I was so stupid, so dense about that Greene woman. Woman? No, monster, snake, serpent – a murderer, for heaven's sake! You knew and tried to warn me, but I wouldn't even listen to you. I'm sorry, Mike."

"It's okay, Marty," I said with asperity. "No one would listen to me about Lynette. Her beauty got in the way of their brains. She even fooled me at first," I admitted after a moment's silence. "When I compared her to Faith, I was sort of wishing Ron would have married her instead."

"But, Mike, that Faith is a real keeper – and beautiful to boot."

"I know that now, Marty. I was just momentarily blinded by Lynette's beauty, like you and a lot of other people."

"Well, Mike, I'll tell you something I probably should

have told you a long time ago. When it comes to keepers, you're quite a catch yourself."

Marty's eyes fell away from my face and traveled around the whiteness of the bed linens. I realized what an effort it must have been for the proud, self-sufficient ex-actor, star, and rodeo champion to apologize to me. Apologies were probably about as rare in Marty's life as placer gold – those unexpected gold nuggets hidden in the desert sand in dry washes and beds of quartz crystals. He wasn't in the habit of getting himself into pickles.

I smiled: Marty had called me – forty-something me with too-big eyes, a too-abundant body, and pretend-red hair that flew into every style except an attractive one – a keeper! My smile was so wide that it stretched my face and hurt the corners of my lips. I knew that smile had started from inside my heart and spilled out to spread over my face like warm peanut butter. It was probably popping right out of my eyeballs.

Fortunately, Marty didn't notice. He was still reading the whiteness of the bed linens, as if they could explain his foolishness. "Anyway, Mike," he added after a short silence. "It's sure nice of you to forgive me about every foolish, stupid thing. And ..." He looked up at me suddenly. Without warning, Marty's fabulous dayflower-blue eyes, with their pulsing yellow centers, were locked on me in an attempt to read my too-big, greenish eyes, and I felt my face flush. "Mike," Marty said, as if he enjoyed repeating my name.

M&Ms for sure!

"You know I don't mind about your pickles, right? You know I just like to kid you about that, don't you?"

Again at an inopportune time, the floor nurse returned, waltzing around the machines at Marty's bedside in an effort to check his vital signs. She cast a suspicious look at her patient, wondering no doubt why anyone in a hospital bed would be talking about pickles. She tested him with the portable thermometer she carried in the pocket of her smock. I figured she thought Marty might be running a fever and that his medical condition was causing him to become delusional about food.

I smiled back at Marty, afraid he could read the love spilling out of my eyes, yet powerless to hold it back, and at the same time kind of hoping he would accurately read it. I was too bashful to speak, but I had been reining in my secret desire for so long that now it had rebelled and broken free.

"Actually, Mike, besides liking you," Marty said after the nurse left, "I admire you. You're brave, smart, kind, generous, and you know how to trust and obey God. I reckon a man would have to walk through a lot of desert sands to find another woman like you. I even like your pickles. They add zest to life. I think it's about time we got to know more about one another than just being able to recognize each other from a distance. I've known what you look like on the outside for years, but I know more about the characters in the books you've written than I know about you. Since I'm supposed to be out of here tomorrow and we're pretty sure Ryan has been found already – or will be soon – let's make a date for Friday's seafood buffet at *The Spanish Tile*. I reckon that's about as good a starting place as any. I should be pretty handy on those crutches they threaten to make me practice with by then. I know we've made plans for Friday's seafood buffet before, but unless I'm mistaken, it seems we usually get interrupted or sidetracked – by pickles, as I recall!" He chuckled. "This time, let's make a date for Friday's seafood buffet at *The Spanish Tile* ... and keep it."

I nodded and managed to say in a voice not at all like my own, "Great! I'll be there." Marty's praise had confused me. Dancing chocolate bars of every shape and description seemed to be whirling around in the room with us or perhaps just whirling around in the melange of my thoughts. Not knowing how to respond to anything else Marty had said after I had accepted his invitation, I said nothing. I opened up the book and began reading.

"I hope the story won't bore you, Mike," Marty interjected. "It interests me because of the horse-training angle. I like to read up on horse-training and learn all I can. Knowledge makes a person better at anything they do – even training animals."

Partly, no doubt, because Marty's praise had awed and confused me, I never did understand the story. The part I read had nothing to do with training horses – or if it did, I failed to grasp the concepts introduced. I gathered that the book was a Western. The writing was poor, and the author seemed to be making an attempt to parallel a young boy's coming of age to his stallion's discovery of the attraction of mares. The author took great pains to describe the desert setting of the story, right down to cacti, roadrunners, and rattlesnakes, yet the description did not ring true. The desert setting of the book seemed a wasted effort to add enough words to the pages to finish the confusing tale. Part of the writing embarrassed me. I found myself skipping graphic details of the stallion's quest for new mare flesh. Whether or not Marty was familiar with the book and knew how much I had skipped, I never learned because he fell fast asleep.

Marty looked almost like a young boy when he was asleep. The cinnamon-colored hair he usually kept so neatly groomed fell across his forehead in careless locks. His face looked unlined and smooth. Only the mustache, sparkling with occasional white hairs, spoiled the childlike image. And, of course for me, asleep or awake – Marty held all the sexual attraction that God intended for one man and one woman to share and enjoy as a reward for marriage.

I hated to leave while Marty was asleep, but when I talked to the floor nurse, she urged me to go.

"We've given him pain medication. He's likely to sleep through much of the day. I'll tell you what ... if you follow me down to the nurses' station, I'll find you some paper and a pen. You can write a note for him."

Armed with pen and paper, I marveled at the continuing blank space beneath my fingers. I, a writer who zipped Pastor Garth Seymour through page after page of mystery, was unable to pen a short note to Marty. But this was different: My heart rode on every stroke of the pen, and I quit breathing when I remembered the pulsing yellow center of his blue eyes looking into mine with ... What? At least a deeper affection and appreciation than he had ever shown towards me before.

After some arrangement of words finally appeared on the blank paper, I propped the note up against Marty's book, so he would see it when he woke up. Then I left, knowing he needed his rest.

My feet practically flew me out of the hospital to the parking lot, where I could use my cell phone without disturbing Marty. I had to know about Ryan, and I hoped he'd already been found. I wouldn't have it any other way.

Chapter 15.

I missed my Friday date with Marty at the seafood buffet – again. He had developed an infection in his leg and remained hospitalized. He demonstrated himself to be a very impatient patient.

Even worse, Ryan still had not been found. Even by Monday, when most of the volunteers were forced to abandon their searches and return to their jobs, Ryan was still missing.

True to Faith's predictions, Ron left her and Alex with me and returned to work. "I'm just a phone call away," he reminded us before he left. The frame of his body spoke his reluctance to leave us even as his words did not.

Donna and I went everywhere together. Amazingly, I found I was looking forward to her departure on Wednesday. Either distance and time had grown us apart, or else my best friend possessed personality quirks that I had never noticed before. All of us at the table cringed when Don blew her nose during meals. She cleared her throat frequently, whether or not she was speaking. When she was sitting, Don tapped her foot against the floor or kicked furniture. When she was standing, she walked around touching things and plucking at them, even in stores. Her constant agitated motions began to wear on my nerves. After that first day of fixing breakfast for us, Donna seemed content to sit back and let us wait on her.

Even worse, Donna had picked up unfortunate expressions like "Kick butt." She used these constantly – and inappropriately – in conversations.

When Faith heard Alex say he wanted to go to jail and "kick butt," she corrected him.

"Grandma's friend says that," Alex said defiantly, "and that's what I want to do to that mean woman who stole Bubba. I want to kick her butt!"

Faith sent Alex to his room.

Donna, however, laughed uproariously, unable to comprehend why Faith objected to Alex's word use. "I want to kick her butt too." Donna laughed. "What's the big deal? It's not like using bad words."

But to Faith and me, it was exactly that.

After Donna and I caught each other up on news and important events in our lives, Don monopolized conversations. She talked incessantly, as if she was using a prerecorded script. I could guess what she was going to say next even before she spoke. Her conversations were limited to two topics: her grandchildren and how her daughter had disappointed her. I felt sorry for Donna's sons, as they were apparently doing well in their lives and therefore were not fitting content for discussion. As much as I hated to admit it, Don seemed to revel in her misfortunes and take great comfort from her misery.

When I was able to slip away from Donna for a few moments at a time, I fell down on my knees and thanked God for two things: that Ron had not married Irene and that God had put Faith and Ron together. Then, of course, my prayers turned to Ryan and pleas for his safety and return.

What irked me most about Donna was that she seemed to remember for only short spurts of time that Ryan's disappearance was the impetus behind her arrival at Three Prongs. Donna was bouncing with energy, able to sleep soundly at night, unlike the rest of us, and she was eager to visit old haunts and gab with old friends. This was only natural, and I could not resent it. I did, however, resent the long face she drew down over her countenance when I mentioned joining a search party. Once, Don had been eager for anything that might pass as adventure. Now, she liked to sit and drink coffee, clearing her throat for no reason and drumming her feet against any obstacle they could strike. Worse yet, she expected other people to bring her the coffee and even refill her cup!

Donna had even treated Jared rudely, expecting him to act as both messenger boy and slave.

Ron and Faith had talked to Jared about their willingness to adopt him, and Jared had drawn himself up proudly and thanked them. "But I have a dad," he explained, "a real dad. He's letting me stay here with Miss Mike while I finish school so I can go on to college, but I could move in with him."

"I shouldn't think you would want to be around Zolly Gilmore," Donna had said with supreme lack of empathy for how her words might hurt Jared. "He runs a bar and peddles misery to people who haven't got the brains to resist. That man's a real turd."

"That man happens to be Jared's father," I had told Don icily, "and Jared has every right to be proud of him as a father, regardless of what kind of a business he runs. He's a good businessman and has made a small fortune from his bar. That is something in itself. While you are in our house, you will show respect – and don't use offensive words like 'turd,' or Alex will pick them up."

Jared had thrown his arms around me, tears shining in his eyes, and fled from the room.

Donna, on the other hand, had looked at me as if I had grown horns in my head and sprouted whiskers around my mouth. She had vented her anger against me for most of the rest of the day by pointedly ignoring me and treating me to large doses of silence – which were indeed golden.

Marty, meanwhile, had been more seriously injured than he had at first realized, and the infection in his leg worsened. He remained hospitalized.

Don and I visited him daily. We never stayed long because her nervous rambling around the room and constant plucking at things seemed to irk Marty. After ten minutes of her rearranging his room, Marty would wink at me and drop his head back into his pillow, pretending sleep. When Don saw that Marty was sleeping, she would grab my arm excitedly and whisper in a voice that could be heard down the hall, "Let's go, Mike. He's finally asleep."

Donna's actions at the hospital fostered deep disappointment in me. Other than finding Ryan, the second most important thing in my life at that moment was visiting Marty. During our short visits that week, I was slowly learning more about him: his favorite books, movies, and music. I learned what his hectic life had been like in Hollywood and why he had left, why he had never remarried after the unexpected death of his first wife, how he had found

Three Prongs, and why he had stayed. Every new detail I learned about Marty was compatible with some facet of my personality. Even with Donna's interference, the colored M&Ms of my imagination were spinning together into a pattern with real substance for the first time.

One of the newly learned details about Marty that I treasured most was his adamant refusal to judge other people on any other basis than the one they, themselves, provided as proof of their character. He had been one of the first people in his profession to welcome black horse trainers and to work with them. Marty had never put a difference between himself and another person because of the color of their skin or different education levels or back-grounds. Marty, himself, was a college graduate with two degrees, yet he had waged a successful battle to obtain a position at his studio for a Hispanic youth, a high school dropout who had shown skill and dexterity in planning and executing stunts and in working with animals. After the popularity of Western movies faded, that young man had gone back to school. He was now a veterinarian with his own practice, and he still kept in touch with Marty.

"I've taken my horses to him," Marty explained, "when I've been in California for a stint. I'd trust that young man with any of my horses, even Cactus. He's good."

I hid my smile, knowing that like Marty and me, that "young man" would be forty-something.

Marty had been equally inclusive when it came to involving Native Americans in Three Prongs celebrations and encouraging them to keep their culture alive. "Cowboys are only half the story," he had told countless people who brooked opposition. "The Indians are the other half, and they were here first. They have been villainized for years, called 'red savages' and the like when the truth is that this was their land. No one gives them credit for discovering aspirin and chewing gum and teaching pioneers how to treat wounds and set broken bones. And their beautiful craftsmanship should be preserved. It's not limited to those touristy bead coin purses some people think of as 'Indian.' It is so much wider and richer than that."

Donna's boredom with Marty – how could any woman be bored or indifferent around Marty Richards! – was not the only thing that disappointed me about my former best friend. I had taken to stopping by the auto dealership, even though it was not located along the shortest route to the hospital, to visit my dream truck, and she thought me foolish. "Why would you want a bright yellow thing like that, Mike?" she asked. "No one else is driving anything that looks like that. You'd be the only one in Three Prongs with a yellow truck."

"Hello."

"Wouldn't you feel stupid?"

"No. I would feel different, unique, like I'm my own person."

"Mike, you are unique all by yourself. You don't need a yellow truck to be different."

"I like the truck, Don. It's me."

"I don't think it's you. I think it's a joke! Why don't you get a nice white one like everyone else drives? Or that pretty brown color? Why would you want something that advertises you from a mile away? It must be nice to be rich enough to go shopping for a new vehicle. I know I don't have that kind of money to throw around."

"Well, remember how long I drove Old Blue. I think –

"I'm borrowing a car from Eddie, thanks to the mess that daughter of mine has made of her life. It's a sad thing when parents can't enjoy their advancing years because their kids let them down."

I gave up explaining to Donna how I planned to finance the new truck. She was off on her favorite topic about how rotten her life was because of Irene, and it was clear she had no real interest in my life.

With a hidden sigh of relief, I hugged Donna on Wednesday, thankful she would be driving herself to the airport. I waited until I was sure she was gone, then prepared to leave for San Antonio to visit my truck and see if Marty was ready to leave the hospital. I had promised Marty I would take him home as soon as his physician released him.

Faith grinned at me. "I know Don's your best friend, Mom, but I'm kind of glad to see her go. I don't think I could take one more day of hearing how terrible her life is because everyone else is plotting to make her suffer … and hearing her blow her nose during meals and clear her throat all the time about gagged me. Of course, what Ron and I object to most was some of the near-profanity that came tumbling out of her mouth."

I laughed. "I hate to admit it, but I'm glad she's gone too!"

"Why is she your best friend? I don't see that the two of you have very much in common."

"*Was,* not is, my best friend – and I don't remember now how we got to be best friends. I'm not sure if Don's changed or if I've changed or if we've both changed, or if it's just a trick that time and life have played on us. In any event, with all her whining about not having money, I don't expect to see her again for a long time."

Impishly, Faith suggested, "You could send her money to come back for another visit. You sure made an impression on her as being very rich, since you're planning on buying that new truck. I know! You could buy all of us airline tickets for vacations somewhere since you're so rich!"

"Not another word, daughter, or I might be tempted to disinherit you!"

Faith laughed. She smoothed her light brown hair away from her face and sighed in relief. "I'm glad to hear you say you're glad she's gone, Mom. I hated to see Donna go because I was afraid you would miss her and be sad. I know with ... Ryan still gone and ..." Faith's voice dropped to a whisper, and she determinedly wiped tears out of her eyes. "I know with Ryan still gone, we're all still lacerated inside. I didn't want you to be hurting even worse."

What an awesome daughter-in-law God has given me!

"I have an idea!" Faith exclaimed suddenly. She looked more alive and excited than she had since I'd shown up with Ron's new sign painting brush. "Let Alex and me go to San Antonio with you. We'll go by that car place you've been talking about and help you get your yellow truck." She laughed again. "I don't think Ron really believes you want a yellow truck. He thinks you're just kidding. Anyway, I'll drive the car back here for you. Then, when Ron gets here this evening, we can take the car back to Sheriff Cruz and Anna."

"Faith, thank you! What a marvelous idea! But we can't. You need to stay here in case Ryan is found and someone calls."

"Don't argue. You're always doing things for other people. It's about time someone in your family – meaning Ron or me – did something nice for you. The sheriff's department has my cell phone number, Mom. We've been waiting for that phone call day and night for five days. I scarcely think it's likely to come now while I drop you off to get your new truck."

"Faith … I don't know."

"Well, I do. Let's go." Faith laughed when I looked at her questioningly. "Oh, Mom, it will be worth it! From what Donna said about your yellow truck, I can't wait to see Ron's face when he drives up and sees it! We need a bit of humor around here, don't you think?"

"Enough said. Let's go!"

So we went, and Faith passed the test – which she didn't, of course, know that I was administering.

"Mom! It's beautiful!" Faith exclaimed when she saw the yellow truck. "It matches you. It's perfect. I can't picture you driving anything else. This is you!"

Alex jumped up and down in the car seat clapping his hands. "I like yellow! Like Big Bird! Like baby ducks! Like Texas roses."

Faith and I laughed over his comparison of the yellow truck to the song "Yellow Rose of Texas."

"Where did that come from?" Faith asked, wrinkling her nose playfully. "That wasn't your ex-best friend Don. All she could talk about was how miserable she was in Georgia and how brave and unselfish she had been to go there and take care of her parents, only to be rewarded for her efforts by having a daughter like Irene!"

Fortunately, I was an old hand at driving a straight shift. By the time the yellow truck nosed into a parking space at the hospital, I was growing proficient at changing gears, even at one traffic light that had left me stopped on a steep incline. God, I decided, was smiling on me. When I rushed into Marty's room, he was sitting in the chair in his room, fully dressed.

"Mike!" He looked past me with dread, then sighed in relief. "Is she really gone now? Or did she stop along the way to torment someone else?"

I laughed. "Yes, Don's really gone. And I see you're really ready to be released."

"I've been ready since they brought me in here. I just had to wait for the hospital's readiness to catch up with mine. Look, Mike!" He motioned to the white, gleaming cast thrusting his blue jeans apart along one seam. "They cut my pants to get them on over this ridiculous cast! How am I supposed to ride my horses with this heavy thing throwing me off balance?"

The floor nurse, pushing a wheelchair into the room for Marty's trip out of the hospital, answered. "You are not supposed to ride horses, Mr. Richards." She waved a yellow sheet of paper. "These are your discharge orders. I'm going to read them to you now. One of the things I will be reading is how much you need to limit your physical activity for now."

Marty groaned. "Out of one prison into another. I knew I didn't want to come here from the start."

"At least you still have your leg," the nurse reminded him. "Without us, the infection would have become so virulent that your leg might have been amputated to save your life."

Once he was wheeled out to the patient discharge area, Marty passed the test. "Why, Mike! You've needed a pickup truck for years! And bright yellow like an M&M. It suits you and your sunny personality – a right pretty truck, almost too pretty to put to work."

I helped Marty into the front seat and made sure his seatbelt was fastened. "It's a work truck," I assured him. "I didn't spend that much money on a truck to leave it parked outside my office or drive up and down Main Street."

Marty laughed. "Reckon this little yellow love will help you dish up all sorts of pickles. And speaking of food, Mike, don't forget our date Friday – seafood at *The Spanish Tile*. We had to miss it last Friday because of this dang-blasted busted leg, but no excuses for this Friday. Seafood it is!" Then he added, "You can bring Faith and Alex with you. I'm sure sitting around waiting for a phone call about Ryan is about to drive poor Faith plumb crazy. It would me. Of course, I reckon sitting around a spell is all I'll be fit for until this leg heals up, from what that nurse said."

"She also said your leg seems to be healing well. You won't be sitting around for very long, I'm sure."

"And these sticks," Marty complained as I climbed into the driver's seat. "They said I needed them to keep the weight off my leg and make it easier for me to get around. I can't even figure out how to use the blasted things right! They made me practice in the hall over and over again because I couldn't get it right. They said it's for my safety, but I kind of got the idea it was for their amusement. They lined up and laughed at me! I still don't have it right, but they must have gotten bored watching the show because they finally decided to send me on home. I bet I could ride Cactus around town easier than learn to walk with these sticks. Riding Cactus would keep me off my leg."

"You've been released into my care," I said with mock sternness, "so you better behave. If you get hurt again, they'll hold me responsible. They might even force you to marry me so I can watch you twenty-four/seven."

Marty laughed. "Reckon that would be less painful than learning to crash around on those sticks. Say, Mike, what do you reckon that kid of yours is gonna say about your new yellow plaything?"

I laughed. "Faith and I both plan to be outside waiting for Ron to show up so we can watch his face."

I dropped Marty off at his house. A neighbor had been feeding Marty's cats and hurried over to check on Marty when we pulled up into the driveway. I left Marty in his neighbor's care and slipped away.

It was about time I did some serious searching for Ryan on my own. I had let Donna – and even Marty – hamper my efforts, and now there was no excuse. I would find a quiet place to pray and ask God where to find my grandson. I thought about my Three Prongs office, then dismissed that thought; I hadn't been there since the Friday before Ryan's kidnapping. When people saw a vehicle parked there – especially a bright yellow truck – curiosity would bring them. Instead of praying and seeking God's wisdom, I would wind up answering questions and accepting condolences. Clint Flavors always said the river was a good thinking place. Perhaps taking advice about thinking from someone who had connections missing in his brain was foolish, but the river would at least be quiet and peaceful.

However, on the way to the river, I discovered an impromptu praise and worship and prayer service for Ryan on the courthouse lawn. Churches in the community had banded together to organize the noon service. Tears washed unhindered down my face as I saw evidence of community support everywhere I looked in Three Prongs: blue ribbons, posters, and banners proclaiming, "Help Bring Ryan Rice Home! PRAY!"

Donna and I had attended a prayer service for Ryan

at our church, but Donna had been more interested in meeting and greeting old friends and making new ones than she had been in praying. She had proven to be a distraction. On the courthouse lawn, with joyful worship music rising up to tickle the leaves of the live oak trees and startle the pigeons on the courthouse dome, I could feel God's closeness. Not even all the people who were fasting during lunch and spending their lunch break in prayer and praise for Ryan were as much of a distraction as Donna had been. Those people were present because they shared the pain of a child-bereaved family and because they believed in God's power, authority, and ability to answer prayer and bring Ryan home. Donna had attended the church service merely to be with me.

I tried to slip away from the crowd before too many people discovered me. Bea, however, I could not avoid. She drew me aside and plopped me down on the top of the retaining wall at the courthouse lawn. "How's Marty?"

"He's home from the hospital now."

"Good. I wish I could have visited him while he was there. I heard you did."

I nodded.

"Well, some of us have to work. Part of my work at the moment is covering your grandson's disappearance." She gestured to the closing service on the courthouse lawn. "It does one proud to live in a community where folks band together for something like this. That's what I'm doing here – pictures. Can't get Nat back to work. He stays out on search teams with his dad. Don't worry, Mike. I understand. I'm thankful your family's getting all this support. I'm not going to fire Nat. I just hope –

"We all do."

Bea looked contrite. "I'm sorry, Mike. How awful of me."

"Not at all. You have a business to run. Ron's had to go back to work too."

She nodded. "Well, I'm glad to know Marty's okay. Did you hear about Hyacinth?"

"What about her?"

"She was coughing and had some chest pains, so she went in to her doctor for a check-up. Lung cancer."

"No!"

"Yeah. Not a pretty picture, that. The docs say they caught it while it's still in just one lung. They're going to try to remove part of the diseased lung – surgery, chemo, radiation, and the works. But lung cancer has one of the poorest survival rates of all cancers, so it still doesn't look good for her. She's been hiding out at her art colony, avoiding people. No one has seen her in town for nearly a week. She found out last Thursday. I don't think she's left her hill since then, not even to eat at *The Spanish Tile*. I haven't had time to go see her. I tried to call her a couple times, but she leaves the answering machine on."

"Why would she avoid people? It sounds to me like she could use some help."

"Now, Mike, don't go mixing yourself up in someone else's business. We haven't solved your last pickle yet! There're plenty of deadbeats at the colony to help Hyacinth. Besides, she's really mad at you."

"At me? Why?"

"She hasn't forgiven you for that embarrassment about the dog-fighting ring, I hear. It's true no proof was found at her place, but Sheriff Cruz let her know that he knows she was involved and that he's watching her. People who have heard about the incident are pretty much shunning her, and she blames you."

"I'm glad to take the blame for shutting down something as nefarious as a dog-fighting ring!"

"Yeah, and I would feel the same way, but it's Hyacinth. One reason she's so put out with you is Marty."

"What about Marty?"

"It's been all over town how you've been visiting him in the hospital. Hyacinth knows Marty has heard about the dog-fighting ring and that he has probably guessed she was involved in it. She's afraid he won't have anything more to do with her. Just between you and me, Mike, I think Hyacinth's stuck on Marty. I think she intended to install him up on her little chunk of hill country as a love slave."

"She did," I said grimly. "She bragged about it to me. She didn't want to marry him, just keep him."

"I figured as much. Marriage isn't exactly her style. If I were you, Mike, I'd steer clear of her until she decides to be sociable again. If you try to force her, she'll just be angrier."

"But, Bea, lung cancer is never a good prognosis, as you already pointed out. How sick is Hyacinth? How long does she have? Someone should do something to help her if they can – at least to make her more comfortable."

Bea sighed and fluffed her dark bangs away from her face with puffs of air. "Me and my big mouth," she muttered. "I knew I shouldn't have told you. I thought maybe you'd be too taken up with Ryan gone and Marty in the hospital to get mixed up in Hyacinth's business."

"I never get mixed up in other people's business, Bea. You know that. I'm just sorry for Hyacinth. All that yoga and exercise and eating salads to keep thin and look good, and now –

"Like she says, she'll look good in her coffin."

"Bea!"

"Mike, I know you've heard her brag about that. I'm just repeating what she's said all over town."

"But at a time like this –

"At a time like this, I think you should get back to the ranch and wait to hear about Ryan."

"I've done that all week. Now I'm going to look for him myself."

"Good luck, but I don't see how you can make out any better than all these people who've already been searching. How will you know where to start? Anyway, I've gotta run. Lunch is nearly over, and there's no one covering at the office." She motioned to the dispersing crowd. "Everyone came here."

"Thanks, Bea."

"For what? For letting my employees make their own choices about how they want to spend their lunch break and whether they wanted to eat or pray?"

I returned her grin. "That ... and for being a good friend."

"Speaking of friends, has Donna Johnson left yet?"

"Yes, early this morning."

"Bet you were sorry to see her go. Did you ever get over the fact that Ron married Faith instead of Irene? You were pretty riled about it at one time."

"That was long ago, Bea, and I'm over it now." Even I heard the hint of anger in my voice.

Bea looked at me skeptically, shook her head, then trounced off down the sidewalk. Bea had no way of knowing, of course, that my momentary anger had been sparked by a mention of Donna Johnson and was not guarded resentment that her daughter and Ron had not married.

I slipped into my bright yellow truck, wishing my mood and emotions could match such brightness and wondering if they ever would. I was thankful I had surprised the gathering on the courthouse lawn. I realized now that other people cared about our loss and were willing to share our grief and bind our hope into their hearts. That made each breath of air a bit easier to inhale, even knowing that oxygen prolonged pain and suffering.

It had seemed to Ron, Faith, and me that life for everyone else had trundled along on smooth tracks while our family had been derailed and pitched into a convoluted nightmare. We couldn't wake up from the bad dream. We were afraid to allow mornings to rouse us too fully. If we ever snapped to full wakefulness, the knowledge that Ryan really was missing would be fatal to all of us.

For other people, the sun went down at night on the old day and rose again to birth a new day. For us, there was no newness. We had the same constricting pain in our chests, the same tight faces from holding in our emotions and attempting to be strong for each other, the same fatigue and despair that short snatches of sleep could not remedy. We were walking missing persons. Each of us walked around pretending to be whole while disabling pain oozed out of the hole in us; something was missing because Ryan was missing. We were always hungry, but it was a hunger fed by a famished spirit, and food could not fill the emptiness.

Even Alex was quiet in his play, indifferent in his taste for food, and inconsolable when it was time for bed and Bubba was still missing. We were injured people, hurting people, incomplete people, frightened people. We couldn't be normal people, as others around us were, because Ryan's abduction and disappearance had warped us as surely as heat pouring through the windshield of a vehicle would warp a plastic container.

Not daring to believe in miracles – because other people had experienced miracles, and what would that say about our family's worth in God's eyes if we didn't rate a miracle? – I headed for the river. I needed some place to go and cry, somewhere to pray, somewhere to be alone and fall apart and wait for God to put me back together.

I had already parked the truck with its hood sheltered by the lacy shade of a cypress tree before I spotted Clint

Flavors; I wouldn't get to be alone and fall apart yet after all. It seemed rude to get in the truck and drive away again since Clint had stuck his fishing pole into a forked stick along the bank and was staring at me.

"That you, Miz Rice? That your truck? It's yeller, ain't it?"

"I thought you were working for Thor, Clint. What are you doing in Three Prongs fishing?"

"I tried to help, Miz Rice. I wanted to find him on account of all you done for me, but they wouldn't tell me what to do. They're not working, you know. They're looking. I'm a good worker ... strong."

"Thor and his crew took the week off to look for Ryan?" I asked. "And you wanted to help in the search, but no one told you where to look?"

Clint nodded and brushed his dark hair, sprinkled with white glints from the noon sun, away from his cactus-brown face. "Yup, and I even told her. She call you, Miz Mike?"

"Who, Clint?"

"I told her about you missing your baby and to call. She was all flip-flopped over it, because of Vinny."

I almost left Clint Flavors to his fishing, which would have been the greatest tragedy of my life. In fact, I had turned on my heel to flee back to the relative sanity of the yellow truck when I stopped and turned back. "Clint, has Vinny called you from jail? You do know she's in jail, don't you? For taking Ryan?" I didn't see any point in trying to introduce the truth to Clint Flavors about Lynette Clarissa Greene's other crimes. I didn't think the windows of his mind could hold back all that information without popping out and breaking.

Clint nodded. "Vinny's bad. I used to think she was good, but now I know she's bad. She took your baby. She left your baby with her."

My heart stopped, and I quit breathing.

Clint was looking out across the Three Prongs River, his empty eyes absorbing scenes that were hidden to me.

I spoke very carefully, afraid that if I pushed him, Clint would slide off to those distant shores that I had no way to reach. "Clint, do you know where Vinny left Ryan?"

"Yup. I done told her to call. She ain't called you yet?"

"Who, Clint? Vinny, or someone else?"

"Vinny can't call! Vinny's in jail, and they won't let her out. She's bad. She's mean. I used to think Vinny was good. She's not. She's bad."

I dug my fingernails into the palms of my hands to keep from lunging at Clint and shaking him. I forced my breathing to slow down. I found I could do nothing to stop the crazy thrashing of my heart against my ribcage. "Clint, do you know where Ryan is? Where is Ryan? Is he okay?"

"She said Vinny left him there, told her it was a baby she didn't want, a baby she had when she didn't have no husband – that the husband had the baby and brought it back. So she asked if she would keep it for a little while, and she did."

"Clint, who has Ryan?"

"She was just trying to help Vinny. Vinny lies, you know. She lied to her. She didn't know Vinny lies. It's not her fault, but I told her about Vinny's lies. I told her Vinny's bad. I told her to call you. You're good, but that Vinny, she's bad."

I gritted my teeth. If Clint hadn't made himself more understandable to "her" than he had to me, no wonder no one had called us about Ryan! I tried again. "Clint, did Vinny leave Ryan with someone? Did Vinny tell someone Ryan was her baby?"

He looked at me with surprise. "I done told you that, Miz Mike. I done explained it, and I explained it to her, too, but she didn't understand."

"Where did Vinny leave Ryan?"

"Vinny ain't her name now, Miz Mike. She lies. Her name is Lynette. That don't even sound like Vinny. Her name never was Vinny, but she was my girlfriend before I knowed she was bad. I wouldn't want her back now that I know. Vinny, she was right purty, but only on the outside where you could see. She wasn't no purtier than a catfish gagged on a worm on the inside."

If I hadn't been so frantic about Ryan, I would have appreciated Clint's description of Lynette. I sank down on the bank next to Clint because my legs would no longer support me.

He smiled aimlessly at me. "It's okay if you sit there, Miz Mike," Clint Flavors said generously. "Vinny's in jail. She won't see us and think stuff about you trying to be my new girlfriend. Vinny ain't my girlfriend anymore anyways.

She's bad. She's catfish ugly. I like catfish to eat – not to look at like a picture. I done throwed her pictures away now because I see the outside over the inside, and it's catfish-gagged ugly."

"Clint, this person named Vinny who is really named Lynette, where did she leave Ryan?"

And then, while law enforcement officers from agencies, including the Texas Rangers and the FBI continued their search for the kidnapped boy, Clint Flavors, who many said wasn't the brightest crayon in the box, solved the mystery. He considered me with flat, dark brown eyes. "I done told you, Miz Rice. She has him – only she don't know it's him because Vinny done lied to her, and she believed Vinny."

I forgot myself. I forgot how Clint Flavors could slip away like egg white spilling out of a shell. "Who has Ryan?" I yelled into his face, startling him.

He blinked at me in hurt surprise and with resentment just beginning to register in his eyes. "Her ... that Hyacinth."

Chapter 16.

Without thinking to call anyone, I scrambled back to the truck, jerked the door open, and leapt inside. Clint looked after me with flat brown eyes that noted I was in a hurry and wondered why.

My emotions were so tangled that they trussed my coordination. I clashed gears wildly in my new truck before I finally managed to squeeze out from under the shady canopy of cypress tree and head for the art colony. When I looked in the rearview mirror, I saw Clint staring in my direction. Even though the new truck was bright yellow, I wasn't at all sure that Clint saw it as he stared after me.

Hyacinth Walker met me at the door of her cabin. Her haggard face grew more lugubrious when she saw me. "So, Clint Flavors was right," she said wonderingly. "I didn't quite understand what he was trying to tell me, but I think I have what you want in here."

I followed her slim body into the next room and let out a whoop of joy that startled even the paint on the wall.

Ryan sat on a small chair in front of a television set, watching a Walt Disney movie. When he looked up and saw me, he repeated my whoop. He jumped up and ran across the room and threw himself into my arms.

I hugged him so tightly that he yelped.

"Grandma, quit squashing me! Where's Mama? Where's Daddy? Where's my Alex? Why didn't you come get me, Grandma? I've been here since day went to dark and dark went to day, and she only has this movie and one more movie. I got to paint, but then day went to dark, and Mama didn't come." Ryan grabbed the material of my blouse and pulled it up around his small face and burst into tears.

My own tears splashed on top of Ryan's head as I rocked him in my arms.

Even the usually callous Hyacinth looked close to tears. "I guess I'm in a lot of trouble." She sighed. "I don't suppose you can say you found him on the river or something."

"Hyacinth, I don't know exactly what happened, but Clint seems to feel it wasn't your fault."

"Clint? Clint Flavors? Who in their right mind would listen to him? His elevator stops between floors, Mike."

"Clint solved the mystery of Ryan's disappearance," I reminded her gently. "A lot of other people with working elevators are still looking for him. When you explain what happened to Sheriff Cruz –

"He's your friend, not mine. He hates me."

"I don't think Brent hates anyone, Hyacinth. He is serious about upholding the law. I know you haven't always been on the same side of it that he has, but I don't think he's a small enough person to let personality clashes alter his good judgment."

"Yeah? When I've held rallies in an attempt to get him replaced, to get someone else to run against him for sheriff."

"Oh that. Well, no offense, Hyacinth, but those rallies didn't draw much of a crowd. Besides, like I said, Brent is a fair man. He judges things by what the law says, not how he feels about things."

"Whatever."

"I'm sure he'll go easy on you if you just explain ... everything."

"Everything? You've been talking to Bea, haven't you? She's called here and left messages for me. I don't want to talk to her. I don't want to talk to anyone. I don't want pity."

"Perhaps what people want to offer you is help."

"I don't need help. I'll be fine, and I don't need your religion pushed down my throat either, Mike. I saw that look flit across your face. As you pointed out, I have my own beliefs."

"And you've every right to have them, Hyacinth. I just thought that at a time like this, you might want more than beliefs – like a real, living Jesus you can talk to."

"You thought wrong. Don't come around here sticking your nose in my business, or it's likely to be chopped off. That would rather ruin your appeal for Marty. He's a man who likes a woman to ride easy on the eyeballs."

"Hyacinth, I need to make some calls. There are a lot of people taking time off work to look for Ryan. I need to get word to them that he's been found. I left my cell phone out in the truck."

Ryan had quit crying and was holding me so tightly around the neck that I wasn't sure I would be able to talk, but I owed it to the searchers to try.

Hyacinth gestured to the phone near the sofa. She walked over and switched off the movie. "I'm glad you're here. I was getting as sick of that movie as he was."

I sat down on the couch, loosened Ryan's grip around my neck, and called Faith. For a moment, I thought she'd fainted again, but then her quavering voice came over the phone line, asking to speak to Ryan, and I passed the phone receiver to him.

"Mama! Mama! Mama!"

"Ryan! My Ryan!"

I had a hard time parting Ryan with the phone receiver so I could call everyone else.

Sheriff Brent Cruz instructed me to stay put. He arrived within a few minutes. He was gentle as he questioned Hyacinth, and I knew Bea had spread the word about Hyacinth's illness. "So basically," he said, "you thought you were keeping this child for an unwed mother, Lynette Greene, whose husband had tired of him and dropped him off?"

Hyacinth nodded.

"What about the boy? Didn't he tell you who he was?"

"Yes. He kept saying he was Ryan. I already knew that. That was what Clara called him."

"But didn't you know about the missing boy? Didn't you make the connection?"

"Not until Clint told me today when he came up here to ask if he could go fishing in back of the cabins. I haven't been in town lately. I guess you probably already know what I found out from the doctor. It sort of ... knocked me over. I haven't wanted to go anywhere and see anyone or have anyone asking me a bunch of questions." She looked defiant. "I don't want pity."

"How about help?" Brent asked, as I had. "You may find you need some help. We all do from time to time."

"Are you going to arrest me?"

"Can't think of a reason." He looked at me. "Can you, Miss Mike?"

I shook my head.

"The boy looks fine," the sheriff said thoughtfully. "I can see you've taken good care of him. You didn't take him. We know who did that. You didn't know who he was or that he was missing. Nope, I don't believe there's any charge worthy of an arrest."

"But when Clint told me, I didn't call."

"Did you believe Clint?"

"Well, Clint's honest. I know that. It's not that I didn't believe him. I just couldn't quite figure out what in the world he was talking about."

I hid my smile, remembering my own recent and frustrating effort at trying to understand Clint Flavors all too well!

Hyacinth added, "I was trying to figure out what he had been trying to tell me when Mike showed up at the door. When I saw Mike, I understood right away."

"Confusion is no crime that I know of," Brent said cheerfully. "When it comes to understanding Clint Flavors, well ... I guess we would all be guilty of confusion at times."

Hyacinth stomped her foot. "I don't want sympathy! I want to be arrested!"

"Well," Brent said, removing his Stetson and scratching his dark hair, "I have shelves of law books over at the courthouse. No one uses them much anymore with all the information they can find on the Internet, but you're welcome to come over and browse through them and see if you can find something I can arrest you for. Meanwhile, I've got to get this young man home to his mother. If we can borrow your phone, Hyacinth, I'll call Faith and see if she will meet us in town. A whole heap of folks are ready to hold a parade down Main Street in Ryan's honor." Brent smiled at Ryan. "You and your mom can ride on a fire truck in the parade."

Ryan wanted no parade in his honor, and not even a ride on a fire truck could tempt him. He rubbed his eyes and sobbed, "I want to go home. I want mama. I want my Alex. I want Daddy. I want to go home with Grandma."

Brent rubbed Ryan's back gently. "Hush, son. We won't have a parade for you if you don't want one. We have too many parades in Three Prongs anyway. It ties up too much of my manpower when deputies are out there stopping traffic and rerouting it around Main Street." Before we left the art colony, Sheriff Brent Cruz turned back to Hyacinth Walker. "Thanks for your help,

Miss Walker. Remember, friends return the favor. If you need help – you call. I realize you can hide up here on your island, but sometimes the water rises and the island shrinks in size. If you have a hankering to get off for a spell and test your land legs, come on down into our world and let us help."

Brent's words seemed to have reached Hyacinth's as mine had not – and yet Ron and Bea seemed to think that I stuck my nose in other people's business. Hyacinth actually smiled at the sheriff, and I imagined that was a first.

I found out later that when they were deprived of Ryan's victorious ride on a fire truck, some of the volunteers had wanted to parade Clint Flavors down Main Street as a hero. They even considered putting him on top of one of the EMS units. Like Ryan, Clint shook the idea off like water avoiding an oil filter. "I got to get to work," he told everyone proudly. "Mr. Dean's done hired me out at his ranch. He needs me to work now that the looking's over. It was Vinny that done it. Vinny's bad."

Bea had laughed when she related this to me over the phone. "Only a few of us know who Vinny is," she explained, "so parade organizers thought Clint had slipped into his own world again and decided the whole parade idea was a bad one if the hero was going to slip away from them into a place they couldn't visit. I know one thing ... I'm sure glad to have Nat back. His dad brought him into the paper as soon as they received word about Ryan's recovery. Nat's going to get his driver's license next week. Thor bought the car you borrowed from Anna and Brent. Nat said he had taken a fancy to that car because every time he drove it, he would remember a crazy lady xenia who'd rescued him from San Antonio. I don't have any idea what he meant by that."

I did, but I didn't tell her.

By bedtime on Thursday evening, Ryan and Alex were already arguing again like normal siblings often do. "You have to let me pick the story," Ryan told Alex, climbing up into Ron's lap. "On account of I got missing and found again. You gotted here before I did. You gotted to choose first."

"Got," Ron corrected.

"He gotted missing too?" Ryan asked.

Faith and I laughed and hugged each other. Jared

settled the brief argument by selecting a book he liked and reading it to the boys. Ron smiled at me from across the room, and I knew he had forgiven me for sticking my nose into Jared's business.

After the boys were asleep, Ron joined us in the kitchen, where Faith and I were leisurely washing dishes and enjoying each other's company. "Well, Mom," Ron said, "in a way, we have your predilection for sticking your nose into other people's business to thank for getting Ryan back."

"Ron! What a terrible thing to say! I never stick my nose in other people's business. I stay quite busy enough on my own. You apologize to me this instant!"

Faith giggled. "Oh, Mom. Think about it. Ron's right. If you hadn't been helping Clint get over his broken heart by letting him stay here, you never would have learned the truth about that Lynette monster. And if Clint hadn't learned to trust you when he stayed with you, he probably wouldn't have told you about Ryan. He had tried to tell Hyacinth, but she wouldn't listen to him. He might have just dropped back into his own world and never said anything to anyone else. I don't think he was even sure the little boy Hyacinth had was our missing Ryan. He just knew Lynette had lied about the child because she had lived with him for several months and had no child then."

Ron laughed. "I know Hyacinth has gone a bit nuts over the yoga angle, but it's funny, isn't it? She has two college degrees and several art school diplomas, yet in the end, Clint Flavors was smarter than she was. She actually believed Lynette and trusted her right up until the day you went thundering into her house to rescue Ryan, Mom."

"I didn't thunder! I was –

We all looked at each other and broke into shared laughter. How wonderful it was to exercise the gift of laughter again.

"I'm still mad at you, Mom," Ron added sternly. "Sneaking off to buy that monstrosity of a bright yellow truck without even asking me what I thought!" He shuddered. "It hits me all over again every time I pull my old truck up into the driveway and see it there, kind of like an uncovered electrical wire that keeps on shocking. And, Mom, how did you get to San Antonio to pick the thing up and still get Brent and Anna's car back to them? I understand Nat bought that car . Bea told me when she called here for you last night."

Faith and I exchanged smiles. I never answered Ron's question directly. "Ron," I said with a saccharine tone of voice, "I'm still the parent, and you're still the child. Parents learn early in their roles to be resourceful. You and Faith have learned that already, haven't you?"

Jared hugged all of us. "Well, Miss Mike. I'm sure thankful for how you've helped me out … and I like your yellow truck!" He glared at Ron, and even the kitchen seemed to share in our laughter, fueled in part by relief and joy at God's faithfulness in having brought Ryan safely home.

True to his word, Marty met me at my office on Friday morning so we could savor the seafood buffet at *The Spanish Tile.* He was an hour early. He settled into a chair and smiled at me.

I could have sworn chocolate drops danced around the room.

"Go ahead and work, Mike. I just want to sit here and watch. Do you mind?"

Did I mind? Well, perhaps I did. I couldn't breathe. I couldn't type. I was finishing the cover letter to send with my newest manuscript, Pastor Garth Seymour's seventh book, which was finally completed. The letter should have taken only a few minutes to type, but with Marty's virile presence at such close quarters, my fingers found all the wrong keys and even got stuck in the spaces between keys. I spent so much time backspacing and correcting my work that I still hadn't finished the letter when it was time to leave for *The Spanish Tile.*

Fortunately, Marty saw my fingers playing over the keys and had no idea of how scrambled the words – and my thoughts were. "You're a talented woman, Miz Michal Rice," he observed. "I think I left that out at the hospital when I was rattling off that list. No doubt about it, you're a keeper. Well, let's mosey on over to get some grub. If you don't mind, I thought we'd walk. I'm still put to a bit of a challenge with these sticks the doc gave me. With all these inventions and contraptions – like that computer you're using – I don't know why they haven't come up with something better than crutches. Who do we know in Three Prongs that's good at inventing stuff?"

Ron would have told Marty his mother was good at inventing mysteries to get tangled up in, but I was certainly not going to admit that to the man who thought I was a keeper!

Our progress down Main Street to *The Spanish Tile* was slow. As Marty had predicted, his skill on crutches did not match his skills as a horse trainer. I didn't mind the slow clatter down the sidewalk. Colorful M&Ms somersaulted though my mind the whole way. Marty and Mike! I'm a keeper, he's a keeper, and life is good! The empty, gaping hole that had kept me hungry, the one food could never fill, had healed with Ryan's return. The occasional antagonism I had misdirected at Faith over the years had evaporated. A sunny yellow truck sat in front of my Three Prongs office. Ron and Faith had encouraged me to keep the office in town so I could write without interruption. Alex and Ryan were already rowdy, and now Faith was beginning to show off the secret life that grew inside her as her flat stomach heaved up into the roundness of ripening fruit.

We stopped at the corner of the restaurant to let Marty rest. "You should try this, Mike," he puffed. "God never designed the armpits to hold up the weight of a person's body. It's more work than riding saddle broncs in the rodeo."

"I think those handles down below the armrests are for holding your weight off your shoulders," I suggested helpfully.

"You want to try?" Marty asked indignantly.

I laughed. "Not unless you want to pick me up off the sidewalk!"

"Nope. I don't want to do that, but I know what I would like to do." And right there on Main Street, with vehicles rolling past on the street and people easing around Marty on his crutches, Marty bent over and kissed me. Fortunately, my back was solidly pressed against the hard rock corner of the building, or I would have fallen. My legs turned to liquid, both from shock and from the physical thrill of lip contact with Marty. I still felt shaky by the time Marty shoved both crutches into one of his wide hands and used the other hand to pull out my chair for me at *The Spanish Tile*.

Marty had kissed me! Mundane, forty-something me, who was a bit too wide for my height and had missed out on both red hair and green eyes! Marty had kissed me, and now we were sitting together at a table in *The Spanish Tile* restaurant, in plenty of time for the seafood buffet. Life was perfect. It couldn't get any better than this.

Marty and I held hands and prayed. An electrical current seemed to flow from his fingers to mine. He held my hand warmly for long seconds after we had finished praying. I smiled mindlessly at him, trying to remember how to breathe. No, life can't get any better than this!

Our waitress arrived with iced tea and silverware. She was pert and pretty, with a flawless figure and a sparkling personality. I didn't mind, as jealousy and I were strangers. I had never been a jealous person, just like I always minded my own business. Besides, my M&M theory had been proven as fact now and was no longer subject to debate. Not even Bea or Hyacinth could steal the rainbow from my sky or steal the chocolate flowers rioting through my mind now. Marty had kissed me! Marty and I were finally together at Friday's seafood buffet at *The Spanish Tile*. Life couldn't possibly get any better than that.

"Bit of a change on the buffet today, folks," the perky waitress said with a Texas-sky-wide smile. "No seafood. Barbecue with all the trimmings – you know, like onions ... and pickles."

THE END

The Author

Inconveniently, writing is not something that I have ever possessed; it is something that has possessed *me*.

As a five-year-old I lived for show-and-tell days at school when the students brought things to class and talked about them. I never had anything to bring – but, boy, could I ever tell!

Me: *A camel followed me to school. I tried to ride it, but it had slippery hair and I fell off.*

Or: *I didn't forget my lunch today. There was a lion in the front yard. He roared at me, but I wasn't afraid. I knew he was hungry. So I gave him my peanut butter sandwich.*

Or: *I didn't fall down on my way to school. This big bird with colorful wings landed on my shoulder. I caught it and went flying with it – but it dropped me. That's why my knees are bleeding.*

A parent-teacher conference ended my first grade story-telling career. I was instructed not to tell any more lies.

When I was in the fifth grade, my father got an advance on his first book and came home with a pony. That was a bit of an incentive to write. But the real incentive?

Me: *Dad, what's your book about?* Him: *A boat-going detective who makes a lot of money.* Me: *Is it true?* Him: *No, it's just something I wrote.*

That settled it. If a person could get paid for telling lies on paper, that was the job for me!

I received my first rejection slip on a children's picture-story book, *Hubert, the Friendless Snake,* before I graduated from high school. Other rejection slips followed, along with a few successes. But no matter how many rejection slips I received for how many different genres, I kept writing, because like Jeremiah 20:9, *His Word was in my heart like a burning fire shut up in my bones; I was weary of holding it back and I could not.*

My father – an atheist – had written four worldly novels. I wanted to write to glorify the LORD – entertaining books that would prove that Christians could have fun! Sunpenny Publishing has given me the opportunity to do that.

The worst day in my life was the day when: my mother died in Florida and I couldn't go because the Texas hospital was sending my terminally ill husband home to die; I lost my job; our loveable sheepdog died, and my truck caught on fire in downtown San Antonio. What doesn't make you bitter makes you better, and after surviving a day like that the possibility of rejection slips lost its fear, and I started writing again.

I am now married to a gifted and talented writer in his own right (and a wonderful husband!), Alan T. McKean, who has spent 30 years (so far) serving God as a minister. We live on the lovely Black Isle in Scotland. I am also blessed by having a son, Luke Parker, who walks after God and serves the United States in the Marine Corps. He and his wife, Dr. Delight Thompson, have a bright and talented daughter, Dulcinea.

Yes, all grandparents think that about their grandchildren. But in my case – it's true. And, no, this isn't another lie on paper!

Rose & Crown

blue
freedom

SANDRA
PEUT

SAMPLE CHAPTERS

Blue Freedom

by

Sandra Peut

ISBN# 978-0-9555283-5-4

"A thrilling mystery of exciting anticipation, witty antics and laughs, with heart-felt truths all in a 'what happens next' plot. Simply and elegantly written - your imagination is caught in the perfect 'Pacific' drama which just keeps getting better to the very end."

- Elizabeth Findlay, Scriptwriter/Magazine Producer

Prologue

Somewhere in the Pacific Ocean

He never should have swum off alone. What had at first appeared to be a shallow indentation in the coral-encrusted rock had turned out to be a cave. The diver had spent almost twenty minutes exploring the cavern and its colourful marine life – but when he emerged, the rest of the group was gone.

Checking his diving watch again, he fought against the rising panic. Everything he had learnt in his years of scuba diving flashed through his mind. *Stay calm and breathe normally. Stay in the same place and wait to be rescued. Never swim away from your diving partners.*

He'd been completely stupid. But the inside of the cave was so fascinating, and he'd wanted to take a closer look so he could describe it to his fiancée. With her writer's creative appreciation of all things unique and beautiful, she would love it.

Now he wondered if he would ever see her again.

He'd still had some oxygen left in his tanks, but had discarded them, along with the weights in his diving belt, after he surfaced. There was no sense in trying to tread water or swim with all that weight on his back. And even without the oxygen, he had little hope of reaching land, over ten kilometres away.

He would just have to swim. And pray.

The alarm had surely been sounded by now. His rescuers had probably already begun the search.

Chapter 1

Brisbane, Australia

4) The Blame Game

The final, and perhaps most damaging, form of self-sabotage is that of blaming ourselves. "We all recognise we're our own worst critic," says psychologist Dr Sarah Green. "The problem is that external messages – such as those from media advertising, and even from family and friends – can serve to reinforce our own negative thought patterns." The key, according to Dr Green, is deciding to be kinder to yourself. "By making small, positive changes to the way you think and speak, it can be possible to stop negative self-blaming patterns." Learning to change old habits and eliminate these four areas of self-sabotage can help you move on into the successful and confident future you deserve.

"There! Finally finished!" Bella Whitman typed the last few words with a flourish, before moving her neck around in slow circles in a vain attempt to work out some of the knots. "Typing gives me cramps," she complained, lifting her arms up to the ceiling in a languorous stretch.

"Well, writing is your chosen profession," Krista – her housemate – reminded her as she padded past the kitchen table to the refrigerator. "You just have to put up with the occupational hazards that go along with it," she mumbled around a bite of apple.

"You can talk!" Bella retorted, leaning back in the chair, her eyes closed. She lifted up the tangled mass of her chestnut curls, allowing the air to cool her neck. "Sticking people with needles every day sounds pretty hazardous to me."

Krista reached over and playfully tugged her friend's hair. "It's called phlebotomy, for your information. And at least it's a job with a steady income." The end of her reply faded as she walked through to the lounge. Bella smiled. Krista was no doubt watching her favourite afternoon soap on TV. Like clockwork.

Bella sighed wearily as she began gathering up her paperwork, now strewn across the table's surface. She enjoyed being a freelance writer – loved the freedom, the challenges, the chance to express her creativity. But the constant pressure of deadlines and lack of secure income took their toll.

"What I need is a holiday," she murmured, rubbing her blurry eyes. Her last holiday had been a couple of years ago, right before –

Bella squeezed her eyes tightly shut, trying in vain to block out the memories of Andrew. His smile, those chocolate brown eyes, the way he would look at her just before they kissed ...

But then he was gone, disappearing so suddenly, leaving Bella alone and crying on a Pacific island beach. Wondering why the men in her life were always taken from her prematurely – asking the heavens what she'd done to make God so angry.

As Bella started making dinner in an effort to distract her thoughts, she realised she was still asking those same questions now, a couple of years on. Memories swirled about her as she sliced an onion. She couldn't be sure if her tears were from the fumes or her depressing thoughts.

With a sigh, she put down the knife decisively. "I need a change," she announced to the kitchen walls. "They say a change is as good as a holiday – don't they?"

"Are you talking to yourself again?" Krista's head popped around the edge of the door. "Writers," she mumbled to herself, shaking her blonde head in mock frustration as she came all the way into the room.

Bella ignored the comment, choosing to focus on the diced onions now frying in a pan.

"I just saw a new magazine advertised on the TV," Krista casually mentioned, sneaking a carrot slice from the cutting board. "It's called Healthy Lifestyle, and it's published right here in Brisbane."

Bella lifted her head and looked at her friend. "A new magazine? That might help." Work had always been a source of welcome reprieve.

"Help what? And haven't you conquered enough magazines already?" Krista asked, chomping on the carrot. "Never satisfied ... it must be a writer thing," she flung over her shoulder, returning to the TV.

Bella smiled to herself as she emptied some tuna into the pan. She would make some enquiries tomorrow.

Two days later

A sharp rap on the open office door interrupted Ethan Gray's busy focus. He sighed impatiently, lifting his eyes from his weekly planner to glare at the unwanted intruder. "Make it snappy!" he barked.

The usually self-confident office assistant visibly shrank before the editor's obvious irritation. "Umm ... Gemma's asked me to tell you that because of the big fitness-wear fashion shoot next week, we've had to reschedule October's planning meeting to this morning. Nine-thirty." She hesitated. "Is that okay with you?"

Ethan checked his planner, noting his 9:30 am appointment with a freelancer – Bella Whitman. "Shouldn't be a problem," he replied without looking up. "There's nothing here that can't be put off."

The woman turned with a relieved smile, and started to walk out through the doorway. "Susan," Ethan called, halting her in her tracks. The editor's voice was like granite, hard and brittle. "I expect to be given more than fifteen minute's notice of any future schedule changes. Understand?"

Susan stammered her assent before hurrying from the room. She almost tripped on her ridiculously high heels in her haste.

Ethan smirked as he observed her discomfort. Women! They were only good for one thing.

Chapter 2

Brisbane, Australia

With a screech of brakes and a sharp jolt the train pulled into Central Station. Pneumatic doors wheezed open as Bella hurriedly grabbed her shoulder bag, water bottle and coat. Although the blazing sun promised a warm spring day, she never could trust those air-conditioned office buildings.

The rush of commuters streaming from the train caught Bella up in its midst, carrying her out onto the platform and up the escalators to the street level.

She waited with the crowd for the traffic lights to change. It was a gorgeous day. The cloudless sky, as yet untinged by city smog, reminded her of the cornflowers in her grand-mother's garden. A slight breeze played with wisps of her hair that had strayed from the high chignon. With a sigh of annoyance at her unruly curls, Bella attempted to tuck the errant hair behind her ears as she crossed the street. She was beginning to feel anything but professional, and the interview was less than an hour away.

Bella continued down Edward Street, which fell steeply towards the city. A few minutes later, with her feet already beginning to ache from the high heeled sandals she'd care-fully chosen to match her ivory suit, she found herself at a small café and tumbled into the nearest seat.

She caught her breath while waiting for the waiter to bring her order of a skinny cappuccino and blueberry muffin. She had just under an hour before her interview with Ethan Gray, editor-in-chief of *Healthy Lifestyle*. Strangely, her stomach twisted in knots just thinking about it. Bella was normally confident and self-assured—or, at least, she managed to convey that impression to those around her.

Perhaps it was because she seriously wanted to make a good impression and obtain some new avenues of work. Life seemed so ... so *unfulfilling* at the moment, and she didn't quite know why.

Actually, she had a fair idea, but Bella had always shied away from being too brutally honest with herself. Now though, the sentiments crowded in ...

It had to have something to do with Andrew, she thought, stirring sugar into the frothing cup the waiter set before her. She'd never felt the same since he had gone; she was stuck in limbo, a prisoner of her past.

Her eyes flitted around the café, scanning desperately in an attempt to distract her from the painful images threatening to invade.

A man two tables over caught her eye, mainly because he was obviously wishing he was somewhere else. His toe tapped restlessly, causing the waves of his windswept blonde hair to bob in time to the rhythm. He sighed, checked his watch, then looked over to the door.

Their eyes met for just a moment, Bella noting that his were an oceanic shade of blue. She thought she detected the hint of a smile on his lips before he rose and walked out onto the street.

He must have been waiting for someone, she thought, an unexpected twinge of envy causing her to frown. It had been a long time since she'd had a coffee date or dinner with a man. Too long.

Bella remembered the last time only too well: kissing Andrew goodbye at the pier, making dinner plans for later that evening at their hotel restaurant ...

"I'll be back in four hours," he'd reassured her. "Sure you don't want to come?"

Bella wrinkled her nose. "You know how I hate sharks."

"Well, I'm sure you'll be able to find something to amuse yourself with." Andrew's brown eyes twinkled.

"I don't know," she pretended to pout. "There's hardly anything to do here—only swimming, or going to the gym, maybe a massage in the day spa." She grinned, giving him a playful swat on the shoulder as he turned to go. "I'll miss you," she called after him.

Andrew looked back at her with his dark eyes, blew her

a kiss ...

And that was the last time she ever saw him.

The loud cry of a hungry toddler at the next table rudely jerked Bella out from beneath the dark clouds of past memories. A glance at her watch sent her into a mad panic. *Nine twenty-five!* She drained the last of her now lukewarm coffee, stuffed the untouched muffin into her bag, and raced down the footpath towards the imposing office building that housed *Healthy Lifestyle*.

Too late, Bella realised she had left without paying for her snack! Her cheeks flamed with embarrassment as she determined to return and pay her bill. But not now ... it would have to wait until after the interview.

It was 9:35 am by the time she stepped out of the elevator at the 10th floor suite of offices. She felt hot and frazzled, not at all like the organised, professional image she had hoped to project.

"Excuse me ..." Bella approached an efficient-looking secretary behind a marble-topped counter. The woman, identified as Susan by her gold name badge, seemed perfectly suited to the opulent surroundings. Her blonde hair was swept up in a classic French roll, and her tailored suit cried out 'expensive'.

Susan looked up from beneath long eyelashes, examining Bella as though she was an unwelcome insect.

Bella rushed on: "I have a nine-thirty appointment with the editor, Mr Gray. I'm a little late."

'Miss Perfect' gave her a decidedly blank stare.

"Umm ... there should be a record somewhere." Bella self-consciously smoothed her hair down with one hand. "I confirmed the appointment just yesterday. My name's Bella Whitman ... if that helps ..." Her voice trailed off. She doubted if anything short of her being a celebrity, or a Pulitzer Prize winner, would get her past this woman.

The receptionist was clicking through screens on her computer. A light suddenly went on in the skillfully made-up eyes, and her whole manner instantly changed.

"Of course, Ms Whitman," she purred. "You *were* booked in to see Mr Gray this morning." Bella let out a breath she didn't even know she was holding.

"However," the woman paused for effect, her gold pen

pointed at Bella from her manicured fingers, "Mr Gray has had to attend a rescheduled meeting this morning. Last minute, you understand. He must not have been able to reach you." She shrugged, almost as if to blame Bella for being out of contact. "He now won't be available until after lunch. I suggest you make a new appointment for another day." Her tone softened slightly at Bella's disappointed expression. "He *is* a very busy man, you understand."

Bella was more than disappointed. She was frustrated, even a little angry. This was the last thing she needed right now. But she wasn't going to give up this easily.

"Could I make a new appointment for later today?" she asked, attempting to keep the tense edge from her tone.

The secretary's voice was almost sympathetic. "I suppose you could wait here if you have the time. Mr Gray sometimes has a few minutes to spare between meetings, and he usually walks through here to his office."

Bella gave her a sceptical smile.

"Maybe—just maybe—you might be able to catch him this morning." Her small attempt at being helpful seemed to leave Susan feeling exhausted, and she merely nodded at Bella's thanks.

With a sigh, Bella settled down onto the black leather couch opposite the counter, glad that she had brought some articles to work on. She wasn't very hopeful about her chances, but maybe she could grab the editor at lunch. The man had to eat sometime, didn't he?

Ethan Gray looked at his watch for the fifth time, barely suppressing his growing irritation. While planning meetings were vital in running a publication, the other editorial staff completely lacked focus. They would much prefer to discuss wishy-washy topics like the quality of the graphics, than real issues such as the summer holiday feature.

He had managed to keep them vaguely on track, addressing eighty per cent of the matters on the meeting agenda. But when he noticed Gemma, the fashion editor, filling in assistant editor Chloe on her upcoming wedding plans, he lost all patience.

"Okay, everybody!" he barked—a little too harshly, perhaps, but they needed to show some respect. "That's it for today," he continued over the rustle of papers being gathered together. "We'll have a follow-up meeting on Friday. Check your e-mail for the time."

One-thirty! Ethan fumed silently as he strode from the room, oblivious to the annoyed glances shared between his co-workers. You would think they had nothing else to do but gossip all day!

He dumped his organiser and notes on his desk, and nodded to Susan on his way out. "Lunch. Back in an hour."

"Mr Gray!" she called after him, pausing at his audible sigh of frustration. "Uh ... there's someone here to see you. Ms Whitman—your nine-thirty appointment."

Ethan's lips had already begun to form a negative reply, when he noticed the attractive woman seated on the reception couch. Wisps of chestnut curls framed her oval face, with creamy skin, a soft blush, and bright blue eyes that looked up at him expectantly—all counterpointed by an elegantly tailored ivory skirt-suit covering a body that curved in all the right places.

"Ethan Gray," he smiled, cranking up the charm as he extended his hand. "How would you like to join me for lunch?"

END OF SAMPLE CHAPTERS

"BLUE FREEDOM" is available from all good online stores, or better still, support your local brick-and-mortar bookshop by ordering through them!

ISBN# 978-0-9555283-5-4

Rose&Crown
Inspirational Romance
www.roseandcrownbooks.com

(an imprint of the SUNPENNY PUBLISHING GROUP)

ROSE & CROWN, BLUE JEANS, BOATHOOKS, SUNBERRY, CHRISTLIGHT, and EPTA Books

MORE BOOKS FROM the SUNPENNY GROUP
www.sunpenny.com

Dance of Eagles, by JS Holloway
The Mountains Between, by Julie McGowan
Just One More Summer, by Julie McGowan
Going Astray, by Christine Moore
My Sea is Wide, by Rowland Evans
A Little Book of Pleasures, by William Wood
If Horses Were Wishes, by Elizabeth Sellers
Far Out, by Corinna Weyreter
Watery Ways, by Valerie Poore
The Skipper's Child, by Valerie Poore

COMING SOON:

Trouble Rides a Fast Horse, by Elizabeth Sellers
The Stangreen Experiment, by Christine Moore
Someday Maybe, by Jenny Piper
Breaking the Circle, by Althea Barr
A Devil's Ransom, by Adele Jones
Blackbirds Baked in a Pie, by Eugene Barter
Sudoku for Sailors
Sudoku for Christmas
Sudoku for Birdlovers